A FLORENTINE REVENGE

Christobel Kent

sphere

SPHERE

First published by the Penguin Group in 2006
This reissue published by Sphere in 2018

1 3 5 7 9 10 8 6 4 2

A CIP catalogue record for this book
is available from the British Library.

ISBN 978-0-7515-7118-9

Typeset in Bembo by M Rules
Printed and bound in Great Britain by
Clays Ltd, St Ives plc

Papers used by Sphere are from well-managed forests
and other responsible sources.

MIX
Paper from
responsible sources
FSC® C104740
www.fsc.org

Sphere
An imprint of
Little, Brown Book Group
Carmelite House
50 Victoria Embankment
London EC4Y 0DZ

An Hachette UK Company
www.hachette.co.uk

www.littlebrown.co.uk

In memory of Bruce Johnston,
1950–2005

Acknowledgements

I would like to thank Camilla Baines for allowing me to steal a little of her life as a hardworking, intuitive and enormously knowledgeable guide to Florence, as well as for nearly twenty years of loyal, generous, unstinting friendship.

I have in this book tried to be as accurate as possible when describing Florence's streets and palaces, but some locations, most significantly the Palazzo Ferrigno, the Olympia Club and the Hotel Regale, are entirely the products of my imagination.

Prologue

Across Europe it had been the hottest August for seventy years and in Florence the days were scalding, the city's streets deserted until night fell. The visitors sought out air-conditioning, sitting in their expensively chilled hotel rooms looking out at the cloudless, blue-white sky, or wandering in the discount designer shopping malls on the outskirts of the city. Almost all the Florentines had gone, to the sea or the mountains if they could afford it, to relatives down south or closer to home, to the woods and waterfalls of the Casentino. Only the very old, the very poor or the frankly mad were on the streets, and even they could only be seen in the early morning, wandering slowly, stunned by the night's heat.

All month it never cooled down at all, not even at four in the morning, and the tally of deaths crept up, stealthy, ominous, inexorable: old people, babies, pregnant women. In the company of a handful of Italian drifters an American boy drank two litres of red wine on the steps of Santo Spirito one evening and the following morning was found dead between parked cars by the street sweepers. He had vomited, become fatally dehydrated and, his new-found friends having dispersed, suffered multiple organ failure before the sun even came up.

In the suburbs of the city, Galluzzo and Sesto Fiorentino, Scandicci and the Isolotto, the villas breathed quietly in their green gardens, nestling among orange trees and feathery, tropical foliage, but there was no wind. The suburban swimming pools – and there were many of them slotted in alongside sports centres, motorways and housing projects; public and private, grubby or smart – were full. The bodies were packed tidily, this being Italy, but packed all the same, laid out under rows of umbrellas on a new season's bright towels, side by side like sardines. In contrast to the baked, silent city the air here was cacophonous with splashing, whoops and screams and the hoarse shouts of teenage boys.

In among the Italians at the Olympia Club at around two that long-ago afternoon, when no one without air-conditioning could bear to be inside any longer, there had been one or two foreigners, those who had been taken by surprise by the heat: campers, budget hotel guests. A handful of Germans, an orderly French family, and a young English couple with their small daughter. At their holiday villa the rented pool had cracked in the heat and drained dry and in desperation the owner, had arranged temporary membership at the Olympia for them. It wasn't an upmarket place, for all it styled itself a country club; the bare-chested barman spent most of his time leaning across the bar to chat up pretty foreigners, and the girl who handed out the baskets for their clothes was an anorexic seventeen-year-old who hardly looked up from her magazine when they arrived.

The English girl was seven years old, her fine brown hair bleached by the sun and her skin darkened just enough to show the outline of her miniature bikini. She ran between the bodies to get an ice-cream from the bar, and came back triumphant, her prize already melting in one hand and the change sticky in the other. She had been so pleased with herself, and this was Italy, after all, where no harm could ever come to a child, that when she said she needed to go inside, *Need the loo, Mummy, I know where it is*, they had sent her off. Had they watched her go, smiling at her independence, her determination? Had they congratulated themselves on not wrapping her in cotton wool? These were questions no one could ask, and they gave no interviews afterwards, volunteered no information.

What was clear, though, was that after no more than five minutes the girl's mother, having felt some stirring of silly anxiety, some familiar, ridiculous misgiving, had got to her feet and carefully picked her way between the sunbathers to find her daughter. She had walked on the dimpled tiles past the drained indoor pool, huge and echoing and empty, beneath the dry showers, over slatted boards and into the silent changing rooms. She called the girl's name and held her breath, always fearful, for the moment when she would hear the small voice call back and all would be well. But there was no reply.

Chapter One

A week later the child's body was found in the river to the south, caught in an overhanging branch five miles out from the city where the river flowed clear and green between steep, wooded hills. A pretty spot, although for a long time afterwards no one went there, not for pleasure, not to admire the view. Celia Donnelly, twenty-one years old, had only just arrived in Italy, and it had been all over the local papers, a headline pasted outside every newspaper stand in the city when it happened; among the first words of the language she absorbed were those for abduction, murder, drowning. Across the half-empty city those left behind in the heat came out to mourn; flowers appeared at dusty shrines to the Madonna, begging for her intercession; there was a look of confusion, almost shame, on the faces of those who brought them. Suspects were called in, the first of them within hours of the girl's disappearance, but no arrests were made, no charges filed. The case remained unsolved.

Nearly fifteen years on, Celia lay awake in the darkness and listened. The child that cried every night somewhere along the street had not yet started up; if she dropped off soon perhaps tonight she'd sleep through the sound. The crying always went on for a long time, more than an hour; Celia could not tell the child's age, or sex; the sound was not verbal, as far as she could tell. She sometimes wondered if, like her, there were those who thought of the child abducted so long ago when they heard crying like that in the night, and it bothered her obscurely that she still barely knew her neighbours, wouldn't know if she had seen the crying child in the street. After close to four months back in the city she still found herself wondering when she would begin to feel at home here.

Outside for the moment the only sound was the rain falling softly on the terracotta roof over Celia's head. It had been a long, damp, mild autumn that had lasted all through November, and well into December it was still raining. But they said the weather would change soon, perhaps tonight.

It had been a busy week, and there was more to come. Only yesterday Celia had been up at Como, showing the Liberty villas to a group of peach-soft ladies from Charleston, listening to their sweet Southern accents exclaiming over the wet green lawns, the dark mountains shrouded in mist. It was always hard work when the weather was bad, although in the case of the Southern ladies it had turned out to be nothing a little shopping wouldn't cure, and she'd sent them home with handblown glass, pigskin gloves and embroidered velvet handbags. And besides, Celia knew yesterday's group already; they'd been in Italy a year earlier and at the airport in their pastel suits had fallen on her with little cries when they saw her again, pressing their soft, scented cheeks against hers, teasing

6

her that she still wasn't married. *How about that nice driver, what's his name? He'd be my type, I can tell you, if I was twenty years younger.* They were talking about Gabriele, the handsome, laid-back Roman coach driver; lazily he'd smiled at her when he heard them talking.

It might be different, though, on Friday, a different thing altogether. She didn't know them, did she? She knew almost nothing about them, except that they were rich, but then, most of Celia's clients were. The usual long weekend in Florence to celebrate a birthday, just a matter of hotel bookings, some gallery visits, a guided walk, all booked. Friday and Saturday Celia would be guiding them, Sunday they'd have to themselves: Mr and Mrs Lucas Marsh. There was no point in going over it, Celia knew that from experience, no need to lie awake worrying over unforeseeable complications. Just a job, like any other. Leave it. Tomorrow was her day off, and there was no need to waste it wondering about a job. As long as the weather improved.

The sound of the rain became lighter, softer, and it seemed to Celia that she could feel the temperature outside dropping even as she lay there, but she didn't get up to close the window. In the summer, just after she'd moved in, there had been a gardenia in the courtyard below, and nicotiana spilling out of a big cracked terracotta pot, and their scent had found its way up to Celia's high window. There was an engraver's studio down there, and in the fine weather the students had laid their work out on trestles to dry under an awning between the pots. They needed the awning because you could never tell in Florence: even on summer nights great thunderheads could balloon up out of nowhere and open over the city like bombs, drenching the lush private gardens and lines of washing left out to dry.

Could she adjust to being back here, among all this unadulterated life? Celia thought of the lime trees she'd seen in the little square between the tiny attic and the Arno, and high up under the roof she turned over in the darkness and thought of lime blossom. June, when the trees would be in flower, seemed a long way off now; the fresh December air smelled only of cold stone and water. The rain had stopped and the temperature was still falling, but still she didn't close the window. Pulling the quilt up to her chin, Celia lay in the cooling air and listened to the sounds from outside. She could hear someone laying a table below her for a late supper, cheerful voices calling each other to the table. Celia reached up a hand and pushed the window to. Now she could only hear the small sounds inside the flat, the comforting flare of the geyser as it warmed the radiators, the tiny scrape of pigeons on the roof. *Perhaps it is turning into my own place after all*, she thought dreamily, *perhaps this is where it begins to go right*. She thought of tomorrow, a day to herself, the first for a long time. And she drifted, at last, into sleep.

Out to the west along the river, quite suddenly the grand façades of the city dwindled into nothing and anonymous apartment blocks and seedy parks fronted the Arno. The great dark band of Le Cascine, a pleasure garden from the nineteenth century whose tree-lined avenues might once have rivalled Hyde Park, lay along the river to the north, visible from every vantage point around the city, black and mysterious as a mythical forest. Close up it was less picturesque; Le Cascine wasn't a pretty place on a night like this, its ranks of sodden black trees dripping in the rain, and it was hard to see who, other than those with an urgent need for privacy, would be tempted down its dank alleys and paths strewn with hypodermic needles. At the centre of the park was a squat, scruffy compound, a handful of low-lying buildings surrounded by a fence. This was Le Pavoniere, an open-air swimming pool whose fin-de-siècle pavilions were looking their age, all peeling paint and lopsided shutters, although the pool itself was a cracked relic of the seventies. Le Pavoniere had a neglected air even in the summer but on a wet night in winter, lit only by the distant yellow gleam of the embankment lights, it was dismal. The dripping, dilapidated iron railings around the pool were crudely chained and a broken plastic sun-lounger lay on its side in the grass grown long and ragged after a wet autumn. There was a wind and the bare, drenched trees stirred and rattled. The pool itself was drained, although a couple of inches of green, brackish rainwater had collected at one end and it was slimy with fallen leaves. At the centre of the drained pool the leaves seemed to have collected into a heap, a dark, humped shape that even in the flickering yellow light looked too oddly substantial to be just wet leaves.

Sometime during the night a fight broke out between two homeless alcoholics lying in the lee of the pavilions in a hopeless attempt to shelter from the relentless rain. At one point the heavier man flung the other against the pool's link fence, where a dim yellow security light that had flickered and fizzed all night flared briefly into bright white life. For a moment both of them stood there, blinking and cursing and mumbling in the glare. Then the big man grew still suddenly, shaking off the other, raising a hand and pointing through the fence. At the bottom of the pool was not a heap of wet leaves but the figure of a kneeling man of late middle age, hands behind him. Although he was bent forward over his knees the man's head was flung back at an odd angle, a position that even a pair of sodden drunks could see was wrong. In the sodium glare the stain that spread across his farmer's checked shirt shone black, and his eyes stared sightlessly up into the overcast night sky.

Chapter Two

Only twenty-one, barely out of university with her degree in English, some night classes in art history and half a year's temping while she looked for a job, Celia had come to Italy, it seemed to her now, out of a kind of panic. There'd been a boyfriend who'd fizzled out after university, under the pressure of finding a job and somewhere to live, the anti-climax of the real world. And then Celia's father died suddenly of a heart attack, fifty-five years old, and her mother shut herself up in the house, saying she didn't want to talk about it. With what seemed to Celia now like monumental self-absorption she'd taken her mother at her word and had left the country. At twenty-one, she thought as she looked back, you couldn't stand still, you didn't want to be held back by things like parents, or mortgage payments, or responsibility. It was almost a law of physics, something to do with momentum, or biology, perhaps.

There'd been Kate to consider, too, of course, but she was

just a worry to Kate, just an aimless younger sister who seemed unable to decide what to do with herself. Looking back, it seemed to Celia now that maybe it was Kate who'd been the odd one, with her life already mapped out before she'd got to twenty-five. Celia had arrived one morning in another strip-lit office and found herself thinking of her mother as she tried to fit her possessions in on the desk top among someone else's, camping out, temporary. Her mother whose life seemed to be over already without ever having visited America, or India, or even Spain. She had stared at the blinking green cursor on the computer screen for a full ten minutes thinking, *This can't be all there is.* Someone had asked her impatiently if she was all right, did she need anything, and without answering Celia had gathered her things together and walked out.

So Celia blew her meagre savings on a course in English language teaching – a move everyone had sighed at, another change of career, money down the drain – and got a budget flight to Italy almost at random. She'd gone to a party where everyone was complaining about work, and someone had mentioned Jo Starling, the school rebel, who'd gone to Florence and never come back. Celia had never been further than windswept Calais on a school trip before then, but then, not many people had; Florence sounded distant and exotic, and she got hold of Jo Starling's number.

'Hey,' Jo had said incuriously as she opened the door of her flat in Santa Croce to Celia six weeks later, as though she lived around the corner and had just popped in for a gossip. She had red lipstick on and an old silk scarf wound around her head; behind her the dim flat smelled musky, of scented lilies and coffee. Jo had had a touch of the Bohemian about her even at school, rising above the jeers of teenage boys directed at her homemade skirts, her hennaed hair; here, it seemed, she had found her element. 'Come in, then,' she said. And Celia had marvelled at how different things were here.

That first sweltering August night on Jo's uncomfortable sofa turned into a week, then two, but soon Celia realized that her presumption that it would be fine to camp out there indefinitely without a job or a prospect of one and a backpack full of unsuitable clothes had been careless. It had lasted six weeks; the flat had been gloomy and stifling and too small for two women. Then Jo, who when Celia had arrived had been loudly proclaiming the bliss of living without a man, the heaven of not being in a relationship, grew bored with her freedom. She started seeing the young mechanic who'd fixed her scooter when a delivery truck reversed over it on the pavement, and Celia's days in her flat were numbered.

So Celia had moved out. Even then, finding somewhere decent in the city had been a nightmare and for one, then two, and what turned into four years she'd endured a succession of short lets and gloomy, airless, mosquito-infested bedsits before giving in, and moving to the guilty comfort of the suburbs. *A cop-out*, said her friends; *premature retirement*. But it was so easy. In days Celia found a pretty, modest villa with a new kitchen and a bit of garden, built by a butcher for a son who preferred to travel the world. She was out of the smell and the din and the dirt of the city, the refuse trucks at six in the morning, the wail of sirens, the pollution. She was safe.

Celia still saw Jo now and again, the odd white hair in her shiny black ponytail these days and still living in Santa Croce, still teaching violin to the small children of the Florentine upper classes and doing some careless proofreading on the side. That was what happened in Florence; you slipped into a

13

comfortable groove, there seemed no need to change things, to progress. The old friends back in London or Manchester who were always restlessly improving themselves, working their way up, getting on the property ladder, going to evening classes to get a law degree or study another language, seemed impossibly, crazily ambitious from this distance. It seemed that in Italy, for the foreigners camping out here at least, there was no need for any of that ambition: you could live pretty well on not much money; coffee and wine were cheap, and the sun was free. Until it all went wrong, of course.

For Celia it had all gone wrong this summer, fifteen years on, and she supposed that wasn't too bad a run of luck, for Italy. But it had gone wrong in August, the month in Italy when it was most difficult to set anything right, to have a dripping tap mended, to find a new job or a new flat. After more than ten years happy in her suburban villa, Celia's landlord had said breezily halfway through July that his errant son was getting married, and he'd need the house back.

She put out feelers, that was how you had to do it here; asked around. Something would turn up. She begged some cardboard boxes and began to pack ten years' worth of accumulated household objects, steeling herself against the changes that came over her beloved little house, the pale patches that appeared on the walls as her pictures came down. *This is nothing*, she told herself. *It's just a house.* But the truth was, Celia was right back where she'd started.

Chapter Three

Beate had found Celia the flat in the end, less than a week before time ran out and with the landlord's son calling every other day to let Celia know exactly when his removal firm planned to turn up. Beate, who had much grander friends than Celia, who had no need to help her out at all, just called her up one evening.

Half-Italian, half-Swedish, and of unguessable age, Beate was one of those people who always made you feel better, just by saying your name. In the complicated hierarchy of the guides of Florence she occupied a privileged position, and not merely because she had studied fine art at the Accademia and history at the Sorbonne; she had something else, too, a quality more rare and sought-after than erudition; something like grace. Tall and dark-skinned, with corkscrew white hair that fell to her elbows and armfuls of bracelets like Nancy Cunard, Beate was recognizable from streets away, never with a gaggle of clients, only ever a select two or three. She would be talking to them warmly in her high, clear voice, her gestures intimate as she laid her long brown fingers on a client's shoulder or vivid as she swept her arm wide to show the drama of a landscape or the grandeur of a palace.

When Beate phoned, Celia had that moment walked in after a sweltering day in the city; her heart had just dipped at the sight of the house that was no longer her home, her possessions in boxes next to the door. She let her satchel fall to the floor beside her, sat down, picked up the ringing phone; she could hear the champagne in Beate's voice and wondered where she was. Like her age, Beate's financial position was mysterious, a matter of some conjecture among the others – although prestigious, being an accredited Florentine guide was not well paid – but one thing was certain: she had expensive tastes. Tonight, Celia thought from the background sounds, some ululating Moroccan music and the hum of conversation in languid African accents, Beate was probably in the Caffè Maroc. It was one of her favourite hangouts, a private club in the Oltrarno done up to look like a medina, all mosaic tiles and fountains and heaps of cushions. They might even have hookahs; Celia could imagine Beate with a hookah quite easily. She looked at her watch. Even at five on a Monday afternoon.

'Sweetheart.' Celia sat down at the table, wiped the sweat from her forehead. She'd had a hot day showing fourteen Americans around the Museo della Scienza; no airconditioning. 'Yes.'

'Are you still looking for a place?' Beate put the question lightly, pretending Celia wasn't desperate, pretending, kindly, that this was a mere nothing, a tiny favour between friends. 'I know you don't want to live in town but – well, it's a nice area. And if you want it, it's empty straight away. I don't know how long for – he's – what is he?' Then the line had gone muffled as though Beate had her hand over the phone, talking to someone. Beate's current boyfriend was an industrialist called Marco, a handsome, silver-haired sixty-year-old. The soft, hoarse voice came back. 'He's Venezuelan, Marco thinks. Anyway, he couldn't renew his *permesso di soggiorno*, he's overstayed and you know how that seems to annoy them. God knows when they'll let him back in and in the meantime, the flat's there. I think it's even furnished.'

A week later, never having set eyes on it before, Celia had opened the door on her new home. The key had been left for her at the bar on the corner, the last in a succession of casually miraculous arrangements, or almost the last.

Gabriele had offered to bring up her stuff in his van. There was something about Gabriele – perhaps it was because he was from Rome, where they were less fastidious and readier with a smile – but whenever she knew he was to be her driver on a tour – and they'd been to Sicily together, Verona, Elba – she knew she could relax. They simply got on; Gabriele seemed as happy to have her as his guide as Celia was to have him at the wheel, capable, laid-back and cheerful. As she stood there she heard him come up the stairs behind her, three boxes balanced in front of him. 'Go on then,' he said. '*Forza.*' Closing her eyes, willing the key to catch, Celia had turned it one last time and the door opened.

A corridor with a dusty terracotta floor led away from her, and a shaft of light slanted down from an odd little window high up on the right. She stepped inside, passed a dark bedroom to the left and then saw more windows, more light. And although balls of dust had collected in every corner it had a good smell; clean, empty, as though the Venezuelan had barely inhabited the place. Celia's landlord, Beate had said, was a bookbinder on the other side of town, and as long as the rent appeared in his account every month, he didn't care who lived in the place.

In the kitchen Celia leaned across the table, pushed the window open, and caught a glimpse of a tall, slender bell-tower with cut stone corners and Roman arches. Even before she'd taken in the view, her hand still on the window frame, she heard another window pulled to sharply in response; already she was invading someone's space. She looked out cautiously to see who it might have been and saw windows everywhere, the nearest practically at her elbow, but couldn't tell which had been affronted by her presence. Neighbours; she'd never had to think about neighbours before and now she had a dozen.

She'd been here three months when he phoned, but the place still felt nothing like home, nothing like her place; with the bare terracotta floors and high ceilings it had the empty, impersonal feel of a short let, not much more than a hotel room. Lucas Marsh. Someone had recommended her, he had said, although afterwards Celia hadn't been able to remember who.

She remembered liking his voice. It was to be a birthday celebration for his wife, short notice, three weeks, but he said straight away that he'd send her an advance, a generous sum. He sounded like a man used to things running smoothly but he was not rude or bullying, as very wealthy clients often could be. He asked her to draw up an itinerary, made a couple of suggestions that indicated to Celia he already knew the city, and she thought, yes, I suppose I could do that. Straightforward enough, a walk or two – she offered Fiesole and San Miniato – restaurants, the Uffizi. The only tricky request was for a dinner

18

he wanted her to arrange on the Saturday, somewhere private, exclusive, with a good collection of paintings. It would be a challenge. There was only one little thing that had seemed odd to her at the time, and even that was explicable, she supposed. She'd asked how old his wife would be.

'Why do you need to know that?' he'd asked, and she'd heard something in his voice, an edge, a sharpness, although it had, Celia thought, been a perfectly reasonable question. It had to be a special birthday, didn't it? Flustered, she'd tried to get out of it.

'I – I didn't mean, I'm sure—'

'Thirty-two,' he'd said shortly, and there'd been a pause while Celia digested the information. Not a particularly special birthday, then. When he spoke again his voice was just as it had been to begin with, calm and easy; it wasn't the kind of voice you said no to. And thinking of the hole in her bank balance moving house had left, and of the bills gathering behind it, jostling, asking to be noticed, Celia had of course said yes. The thing about being a freelance was, you couldn't afford to turn anything down, whatever kind of funny feeling you had about it. Just another job.

When Celia tried, later, to recall the precise timbre of Lucas Marsh's voice, she found it inexplicably difficult. She could only remember, and for some time, the feeling it had given her, that kind of churning in the stomach when you wanted to impress someone and you knew they wouldn't be easily won over, something complex and guarded in that voice that was intriguing. She began to look forward to the weekend half with unease, half with excitement. Never a good idea to get a crush on a client, not one with a wife, in particular, but still . . . it wouldn't be boring.

Chapter Four

The day dawned bright and cold; out at Le Cascine striped police tape fluttered in the wind, strung between trees, and a white polythene tent had been set up in the drained pool. At the entrance to the park, half a mile away, police cars were turning away the vans loaded with cheap clothes, cheeses and hams that were arriving for the weekly market. One of the fighting drunks from the night before had been taken off to hospital to have a cut on his head sewn up, but the other, sober for the first time in years, was sitting in a mobile forensic unit, wrapped in blankets. His hands shook as he drank the glass of tea someone had brought him. 'Throat cut like a – like a pig,' he kept repeating, 'like they wanted all the blood out of him.' Patiently a stocky policeman, who'd been up since five, sat beside him and waited for him to start making sense.

Celia could tell the weather had changed even before she opened the shutters, by the quality of the light that spun and danced through the slats. The light changed everything. She listened for the sound of the child crying, but heard only the whine and roar of the morning rush hour on the Lungarno, helmeted girls perched on *motorini*, delivery vans that had to be out of the city before nine. Celia thought it must be after eight but she didn't have to get up, not today. She pushed the thought of tomorrow away, into the future, stretched, and opened the window.

It was breezy and cold, but not bitter, not yet. The sky was cloudless and cornflower-blue; Celia looked to the north and saw the hills across the rooftops, visible for the first time in more than a month and rising in shades of indigo, one behind the other. Celia had hardly been here since she moved in, it sometimes seemed, in and out of the city on jobs: Verona, Vicenza, the ducal palace in Mantova, the Palladian mansions of the Veneto, Greco-Roman ruins in Sicily.

She filled the coffee pot and put it on the stove, and as it began to bubble through, the phone rang.

The cleaners came in at eight-thirty, and behind long dark blinds pulled down the full length of the plate-glass windows to protect the public from the sight of the shop floor looking anything less than perfect, they went to work. They had a battery of equipment, a dozen different kinds of brush to fit in every cranny, behind radiators, soft cloths, vinegar, bicarbonate, packets and bottles stacked cheek-to-cheek in their plastic buckets. To and fro the team of cleaners moved, synchronized over the dark wood floors and pale, velvet-smooth carpet like a forensic team, sweeping, polishing, vacuuming, picking up fluff, filling scratches in the wood, every tiny scrap of evidence of the previous day's custom eliminated.

By the time Luisa arrived for work, usually at nine-thirty, the cleaners would be out at the back changing out of their overalls, having even erased the evidence of their own presence. This morning, though, she'd been early; Sandro'd had a call just after five and he'd been up and out like a shot, not bothering to tell her, naturally, what all the hurry was for. She'd been able to tell from the one side of the telephone conversation she could hear that it wasn't nice, but was it ever? Police business. 'Shit,' he'd said. 'Shit, shit.' Then he'd got his uniform on, taken it down from the wardrobe where it had hung every night of their married life, the shirt too tight these days; he hadn't bothered to shave. Luisa hadn't been able to settle after that, had lain awake in the bed. Had it been all her fault? Was it his job? It was an evil time of day, she'd decided long ago, that hour just before dawn when the world seemed thin and sour and grey; nobody's marriage could look perfect in that light.

It wasn't a bad marriage, that was what she told herself. It might not have been what she'd dreamed of, gazing into a jeweller's window at the age of nineteen, but didn't everyone have to deal with disappointment? Sandro never hit her, did he? Had a steady job. Deep down she knew, though, that if he had been a cabinetmaker or a bus driver instead of a policeman things might have been different; deep down she knew that – what was it, fourteen, fifteen years ago now? – something had changed. She'd been forty, a dangerous age. She could see now that that was the age at which the world begins to narrow for a woman, possibilities shut down, one by one. And there had been a little girl, abused and thrown in the river. You couldn't talk about that over dinner, could you? You couldn't go on as if nothing had happened, but that was just what they had done.

22

At nine forty-five Luisa gave the window display the once over, then raised the blinds; her first job every day, letting in the light and allowing passers-by their first privileged glimpse in at her merchandise. She thought of it as hers, although she was just as much a servant on the shop floor as the cleaners; she had herself begun her life in this shop, however many years ago – forty, near enough – as a cleaner. It had been different then, though, she thought wistfully. You were more a part of it, everyone in the same little team, and of course the shop had been smaller, more intimate. Carefully Luisa cranked the blind up, and the cold, pale northerly light from the broad street flooded the room.

When Luisa had first come to work in Frollini it had been a good dress-shop, no more, half haberdashery, half dressmaker's, with accommodation above. The back wall had been covered in little glass-fronted wooden drawers that slid out to reveal handmade silk lingerie and cashmere twinsets from Scotland. In the window in those days there would have been a handsome wooden mannequin dressed in a *tailleur* or black cocktail dress, perhaps a pair of shoes and matching handbag. Girls like Luisa out for a *passeggiata*, seventeen-year-olds in homemade dresses swinging straw bags from the market, would stand at the window and dream of growing up and wearing something so perfect, so sophisticated. Things were longed for, postponed and saved for, and once bought, they were treasured for ever. Not today. Luisa watched as half a dozen schoolgirls sashayed past down towards the Ponte Vecchio, the *scuola superiore* in low-slung jeans, and clicked her teeth.

It was a different world, and Frollini was a different place these days, but it wasn't all bad. The window was a glittering treasure box, chiffon and devoré and sequins all year round, and all colours of the rainbow, cyclamen and emerald and violet. Inside though, as Luisa turned away from the window to examine the cleaners' handiwork this morning, the room was as pale and empty as a church – that was the style now. A few carefully selected garments – charcoal, ivory, perhaps a tiny splash of colour here and there, just to tempt – hung on rails tucked away into white alcoves, and a long glass display case presenting handbags as though they should really be in the Uffizi ran the length of the room.

The customers had changed too; they were no longer nit-picking, penny-pinching Florentine aristocrats who complained about the quality of lining fabric and moaned about the demise of the lady's dressmaker; they came from all over, from Germany and England, Japan and America, and to Luisa they seemed fabulously, stupidly wealthy. They bought up whole window displays, a designer's entire catwalk output, and left the shop with so many big white ribboned bags they could hardly get through the door. And as a result there was no longer just one Frollini but instead a little chain, four three-storey emporia in choice locations across the city, but this one, the first, the original Frollini, Luisa's empire, was still the best.

Luisa looked out into the street. She liked this time of the morning, when she was alone on the shop floor before Beppe arrived to go up to menswear, before Gianna took up her position at the cash-desk. Opposite the shop in the straw market the stall-holders, jackets pulled up around their ears in the morning chill, were wheeling up their stock on trolleys, hanging up handbags and fringed shawls with their long-handled poles. *Can't stand here all day*, thought Luisa, reminded of the boxes of her own new stock that had arrived from Milan late last night and were waiting to be unpacked. *Work to be done.*

24

On her way down to the *magazzino* Luisa stopped off in the ladies to make sure she was presentable. It was no more than a tiny cubbyhole but the mirror was softly lit in there, and flattering; she looked a little tired perhaps, but nothing catastrophic. Hair neat and dark still, thanks to her hairdresser, back off her face; pearls in her ears; ironed white shirt; the same straight navy wool skirt to just below the knee she'd worn to work, day in, day out, ever since she could remember. Luisa washed her hands carefully out of habit, smoothed her skirt over her solid hips and frowned briefly at her reflection, glimpsing her own mother in the look she gave herself. Suddenly impatient, she whisked out of the door and on down to the stock room.

There were six boxes waiting for her like Christmas presents, light as air, filled with cellophane packages. Party dresses from a new supplier. Luisa studied them, judging the quality; strapless tulle, with silk underskirt and satin ribbons around an empire waist, they came in good, bright jewel colours, scarlet and sapphire, purple and sea-green. *Better get them out quick*, thought Luisa, planning a window already; she knew just the shoes, a velvet corsage; *not long till Christmas*. She gathered an armful and hurried back up to the shop floor.

Celia stamped along the river, shoulders hunched, trying to walk it out of her system and not altogether succeeding. The phone call had been from Kate. Involuntarily she sighed. Kate.

Perhaps it was the same for all sisters. One of them, after all, had to be older and wiser and unable to refrain from administering advice. One of them had to have done everything before the other, although in Kate's case, all she'd done was hold down a good, dull job in a publisher's production

25

department for a steady, unwavering ten years, got married, had two children in quick, efficient succession. Kate was now in the business of ordering her children's lives and there was no doubt, she was good at it.

Celia was fond of her nieces; she'd flown home when each of them was born, loaded with small and impractical presents, baby clothes that turned out to be the wrong size or season, marbled photograph frames, for each a heavy brass stamp with their initials. Flora and Imogen, both of them small, dark, serious children that reminded Celia of herself. She wrote to them when she remembered their birthdays and sent them postcards, but as she posted the parcels she couldn't help but imagine Kate standing impatient at the breakfast table as the girls opened them, arms folded, imperfectly suppressing disapproval.

Kate did try not to criticize, Celia could see that. But whenever she phoned, which wasn't often, there was always that prickliness between them, palpable even down the telephone line, like a pair of cats, each wary of what the other might come out with, each knowing how easily offence might be given and taken. And the fact that Kate's unspoken reproach – *What are you doing with your life, out there? What have you got to show for fifteen years in the sun?* – was beginning to look justified, didn't make it any easier.

She'd called to ask what Celia would be doing for Christmas. Her first words, though, and the tone in which they were delivered, were typical.

'Oh! You're in, then.' Wearily Celia sat down at the table, the phone on her knee, and heard in those few words everything Kate believed her younger sister's life to be; irresponsible, gadabout, a life spent at parties and in restaurants, frittering away her youth. Pleasing herself.

'Have you been trying to get hold of me?' she said. 'I've been working, mostly.'

'Right,' said Kate, disbelieving. 'Anyway,' making an effort, now, to be friendly, 'how's the new place? You've fallen on your feet there, haven't you?'

'I suppose I have,' said Celia, looking out across the roof-tops. 'Yes.'

She pondered Christmas; she hadn't thought about it much. Usually she just stayed home and read, enjoying the silence; if she got restless there was always work – even on Christmas Day you could get a job if you wanted one. She hadn't been back to England for the holiday, she realized, in two years. 'Three, actually,' said Kate, and Celia knew she was probably right, she almost certainly had it noted down somewhere. 'Flora was five when you last came.'

Three years. Celia felt a momentary tightening in the pit of her stomach at the thought of all that time gone, so easily. 'Are you sure you want me?' she said, warily. 'Haven't you got enough on your plate?'

There was a pause, and an almost imperceptible sigh. 'No, I mean yes, of course I want you.' For a second Kate sounded uncharacteristically tired, the bossy edge replaced with some-thing flat and defeated. *Is it me?* Celia wondered. *Is she really worried about me?* Or something else? Not John, Kate's husband, that was for sure, a solid, hardworking, unworldly man quite devoted to his family. Flora and Imogen?

'Is everything all right? Girls all right? No one's ill?' she blurted, sounding even to herself like a hopeless, impractical, panicking younger sister.

'No, no,' said Kate. 'Everything's fine, we're fine.' She seemed to hesitate a moment.

'Look,' she said. 'I know it's not, whatever, not fashionable or something to say this kind of thing, but you know by the time I was your age I'd had both the girls? It's not something you can put off for ever. You're not—'

'Not getting any younger,' said Celia, putting her face in her hands. 'I know.' *I'm thirty-five*, she repeated to herself, like a mantra. *Not fifty-five. Shut up, shut up, shut up.* It hadn't got any better, after that.

Out in the air Celia stopped now, her feet aching with stamping against the cold, hard pavement, and made a conscious effort to dissolve the tension in her stiff, angry limbs. She leaned on the rough stone parapet and looked down at the river, its surface glittering in the late-morning sun. A lone sculler bent over his oars, the tiny narrow craft skating smoothly across the green water towards the Ponte Vecchio. Across the river she could see the crowds clustered around the Uffizi, the souvenir stalls and pavement vendors, but on this side it was quiet, rush-hour past. Celia straightened, looked across at the huge terracotta dome of the cathedral rising over the rooftops, the golden ball and spire that surmounted it glinting in the pale light, tiny figures on the viewing platform. She stretched, willing the tension out of her shoulders, and took a deep breath. Coffee, she thought.

The Caffè Maioli was one of Celia's favourite places in the city; she had come here even when she lived in Galluzzo, stopping off on her way in to work for a dose of warmth, half-listening to the barmen's banter. It was open every day, even Ferragosto, even Christmas; it fleeced tourists without mercy but once you were recognized, it was a different story. Its interior was bright with gleaming marble and it was famous for its patisserie; beside the bar stretched a long glass cabinet stacked with cakes and pastries: fruit tarts dusted with icing sugar, tiny profiteroles, mille-feuilles layered with crème Chantilly and custard.

Behind the bar was a photograph from August 1947 of what appeared at first to be a desolate, bombed-out street, no more than a heap of blackened bricks. This was the Via Guiccardini, where the Maioli stood; three years after the German with-drawal from the city, as the Allies had advanced, it had still stood in ruins. It was here, at the southern end of the Ponte Vecchio, that the Germans had planted mines and the great palaces of the Via Guiccardini had been reduced to smoking rubble. But if you looked closer at the old photograph you could see a blurred white square in one corner, a little sign pasted on to what remained of the bar's wall: *Caffè Maioli. Aperto.* Open for business.

Pasquale looked up from his Gaggia as Celia came through the door, unwinding her scarf, and he inclined his head, smil-ing. That flirtatious little smile of his, a twitch at the corner of his mouth, a crinkling around the eyes, just for her. Just for her, and the rest. Without a word as Celia stood at the bar, pulling off her gloves, he placed a cappuccino in front of her on the marble, a heart shape forming in the foam. Then he folded a paper napkin around a warm brioche from the tray just brought down from the bakery upstairs and tenderly presented it to her. Celia rolled her eyes, but she took the pastry.

She pushed a little pile of coins towards Pasquale across the bar, and sliding them into his hand he nodded past her to the doorway; she turned, and there was Beate.

Dressed in something long and dark, a heavy piece of embroidered cloth thrown over her shoulders, Beate walked through the door, her fine-boned, golden face a little crumpled with weariness, eyes unfocused as though she were thinking of something else. Celia realized she'd hardly seen anything of Beate in the last couple of months, and felt a pang of remorse. It wasn't as though they had a regular arrangement to meet and after all, that was how things were when you were a free spirit, a freelance, that was why they were all here, Celia supposed, remembering her conversation with Kate. They didn't want to be bound to routine and duty and obligation. But perhaps freedom wasn't everything, she thought as she took in the dark circles under Beate's eyes; perhaps it won't be so much fun being free ten, fifteen years down the line. The door swung shut behind her, keeping the steamy warmth inside, Beate looked across at the bar with an automatic smile for Pasquale, saw Celia and her smile spread, the weariness suddenly all gone.

There had been a time when Beate and Celia had been in here together most days, stopping in for a coffee if they passed each other on the corner on the way to or from a job. In the cool early mornings it was handy for the Uffizi, at the end of the day for one of Pasquale's surprisingly strong red *aperitivi* and five minutes' winding down before the journey home. There was a particular table, tucked in around a corner, that was more or less reserved for regulars, and by unspoken agreement they sat there now.

Beate threw her things down, dropping the big velvet bag she lugged everywhere on the floor and shrugging her coat and scarf gracefully on to the back of the chair. She had ordered a caffè latte, not her usual black coffee, and took a sip a little gingerly as though it were medicine. She looked up at Celia with a grimace.

'It is supposed to be good for you, isn't it?' Beate said. Her voice was musical with a mixture of accents, Swedish, Italian, a little West Coast American from a long-ago boyfriend. 'I think I need nourishment. Or something. Do you think I am getting too old for all these late nights?'

Celia laughed, her reflex when Beate joked about being old, but of course one day it would be true, Beate would be officially old. And so, eventually, would she. Would she be alone, like Beate? Because Marco didn't count for much, she realized. He wasn't in it for the long haul with Beate. Thoughtfully she took a bite of her brioche.

'So,' said Beate, 'not working today? You must have been so busy, I've hardly seen you.' She spoke cheerfully.

'Yes,' Celia said. 'A lot of tour-leading, out-of-town jobs. For the money.'

Beate grimaced sympathetically. 'Poor thing,' she said. Tour-leading – making arrangements, riding on coaches, not proper guiding – was a bit of a slog, it was agreed, with too much time spent away in hotels and no home comforts.

Celia shrugged. 'Oh, it makes a change,' she said, feeling sanguine for once, 'and I'm back in the city now. I've got a three-day job, starting tomorrow.'

Beate patted her hand. 'Good,' she said. 'Good.'

'And the flat's terrific, Beate,' said Celia suddenly. 'Really. I don't know what I would have done—' she broke off, not wanting to sound too hopeless. 'Really. You're amazing.'

Beate smiled a little. 'I'm glad you like it,' she said. 'I only went there once, with Marco, to see the Venezuelan's paintings.' Her mouth turned down a little. 'Hideous. I hope he took them all home with him, for your sake. But I thought the flat was sweet. A bell-tower, isn't there?' She pulled a pack of cigarettes and a heavy old Zippo out of the depths of her bag, and lit up.

31

'Yes,' said Celia. But Beate was looking back over her shoulder, wafting her smoke away, and didn't hear; when she turned back she said brightly, 'So, who've you got tomorrow? A big group? Or something nice and intimate?'

'Oh,' said Celia, pondering the answer to this question. 'Not a big group. A couple.' She felt a stir of unease she had been suppressing since she'd taken the job on, at the thought of three days playing gooseberry to a high-powered marriage. Intimacy didn't sound very inviting. 'A birthday, a long weekend to celebrate the wife's birthday. The husband's pretty big in something, I don't know exactly what. A banker, I suppose.'

'Oh, yes,' said Beate, taking another sip of her caffè latte. The ones you needed the private room at the Ferrigno for? You never told me their name. Marco might know them.'

'Marsh,' said Celia with an involuntary sigh. 'Mr and Mrs Lucas Marsh.'

'Oh,' said Beate vaguely, setting her coffee down and frowning as though in an effort to remember something. She repeated the name softly and in her musical voice it sounded mysterious and strange. *Lucas Marsh*.

Chapter Five

The shop could not have had a more favourable position; on the corner of the Piazza Signoria in the early mornings the crenellated shadow of the Palazzo Vecchio's slender tower fell practically to its door, and every tourist, every worker in the city had to pass Frollini's windows on their way anywhere. For some shops the location might have been a licence to pad out the stock with cheap stuff made in some Chinese factory, or to mark up the prices at random, but not Frollini, and particularly not Luisa.

For special displays she favoured the window that faced down towards the bridge; the street on that side was broader and encouraged a more leisurely stroll past. It was here that she had set up her party dresses, and it had taken her longer than she had expected; Beppe had already let himself in, calling a greeting before retiring upstairs, and behind him Gianna, complaining about the cold, fussing about in her little nest behind the cash-desk with shawls and scarves. Gianna never dressed sensibly enough, that was her problem, thought Luisa, with those low-cut blouses behind the till; she leaned around her display and called across.

'Nearly done.' Her back to the glass, Luisa sat back on her stockinged heels to survey her handiwork.

She had decided on green as her theme, with a splash of scarlet; a grassy-green tulle dress with a turquoise satin under-skirt and ribbon waist, a pea-green velvet clutch bag, a pair of emerald crocodile pumps with high heels and round peep-toes. The red dress, she thought judiciously as she looked the display over, would be the one that sold best, crimson over a magenta underskirt, a velvet corsage in shades of plum pinned to the bust, satin shoes to match. Red was a Christmas colour; it was hard to sell at any other time of year, but at Christmas it ran out of the shop. Luisa liked the green, though – unlucky for some but somehow it had caught her imagination, fresh and new and romantic, a fairy colour. Carefully she set the card listing the prices in the corner of the window, filled out in her old-fashioned copperplate script; two weeks' wages on a pair of shoes.

There had been a time when Luisa might have gone without food for a fortnight for those shoes with their stacked heels and peep-toes. But these days she wore little flat pumps to save her legs. In the window she straightened her back, stiff from her cramped position on the narrow display ledge, and became aware of a figure stopping outside, looking in. She'd finished just in time. Carefully Luisa stepped back into the shop past the window's backdrop, tucked her shirt smooth behind her waistband, buttoned her cuffs and, transformed once more into little more than a part of the shop's fittings herself, discreetly looked out at her display's first audience.

A girl stood there, looking at the green dress. Perhaps not quite a girl, maybe thirty, thirty-five, although from Luisa's vantage point, at closer to sixty, thirty seemed impossibly young. Watching the look she gave the dress, with a tug Luisa remembered being thirty herself, that threshold into adulthood; in her opinion it wasn't eighteen at all that marked maturity, you stayed a child all through your twenties. At thirty you were beginning to wonder if you might not be getting too old for strapless party dresses, even though they still drew you, still promised happiness, dancing, opportunities. At thirty you began to glimpse age, began to see where things might end. Luisa had married at thirty.

The woman on the pavement liked the dress, Luisa could see that, and it would suit her. She had pale, translucent northern skin, not Italian, with dark hair tied back; she was muffled in a good dark coat but wore no gloves – an Italian would certainly be wearing gloves – and her face was young, unmade-up, with strong, high-arching eyebrows; it was a good old-fashioned face. *No children*, thought Luisa, who made a game of wondering about such things; no husband. The woman looked at Luisa as though she was calculating, *Could I afford that?* Not, *He could buy me that for Christmas.* She didn't even need to look at the prices, either, to know it was out of her league, but still she was frowning, wondering what she might do without, and for how long, to compensate for this wisp of sea-green nothing. Luisa wondered if she would come into the shop; probably not.

As though in answer, just then the woman turned, as if to move on. The morning sunlight fell on her face and Luisa leaned forward a little; did she recognize her? She turned back for one last look at the green dress and Luisa considered the high arch of the eyebrows, the blue eyes; she had an excellent memory for faces and liked to be able to remember a customer. Rude, she always thought, to forget them after that brief connection you made over the softness of a suede handbag or the perfect colour to suit a complexion. And then the young woman looked straight at Luisa and smiled, a shy, conspiratorial smile that lit her face; she shrugged as if to admit, they both knew that dress was out of her league, but she could look. *Yes*, Luisa pondered, sure of it now, *I have seen you before*. One of the guides. And she smiled back.

On the pavement Celia turned away from the window, the image of the dress imprinted on her unconscious memory, filed away under *unattainable*. She had seen the woman standing there for some time behind the window display in the shop's creamy interior with her hands behind her back, solid, helmeted with black hair, watching her. Celia had been in there once or twice, having recommended the shop to clients; she knew they wouldn't be ripped off in Frollini, and they sold good, well-made clothes, catwalk stuff but judiciously selected, so she knew they wouldn't be disappointed either. She liked the atmosphere in there too – it was faintly old-fashioned, despite the modern fittings. But Celia would always stand back once she'd taken them in, self-effacing, trying to disappear, trying not to be taken for a paying customer. These clothes, after all, weren't within her reach. She walked on towards the Palazzo Ferrigno, where Lucas Marsh and his wife would be having dinner on Saturday night.

He didn't want a restaurant for that night, he said; he would leave it to her. But finding somewhere for them to have this particular dinner had, surprisingly, been the hardest part of the job.

36

'He wants good paintings, and privacy. A private dining room,' she'd said to Beate, at her wits' end. She'd thought when she took on the job that the Corsini would have had something; it was a vast place and so impossibly expensive that she thought they couldn't be booked. But no, it had been quite out of the question, the *direzione* there had said haughtily. Beate had thought a bit, then suggested the Ferrigno; it wasn't generally open to the public, still in private hands, but Beate, who had the best contacts in the city, had got her the dining room at three weeks' notice.

'Good paintings, yes,' Beate had said consideringly. 'Some lovely Titians, and certainly it's private, plenty of people don't know it exists. I've heard a rumour they've had royalty there when they're keeping their heads down, isn't that what you say? It's a funny sort of place, though, very old-fashioned.'

Celia had leapt at it; old-fashioned, surely, was what was wanted. But it *was* a funny sort of place, Beate was right; *no*, the administrator had said when she telephoned to confirm the reservation, she couldn't come and check the room, they were very busy. Some of the paintings were in restoration, others were being rehung – it was a carefully controlled environment. She should pay in advance, submit any specific requests in writing, and sometime in the interim they might be able to arrange a visit. But they had never had any complaints, she finished, with just a suggestion in her voice that she was ready to take offence.

It had been a risk, but Celia had seen the building from the outside and knew it to be beautiful, and besides, she had no choice. So she sent the money and a letter requesting the terrace for drinks and the best paintings available. When she sent the itinerary to Lucas Marsh, he had seemed more than

37

satisfied; Titian, he said, was exactly the painter he had been thinking of, and she had relaxed, warmed by his approval. Now, though, after what Beate had said this morning in the bar, something whispered to her that she had better be sure of every detail. It wouldn't do any harm, now would it? Even if she had to just turn up on the Ferrigno's doorstep and insist.

The mention of Lucas Marsh seemed to have set something off in Beate that unsettled Celia and left her thinking, *These people are out of my league.* She started mildly enough, typically of Beate, who was not one to barter explicit gossip, not having an envious bone in her body. She liked to believe the best of people, and had a good word for even the most spoilt of the city's wealthy itinerants, the wastrel scions of noble Florentine families or empty-headed heiresses from Hong Kong or Park Avenue. 'So generous,' she would say, or, 'A lovely person, really, just a little, *unfocused.*'

'Oh, I'm not sure, but I think Marco does know him,' she'd said at first, vaguely, to explain how she knew who he was. 'Or know *of* him, you can't tell with Marco, such a name-dropper. Have I seen him in one of those magazines?' She put her head on one side. 'Yes. He's got a pretty wife, I think, but I can't picture him, not exactly.'

'Do you know what he does?' Celia had asked, curious.

Beate had shrugged. 'Oh, these magazines, they never actually say, do they? What do any of them do? And I have never actually met him myself, I don't go to London. I have a feeling he might be a lawyer. Marco did speak about him once, now I come to think of it, when he went to England for one of those big forums they go in for. He was impressed, by how rich he was, I expect.' Beate rolled her eyes. 'What do they call themselves? The Association of Directors, something like that. What does that mean? A lot of rich men get together in an expensive hotel or one of their clubs and talk about, I don't know, how to get richer. Why not to sell here, why to go there, expanding markets. War zones. At least Marco's not into all that, not really.'

Celia had nodded, wondering if Marco really rubbed shoulders with these people, if Lucas Marsh could really be one of those exploiters she'd read about, a man who sold cigarettes to Chinese children, or arms to Sudanese warlords. Or if Marco just told stories he thought would impress Beate when he came back from some conference; Celia hoped so. Then Beate shook her head a little to leave the subject behind and smiled.

'We have to see more of each other, sweetheart. Don't you think? Let's have a drink tonight?' And Celia had agreed, then waved goodbye and watched Beate saunter off, ringleted hair shining silver in the light down the Borgo San Jacopo towards her flat.

Still, Celia decided, her thoughts returning to work as she walked through the straw market, past the shiny-snouted bronze of a boar, his fountain filled with pennies made golden by the heavily chlorinated Florentine water, and down into the comfortable gloom of the Via Porta Rossa, *it's only a weekend*. By Monday Lucas Marsh and his wife would be gone, whisked back out of her world, without a trace, and besides, despite her apprehension she was more certain than ever that it wouldn't be dull, a weekend with them.

Leading down to the Ferrigno, the Via Porta Rossa was busy. A handful of shop owners – mostly elegantly dressed men in late middle age, practised in the art of flattering foreign ladies of a certain age – were standing in their doorways, smoking fastidiously, chatting, watching for custom. It gave the road the air of a rather raffish drawing room rather than a city street.

The sight of the Christmas decorations going up took Celia by surprise; it was, she supposed, thinking of Kate and her telephone call, well into December already. And it was getting colder; here in the shadow you could feel the stones of the street beginning to take up the air's chill, settling into winter. At the far end of the street a broad strip of sunlight fell down the Via Tornabuoni on to the tall marble column that stood between the great church of the Santa Trinità and the scalloped façade of the Palazzo Salimbeni and it gleamed pink and white. This was the seductive city at its most ravishing, a place so lovely it was hard to believe anything unpleasant could ever happen here, no drug deals in the shadow of these exquisite palaces, no prostitutes haunting the ring roads, no bodies found floating in the river.

Celia crossed in the warmth, past a swathed beggar who sat outside the church with her hands held out, folded across each other, and a crudely pencilled message on a piece of card in front of her. *I am poor*, it read, *I have nothing. Have pity*. Celia wondered where the woman went at night, thought of the uncharted grey hinterland to the city. She dug in her pocket and dropped a handful of *centesimi* on to the fold of cloth in front of the rocking figure, then went on down the Via del Parione, where the Palazzo Ferrigno lay. It was narrow, too, and dark, but emptier than the Via Porta Rossa and grander; this was where the very rich kept their little pieds-à-terre, the wealthy Americans who liked to have a place for shopping or dipping into the galleries, the young men who worked for Gucci. Celia stopped outside the doors of the Palazzo

40

Ferrigno, open to reveal a lavishly huge, empty courtyard, a symbol of wealth here where land prices were impossibly high.

Daunted, she made her request with elaborate courtesy. The concierge, a heavy-set, taciturn man with sleepy eyes, didn't seem particularly interested, but the building's administrator, a brisk, smart woman in a suit and pearls, appeared in minutes. As the woman looked her over with a professional eye, Celia resisted the temptation to check her shirt front for breakfast crumbs.

'Yes?' the administrator said, frowning slightly. 'May I help you?'

'I simply wanted to confirm the arrangements for Saturday evening,' said Celia, fixing a smile, thinking, after all, this is costing them five thousand euros. 'The dinner for Signore Lucas Marsh in the Titian room?'

'Yes,' said the woman slowly. 'It is confirmed, really there is no need – they should arrive at seven, for drinks, that was the arrangement?' There was some flaw in her composure; she looked puzzled. 'You are the guide?'

'Yes,' said Celia, trying to maintain a polite smile; some of the officials she had to deal with did seem to find it difficult to believe that she had the necessary qualifications, being English. 'Celia Donnelly.' She held out a hand.

'Of course, yes, of course,' said the administrator, taking her hand distractedly. 'Paola Caprese,' but she didn't seem convinced. Celia rose above it, concentrated on producing her most elaborately polite Italian.

'I would like to have a copy of the menu, please.' She smiled, and Paola Caprese inclined her head. 'Certainly,' she said.

Celia persevered. 'And I would like to see the room, if that could be arranged?' The administrator compressed her lips, but she gave a stiff little nod and turned on her heel.

'Please,' she said over her shoulder. 'Follow me.'

They didn't enter what looked like a grand lobby but instead went through a small door off to the right of it. A narrow wooden service staircase led them up through the centre of the building; as they passed through a corridor on the first floor Celia glimpsed a little boudoir inlaid with mother-of-pearl, then an enfilade of panelled rooms stretched away from her, each flooded with light reflected up from the river below. She felt as though she had been transported into an earlier world, had become her equivalent four hundred years earlier, a humble servant confined to tiny spaces and back rooms, a dumb witness to all this lavish beauty.

Eventually they emerged at the top and crossed a landing where a grand staircase of *pietra serena* came out, meeting them; presumably this was where the Marshes would arrive, although as she looked down its wide, cold grey length Celia found herself preferring the mysterious, wood-scented confinement of the service staircase. Overhead a huge glass cupola shed a blue, wintry light on the landing.

'Here,' said the administrator shortly, gesturing towards a panelled oak door opposite them on the landing and permitting herself a brief, polite smile. She pushed the door open. 'Please.'

Celia entered first a small, panelled ante-room with two sets of long windows that opened on to the Palazzo Ferrigno's terrace. Through the windows on the flagstones outside she could see stacked chairs, a brazier and some terracotta pots, their contents shrouded under sacking. The administrator followed her gaze.

'For the *aperitivo*,' she said. 'If there is not rain, at least.' Celia nodded and turned towards a set of panelled double doors at the far end of the ante-room that could only lead to the Titian room. 'Yes,' said the administrator to her unspoken question and walked briskly ahead of her, swinging open both doors at once with Celia in her wake.

The room was not large but it had a high, vaulted ceiling; it was warm and had the rich, mysterious smell of a church, bitter herbs, incense and wax. The floor was set with red hexagonal tiles so old they undulated underfoot, and a long oak table sat in the centre of the room, set with one or two pieces of old silver. There was a single huge, floor-length window facing south, framing the cypress-studded hill of the Parco Strozzi on the far side of the river, as it rose black in the mist against a pale sky. Slowly Celia looked all around the room, taking in its perfection. She felt the administrator eyeing her, watching despite herself for a reaction to her prize, and she nodded.

'Well,' she said, smiling in wonder. 'It's perfect, isn't it?' She hesitated. 'And the pictures? The Titian collection?'

The woman shrugged slightly, the merest trace of apology. 'Two are still in restoration. Another is really too fragile for anything but a private viewing, under particular conditions. But there is still one, and it is a magnificent work, it is agreed; the jewel of the collection. *Madonna dei Gigli. The Madonna of the Lilies.*'

Celia subdued her frustration; this was the kind of thing that happened. Was it part of the charm of Italy, the fact that you could never be sure of anything? Until you were there, on the spot and on time, only then would you know that whoever you were meeting would turn up, what you wanted to eat would be on the menu, what you wanted to see would

43

be hanging in its rightful place. She looked around the walls of the room; they were still beautiful, even bare of Titians, painted with peacocks and vines and hummingbirds; on the wall facing the window hung a faded red linen curtain, behind which must be the Madonna.

Celia had heard of the painting, vaguely, remembering it as a kind of votive work, the subject the patroness of some lost cause or other. She remembered it as pretty, but it was of course impossible to tell anything from a print in a book, however expensively reproduced – that was why people bothered to come all this way, fight through the crowds, employ a guide. She felt irritated that she hadn't been able to come earlier and do her homework properly, but at the same time she felt a stir of excitement; suddenly she felt sure that this painting would be worth it, worth all the delicate negotiations, and the money; worth the wait. The administrator followed her gaze and after some hesitation crossed to the far wall. Celia followed.

It was not a large painting, perhaps a metre across, but it was quite extraordinarily beautiful; involuntarily Celia took a step back. The Madonna, unusually, was not quite upright, instead half-reclining on a dark red chaise, the child nestled in the crook of her arm contemplating his fingers, which were interlocked; it was a startlingly natural, sensuous pose. A piece of heavy golden cloth embroidered with tiny flowers was draped across the divan; in the background, behind the Madonna's left shoulder, a balcony was golden in evening light. A dark myrtle tree stood beyond the balustrade, its narrow pointed leaves brushing the pale stone of the balcony. The room in which she sat seemed like a bedroom or a boudoir, a place of intimacy rather than religious contemplation, and on a dark wooden chest in one corner lay a handful of pale, papery lilac iris, the Florentine lily of the title. The Madonna herself, her skin very pale, her hair, which was very black, parted in the centre, tiny pearls in her ears, looked up shyly but candidly, exactly as a new mother flushed with pride might look up at her child's father.

Celia and her guide stood united in contemplation; Celia realized she was holding her breath. Any anxiety she might have had about the absence of the other Titians had entirely evaporated; this was enough for anyone. She could not imagine what it would be like to sit with someone you loved in this beautiful, intimate space, this little jewel casket of a room set in the palace's great empty luxury while a Titian Madonna – this Madonna – looked down from the wall. Lucky Mrs Lucas Marsh; Celia wondered if she would appreciate it.

'Who was the model?' she asked the administrator in wonder, unable to believe she had never seen this picture before.

The administrator smiled a little. 'Ah,' she said. 'A long story. The wife of one of the Bardi, a minor noblewoman of Florence, not important, not historically you understand. But it is quite clear that Tiziano – Titian – was in love with her. He revered her; he might have made her a Venus, but he made her a Madonna, he put the *giglio* – the flower of Florence – as a tribute to her, to the city.'

Celia nodded. 'And what happened?'

Paola Caprese frowned a little. 'It is not known; only speculated. That the child may have been his, although I think not.' She turned away, looking out of the window. 'And in fact there is not, what do you say, a happy ending; the child died, in an epidemic of some kind, it may have been influenza, shortly after the painting was completed. The husband locked

45

the painting away; it was rumoured that he had burnt it. In his grief.' Or jealousy, thought Celia, nodding. She remembered the story vaguely, was surprised by how affected by it she felt now that she had seen the painting, by the expression in the eyes of a woman who had lived centuries ago.

'Thank you,' she said to the administrator, suddenly feeling an excess of gratitude, a feeling of having been greatly privileged in being allowed to see the painting. *Not a bad job, after all*, she thought.

The woman nodded. 'So,' she said, crossing to a Chinese lacquer chest that stood in the corner of the room, and opening a tiny drawer from which she withdrew a sheaf of thick, printed papers. 'The menu, for confirmation. If there is anything else, certainly I shall be delighted to help you.' But from the brisk manner in which Celia now found herself ushered to the door she understood that she had already exceeded her entitlement to gracious service from the Palazzo Ferrigno.

Out in Le Cascine the trees cast a cold shadow, and the wind blew the leaves in eddies around the pathologist's tent that still stood in the drained pool. The vagrants had gone, a place found for them for the night in a shelter near the station, and so had the scruffy handful of potential witnesses the policemen had managed to trawl from the wooded avenues of the park. A drug addict with glazed eyes they'd found on a bench, the proprietor of an all-night food kiosk on the edge of the park, his eyes darting to and fro as he answered in monosyllables, *No, he hadn't served anyone unusual, the usual clientele.* But then none of his clientele could be called polite company: a couple of hookers, some Albanesi drinking beer and high as kites on something, a big Nigerian, a nightclub bouncer on his way home. The body had gone, too, off to the pathology lab in the north of the city, where it lay on a dissection table in a white-tiled room, the countryman's clothes removed and set aside for forensic inspection. A plaid shirt stiff with dried blood, a pair of heavy, polished boots.

Two policemen stood on the edge of the trees. 'I don't get it,' said the taller policeman, who was called Pietro. He sounded gloomy. 'I mean, no one's going to miss him, but why now?'

The stocky policeman shook his head, not answering. He stood on the edge of the trees and gazed down the silver ribbon of water to the west, where the great struts of the Viadotto dell' Indiano rose from the misty wasteland of swamp and rushes like the halyards of a ghost ship. He looked pale with sleeplessness and grim, and seemed to be staring at something beyond even the setting sun. 'Let's go, Sandro,' said Pietro, clapping him on the shoulder, and after a long moment the policeman put away the fluttering pages of his notebook and turned after him into the dark trees.

Chapter Six

In December the sun already hung low in the sky by three o'clock in the afternoon, and by not long after four it was setting. From the Ponte Alle Grazie you could see a white-gold disc hanging just above the horizon through the central arch of the Ponte Vecchio, silhouetting the heads of tourists as they passed endlessly up and down. As it set, the sun shone down the length of the river flowing west, bathing the façades that fronted the Arno in the last of its warm yellow light, gleaming off the inlaid façade of San Miniato up on the hills above San Niccolò, then it was gone.

At her till Gianna stifled a yawn. An hour until closing. Luisa walked the length of the showroom, turned back towards the door. It always grew cold in the shop as the sun sank behind the Borsa and left the façade of Frollini in shade, but Luisa was in no hurry to be home.

Luisa knew that Gianna and Beppe thought of her as old-fashioned, plain-speaking; an ordinary person of the old school who believed in eating properly and doing everything by the book. It was a generation thing; even though they were only ten years or so younger, the world had changed in those ten years and they thought of her as old, thought she'd been like this for ever. Everyone knew she was married, no children. She wasn't given much to talking about her husband, either, not even the sort of good-natured grumbling practically obligatory in every marriage; a sign, they thought, of old-fashioned discretion. But Luisa had a secret; she was the girl in the postcard.

Among the black and white cards displayed everywhere in the city – little snatches of nostalgia, rain-soaked panoramas, lads on Vespas, ragged children running through the market stalls: street life from another world – there was one of a young woman, narrow-waisted in a fitted sweater, tight skirt and heels, looking in at a jeweller's window on the Ponte Vecchio at dusk, the glitter of treasure reflected in her dark eyes: Luisa.

When Luisa saw that face it was as though she was looking at a stranger, and as for the tiny waist Sandro could once span with his hands, where had it gone? Was it still there somewhere, underneath the comfortable thickness of middle age? But she could remember the feeling still; now and again it came back to her, fresh and heady like the smell of hyacinths in the dead of winter. The feeling, as she looked at that emerald necklace, of being poised on the edge of something. *Will I be handsome, will I be rich?* Behind her the crowds had been flowing past as they did today when slowly she had become aware of an unmoving presence among them, heard the solid click of the shutter and turned. He'd flashed her a charming professional smile, tipped his hat to her and was gone.

The picture hadn't gained currency for thirty years or

49

more. It had been published in a small collection, gone into an archive to be rediscovered three decades later by an enterprising printer and published as part of a nostalgic series. She sold well, did Luisa; she thought sometimes someone might recognize her and exclaim over her image that was considered pretty enough to be bought and posted all over the world, but nobody ever did. Luisa wasn't sure any more if her secret warmed her or brought her pain as she stood, square-hipped in her plain dark clothes and flat shoes, and watched the crowds hurrying home on a cold December evening.

Celia met no one in the gloom of the stairwell as she hurried down the stairs. In nearly four months she had passed other residents of the building, which contained seven apartments, on these stairs only once; a smart, youngish couple in matching heavy-framed, wraparound glasses who didn't seem eager to make friends. Pushing open the door at the bottom of the stairs, Celia stepped on to a street where the evening had begun. Someone was going into the bar opposite as she emerged and as the door opened the sound of music and voices was briefly allowed out. Through the steamy window as she passed Celia could see a couple standing at the bar, heads close together, drinking from tall glasses. Did she miss it, being a couple? She wasn't sure.

For a long time Celia had been quite happy on her own. Seeing Jo Starling, for one, negotiating all the responsibilities and nuances of a relationship with an Italian, it had felt like freedom, rather than solitude. No one to tell her off for not having a shoe cupboard, or a tablecloth on the table, or the right kind of coffee machine. Then she'd met Dan.

Kate had thought Celia would marry Dan; if she was honest,

even Celia had wondered about it. From the day they met, at a cocktail party organized by the British Council for the local English-speaking community, Celia had felt completely comfortable with Dan Strickland, as though she'd always known him. Stocky and dark, Dan was very clever, and very funny. A poet himself, and a jobbing journalist on the side, he knew everybody in Florence – Nobel prizewinners, struggling painters, impoverished academics, alcoholic language teachers – but still he had been impressed with Celia's official accreditation as a guide, and she'd felt herself melt. Close to five years working in language schools and travel agencies while she studied and prepared for the *concorso*, the infamous open question session that had to be survived to become a guide to the great, incomparable city. 'Rather you than me,' he'd said admiringly, and looking up at her over the rim of his glass. 'It's supposed to be like the Spanish Inquisition, getting past the Academy.' And over the course of that evening, as she moved under the coffered and painted ceilings of the Palazzo Strozzi, in all the din of over-excited conversation, Celia had become aware of his sharp brown eyes on her now and again. And when the crowd began to thin out, friends drifting off in groups to go and eat, the happily married going home to their families, Dan had appeared at Celia's elbow at precisely the right moment, just as the pleasure of the evening hung on the point of evaporation.

'Come on,' he said. As she descended the broad marble staircase on his arm Celia had felt as though she was floating.

For three years they'd been a couple, going to parties together, mixing, drifting, finding each other in corners to report back, meeting for breakfast under Pasquale's eye, walking in the Boboli on Sundays, talking. Gossip, argument, helpless laughter; the pleasure of a proper conversation and a shared culture had been thrilling. They had never actually lived together properly; perhaps that should have told Celia something. But she had agreed with him, hadn't needed persuading that they both needed their space.

A couple of weeks short of the third anniversary of their first meeting Dan started sleeping with a well-bred Florentine girl from one of those noble families, a Ricasoli or a Torrigiani. Allegra. She was haughty, with a swinging walk and long dark hair, fine bones, tendons like piano wire; in addition, she was only twenty-one and indiscreet, so Celia found out what was going on very quickly. It was difficult to get emotional with Dan, though; he was too sharp. You couldn't break down and reproach him, which was probably just as well. And it had always been part of his appeal after all, that chip of ice in his heart, that sharp tongue, and three years had been a long time, in his book; she hadn't done badly. Occasionally while they had been together Celia had glimpsed, or thought she'd glimpsed, something else, a secret tender spot that all his cleverness was there to disguise, but then it would vanish and he would become irritable. Perhaps that prying glance of hers was what had sent him off, in the end; she'd never know.

As she left the bright windows of the bar behind and set off down the dark, narrow canyon of the Via dei Bardi to meet Beate, Celia pulled her coat around her, the fur collar soft and warm against her cheek. She loved this street, so silent, so beautiful, so dark; anything might happen here. She shrugged off the thought of Dan. The truth was, she told herself, although she often missed talking to him, she did bump into him now and again, in the corridors of the Uffizi, in the paperback exchange, and that was probably enough.

Beate had wanted to meet in a new place on the river, the Scarlatti; a sleek modern bar with a restaurant at the back about fifteen minutes' walk away. 'Marco likes it,' she'd said. 'He'll be along for ten minutes or so, then he's got people to see. You don't mind?'

Celia had shrugged; she'd have liked to see Beate alone, and in her flat, for once, she realized, somewhere relaxed. But she liked Marco well enough. He was well dressed, courteous, laid-back; he smelled good and was generous to Beate, so how could she object to him? He did sometimes seem so detached as to be somewhere else entirely, but then perhaps that was businessmen for you, they kept part of their thoughts for business, always. Celia found herself thinking of Lucas Marsh as she emerged from the Via dei Bardi on to the Lungarno, where the bright lights strung along the embankment were reflected in the dark surface of the river below. She assumed he would be like that, detached, distracted. Was that why he was arranging this lavish weekend, to compensate his wife for his absence? Celia wondered if they had children, where they might be.

The Scarlatti occupied the ground floor of a solid, nineteenth-century building set back a little way from the river; what was called a piazza on the map was in fact barely more than a wide stretch of pavement. The bar's exterior was anonymous, sand-coloured, with a wide plate-glass frontage tinted against the sun and inquisitive passers-by. When Celia peered in she could see that Beate was already there, leaning back on a pale leather banquette, gazing at something far off. Her thick white hair was in a heavy plait over one shoulder, one long, slender brown arm stretched on to the table, fingers resting at the base of a tall wine glass. Marco was next to her, frowning into a mobile phone display, in front of him

53

a tumbler of mineral water. Celia pushed open the heavy glass door.

Beate turned her head and raised a hand, beckoning Celia over; Celia smiled back and began to remove her coat in the warmth. It was still early and apart from the three of them the place was almost empty; behind the long, curved bar the white-aproned barman was restocking a wine rack that went from floor to ceiling. Celia recognized him from somewhere. They moved around the city mysteriously, the good *baristas*, floor managers, wine waiters; when a new place opened up there they'd be, giving it the imprimatur of quality, speaking their perfect, courteous English. 'Salve,' she said to him, and the barman narrowed his eyes, placing her, then smiled. Leonardo, that was his name. *Leo.* Celia nodded towards Beate's table and asked for a glass of white wine. Leo inclined his head, and Celia wondered whether she should have specified a grape variety and vintage; it was that kind of place.

The lighting in the bar was dim, uplighters on the cream-plastered walls, and Celia's eyes took some time to adjust, but it was, she saw in the long mirrors that ran along the length of the leather banquettes, a flattering light. This was a place for the older, wealthier client. Celia slid behind the pale wood table beside Beate, who laid an arm along the seat back and pressed her cheek against Celia's. She smelled of wine and the heavy scent she always wore, old-fashioned, sweet. Marco put down his mobile phone and regarded Celia with new interest.

'Aha,' he said. 'I hear you are a high-flyer, these days, Celia. Lucas Marsh, eh?'

Celia's heart sank a little; she didn't want to be reminded of how big a deal Lucas Marsh was. She nodded, aware of Marco's eye on her, but just then the barman came over with a little tray, set down her own huge glass one third filled with wine, and some little bowls of the tiny olives that came from Liguria. 'The wine is from Sicily,' he said politely. 'I think you will like it.'

'So,' Celia said reluctantly once Leo had left. 'What is all this about Lucas Marsh? What exactly is it that he does?' She took a sip of wine; it was full-flavoured, aromatic stuff, and she felt it burn as it hit her empty stomach.

Marco gave an elegant little shrug of his broad, tailored shoulders. 'That would be telling, as you say.' He smiled, and took a draught of his mineral water, frowning down at the ice-cubes in the glass in mock dismay. 'Tcha,' he exclaimed. 'I didn't ask for ice. Everything here is for Americans now.' He said something over Celia's head to the barman that she couldn't follow, but the man just smiled a little and went on polishing the big glasses that hung along the bar. It was just a distraction, anyway, keeping her in suspense. Perhaps he regretted letting on that he knew anything about Marsh, or perhaps it had all been bluff, pretending he knew more than he did. Suddenly Celia didn't feel like letting it drop; after all, this would probably be her only chance to find out anything about the Marshes, and the wine had made her reckless, and curious.

'Come on, Marco, either you know or you don't.' And she took another drink.

Marco made a little wagging, equivocating movement with his neat, distinguished head as if to say, *Maybe. Maybe, maybe not.* Then he relented. 'Okay,' he said. 'Lucas Marsh is a lawyer. A good lawyer, and I think a charming man. Very nice, very rich.' He paused, looking at Celia, wondering if that would satisfy her. She laughed.

'Very illuminating,' she said. 'You can do better than that.'

Marco just smiled, taking a sip of his water; the ice-cubes rattled against the glass. Beate leaned against him, pressed her cheek against his, draining her wine. 'Spill the beans, darling,' she said, setting the glass back on the table. 'What good are you if we can't get the inside story?'

Marco shrugged. 'The truth is, I don't really know much about him personally, not anything . . . concrete. Lucas Marsh is one of those people who gets very rich and no one's quite sure how he's done it. He's tough though, that's for sure; he works for some pretty intimidating people, big boys from the East. Russian money.'

Celia frowned. 'Is he a crook?'

Marco made hushing movements with his hands, looking offended. 'No, no,' he said, but in a tone of voice Celia recognized as particularly Italian, a tone that meant, the truth is a flexible substance, words can mean one thing, or they can mean quite the opposite. He clicked his teeth. 'Lucas Marsh – well, I have a theory there's something going on there, something in his past, it's often the way with rich men, there's something that drives them. You know?'

Celia wasn't sure that she did; suddenly Lucas Marsh was all of a piece with the groups of *carabinieri* that seemed to be everywhere these days, bringing menace to the lovely galleried courtyard of the Uffizi, walking among the crowds. What was the world coming to? She gazed out through the tinted glass; on the other side of the river the proud, golden façade of the Palazzo Ferrigno rose above the river, its windows dark and shuttered tonight. It suddenly seemed a sinister place, somewhere you could imagine poisonings or assassinations plotted in its rambling corridors.

Marco's ten minutes came and went and he showed no sign

of leaving; having Lucas Marsh as a client had obviously conferred greater status on Celia than she had ever enjoyed in his eyes before. She found this quite amusing and they chatted on quite happily, although Beate didn't contribute much; it was only when she looked at her watch that Celia realized it was ten o'clock and there had been none of the catching up she'd planned. She was disconcerted.

'Oh,' she said unhappily. 'Beate, I didn't realize – I've been jabbering on—'

'Never mind,' said Beate, waving away her apologies; she was incapable of taking offence, perpetually agreeable. 'There'll be another time.'

Marco stood up, frowning. 'But I must go,' he said, looking at his watch. 'I'm flying to Berlin in two hours. You can chat now, surely?' He pulled on his coat, lifted a hand in farewell, but before he got more than a couple of paces he turned back.

'You might be careful, though,' he said consideringly. 'Didn't he ask for security of any kind, a heavy or two? Men who are that rich attract attention, if you know what I mean. And not always the right kind of attention. Things ... can happen.' Then he was gone.

Celia turned to look at Beate, who was lighting another cigarette, watching Marco's back disappearing through the glass doors. 'I've got to be up early,' she began uncertainly, apologetically, feeling tomorrow weighing on her already as Marco's words settled in her mind.

Beate took a deep drag on her cigarette and patted Celia absently on the hand. 'Of course you do,' she said with distant kindness. 'Off you go now.'

*

It was eight-thirty by the time Luisa let herself into the building in the crowded, narrow streets between Santa Croce and the river. When she came to her own front door, anonymous green-painted steel, triple-locked, with her husband's name beside it, she involuntarily held her breath as she always did until the lock turned once, twice, three times, the door was open and she knew if he was in or not. The hall was dark and cold and Luisa felt its chill air settle across her shoulders like a weight as she put down her bags in the kitchen. She felt like a different person here, large and clumsy, as though she took up too much space. She went into the kitchen, turning on lights. She felt it descend on her, the dimness, the gloom she'd felt in bed early this morning, and fought it.

There was stale smoke on the air and there were two cigarette ends in the ashtray on the oilcloth; he'd been back then and gone out again. Luisa emptied the ashtray into the bin, wiped it out with a cloth and set it back on the table. Still standing, she unpacked the shopping – bread, black cabbage, sausage, fennel seeds – focusing on what she had to cook. *That's what married life is all about,* her mother's voice scolded her out of the past, *none of that romantic rubbish. Food on the table.* As she took out onions, carrot, celery, garlic, began to dice the vegetables, put a flame under the frying pan and the mingled smells of herbs and olive oil rose to fill the air, Luisa's shoulders relaxed a little.

She stood there with her coat still on, slicing the long blue-black leaves of young cabbage and skinning the sausage, getting out bowls, boiling water. She fell into a rhythm but at the same time it was almost as though she was working in her sleep; the door opened behind her but she didn't turn around. She could feel the cold air of the hall come into the room and she knew

58

Sandro was taking off his cap and setting it on the sideboard. There was a clunk as he unbuttoned his heavy gun belt – empty, of course, the gun already signed in back at the station – and set it beside the cap. Next he would lay out the evening newspaper on the table and ask her for a beer; she heard the slap as the paper went down, the scrape of the chair, but he said nothing. There was a sound, but it was not articulate, a choked sort of noise, and then she turned.

'Take off your coat,' said Sandro; he often sounded like this, exasperated, but this time there was a despairing edge to his voice too. Luisa set down the knife and took off her coat. She lowered herself into a chair beside him. He pushed the paper across to her and leaned back to take the bottle of amaro from the sideboard, and a glass. Luisa frowned down at the headline; something about a body found in Le Cascine. She scanned the paragraph beneath it, squinting; she needed glasses. The body of a man aged between sixty-five and seventy, not yet formally identified. She looked across at Sandro, questioning. He didn't look at her, just threw his head back and swallowed the viscous amber liquid. He poured another.

It's Bartolo,' he said, his voice rough with the alcohol, staring straight ahead. 'Bartolo's dead. Looks like he cut his own throat.'

Luisa pushed her chair back. 'Bartolo?' she said wonderingly.

'He did it in Le Pavoniere, would you believe it? In a swimming pool.' And then Sandro laughed, a harsh, bitter sound.

'Killed himself?' Luisa couldn't keep the disbelief out of her voice.

Sandro looked directly at her then. He sighed. 'They'd done another DNA test,' he said with reluctance. 'New technology, some new technique from Sweden to extract the stuff from degraded or incomplete samples.' He looked away. 'The papers

59

got hold of that, they're saying it must be to do with that, he knew the writing was on the wall so—' he broke off, drew a thumb across his own throat.

Dumbly Luisa nodded, listening to all this as though Sandro confided in her every night when in fact he never spoke a word. In reality Sandro had stopped talking to her about work or even any other thing that happened between his leaving the house and returning to it at night, somewhere around fourteen years since. She knew who Bartolo was, though, from all that time ago.

A man with a smallholding on the edge of the city, a crumbling farmhouse and a handful of fruit trees sandwiched between a new housing development and the motorway, Bartolo's scruffy patch also happened to adjoin the Olympia swimming pool complex. He'd been about fifty then, known as a loner; he would, mused Luisa, thinking of the article in the paper, pondering the passage of all that time, be sixty-five or so now. He had often been seen standing beside the link fence around the tennis courts, watching the girls play; he'd even been found wandering by the pool now and again, under the umbrella pines. The land on which the pool was built had belonged to his family when he was a boy, and they thought that must be why he kept coming back.

Sandro had called the anorexic who manned the changing rooms half-witted, as though the lack of food had starved her brain. Luisa had seen her in some hurried news footage, standing on the edge of a group of shouting men, her eyes dark smudges on the screen, staring. She'd said at first she might have seen Bartolo that afternoon; Luisa remembered Sandro telling her that much; the statement had been retracted, though, so it was never made public. She'd turned obstinate all of a sudden, said she couldn't be sure, it could have been yesterday morning. Luisa thought about her now, that girl; had Sandro bullied her, got her in a state so she didn't know which way was up? He could be like that sometimes. She thought of the girl on the television screen and remembered she'd been no more than a kid herself, some skimpy crop-top hanging loose on her, mulish and sulky. It wasn't fair. The heat and panic turned everyone's brains to mush, she remembered Sandro saying with disgust; like getting a sullen child to learn, you felt like shaking them.

So there'd been no proof, nothing but circumstantial stuff; they'd gathered samples of this and that, from his van, from his cantina, the lean-to against the link fence. Hair, skin scrapings, a tattered fragment of cloth that turned out to have come from his mother's apron, caught on the fence.

All this Luisa remembered even fifteen years on. She remembered Sandro coming home at two in the morning for the week the child was still officially just missing – but they all knew, didn't they? A seven-year-old girl, gone a week – and pouring it all out, ranting at the table. *How could no one have seen her? All those nice little houses out there in the suburbs, flowers in the gardens, everything new. Where are all the nosy neighbours when you need them?* Luisa remembered it drying up too, the ranting, when the girl's body was found. She remembered as though it was yesterday the vacant, evasive look in the anorexic's eyes when she appeared on the television, dodging guilt. They'd all been doing that when it happened, that was how it had felt. And looking at Sandro now, at the table, feeling his silent rage in the confined space like electricity before a storm, it all came back to her with the force of revelation. Gingerly she put a hand out to Sandra's shoulder, and he began to cry.

*

At the Hotel Regale the heating generated by a bank of sleek German boilers in the basement blasted through the wide, carpeted corridors, warming every corner of the massive, nineteenth-century building. Two years earlier the hotel, standing at the centre of the city on the Piazza Repubblica, had been subject to complete and lavish renovation, every cornice and balustrade, every antiquated bathroom restored. In reception a gold-buttoned concierge frowned at his reservations book; two guests yet to arrive, on the late flight from London. Mr and Mrs Lucas Marsh, the honeymoon suite. It was almost midnight.

The temperature was falling fast; in the dark hills around Florence snow was beginning to fall, dusting the dark Chianti hills with white, settling on the trees in the steep wooded valleys of the Casentino. Snow almost never fell in Florence itself, melting in the warm air that rose from the buildings before it reached the rooftops and turning to slush, but not far from the centre it was drifting down, in Scandicci and Sesto Fiorentino, the bleak suburbs on the Pisan plain. It was even falling at the airport where a single snowplough and de-icing trucks were slowly moving to and fro on the runways, and overhead a delayed flight from London circled, its winking lights illuminating the whirling flakes as it descended between the dark hills to the plain.

Just east of the airport, between the reedy, garbage-clogged banks of the Arno and a half-built section of motorway, the snow fell on a ramshackle shanty town of rusted containers, corrugated iron shacks and tents. Under an awning of tattered tarpaulin a circle of hollow-eyed, dark-skinned men in heavy coats were playing cards at a folding table by the hissing blue light of a Tilley lamp as the snow fell softly in the darkness beyond them. A humped figure in a tattered sleeping bag leaned against the door of a caravan and watched them, a woman, although you'd have to look closely to be sure; her face was gaunt, almost all femininity stripped from it, though whether from poverty or age it was hard to tell. She gazed at the men with bleary eyes, bloodshot and dull. Overhead a plane roared, and the men looked up, all at once. One smiled and another grunted. It was difficult to say what they were thinking, whether they were dreaming of a passage home or thinking of the day they'd looked up as a plane screamed in to land and as its undercarriage came down they'd seen the stiff, frozen body of a stowaway fall to the tarmac.

The plane was idling now along the runway in the floodlit distance, and the men returned to their game. They all knew the airport, a place stuffed with rich pickings, designer luggage circling on the conveyor belts and limousines waiting with their engines running at arrivals. They knew the wealthy were blind, blinkered by luxury; they didn't see beyond the bright lights of the airport concourse and the padded leather interior of the limousine. They couldn't see out here, into the darkness further out where things moved, insidious and invisible, where deals were done and lives were bartered, sold as cheap as the corpse of the Somali stowaway.

Chapter Seven

The city stirred reluctantly awake in the cold, and as it rose the pale sun gave out little warmth in an ice-blue sky.

Celia woke early; some internal clock had told her that today she needed time. There was no one else, after all, to wake her, and after more than a decade of early starts, collecting clients from airports and hotels, she had somehow trained herself to become an early riser. She needed to look right for the job, she'd learned that early; it was no use being a scruffy English girl with unwashed hair, no make-up and bad clothes. You had to arrive on a job and be sure that the clients knew straight away that you were the guide, that you had authority. And that meant you couldn't just jump out of bed and into the clothes you'd left on the floor last night.

Dressed, hair brushed, she paused, calculating. She'd have to book a taxi sometime, to get them from San Miniato to the restaurant at least. Then she had a thought, and dialled Gabriele's number. *Poor guy*, she thought guiltily as she heard it ring. *Taking advantage, this is called.* But the thought of sweating it out waiting for a cab, when she might have someone she could rely on for moral support as well as a ride, had got the better of her conscience.

Gabriele sounded sleepy. 'Sorry, sweetheart,' Celia said. 'Did I wake you?' It occurred to her that there weren't many friends she could call up at this hour, but she never worried with Gabriele. She thought of the last trip they'd done together, to Fiesole, him rolling his eyes at the talk on the Roman arena he'd heard her give a hundred times before, trying to make her laugh with sidelong glances. 'Just checking you're okay for today?'

As she left the warm flat Celia felt an icy draught coming up the dark stone stairwell from below; shoving open the heavy door on to the street, she felt the cold wrap itself around her, stinging her cheeks. Across the road the bar on the corner wasn't open yet, and she turned in to the Via dei Bardi. It was a long, straight stretch that led her into town, dark and silent in the early morning, and as Celia passed between the massive stone walls of the old palaces they exhaled a deep, sepulchral chill. She had dressed with care in boots, neat wool trousers and a thick, soft, dark cardigan she'd saved for in last year's sales and had been keeping for the right moment; for a bitter morning like this and an important appointment to keep. Soft black lined leather gloves from the Scuola del Cuoio, where she got a discount because she took clients there sometimes. But still she was cold.

Celia thought of the day ahead; she had to meet the Marshes at the hotel, then a morning in San Miniato, afternoon in the Uffizi. She shouldered her bag, heavy with its daily load, the tools of her trade – a Blue Guide, notebook, mobile, water bottle – and kept walking. Her feet were freezing and she thought longingly of coffee.

On the Lungarno in the bright, bitter morning the wind came off the river in gusts and Celia hunched her shoulders against it. She saw a handful of early-morning tourists coming off the Ponte Vecchio, their faces looking pinched in the wind with cold and disappointment. Italy was not after all the land of warmth and eternal sunshine. Celia hesitated on the corner beside the news-stand where the latest headlines were pasted up on a board: *Le Cascine: body found*. A man stood by the kiosk with a copy of *La Nazione* open, engrossed in the front-page story. Over his shoulder Celia glimpsed a photograph, police tents among some trees. She took a copy of *La Repubblica*, paid for it and looked at her watch; she had time for a quick one. She turned in to the Maoli.

The bar was crowded; it was a cold morning and Celia wasn't alone in needing fortification on the journey to work. She hoped Beate was having a lie-in; they had drunk two bottles of wine between them and as she stood waiting for her coffee Celia could feel the effects, a bit of a nagging ache behind her eyes.

People stood around the bar talking, heavy wool coats smelling of dry-cleaning and mothballs taking up twice the usual amount of space, and all the tables were occupied. In a corner sat a woman Celia thought she recognized but couldn't quite place; a solidly built, dark-haired woman in a navy-blue coat with a caffè latte on the table in front of her. She sat stiffly, as though trying to erase herself, handbag over her arm as if she had to be ready to leave at any moment although she'd found herself a seat. Her face was powdered and pale, but there were shadows under her black eyes. Distractedly,

Pasquale pushed Celia's pastry and cappuccino over the bar to her and she picked them up without really looking. She took out her paper, unfolded it and stared at the front page, but the gruesome headline repelled her: *slaughtered like a beast*, it said. Besides, she didn't have time to get stuck into a news story now. She put the paper away again.

At the movement the woman at the corner table looked up and Celia recognized her as the brisk, competent saleswoman from Frollini, the one who never forgot a face. Celia had observed her on her visits to the shop, had seen the notice she took of customers' preferences and the regularity of their visits. It was odd, she looked quite different here, almost lost, and it occurred to Celia that that had been why she hadn't recognized her immediately. She turned back to her coffee, downed it and with a nod to Pasquale turned to leave, and saw that the woman who worked at Frollini had already gone.

The Por Santa Maria, the main shopping street and one section of the arterial route that led from the Pitti Palace on the south of the river up to the cathedral to the north, was already filling up with commuters and early-morning tourists, those with less hospitable hotels, uncomfortable beds and no breakfast perhaps. They walked arm in arm more for warmth than anything else, the budget travellers, teenage girls and Eastern Europeans, but as they passed Celia could see the dreaming city reflected in their eyes, the lovely stone façades and arched windows and the thin, pale light of the winter morning. She thought of Mr and Mrs Lucas Marsh waiting for her at the Regale and found herself wondering how they were seeing the city this morning, whether they would get what they had come for. A weekend away in a foreign city; they wanted romance, glamour, luxury, escape. Celia wondered if the Marshes had had the Italian papers delivered with their breakfast, if they knew a mutilated corpse had been found in what was sometimes called Florence's equivalent of Hyde Park.

As she walked on and Frollini came into view, Celia remembered the dark-eyed saleswoman she'd seen sitting in the corner of the Maoli and glanced in through the window, but it was dark behind the display and she walked on up the street to the massive, monumental space of the Piazza della Repubblica, and the Hotel Regale.

If Celia had looked inside she wouldn't have seen Luisa anyway in the dark interior of the shop. Luisa had let herself in with a hand that shook; as always, she had gone straight to the keypad behind the till to stop the alarm going off, but today it took her three attempts before she managed to key in the right code. When it was done she leaned against the door in a moment of weakness, taking deep breaths of the shop's neutral air, feeling a sudden sweat bead on her forehead. She told herself there was nothing to be done yet, she could stay like this for a moment.

Luisa hadn't slept, that was part of it. The truth was, after fifteen years of grim silence between her and Sandro she'd adapted, grown a new skin. And now was it all going to change? She wasn't sure, any more, of whether that was what she wanted, and what was more she didn't know, by the look of him last night, if Sandro himself could hold up under the strain. What would happen if it all came out, everything he had been bottling up for fifteen years?

There had been something in the way that girl had looked at her, too, that had brought this on; a look not accusing but penetrating, as though she had looked right inside Luisa's head. She closed her eyes and wondered bleakly what it might have looked like to that girl, the knotted pathways in her brain laid down by fifteen years of evasion, compromise, silence. Luisa took another deep breath, trying to get it out of her mind, trying to restore the calm she had, until today, always been able to count on once she was inside this door.

After a moment or two she opened her eyes and saw a face at the glass; she started at the sight, then realized it was the first of the cleaners, tapping and nodding, trying to make herself understood through the barriers of language and plate glass. Wearily Luisa nodded back, pulling the door open, and in they came, filling up the room once again. Standing at the window, she let them get on with it behind her, grateful not to have to talk.

Celia, still six minutes early and killing time in front of the Regale under the eye of the hatted and gloved doorman, watched the *carabinieri* leaning against their van in striped guardsmen's trousers, smoking. Was it her imagination, or were they really everywhere these days? Never when you actually needed them, when Beate was threatened a week or so ago by a drug dealer on the corner of her street, a month back when Celia had been jostled by two dark men so her bag fell to the ground, papers, schedules everywhere, her wallet stripped. The *carabinieri* had bigger quarry these days; they spent less time idly preening, more watching in earnest. Celia had seen an abandoned backpack on the steps of the cathedral surrounded in minutes, prodded with electronic probes; they'd been on the point of a controlled explosion when its dozy owner stumbled back, almost in tears. She thought of the potted olive tree set behind the Uffizi in memory of those killed in the explosion there, however many years before.

Twelve? Something like that. And the world hadn't grown any safer since then.

Today, though, in front of her the piazza could hardly have seemed more tranquil in the pale blue light of early morning, businessmen on their way to work in expensive overcoats and trilbies, a puttering delivery van, a crop-headed man smoking meditatively on a stone bench. Celia's own warm breath clouded in front of her on the frosty air. She turned and the doorman was already there, opening the door in front of her, flashing her a smile as she passed him and was inside.

The foyer was high-ceilinged, full of marble, and sound reverberated around Celia, the click of her boots on the floor and strangers' voices echoing from a hundred smooth, hard, polished surfaces. Celia walked to the desk, set her leather bag on the counter and waited. Eventually the receptionist, a young, dark woman in a fitted black suit who was taking a telephone booking, turned to her with a smile of polite enquiry.

'Ah,' she said when Celia had stated her business, and Celia saw a glimmer of interest in her eyes. 'Yes, Mr and Mrs Marsh, they arrive very late last night.' She tapped on a computer keyboard behind the counter, ran a finger down the screen. 'But they are expecting you, at this hour?'

'Yes,' said Celia firmly, but her heart sank. The receptionist nodded, picked up a phone and dialled, eyes averted. The telephone seemed to ring for some time and Celia envisaged a morning wasted, spent sitting waiting in reception while Mr and Mrs Lucas Marsh got ready, but then she heard a voice, muffled and tinny but calm, on the other end of the line. The receptionist gave her name, then said only, *Yes, yes, certainly, yes.* She replaced the receiver and turned to Celia.

'Room 24,' she said. 'The honeymoon suite. They would like you to go up.' She raised a finger and a bellboy materialized at Celia's side.

The hotel's carpeted corridors were very warm and by the time the bellboy left Celia at the discreet oak door to room 24, she felt overdressed and stifled. The fact that her first meeting with Mr and Mrs Lucas Marsh was not, as she had expected, to take place on neutral ground but in the unusual intimacy of a hotel room – the honeymoon suite, at that – increased her discomfort. She knocked.

Chapter Eight

Celia hadn't made the hotel bookings; that was normal
enough. Generally she was an add-on, an optional extra
brought in by one of the tour companies or travel agencies
she had a relationship with. When she had first spoken to
Lucas Marsh he had made it clear in that voice of his that had
so evaded her since that he would, like most of her clients, be
making his own personal arrangements. She was to book restaurants – for Friday the Quattro Leoni at lunch, somewhere
elegant for the evening, Cibreo perhaps. She'd done what he
asked. He obviously knew the city; he was also, obviously, a
private person. And discreet as she felt herself to be, Celia had
to admit that if she had been asked to book the honeymoon
suite at the Regale she might well have speculated.

The door to room 24 remained closed for some moments;
behind it Celia heard the sound of voices. She composed
her face and waited equably; just as she was beginning to
wonder if she should knock again the door opened. A young

woman – she must be older than she looks, Celia thought, remembering belatedly that Lucas Marsh's wife was thirty-two tomorrow – stood there, half-dressed in a silk slip, woollen skirt and stockinged feet. She was pretty in what Celia could only think of as an old-fashioned sort of way; at once voluptuous and delicate, white-skinned, pink-cheeked, with heavy, glossy black hair twisted up behind her head. She gave the impression of bursting with health; beside her Celia felt like a small, dull, brown bird next to a plump white dove. Celia also realized at that moment that she did not know Mrs Lucas Marsh's first name, as in all correspondence she had been referred to only as an appendage to her husband. In the flesh she did not seem at all like anything so insignificant.

'Celia Donnelly,' said Celia, holding out a hand. The woman held out hers in response and opened her mouth to reply when another voice called from inside the room. It was Lucas Marsh's voice, she knew it immediately, like a scent. 'Emma?'

Emma Marsh raised her fine eyebrows in an expression of comic resignation. 'Typical Lucas,' she said. 'Has to get in first.' She turned and called over her shoulder, 'She's here.' There was no answer, but Emma Marsh seemed unperturbed; she turned back to Celia and smiled, showing small, perfect white teeth. She took Celia's hand and gave it a little shake. 'Come in,' she said, holding on to the hand and drawing Celia inside the room.

Despite all she knew about Florentine restraint and good taste, Celia realized as she entered the room that she had until this moment had a fixed idea of honeymoon suites, even here, as something out of Las Vegas with circular beds, ruched blinds and too much marble. The Regale obviously had a different idea of romance, however; the sitting room she entered was large but very simple, with a wooden floor, rugs, two long dark sofas and a huge window looking south to the ornate inlaid Venetian windows of the church of Orsanmichele. On a long, dark oak table against one wall stood an arrangement of tall arum lilies like ceremonial trumpets, waxy and perfect. It was empty, though, of life; there was no sign of Lucas Marsh.

Off one end of the room a door stood open; glancing through it as she stood there, Celia glimpsed another long window through which pale morning light fell on a corner of an unmade bed, gleaming off a dainty heap of something satin on the floor. Then the light moved and shifted as though interrupted, and registering the silent presence of Lucas Marsh out of sight in the bedroom, Celia quickly looked away.

'I – I could have waited downstairs,' she began desperately. 'Really, if you need more time . . .' Emma Marsh smiled at her again, languorous.

'No, no,' she said. 'I'm really nearly ready. The flight was late last night, and I just overslept. Lucas has been up for hours, always an early riser but me—' She shrugged. 'I'm just lazy. Can't seem to get out of bed.' And as if even the mention of bed was enough she yawned a little, cat-like, putting a small white hand to her mouth. 'Sit down. Would you like coffee? I'm having coffee.'

'I—' Celia hesitated, then gave in. After all, San Miniato was not a strenuous place to begin a day in Florence; they had plenty of time. 'Thank you,' she said, and sat where Emma Marsh gestured, on the dark plum velvet of the nearest sofa. There was a soft knock at the door, and as though Emma Marsh only had to decide she wanted something for it to appear, behind it was another uniformed bellboy with a tray of coffee and miniature croissants.

As Celia took the cup Emma offered her, as she took a sip – and registered how good it was, fiercely strong but not bitter – she couldn't help wondering what she was doing up here drinking coffee, instead of waiting in the foyer. Emma Marsh curled up on the sofa opposite her with another cup, her round white calves tucked under her on the velvet. She resembled, Celia thought with a kind of fascination, a pretty pedigree pet, well-fed, manicured and dainty, bred to perfection, but all the same Celia immediately found herself liking Emma Marsh. She also wondered surreptitiously when she was going to finish getting dressed; as she lay back on the sofa, stretching her pale legs, and took a sip of her coffee she showed no sign of it.

'Isn't this lovely?' she said, sighing happily and looking around with an air of such perfect satisfaction that Celia couldn't help smiling. Plenty of her wealthy clients did nothing but complain about their immensely luxurious hotel rooms; the air-conditioning was too cold, the central heating too hot, the coffee too strong.

'Everything's so nice to look at here, isn't it? So wonderfully, gorgeously beautiful.' Emma stretched. 'I do like beautiful things.' Celia had already worked that out from what there was of Emma Marsh's clothing. The lace on her silk slip was very fine and the skirt, which fitted her so perfectly it must have been made for her, was a heavy, nubbly tweed of colours Celia had never seen together before, electric blue, green, damson. You couldn't judge from appearances, she reminded herself, but everything about Emma Marsh was gorgeous, irresistible.

'Yes,' she said, 'it's a very beautiful city. Have you been before?'

'No,' said Emma Marsh. 'Never. This was all rather last-minute, too. I've been to Milan; Lucas took me to the shows this year – he had some business to do. It is rather a businesslike sort of place, very grey. Have you been?' Celia hadn't. Emma leaned forward and whispered conspiratorially, 'Nice shops. I do like shopping. We will be able to fit some in, won't we? Between all the churches and paintings?'

Celia laughed. 'Yes,' she said. 'I had assumed ... everyone wants to do some shopping.' It was true; for plenty of her clients the culture was a trade-off against a day or two in the designer outlets; sometimes they wanted her along, sometimes they didn't.

Satisfied, Emma Marsh leaned back against the sofa again. 'And Venice,' she said, 'we often go to Venice. So pretty, but it is rather chilly. And damp, of course,' she mused. 'Everything always seems damp in Venice, and it's rather ...' she wrinkled her nose, searching for the right word. 'Spooky? Sinister. All that water.' Celia suppressed a smile, agreeing. 'But Lucas knows Florence,' went on Emma Marsh confidently. 'I don't know why he hasn't brought me before. I practically had to force him.' This sounded odd to Celia, who knew the careful arrangements Marsh had made for his wife's weekend, the effort to keep her amused.

'Hadn't you better get dressed, Emma?' The voice, mild, affectionate, came from the bedroom doorway. Celia had to turn a little to see Lucas Marsh properly for the first time; he stood there, hands in his pockets, looking across the room at them. Celia didn't know what she had expected exactly, but he was a surprise. The first thing she saw was that he was a lot

76

older than his wife, perhaps twenty years older, and whereas couples, Celia had noticed, often resembled each other quite closely – if not to begin with, then they grew more alike over time – Lucas and Emma Marsh were physical opposites. He was tall but very pale, his hair silvery-fair off a high forehead. Celia was surprised to find him attractive, with some combination of assurance and strength in his bearing, without being bullying as rich men could be. He crossed the room and extended a hand; it felt cool to Celia, and light. She thought of Marco's insinuations; could this man have a dark secret? How could you tell?

'Miss Donnelly,' he said carefully. 'I'm Lucas Marsh.'

'Celia,' she replied, uncomfortable. 'Please.' Opposite her on the sofa she saw Emma Marsh sitting up straighter, colour in her cheeks; her husband seemed to have an effect on her composure. For a moment Celia wondered if she was afraid of him, but when she turned from Lucas to look directly at his wife, Emma was smiling.

'Just give me a minute then,' she said, and almost ran on bare feet past her husband and into the bedroom. She didn't quite close the door behind her and again Celia felt herself manoeuvred into an unwelcome intimacy. Just a touch of exhibitionism, she decided quickly, and after all, Emma Marsh had plenty to show off about. She looked down at her polished boots on the rug, aware of Lucas Marsh still standing at her shoulder.

'San Miniato this morning, then?' he said lightly. His pronunciation of the name of the church was very good, not overstated.

'Yes,' said Celia. 'Do you know it?'

He nodded, looking away from her through the window at the red-roofed skyline, and said, 'I thought we'd walk.' It was not a suggestion; the authority, the certainty of being obeyed she'd heard when they had first spoken was audible in his voice. Celia told herself that it was refreshing not to have to make every decision, and the walk to San Miniato was a pretty one.

'It's the best way,' she said, calculating the route they'd take to the river, suddenly not wanting the Marshes to encounter roadworks, scaffolding, anything ugly or jarring. He looked back down at her. 'Better get Emma to put sensible shoes on then,' he said, smiling, and as she looked up at Lucas Marsh Celia found herself dismissing everything Marco had implied about the kind of man he must be.

Luisa ran out for something to eat at around eleven; she suddenly felt ravenous. Sometimes she thought that if she was the kind of woman who could starve herself, turn herself into a kind of martyr, it might help. A saint on a pillar. But Luisa wasn't like that, she was too practical, hadn't been brought up to waste food, and there was some primitive survival instinct that told her, eat, be strong, one day you'll need it. So she put food on the table every night, lunchtimes too before they started doing *orario continuato* in the shop, working through. And after last night she felt hollowed out with hunger, starved, as though something inside was having to be rebuilt from scratch.

Unwillingly Luisa found herself thinking of Sandro's head on her shoulder, the wetness of his tears. It all seemed so new, suddenly, and she didn't know if she was young enough, or strong enough. Had their marriage been so bad, without this drama? Sandro drank a bit too much, but then plenty of husbands did, liked a couple of hours every evening with his friends doing whatever it was they did, playing cards, watching football, she'd long since stopped asking. He'd be back in time for his dinner usually, sat quiet, read the paper. Watched the television. Of course her father had been a different kind of man, easy-going, dreaming his life away in his little workshop; he would never have raised his hand to anyone. Sometimes Luisa felt a tightness in her chest at the thought of her parents' marriage, the softness in it, her father coming up behind her mother as she cooked and laying his cheek against hers; her mother would have batted him away, of course, taken all that for granted. Luisa and Sandro – well, you had to take what you were given in life, didn't you? Things didn't always work out the way you'd planned, you had to make the best of it.

Gianna covered for her; just ten minutes, Luisa said, and they weren't busy, not yet. She dashed into the bar over the road and took a little sandwich, which she ate in two mouthfuls, washed down with warm milk. But then as she was running back out a car stopped at the kerb right in front of her and she pulled up. Luisa stood there in the frosty morning air in no more than a cardigan, the paper napkin she'd used to wipe her mouth still crumpled in her hand, and came face to face with a woman climbing out of the car holding a bundle in her arms. Luisa didn't know her at all; she was pale, with rings under her eyes, but somehow her face was lit, glowing, and with an instinct that had kept her from this kind of proximity for twenty years Luisa started back from her. The woman was carrying a baby, not swaddled in a pram, bundled up to the point of invisibility as they usually were, but loosely wrapped in her arms, a tiny creature with the red, scalded look of the newborn.

Luisa's feet felt numb on the pavement and she wondered for a second if she might fall; not quite understanding, the woman smiled up at her and held out the baby, as any new mother might, to be admired. Luisa only gazed at the mother, whose look turned to puzzlement, then before Luisa could stop herself she did look down at the tiny, compressed red face of the baby framed in the folds of a shawl, the soft mouth moving as she slept.

'Ah,' she murmured, automatically putting out a hand to pull back the shawl, and she felt a burning in her eyes. 'How old is she?'

'Just six days,' said the baby's mother, full of pride. 'We're meeting Daddy for lunch, aren't we?' She cooed down at the baby, then looked back at Luisa, smiling. 'How did you know she was a girl?'

'Oh ...' said Luisa, still gazing at the baby, not hearing the question. 'I ...' She was so close she could smell the child, sweet and milky, see the curve of a closed eyelid, and she swallowed. 'I ...' She felt the woman's eyes on her, felt the mother's curiosity hardening into something else.

'Lovely,' she said, making herself look up, dazed. 'She's lovely. *Complimenti.*' And as she hurried past, she felt the woman turn in surprise to watch her go.

Luisa let herself back into the shop, which was mercifully empty, and came inside with her head down while she composed herself, making a big deal of stamping her feet with the cold.

'That was quick,' said Gianna, but she didn't look up from the magazine she was reading behind the till, so she hadn't seen anything.

What would she have thought if she had? It might occur to her that she didn't often see Luisa cooing over babies, might think, what a shame she never had any of her own, but then plenty didn't. Gianna herself wasn't so keen; she was from a family of eight and had always said, one, maximum, to her husband, and so far there'd been none but she wasn't bothered. Her husband grumbled sometimes but she just reminded him of the expense, the prams and car seats and all that there'd been no need of when they were growing up and just as well, imagine buying all that for eight.

Before she married Luisa had always been someone who talked, to her girlfriends, her mother; she would have said there was nothing she couldn't talk about. But it turned out that some of the things that happened to you in life had to stay locked away; they could not be made better for spilling them out on the kitchen table, an arm around the shoulders and a good cry. They never got better; perhaps that was why she had allowed Sandro his silence for fifteen years. Luisa hadn't had her daughter for very long, not six days, no more than a day and a night. Thirty-six long hours. These things happen.

Luisa felt a tremor, held out her hand to steady it. It was just the cold, and it had given her a bit of a shock, that was all. A baby so small shouldn't have been out on a day like this. She closed her eyes, opened them again on the warm, bright interior of her shop. The door swished and she straightened, hands crossed in front of her and her smile of polite welcome in place.

A mother and daughter came through the door, breathless with excitement, English – very English – with padded jackets and ugly shoes. Well made, but very ugly. 'We're looking for wedding pumps,' said the mother, in English. Luisa, whose English was rudimentary but serviceable within a narrow range of vocabulary – shoes, handbag, evening gown, cocktail dress – responded flawlessly, but it never ceased to amaze her, the presumption of the English that wherever they went, they would be understood. Others did it, French, Spanish, Germans not so much, but the English were something else. She didn't hold it against them, not today, anyway.

'And perhaps something for my mother,' said the daughter shyly. 'A suit, or a dress. For my wedding.'

'Come this way,' said Luisa, and she turned to guide them upstairs. With every step she concentrated on the soothing thought that up there among the rows of pale sweaters, the rails of suits and dresses, heavy satin and wool crêpe, she knew exactly where she was, and there she would be able to find this woman and her daughter everything they needed.

Chapter Nine

To get from the Regale to San Miniato was a walk, at a
leisurely pace, of perhaps forty minutes. The morning was
perfect, crisp and clear, and at this time of year the city was
not too crowded. From March to November the streets, to
the north of the river at least, were threaded through with
tour parties following their guides patiently from the Ponte
Vecchio to the Duomo, across to Santa Croce, back to the
Medici Chapel, and Celia found it hard to see where the
pleasure might be found in the walk. Today, though, as Celia,
flanked by Lucas and Emma Marsh, traced a meandering route
through the cold, narrow streets, they were almost empty.
Overhead a pale sun illuminated the frosty blue of the sky, and
in the calm it seemed to Celia as though the city was revealing
itself to them alone.

'You don't want to go to the Accademia?' she said as they
passed the copy of the David outside the great rusticated façade
of the Palazzo Vecchio, mildly curious that Lucas Marsh hadn't

specified such a visit. Almost everyone did. 'To see the restored original? There's been a lot of fuss over it.'

Emma Marsh, muffled up in a heavy tweed coat that matched her skirt, her cheeks pink with cold above it, wrinkled her nose. 'Not really,' she said, glancing over at her husband like a recalcitrant child. 'Not too much culture. Not too much indoors.' Although they were roughly the same age, Celia marvelled at how like a child Emma Marsh seemed; was it marriage to a powerful man that did it? It might have been irritating, but it was not; all the same, Celia found herself puzzling over Emma Marsh – could she really be as guileless and open as she seemed? Lucas Marsh, wearing a long, dark wool overcoat, stood with his hands in his pockets and looked back at his wife with a hint of a smile.

'Certainly not,' he said gravely. 'We have to get the balance right, don't we? It's your birthday, after all.'

They walked on through the long arcaded space of the Uffizi and beside the river. Emma Marsh chattered animatedly, pointing out a crane perched on a branch in the green water, asking about the terraced formal gardens of the Palazzo Bardini that came into view, tumbling down the hill on the south side of the river. Lucas Marsh said almost nothing, only occasionally responding when Emma took hold of his arm to point something out – a piece of stone carving, snow on the mountains to the west, the golden gleam of San Miniato's façade in the morning sun – but he did appear to be listening intently.

Although in Celia's experience of guiding couples the women were generally more communicative than the men, it was not always this way; quite often the men were insistent on getting their money's worth from her, and had a particular approach, an interest in acquiring facts rather than stories. Lucas Marsh's silent attention was, in Celia's eyes, to his credit; she began to like him in earnest as he walked beside her, hands in pockets. As they emerged from the Uffizi on to the river he also appeared to be taking notice of everything around him, and not only the palaces and views but the banks of the river below, the rowing club, the fishermen hunched over their rods, the passers-by. There was a kind of perpetual tension about him, an alertness, that drew Celia back to him even as she responded to Emma's questioning.

The embankment was busy with traffic; the three of them crossed to the arcaded pavement where arches supported the Vasari corridor. Celia had come this way because she wanted to show them the corridor stretching across the river, the private passage of the Medici that led from their apartments in the Pitti Palace to the seat of government in the Palazzo Vecchio, but even as she launched into her description she felt it might have been a mistake. The embankment was packed, under the arches the souvenir stalls and pavement artists narrowed the pavement even further, and they found themselves jostled by precisely the throng that the corridor over their heads had been built to avoid.

Celia was about to point this irony out to Lucas Marsh, but when she turned to look over her shoulder at him she was brought up short by his expression. She followed his gaze to see what he was looking at; a pair of dark-skinned men, walking shoulder to shoulder through the crowds towards them. Eastern Europeans, thought Celia automatically, falling into an old city habit, assessing provenance and nationality in the streets packed with tourists from everywhere, and after having her pocket picked she was on her guard. The men were bearing down towards them through the crowd; it looked as though they must separate to avoid knocking someone over, but as Celia watched they forged past her, forcing a path between Lucas and Emma Marsh, splitting them apart. Celia caught a whiff of something strong as they passed, sweat and petrol; she saw their raw, red hands, ungloved in the cold. Emma gave a little startled gasp, half a laugh, and Celia saw Marsh's head whip round, following the men; they didn't look back and almost as suddenly as he had turned after them Marsh was back at his wife's side, his hand on her elbow.

'Are you all right?' he said, breathless, no trace of his smiling easiness left. He was, Celia thought, even paler above the dark overcoat than when she had first seen him, and rigid with tension.

'Oh yes,' said Emma, smiling, round-cheeked. 'Fine.' But she had paled a little too. Celia cursed herself for taking this route; she looked down the river after the men, but she could see no trace of them. Staring down the embankment, she thought of Marco's warning.

'Sorry,' she said, turning back to the Marshes, briskly apologetic to subdue her own anxiety as well as theirs, 'we'll be out of here soon. Up ahead the crowds all disappear.' She nodded along the river to the east, the tower of the San Niccolò gate at the end of her road rising in the mist at the edge of the old city. Home, she thought, surprised by her affection for the sight. She side-stepped to avoid treading on cheap posters laid out on the paving stones and, taking Emma Marsh's other arm firmly, announcing her passage with a running patter of *permesso* and *scusate* and *excuse me*, she carved a path through the packed bodies until they were out the other side.

By the time they reached the Ponte Alle Grazie the crowds

had evaporated, and Celia kept up her commentary – on the construction of the Ponte Vecchio, the old wall of the city and the buildings that came into view on the far side of the river – to restore equilibrium. It did happen, she told herself firmly, wealthy visitors were often taken aback by the crowds, the press of humanity. Take a different route back, that's all. She stole a glance at Lucas Marsh; his quiet composure seemed quite restored, but as she continued to talk, describing the reconstruction of the Bardini Gardens to his wife, Celia could tell that what might be taken for calm in Lucas Marsh's demeanour was nothing like it. In that moment on the crowded embankment when he had turned after the men something had been exposed in him, even if it was covered again now. Was it that he was dangerous, or endangered? Celia was reminded of something, of walking the humid corridors of the Reptile Room at London Zoo with her mother, looking in at what appeared to be a patterned rock only to watch it rear and strike at the glass in the space of a single panicked heartbeat.

They crossed the river and turned in to the Via San Niccolò past the great studded door of the Palazzo dei Mozzi. It was quite empty, as usual, and shadowed except for a shard of light shining down its canyoned length. The buildings were so huge and the street so narrow that there was never more light than this; Celia liked to show this particular street to visitors, for its silence and for the variety of its façades. Each one was different, some etched with sgraffito, others ornamented with gargoyles shaped like greyhounds' heads, or mermaids, some plain and sombre and massive, and Celia began to point them out, giving some history as she did so.

'Ooh.' Emma Marsh shivered a little as they entered the gloom. 'It's very quiet, isn't it?'

'Lovely,' said Lucas Marsh, and Celia turned to him, surprised. It was the first time he had volunteered a comment, and as she looked at him standing there, surveying the tall, dark buildings with appreciation, suddenly it seemed that this street was the perfect setting for him. With his ascetic look, his high forehead and long straight nose, even the dark, expensive clothes that fitted his narrow frame with luxurious precision, he might have been a ruthless nobleman in modern dress, a merchant prince, Emma his delicious trophy wife. They turned towards the gate of San Miniato, Emma exclaiming over its honey-stoned prettiness, the geraniums in the window-boxes on the Costa dei Magnoli and the olive groves that rose behind the grey stone of the city walls.

'Now, I could live here,' she said, turning impulsively to her husband. 'These houses are so sweet! Look at their little gardens, the trees . . .' Lucas Marsh nodded, but he was looking back down the street, and Celia had the impression that he preferred the dark, narrow space between the great palaces.

They walked quickly up the last stretch, the rows of stone steps that made up the pilgrims' path of the Monte alle Croci, across the winding *viale* and they were there. It was a stiff climb; some of Celia's more sedentary clients complained bitterly about it, but Emma Marsh's cheeks were only a little pinker than usual and Lucas Marsh seemed barely out of breath. All the same, they stood for a moment in the sun at the top of the steps and looked together, unified in silent admiration, at the red city laid out below them.

These days, Luisa knows, they tell you to cuddle the baby, give her a name, take a photograph. She can't see how that would help. How would you ever be able to forget?

88

They said there was no reason why they shouldn't try again. No reason other than terror, of course, though they didn't know about that. So she and Sandro went on as though nothing had happened, except that as if by silent agreement there was no trying again; there were plenty who said it might have been better if they had separated, but it had tied them inextricably together, knotted and wound about with guilt and confusion. Luisa had gone back to work.

After six weeks she had woken one morning alone in the bed and had seen a bright spring sky through the window where Sandro had left the shutters open on his way to work. At the sight of that sliver of blue she had felt something stir, like hunger, an instinct for survival like a pale seedling working up through the soil, and she had lain very still, not wanting to disturb it. And to her astonishment as she lay there in the thin morning light Luisa found herself thinking with longing of the shop, the rows of wooden drawers with their glass fronts, the folded silk and lawn, and she had cried then. Over the thought of lace handkerchiefs. She sometimes wondered whether if she hadn't gone back to the shop, who knew, she might eventually have left Sandro instead, or he her, but this was how things had turned out. No use crying over it now.

At work one or two whispered to Luisa that they were sorry, but then it was quietly left unmentioned. To begin with everyone understood, then there was no one left who knew what had happened and it turned into an unnamed sadness in her past, an indefinable something. Luisa grew older, she and Sandro rubbed along; she hit forty and knew, this was it, last chance. And then at a swimming pool on the edge of town a little English girl had gone missing.

Chapter Ten

As Celia explained the façade of the church – Roman arches, Byzantine mosaic – and the legend of its founder she saw Lucas Marsh look at his watch and she faltered; was he bored already? But then his attention was back with her; marking time was a businessman's reflex, perhaps. They went inside.

Immediately they were swallowed up in a profound gloom. San Miniato was dark and cavernous inside; when they entered the only light seemed to be coming from votive candles and their glittering reflection in the apse, which was lined with gold mosaic. It was very cold and almost empty; up ahead in the presbytery Celia could see only one other group, a handful of people looking up. There was a click and a faltering light came on, illuminating the Christ figure gazing down from the apse; an echoing, whispered commentary began. Celia turned back.

'Let's start in the sacristy,' she said, and again she thought she saw Lucas Marsh look at his watch. She pressed ahead. This way.'

The sacristy was a solid, square room, half-panelled and lined with frescoes depicting the life of San Benedetto, his miracles and temptations, frescoes lurid with demons and culminating in a depiction of his ascent to heaven on a kind of celestial elevator at which Emma Marsh laughed, a bright, happy sound. Her husband had his hand around her waist and Celia saw that he was stroking her hip mechanically, absently.

By the time they returned to the body of the building the other party had gone and the church appeared to be quite empty; Celia, anxious now to complete the tour without delay, was able to lead them through the building's architecture, the few paintings, the apse, without interruption or observation. She finished the tour in the crypt. Lying not quite underground, behind the raised altar, it was a lovely space, hidden from the rest of the church and with a mysterious, otherworldly quality. The fine arches of the vaulted space were supported by delicate columns plundered from churches and mosques across the Mediterranean, each one different, and as she had expected, Emma Marsh was delighted by it.

Wandering through the columns – fluted, twisted, pink and grey and green – Emma stroked them as she passed, something acquisitive in her touch as though she wanted to take them home with her, asking Celia about their provenance. As she answered, wondering as she did about the Marshes' house in London, imagining it filled with Emma's impulse buys, marble, mosaic, mahogany, Celia heard the heavy creak and bang somewhere behind them of the massive door of the church as it opened. Briefly a little pale daylight altered the gloom where they stood and then died away, the votive candles flickered in a draught that blew around their ankles and subsided. Celia turned instinctively, but of course the door was out of sight of the crypt and she couldn't see who might have come in. As she looked around she did, however, register that Lucas Marsh had gone.

Would you like five minutes to wander around?' she asked Emma, a sudden impulse telling her to find him, anxious about that clock-watching. Had he stalked off, bored, impatient? Emma Marsh nodded dreamily, pulling her beautiful coat around her, small feet in ballet pumps, the sensible shoes her husband had instructed her to put on for the walk. She might have been mistaken for a child.

Celia came around the altar, and saw no one. She looked at her own watch now; it was exactly twelve-thirty, they weren't even running late. She had booked the Marshes' table for lunch for one and they had plenty of time to get there. Celia would drop them at the restaurant, would meet them again at the Uffizi at three. But she needed to know if anything was bothering Lucas Marsh. She climbed the steps beside the altar to the choir stalls and looked around the space; nothing. Quickly she ran back down and crossed the chequerboard marble of the transept to the door, hauled it open and came face to face with Dan Strickland.

Celia gave a small gasp and stepped back inside. Dan looked startled and she glanced away, flustered. Through the doorway over his shoulder she caught sight of Lucas Marsh outside, his back to her, standing at the head of the steps and silhouetted against the red city laid out below. He was talking intently into his mobile phone.

'Celie?' said Dan, and she closed her eyes briefly, leaning back against the door. Only Dan called her that, not even Kate. She opened her eyes again quickly and saw that outside the steps were empty; Lucas had disappeared. She took another step back into the church and Dan followed her inside.

'Are you all right?' he said, peering at her. She nodded dumbly, recovering herself. 'Fine,' she managed. Cleared her throat. 'Fine,' she tried again, smoothly this time, nodding. I'm on a job.'

'Ah,' said Dan, his brow clearing. 'Right.' She could see his face properly now, turned to the light coming through the door; he looked tired, she thought, a day's growth on his chin, and there was more grey in his wiry hair although it still stood up from his forehead, unruly, English. You could never mistake Dan for an Italian, not even from a distance; Celia found herself wondering with a tug if he would ever go back home. If it was home, for any of them.

'How about you?' she said. 'What are you doing up here?'

'Been asked to write a piece on Florentine cemeteries, of all things,' he said, jerking his head back to indicate the space behind the little church filled with marble mausoleums and alabaster angels. 'I suppose they asked me because they're full of English poets.' He laughed. 'Not too bad a commission, actually.'

Celia felt the urge to take him by the arm, sit down on the steps and look at the view, to gossip as they used to. She just nodded. 'So everything's okay? You've been writing. And ...' She hesitated, decided, *Be grown up about this.* 'Allegra?'

Dan laughed abruptly. 'Not much writing,' he said, looking down at his hands. 'Not real stuff. And Allegra – well. Didn't last long, as it happens. She – well. I'm much too old for her. I ...'

'Yes?' said Celia.

Dan looked back up at her. 'I'm sorry,' he said. 'About Allegra—'

Suddenly Celia found herself growing impatient. 'No,' she said. 'Really, Dan. Not now, I mean, it's two years, isn't it? Forget it.'

They were still standing in the open doorway; out of the corner of her eye she detected movement in the dark interior of the church. Emma Marsh came up to them out of the gloom and looked from Dan to Celia, and back again. There was something shrewd and appraising in her glance; Celia had the impression she had the measure of them immediately, and for a moment the childlike quality Celia had seen in her was entirely absent. Then she smiled again, her face bright and blank and open.

'Well,' she said gaily, 'where's that husband of mine got to?'

Fortunately the restaurant knew Celia well enough to hold the reservation for them; aware of how busy the place would be, she took the precaution of phoning ahead when Lucas Marsh seemed to be nowhere to be found outside the church. On a Friday, lunch and dinner, the Quattro Leoni was always packed. She could hear the noise down the line, behind the cheerful voice of Stefano, the maître d'; the long table shared by locals, artisans and antique dealers was always loud with gossip, girlfriends out shopping sharing a lunch, businessmen and tourists, a bustling, happy mixture.

After a long moment spent standing, an awkward three-some, on the threshold of the church, Celia had eventually blurted a vague introduction, and graciously Emma Marsh had taken Dan's hand and given it a little shake. Celia saw him take her in, her lovely, expensive coat, her pretty pink and white-ness, and with a pang she realized that it was Emma Marsh, in fact, who embodied the glowing, healthy Englishness Dan had

94

always professed to love in Celia. But he seemed more awed than anything, letting her hand drop; Emma, perhaps, was out of his league. Beside her he looked small, jaded, a little sallow; *you and me both*, thought Celia with a spasm of fellow-feeling.

'I saw him out here a minute ago,' Celia said, gesturing towards the wide marble steps and the view. 'He can't have got far.' And she stepped past Dan and out into the fresh, cool air.

There had been no sign of Lucas Marsh at the front of the church; they'd wandered around the striped green and white façade into the cemetery and that was where they found him, eventually, walking the narrow, oppressive paths between the tombs at the back. He was still talking into the phone as they approached from behind, staring at a miniature temple in marble, shaking his head. 'No,' Celia heard him say. 'Absolutely not.' He sounded coldly furious, and quite oblivious to his surroundings, to the breathtaking view he might have had if he were to turn around, to the fact that he was supposed to be on holiday celebrating his wife's birthday. Celia wondered if these were the sacrifices Lucas Marsh had to make for his money; she looked at Emma Marsh and wondered if it was worth it.

'Darling?' Emma sounded anxious. She didn't seem a woman made easily insecure. Standing back and pretending to look at the view so as not to intrude, all the same Celia listened – she couldn't help herself.

Lucas turned abruptly at the sound of her voice and snapped the phone shut. 'It's nothing,' he said quickly, but Celia could hear frustration in his voice that came close to anger. 'Just work.' She heard Emma Marsh sigh, not angry but forlorn all of a sudden.

'Can't it wait?' she said plaintively.

'Sorry,' he said, then again with an effort, more gently, 'Sorry, darling.'

Gabriele had been waiting for them patiently under the trees, the engine of his gleaming dark blue saloon purring quietly. Inside the car smelled of leather and Gabriele's aftershave; he was wearing an ironed white shirt and Celia felt a wave of gratitude. Once in the car Lucas and Emma Marsh seemed quite at ease again; Celia told them something about the restaurant, what was good to order, the wine list. 'They speak English,' she said; ordering food in a foreign language seemed to faze a surprising number of high-powered clients.

'Oh, Lucas speaks Italian,' said Emma gaily. 'Don't you, darling?'

'Really?' said Celia, impressed; she should have guessed, of course, from his pronunciation, but it was unusual in an Englishman. A bit of French, some German, but almost none of them spoke Italian. They thought of it as a comedy language, something operatic and full of bluster, and often were quite unaware of Dante, Boccaccio, the *Promessi Sposi*, never mind Calvino or Morante. She was curious suddenly. 'Where did you learn?' she asked.

'Oh,' said Lucas Marsh vaguely, looking out of the window. They were winding sedately through the tree-lined boulevard that circled the city to the south, and the old walls had just come into sight. 'School, you know. A long time ago.'

Celia nodded automatically but she was surprised; he must have had plenty of practice since, she thought, perhaps on those business trips to Milan. 'A Renaissance man, then,' she said politely. 'Many talents.' Emma Marsh beamed at this, holding her husband's arm, but he just went on looking out of the window. Celia could tell from the back of Gabriele's head that he was listening too.

Once at the restaurant it all happened very quickly; smiling, poised, the picture of happy elegance, Emma and Lucas Marsh were ushered inside. Gabriele looked up at Celia enquiringly from the driver's seat. 'I'd better make sure they're happy,' she said in a low voice. 'Thanks, Gabri. Sorry you had to wait.'

Good-naturedly Gabriele just shrugged. 'No problem,' he said. Want a drink later?' She could tell he wanted to gossip, to find out about these two.

'Maybe,' said Celia. 'I'll call you.' Gabriele looked at her then with an expression that, for once, she found herself unable to interpret, but then he smiled, touched two fingers to his temple like an American salute, and he was off, the dark car surging away from her down the narrow street towards the Via Maggio.

Inside the restaurant pine garlands decorated with silvery glass baubles hung from the high beams; the air smelled sweet and resinous and was full of exuberant, festive noise. She'd specified a particular table for the Marshes, secluded but not too far from the action, in a corner beside the window; as she approached they were already seated. Every table in the room was full; along the wall a party of close to twenty Italians were being served with antipasti, the long plates heaped with tomatoes and prosciutto and crostini rose and swooped their way between the heads. All the same, despite the bustle, people had turned to observe Lucas and Emma Marsh and Celia could see, suddenly, that they did attract attention, there was something about them. Not just her, but him too. Perhaps it was just money.

Celia stood, coat on, beside the table. 'Everything okay?' she said briskly, wanting them not to be awkward, as some clients were, about not inviting her to eat with them. She suddenly wanted to be on her own, feeling the intimacy of the Marshes' marriage pressing in on her. Lucas Marsh was scrutinizing the menu; in an open-necked shirt, without the expensive armour of his dark cashmere coat, he looked oddly vulnerable.

Emma Marsh nodded happily. 'Lovely,' she said. 'You are clever.'

'I'll see you at the Uffizi at three, then,' Celia said, smiling, trying to disguise her eagerness to be off. 'Don't be late.'

From behind the till Gianna signalled excitedly to Luisa. Luisa eyed her warily across the showroom; she was showing a nice dark suede bag to an unappreciative Frenchwoman, pointing out the quality of the leather, the lining. The French were not Luisa's favourite customers.

'Excuse me,' she said in her careful, schoolgirl French. Crossing the room towards Gianna she felt uneasy, knowing that her hard-won equilibrium was about to be disturbed.

'What is it?' she said tersely. Gianna pouted and held up the receiver of the telephone. 'Your husband,' she said, raising her eyebrows.

Luisa took the phone and turned so she couldn't see Gianna's inquisitive, perma-tanned, lip-lined face. 'Sandro?' she said, astonished. On the other side of the showroom she saw the Frenchwoman put the suede holdall down and look at it, frowning. For once it didn't seem to matter if the woman bought it or not, if she understood the workmanship that had gone into it; Luisa was looking at her but she hardly saw the woman.

'Sandro?' she said again. 'Are you there?'

'Can you meet for lunch?' His voice was abrupt. 'I've got half an hour. We could have a sandwich.'

Remembering her dash to the bar at eleven, Luisa bit her lip. What would they think? They'd think it wasn't like Luisa to leave the shop twice in one day, and to have lunch with her husband, what was more. Did they even know what Sandro looked like? Not unless they'd been spying at her front door to see who came in and out; it wasn't as though she and Sandro did the *passeggiata* together arm in arm. At the beginning he'd come to collect her after work now and again, what, twenty years ago, but after the baby he'd stopped that, couldn't stand their pitying looks. As if Luisa could.

'Why?' she said, bewildered. 'I mean, you never—'

'I – I don't know,' said Sandro, and for a moment he sounded lost. He exhaled. 'Just wanted to see you.' His voice was gruff now, covering up.

'Where are you?' Luisa said quietly. Suddenly she didn't care what they thought.

'Bar La Posta,' he said, and all at once she remembered that it was in the Bar La Posta that he'd first spoken a word to her, both of them waiting for the post office opposite to open one frosty morning. 'Cold,' he'd said, rubbing his hands together. It seemed so long ago it might have happened to a different person

'Give me a minute,' she said.

To her surprise the Frenchwoman took the bag, and a pair of shoes to match. Luisa escorted her to the till and recklessly instructed Gianna to give her a small discount; the Frenchwoman looked surprised when she realized and gave Luisa a little look, a flicker of gratitude, some tiny warmth kindled. Although she wanted to be out of the door Luisa didn't rush the transaction, it wasn't in her nature. Carefully she wrapped the holdall in its felt bag stamped with the brand, then tissue, then a carrier ribbon-tied, and the same all over again for the shoes.

Only once she had slid the bags across the counter to her customer, accepted thanks and checked that the shop floor was quiet did Luisa turn and whisper to Gianna, 'My husband needs to see me a moment.' Before Gianna could react Luisa reached past her for a jacket she kept up here in case it turned cold on the shop floor and was out of the door. She didn't look back but she knew Gianna would be staring after her, mouth half open and ready to summon Beppe down from menswear to talk this over the moment the door closed behind her.

It was bitterly cold outside, the pavements white with frost; the jacket wasn't half warm enough. Luisa had left the house in boots that morning but had changed into pumps for the shop floor, and before she'd taken five steps in them her feet were numb. She felt silly, like some girl half-dressed in the street who might be reprimanded at any moment by her mother. Awkwardly she half-ran, to keep warm and to avoid the looks she was getting, round the back of the straw market, through a side street and under the broad arcade that ran along one side of the Piazza della Repubblica and housed the post office.

Beneath the high, vaulted ceiling of the portico the sound changed, and Luisa heard the echo of her own quick footsteps on the polished marble. The post office was busy with shoppers, couples in hats, scarves, heavy coats, arm in arm. As she slipped between them Luisa was getting out of breath but she was almost there; then she looked up and saw Sandro's face looking out at her from between two columns and her breath went completely. She saw his expression change as he looked at her; first bemusement, as though he didn't recognize her, followed by a flicker of something else, something softer, that was almost immediately followed by stern disapproval. Sandro reached out a hand and grasped her by the elbow, pulling her out of the crowd.

'You'll catch your death,' he said, with the same note of exasperation Luisa had heard the night before. 'Come on.'

When they went into the bar the woman serving produced a sandwich and a caffè latte for Sandro without being asked; no beer, no wine. He took off his cap and laid it on the marble counter. Luisa wondered if he came in here every day, feeling obscurely troubled by the thought that this woman behind the bar might have more to do with her husband than she did herself. Called upon to choose for herself, Luisa looked distractedly into the glass-fronted cabinet and took at random a piece of filled focaccia.

Without saying anything, Sandro buttoned the jacket around Luisa's waist; it was an old one, and a little tight, and she felt self-conscious. He turned away quickly and ate his sandwich in two bites; Luisa nibbled at her focaccia with little appetite.

'What's wrong?' she asked, sounding more abrupt than she had intended, and she thought she heard Sandro sigh. He wiped his mouth with a napkin as if to disguise the sound, took a swig of his caffè latte and looked down into it.

'Can't a man have a sandwich with his wife?' He looked at her defensively, and she just shook her head at the pretence that this was normal, for them. He looked away. *There's something he needs to tell me*, she thought. He looked back and his faded eyes were frank now. 'I don't know,' he said finally. 'I wanted – it's this – this – the Bartolo thing. The body.' He stopped, the glass of coffee in mid-air, and frowned.

'It's good news, isn't it?' asked Luisa tentatively; she didn't sound like herself, she wasn't used to this – talking. Having her opinion sought. She didn't want to put him off. 'I mean, Bartolo's off your hands?' Then she paused, considering. 'I mean, if he did it, that is.' Then Sandro looked up at her.

'Yes,' he said. He twisted to look over his shoulder, out of the door. 'You see the others, they're happy. Overjoyed. Bartolo was a creep by anyone's standards.' He looked away. 'We know things about him, things that you can't mention in court – anyway. And you'd do it yourself, wouldn't you, if you're honest, we'd love the opportunity, most of us. I'd pull the trigger on a man who did that to a child.' He leaned towards her, intent, his face a couple of inches from Luisa's; this was the longest speech she'd heard from him in years. He was so close she could see the different colours in his iris, green and tawny. There was stubble on his chin, a sprinkling of white among the black, and it made her sad – he used to look after himself so well. 'Yes,' she said, wondering what he was getting at. Earnestly he gazed into her face, searching for something.

'The test results had already come in,' he said flatly. 'The DNA test.'

'And?' she said, confused. He looked away, then back at her. 'Inconclusive.'

'Which means – what? That he didn't do it?'

'No,' said Sandro fiercely. 'That's not what it means. It means their famous new technique wasn't that great after all. The sample was too far gone.' He brought his hand down flat on the counter with a crack that should have hurt him, but he showed no sign. Behind the bar the waitress looked across at them, her mild face showing alarm.

Luisa was more bewildered than ever. 'And Bartolo knew, then? If he thought he was in the clear, why would he ...?' She looked at the waitress and lowered her voice. 'Why would he kill himself?' Did these tests mean anything to old country people? Did they understand? She saw Bartolo as he'd been pictured in the newspaper, his face impassive and hostile at once, eyes tiny and watchful, like a wild boar's.

Sandro didn't look at her.

'I didn't tell him,' he said. 'I knew eventually I'd have to, but I didn't see why – I didn't want to give him the satisfaction, so I shuffled the paperwork, misfiled it. I was just so angry. *Inconclusive*, what does that mean, after all these years?'

'It means you can't be sure,' said Luisa quietly. *Does he think he's responsible that the man killed himself?* she wondered. *Is that what's eating him?* It occurred to her at the same time that someone might find out that he'd kept the test results from Bartolo, and there must be some human rights law against that. *No wonder he's in a state.*

'You're right,' he said savagely and, it seemed to Luisa without thinking, he took her wrist and held it so tight it hurt. His voice was full of contempt, but she couldn't tell if it was for the system, for himself, or for her. 'Oh yes. We have to be sure, don't we?'

Chapter Eleven

Celia was sitting in the Boboli Gardens, on a stone bench under a fragrant, unkempt bay hedge. She could have gone home to eat her sandwich but the sky was such a clear, brilliant blue that she thought she'd take advantage of the daylight; it was very cold, however, and the labyrinth of hedges and alleys that made up the formal garden was almost deserted. Picnicking, strictly speaking, was forbidden in the Boboli, but it would have taken a very hard-hearted keeper to stop Celia eating her modest lunch – a couple of slices of prosciutto in a hard, flatbread roll – on a cold, quiet day like this. After her morning's work it was just what she wanted, something uncomplicated to eat and a place to chew on it in meditative peace. He'd hardly said a thing all morning, had he? And she had chattered; at the time it had seemed just how things were between them, one silent, one vivacious, plenty of couples had that kind of attraction of opposites thing. But at this distance Celia found herself wondering whether there hadn't been something nervous about Emma Marsh's brightness, something distracting about it. Who would she be trying to distract, though, and from what? Who Lucas Marsh had been talking to at San Miniato, that fragment of furious conversation Celia had overheard, the note of anger in his voice when he'd been interrupted, seemed, in retrospect, more complex and troubling than merely a work problem breaking in on an idyllic holiday. And he'd been talking in Italian, hadn't he? For a wild moment Celia imagined Lucas involved in some clandestine deal in the city, a secret double life, a network of local contacts. She wondered, more reasonably, why he had taken Emma to see Milan, a cold, grey, industrious city, and never before to Florence.

In front of Celia the mist seemed to be growing denser; she could hardly see the top of the cedar tree now, from which a heron had flapped heavily away when she'd sat down, and the hedge opposite was grey and indistinct. She stretched, rubbed her hands together in the cold, and looked at her watch. Two-fifteen. Another ten minutes, then she'd make her way across the river to the Uffizi, maybe grab an espresso to warm her up, but for now she was enjoying being here, the mist, the silence, the ghostly emptiness of the park. She fished in her bag for her water bottle and encountered the newspaper she'd bought that morning, unfolded it and looked at the headline.

As she read it the air of the gardens seemed to change. The tranquillity ebbed from the misty air to be replaced by something less benign, and the hedges seemed to draw in around her. The Boboli was fenced in, patrolled, practically an open-air museum she told herself, and Le Cascine was a different sort of park, admittedly, a place open at night for all sorts of transactions, but still. A body. It had been found in the drained

105

pool at Le Pavoniere, and at present the police weren't looking for anyone else – did that mean they thought it was suicide? Celia pulled her jacket around her, feeling the cold suddenly. She hadn't been to Le Pavoniere in years, there'd been no need out in the suburbs where there were plenty of pretty pools, private clubs. She thought back to the last time she'd been there, staked out on a plastic lounger with Jo Starling, years ago; it had been a tacky sort of place, even then. American college girls would climb in around the back without paying, thinking it was a big joke; Celia remembered that scruffy link fence. How had he done it? They didn't say, only that it hadn't been a natural death. He hadn't died of exposure, then.

Celia wanted to get up from the cold bench, she knew she should go, but she read on. There was a picture of the pool from outside the fence, police tape around the gates. In the wintry morning light it looked a desolate place and Celia thought back to that night, the rain she'd listened to on her roof, and thought of a man climbing a fence to get inside an empty pool. Why would you do that? Why a swimming pool? She thought of blood, of mess, would you do it for that reason? She turned the page, still reading. The unnamed man had been a suspect in a murder investigation some fifteen years earlier; there was another, smaller picture on this page and Celia stopped reading the words and looked at it. An old photograph, dated, out of focus, but a picture she knew because it had been on the front pages when she had arrived in Florence all that time ago. A smiling child with straight, shiny hair and a chipped front tooth, in striped summer uniform, a school photograph with painted clouds as a backdrop. A different swimming pool.

Suddenly Celia knew that she should go; she didn't want to

read this story any more. She stood up and folded the paper in a hurry, thrust it into her bag. She felt stiff and cold, and she didn't feel safe.

Stefano walked between the rooms of his busy restaurant: the first room for locals, dark and cosy; the second, with its high ceilings and long window on the piazza, was where he tended to put the visitors. They'd done very well today, it was a good time of year coming up to Christmas, couples on celebration weekends away, they liked to order champagne, a big Fiorentina steak between them, could anything be more romantic? There was one couple today that puzzled him, though; the older man, bloodless, anaemic, looked as though he could do with a steak, and his wife, quite the opposite. Like Biancaneve she looked, Snow White with red lips, black hair, a rosy blush on her cheeks. You'd have thought he'd look a lot happier, with a girl like that opposite him, a nice bottle of Brunello on the table and a weekend ahead of them. She was trying, too, you could tell, almost pleading with him, giving it everything she had to make him smile. Hand on his wrist, stroking him. Stefano thought of his own wife, beautiful, sensible, perched in her frivolous shoes at the front table trying to persuade their youngest to take a spoonful of *pappa al pomodoro*, and he counted his blessings. A happy family.

They left the restaurant at two forty-five, the tall, narrow, dark-coated figure, leather-gloved and austere, with his wife taking quick small steps beside him to keep up. They walked along the Borgo San Jacopo, and she looked in at the dressmakers' windows, pointing something out to him, but he barely responded. They came to the Ponte Vecchio and then he stopped, turned to her.

107

'Look,' he said. 'I can't think about it now. I can't. I didn't plan this.' And he turned and walked on without waiting for her. Emma Marsh stood in the street and looked after him, her face pale and stricken, and as the crowds parted around her on one of the busiest thoroughfares of the Western world she seemed entirely alone.

Inside Frollini, Luisa, stirred up by some secret turbulence she dared not define, was back at her station when they walked past on their way to the Uffizi. She was advising an American lady on the best colour to wear against her skin – not the baby pink, no, not over thirty, it wasn't advisable, only white – and when she turned to accompany her customer to the changing room she saw only the back of Lucas Marsh's head and a fleeting glimpse of Emma Marsh's profile. *Pretty*, she noted involuntarily, *lovely, easy to dress, that one*, and approvingly she noted the colour in her tweed coat, the good cut, even recognized the designer. *Plenty of money, too; they'll be in here before too long.*

Her customer emerged from the changing room, an anxious expression on her face, and Luisa sighed inwardly. Automatically she began to soothe, to persuade, wondering why some women seemed to panic so when you suggested a change. Take off the dull things bought in some dull, expensive foreign department store that they had worn every day for ten years – dark trouser suits, long sweaters to disguise everything underneath, long wool coats – and the most businesslike of women emerge from the changing room like frightened children. Luisa paused, stood, considering the white shirt she had persuaded the woman to try, and thought of her own uniform, her navy moccasins, old coat, dark skirt, always white against the face, and wondered if she'd been doing the same herself.

Luisa moved forward, tweaked the shirt's collar to open it, to show the woman's throat. She tugged at the waistband of the skirt, settling it on her customer's hips. The woman obviously thought she was fat, but she wasn't, only a little padding here and there, nothing to be ashamed of.

'There,' she said, motherly, firm. 'You see?' She watched as her customer looked nervously at herself, saw her realize it wasn't so bad, after all. She saw the woman turn a little in front of the glass to get another angle.

At the till again Luisa could see Gianna scrutinizing her as she smoothed, folded and wrapped with careful movements. She pulled a length of grosgrain ribbon, tied the shirt in its paper, her gift to the client. She looked up and met Gianna's gaze; *let her wonder if I am changed*, she thought.

Luisa couldn't have said how she felt, exactly, it was such a sensation of turbulence, a mixture of dread and exhilaration. To be called out of the shop to see Sandro, to stand with him in a bar eating a sandwich like a proper happy couple, these things had filled her with — excitement. Even though they were talking about terrible things, even though there might be worse to come, at least they were — alive. It was an unfamiliar feeling, she'd spent a long time avoiding anything resembling agitation, upheaval. She could hardly remember what she'd said at all; she had only known that Sandro had needed her, and she hadn't found a way of helping him.

He had seemed to her both angry and afraid.

'Will they find out?' She tried to be gentle; she wasn't used to talking to Sandro at all, let alone like this. 'That you kept the result from him?'

Sandro turned his face to her slowly, his expression unreadable. Eventually he shrugged, as though he didn't care. 'Perhaps,' he said. 'Perhaps.'

Was he trying not to worry her, with this poker face of his? Or was it guilt? She had said something to try to soften it then, something daft about, perhaps Bartolo had spent years feeling guilty, perhaps it was a coincidence that the test result was about to come in. Sandro had looked at her incredulously and she'd felt stupid. 'Not Bartolo,' he said. 'He didn't feel guilty. Paedophiles don't, whatever they say in court, whatever you might read in the papers.'

Luisa had turned cold then, the thought of the child in the river chilling her to numbness, and she'd stared into her coffee. Why, then? The whole thing seemed suddenly obscure and frightening; what was Sandro afraid of? Was any of this in some way down to him? But then he'd put out a hand, a soft touch on her arm to comfort her, quickly withdrawn. 'I—' But then he'd stopped. *He needs time*, she thought, *he's not ready to tell me yet*, and she didn't press him. Afterwards she thought perhaps she should have, should have done it long ago, should certainly have done it then. But that touch on her arm had thrown her; she didn't want to scare him off.

'I might be late tonight,' he'd said then, and she thought he sounded sad. 'Don't worry.' And the idea that he was thinking ahead to how she might feel, just those few ordinary words that probably passed between most couples every day, had made Luisa want to laugh and cry at the same time.

She looked up into her customer's face, handed her the bag and smiled. 'I hope you are happy,' she said. It must have sounded odd because the woman looked startled at first; then she returned Luisa's smile. 'Yes,' she said, with growing confidence. 'Yes.'

Celia had it down to a fine art, getting into the Uffizi. Even on a December afternoon there were queues, pigeons, pavement artists and hawkers cluttering the lovely, pale grey arcades at its entrance, and it was a significant part of any visit to the museum that she should protect her clients from all of that. She always booked tickets in advance, and with a deftness born of long practice she would negotiate the enfilade of postcard shops, book stands and temporary exhibits on the ground floor. Before they knew where they were or where they'd been Celia's clients would find themselves above all that on the third floor of the great gallery and their tour would have begun.

So it was only once she had manoeuvred Lucas and Emma Marsh to the beginning of the long east corridor that Celia paused and had a good look at them. It dawned on her then that as she had led them upstairs, taking the opportunity as she always did to talk her clients through the building's history, the Roman sculptures on the ground floor, the rooms originally housing the mint, neither Lucas Marsh nor even Emma had said a word. She stopped talking, and the three of them stood and looked.

The corridor was pleasantly empty, and a pale, warm light flooded its length from the huge window at the far end, overlooking the Arno. There was a smell of wood and wax, and a combination of sounds that, it occurred to Celia, she would be happy to have as the last music she heard on earth: the sound of footsteps moving slowly over the polished stone, pausing every now and then before shuffling on, and the sound of voices hushed in contemplation. On the gallery walls the

111

paintings gleamed like jewels. Out of the corner of her eye she saw Emma Marsh's shoulders relax a little as she stood there and looked down the corridor, and even her husband seemed changed, softened in outline.

Is everything all right?' she asked tentatively. Lucas Marsh frowned.

'Yes,' he said brusquely. 'Of course.'

'Good,' said Celia quickly, feeling his defensiveness. 'I thought your wife – I thought Emma seemed – tired, that's all. If you don't want to do the full tour . . . ' Lucas shook his head a fraction, thinking.

There is something . . . ' He hesitated. 'Tomorrow morning, we were to go up to Fiesole?' Celia nodded, waiting; she'd made an arrangement for a private visit to the monastery of San Francesco, and a walk in the green ruins of the Roman amphitheatre. She'd worked hard to think of a combination of atmosphere and seclusion.

Lucas went on. 'Something's come up, work. And Emma wants to fit in some shopping instead, if you could show her around.' Standing beside them, Emma said nothing, just smiled a little, the ghost of a smile.

'It's my birthday, tomorrow, you see,' she said, as if this explained it all. Celia wondered if they had argued, if this was the pay-off.

'Of course it is,' she said, although she'd forgotten the reason behind the trip. It had hardly been mentioned since the Marshes' arrival, and there was, she thought, nothing festive about their mood. She smiled encouragingly; the truth was it was a relief. She couldn't work Lucas out – he seemed preoccupied, tense. 'Shopping's never a problem.'

They moved through the rooms, Celia taking it slowly,

not expecting much in the way of response and not getting it. Something had obviously subdued them over lunch, and as she led them past Giotto, Cimabue, Virgins and Infants in brilliant blue and gold, she wondered. Perhaps they had just had too much to drink; they didn't seem the type, but it wasn't unknown among even the most sophisticated of her clientele, and Emma Marsh did seem tired. She was pale, and gazed at the diptychs and triptychs, the saints and Madonnas quite blankly, as though she had no conception of their meaning. As though to cover for his wife's sudden silence, Lucas Marsh spoke now and again, asking Celia about the building's construction, the politics of patronage, but the questions came out stiffly, mechanically and Celia felt the prospect of the afternoon hang around her neck like a millstone. Could it be rescued? In Celia's experience the Uffizi had a kind of magic, something would invariably seize the client's imagination; it might be the smooth, monumental marble of the Medici Venus, a sinister Cranach, an incandescent risen Christ by Uccello or Piero della Francesca. And then she could relax, could know the whole thing had worked.

But maybe not today. As they entered one room after another, Emma remained quiet, listless, barely glancing even at pretty Botticelli, which Celia had hoped might please her. She only seemed to brighten, and then just a fraction, when they emerged from each room into the broad corridor and the last rays of natural light that shone down its length from the great south window.

Are you sure you're all right?' asked Celia on the threshold of the Titian room, unable any longer to ignore her instinct that something was not all right at all. She caught a look from

Lucas Marsh to his wife; at the same time he reached out a hand and set it on his wife's waist as if to steady her.

'Yes,' she said. 'Yes, fine.' She made an attempt to smile but it was half-hearted, and Celia frowned. 'Are you sure?'

'Look!' said Emma Marsh suddenly and she turned sharply away as if to avoid Celia's scrutiny. 'Isn't that pretty!' And she hurried through the door towards the *Venus of Urbino*.

Was this it? Celia watched as Emma stopped in front of the broad, glowing canvas and looked. This was, arguably, the most seductive Venus ever painted, her gaze outward, her long white body gleaming like pearl; her boudoir was rich with brocade and silk and bathed in a soft, dusky light. As Celia watched Emma Marsh she found herself wondering what it must be like to be the modern equivalent of this Venus, the object of a rich man's adoration. She was surprised to realize that she felt no envy at all for Emma Marsh.

As she stood there beside Lucas Celia automatically offered her knowledge of the painting, its significance, its patron, its symbolism. She threw in Mark Twain's New World horror at its depravity; she had no idea whether Emma was listening and addressed herself to Lucas; he smiled absently and nodded but he wasn't looking at her either. He was looking at Emma and the painting together. It might have been painted for her, this Venus; voluptuous, physical, direct. She tried to picture the face of the *Madonna of the Lilies*; something nagged at her, said, *Remember me.* And which painting, she wondered as they passed busts of Florentine noblemen and politicians, Medici, Pazzi and Machiavelli, might represent him? At the moment he more resembled some tortured saint, John the Baptist or a pale, pierced St Sebastian. But he's not a saint, is he? He's a lawyer. A powerful man.

As though he knew what she was thinking, Lucas Marsh turned towards her then, cleared his throat a little and spoke in that voice of his, soft, deep, considered, but always tense, always guarded.

'Is everything sorted out for tomorrow night? The dinner?'

'Yes,' said Celia cautiously. 'I – I'm afraid there'll only be one painting, though. Their Titians are all fragile, most of them in for restoration work.' Plenty of her clients would have had a tantrum over less, and she stole a glance at Lucas Marsh apprehensively, but he just nodded slowly. She wondered what it took to make him angry.

'One's enough,' he said consideringly, nodding at the Venus reclining front of them. Wouldn't you say? As long as it's the right one.' And for a moment, although the Madonna's face still would not appear to her, she remembered that feeling she'd had when she'd been about to see it for the first time, the breathless excitement in anticipation of greatness. 'Yes,' she said with relief, smiling. At that moment Emma turned from the picture towards them, like a child towards its parents; Celia saw that her face was very pale. Emma opened her mouth.

'I think,' she said, faltering, 'I think—' and then, right in front of them and without warning, she swayed a little, her head went back and she crumpled to the floor.

Chapter Twelve

A burly attendant leaped from his stool in the corner of the room, galvanized, and was just in time to catch Emma Marsh's head before it struck the floor. Celia, who had moved more slowly, had found the small, vulnerable body unexpectedly heavy as she grappled with it and had not been able to hold on. But Lucas Marsh had her by then anyway, across his body, on the floor. Sitting back on her heels, Celia was startled by the change in him. His fair hair stood up, wild, and his tall, lean figure, which she realized she had seen until that moment as somehow ascetic, self-denying, was suddenly an electric presence beside her; strong, physical, alive with energy released. 'Emma,' he said hoarsely, and she could hear that he was afraid. He cradled his wife's head, and leaning down he brushed his pale cheek against her dead-white one, up and down.

For a long moment Emma Marsh's eyes remained closed and Celia stared, willing them to open; this wasn't sleep, she had never seen anyone look like this before. Beside her the attendant straightened, got to his feet. 'Signora,' she heard him say to her, 'please,' then something else. But there was a humming in her ears; the words sounded far off and she didn't look up at him. Then Lucas Marsh lifted his head from his wife's, she saw Emma's eyelids flutter and Celia breathed out at last, a long, slow exhalation of relief.

Between them they half-carried her into the corridor, she and Lucas Marsh under one arm each, and down towards the window at the end, while back at his post guarding the Venus the attendant spoke on a walkie-talkie in urgent Italian, gesticulating after them as he spoke. The few other visitors to the gallery gaped at them as they passed, stepping on each other in their hurry to get back out of the way. At first Emma Marsh's body was a deadweight on Celia's arm but as they came into the light Celia felt her beginning to come back to herself. She started to struggle.

'No, no,' said Lucas firmly; at the sound of his voice Celia felt Emma go limp and they lowered her to a wooden bench below the great window. Lucas put a palm to her cheek and she looked up at him. Celia could see that although the colour was beginning to return to her cheeks Emma's eyes were wide and frightened.

I'm sorry,' she whispered. 'I don't know what happened. I – do you think—'

'Ssh,' he said urgently. 'Don't worry. Don't worry.' He turned to Celia, and all at once she had a powerful feeling he would rather she wasn't there. Before he could say anything, she stood up quickly. 'I'll see if I can get a glass of water,' she said, and almost ran down the corridor towards another gallery attendant, female this time, striding purposefully towards them. Celia blocked her.

'A little cold water?' she said. 'I think that's what the signora needs.' The woman eyed her suspiciously, and Celia followed her glance as she looked past her towards the couple as they sat quite still in the window seat. The only small movement was from Lucas Marsh as he slowly stroked his wife's hair, looking over the top of her head to something far away, through the great window. In outline at least, Emma Marsh seemed quite composed now, her hands folded meekly in her lap.

The attendant hesitated a second, then turned briskly, ushering Celia towards the far end of the great corridor. As she followed, by some optical trick for a moment Celia could still see in negative the image of the pair behind her as she had last seen them, a *pietà* silhouetted against the window. And as she walked away from the light and her eyes adjusted to the gathering gloom, she found herself thinking of a different image, that of Emma Marsh's pale, frightened face as she looked up at her husband.

By the time Celia got back to the window with a napkin full of sweet biscuits, two glasses of iced water and the gallery's first-aider in her wake, Emma Marsh's fear seemed to have passed as though it had never been. She was sitting up in the window as though in her own drawing room, looking out over the river and pointing something out to her husband on the hills opposite. Sitting there with her black hair and sweet, small face she might have been a Medici mistress or daughter, framed against the dark green hills to the south.

Diffidently, the museum's medical officer introduced himself. A nervous little man, he took hold of Emma Marsh's small white wrist to take her pulse as though it might rear up and bite him.

'It is quite normal, the pulse,' he said. 'But really, Signora,' he went on with great seriousness, 'we should send you in the ambulance to the hospital of Santa Maria Nuova, not so far away. Just to be sure.'

Emma Marsh laughed quickly. 'Hospital? Don't be silly, there's nothing wrong with me.' The man frowned, looked up at Lucas Marsh for support.

Marsh was looking at his wife with an odd expression of mingled impatience and dismay. 'Don't you agree?' urged the medical man.

Marsh turned away a little as if to hide his expression, apparently deep in thought. Emma stopped laughing, looked at him like a child hoping for a reprieve.

'My wife doesn't need the hospital,' he said. 'She's right, there's nothing the matter with her.' He paused, then spoke softly, almost in a whisper. 'She's pregnant.'

Gabriele didn't sound even faintly annoyed when Celia called him for the second time that day. He was in a bar; she could hear a football commentary roaring in the background.

'Gabri,' she said. 'Is the match nearly over?'

He laughed. 'Second half just started. But it's a terrible game. Torture. I'd be well out of here. I'll pick you up around the back, fifteen minutes.'

By the time they emerged into the Uffizi's crowded courtyard, the light had quite gone. Celia led them around the back of the west wing of the gallery; as they passed the great olive tree in its pot Lucas Marsh paused to look at the plaque. She saw him stiffen a little, frowning down, then he looked around quickly. It was a narrow alley where they stood, ill-lit and quite deserted; it was easy to imagine the car parked unobserved with its load of semtex. Even now, with the *carabinieri* idling in the courtyard of the Uffizi fifty yards away, the crowds in the piazza beyond, it would be so easy. Celia could see what Lucas was thinking but she said nothing. It wasn't, after all, part of the usual tourist tour, and she didn't want to upset Emma Marsh, who was leaning on her husband's arm and looking up at him with a puzzled expression.

'This way,' said Celia, and they walked on, around a corner and away from the little tree, incongruous in its pot, an unignorable reminder of violence.

Gabriele was parked illegally on the Lungarno but quite relaxed; he'd even put a tie on, Celia saw. He got out of the car to hold open the door for Emma Marsh. Celia saw Gabriele give her a hard look, taking in her pallor.

'Are you sure you shouldn't go along to casualty?' she said, leaning in through the window. 'Just to get yourself checked over? I'd be happy to come.'

'No, no,' said Emma, and she looked to Lucas as though for confirmation. 'I'm not – there's nothing wrong with me. I've – I've been feeling tired, that's all, didn't eat much at lunch.'

'I can look after her,' said Lucas Marsh gravely. 'Please. If you could just cancel the restaurant this evening.'

Celia nodded. 'You don't want me to come with you as far as the hotel?'

'There's no need,' said Lucas Marsh. 'Really.'

'We'll see you in the morning,' said Emma. 'Shopping.' She tried a conspiratorial smile, a little tired, but just about convincing.

Celia nodded. 'Are you sure that's still what you want?' she asked. Emma waved her away. 'Well,' said Celia, 'if you change your mind, you have my number. I'll see you tomorrow.' She straightened; with a smooth electric hiss the rear windows went up, shutting her out, and Gabriele glided away from the kerb. Just before the big dark car disappeared around the corner she saw a hand emerge from the driver window and wave. She raised her hand to wave back, but they were gone.

Alone in the dark, Celia leaned against the wall that ran along the embankment and breathed a long sigh of relief. It was very cold, and she pulled on her gloves; along the river the lights glittered in the dark water. From where she stood she could see the glowing windows of the shops on the Ponte Vecchio, like tiny, fairytale cottages from this angle, with little balconies and curtained casements above the shops. She could see customers in some windows, dark-coated men buying jewellery, their wives bright with anticipation beside them. The place was a tourist trap, of course, but from here the old bridge had a magical look, and she imagined those women remembering it sentimentally down the years every time they looked at the coral bracelet, the turquoise earrings, the modest diamond.

Beyond the gingerbread outline of the jewellers' shops Celia could see the big lit windows of the penthouses along the river, where the really wealthy lived. As she watched, a woman in evening dress came to one of the windows, a slender, languid silhouette against the golden light, and drew a curtain across the great expanse of glass. Is that what it's like being rich, Celia wondered, thinking of her clients. You buy the view, then you have to pull the curtain on it in case anyone looks in and sees what you've got, tries to take it. She pulled her coat around her and headed for home.

Chapter Thirteen

Walking home through the quiet streets, Luisa felt as light as a girl. She had no shopping in her bag to weigh her down today; she had spent her lunch break with her husband and not in the market. It was only when she reached her own front door and realized it was almost nine o'clock that the thoughts she'd kept at bay from Gianna and Beppe started to crowd in on her, and she began to wonder what Sandro had meant by late.

Luisa had no appetite, and with no supper to prepare she wasn't quite sure what to do with herself. She stood in the kitchen and looked around at her dull, familiar surroundings; everything seemed suddenly so at odds with the way she felt, all these ugly things she had allowed to accumulate, the net curtains greying with every wash, her mother-in-law's dinner service. She tied on an apron and set to work.

By ten there was still no Sandro but there was a brighter light bulb in the hall and five years of dust had been cleaned from its shade. It was not surprising, Luisa had thought on her stepladder as she polished the glass, that she felt so gloomy every time she opened her own front door. The old coats had been bundled into bin-liners for donation to the convent, the net curtains were in the bin and her mother-in-law's dinner service was stacked in a box, wrapped in newspaper.

On the kitchen table embroidered white linen – from Luisa's own mother as a wedding present, and never used in twenty years – covered the old oilcloth with its reproachful marks of wine glasses and hot pans set down in haste. Everything was clean and bright and although it was very cold Luisa had opened the shutters and even the kitchen window to the street just a crack. She had by then grown warm with working, sweeping, polishing, dusting, moving, but it was also as though the taking down of the grubby net curtains had sparked something. The nets had seemed somehow sinister in her hands, grey and suffocating, and all of a sudden she wanted rid of it all, shutters, windows, curtains, everything that stood between her and the pungent, noisy air of the outside world.

Just as well he's not home yet, Luisa thought robustly as she surveyed her work and felt the bloom of sweat between her shoulderblades, looked down at her work shirt all creased and grubby. She tried not to think, *But I hope he's back soon.* She showered and changed into a clean nightdress, lay down in the wide, cold bed and turned off the light. But she didn't sleep, not for a long time; in the dark her thoughts began to circle, and like an old news-reel, cut and pasted, the day flickered before her eyes. She saw again the look a younger woman had given her in the Caffè Maioli, saw Sandro drinking caffè latte with her in the Bar La Posta; she remembered standing under the arcades on the piazza arm in arm with Beppe and Gianna, showing them a postcard. A rich, pretty woman stepping out of a car, a newspaper headline, and a dead girl resurrected. When at last she heard his key in the lock, called back from the brink of sleep Luisa sat bolt upright in the dark bedroom and all the images collided. *Something's wrong*, she thought.

Celia had stopped for a coffee on the way home, a little treacly spoonful in the bar opposite her flat, on an impulse to go inside into the warm and exchange a word or two with some friendly stranger at the bar. It had been nice; it had done the trick, she felt, as she looked around the bright, noisy room and recognized a couple of faces, neighbours, people she'd seen in the street. Are the parents of the child that cries in here, have they left her asleep in her cot and risked running out for a drink to wind down together? She looked around at the faces, and they all looked relaxed, a Friday night feeling. *Maybe I'll settle in here after all*, she thought. But as she climbed the stairs and let herself into the flat, she felt that caffeine buzz shake up the day's events in her head, and she knew she wouldn't sleep, not yet.

The flat was very warm inside, and Celia opened a window to feel the cold night air; behind the bell-tower the sky was frosty with stars. She put on some music, some old Parisian jazz that was on the top of the stack of CDs she'd unpacked yesterday, and tried to remember where it had come from. She thought Dan had given it to her. For the first time in years she found herself thinking of Dan not with that awful sour mixture of hurt and anger but with something warmer, softer. Poor Dan. Celia poured a glass of wine cold from the fridge, took off her shoes and her thick sweater and lay on the sofa, listening to the music as it filled the room with its muffled, jittery rhythms.

The wine worked on her quickly and Celia realized she'd had no supper; idly she thought, *there's cheese in the fridge, crackers, tomatoes*, but she didn't get up to make anything, not yet. It was a nice feeling, for once, to wind down, to let go. Am I so uptight, she wondered. Perhaps I need to loosen up. And then she found herself thinking of Lucas Marsh, but before her train of thought could cohere into anything intelligible, the doorbell rang.

As she padded down the corridor to answer the entryphone, her bare feet on the soft, rough terracotta tiles, Celia realized that she was feeling rather light-headed, detached enough not to be worried about who might be knocking on her door at close to midnight. A friend; it could be Beate come for a chat, couldn't it? She had to put her ear close to the plastic box to interpret the crackle, and even then had to ask for it to be repeated.

'Sorry?' she said. He spoke again. 'Gabriele?' she said, surprised, pressing the button to admit him. She opened the front door and waited for the dim stairwell light to blink on, its timer clicking down. *Good*, was all she thought, as she heard Gabriele's stolid footsteps on the stairs, *now I can thank him*, and when he reached the top of the stairs she flung her arms cheerfully around him.

'Gabri,' she said. 'What a day! You've been lovely. I didn't say thank you properly.' She felt his hands, light and nervous, on her waist and she stepped back. 'Sorry,' she said, laughing, 'I've had a glass of wine and I'm a bit, well . . . Come in.'

'Well,' said Gabriele, uncharacteristically serious, 'just for a minute.' He was wearing some kind of thick reefer jacket, and a cap, which he took off. 'It's late, after all. I just—' he broke off, looking around the flat as they came into the sitting room.

'No,' said Celia, 'it's fine. Would you like something to drink? A glass of wine?'

Gabriele shook his head. 'No, thanks,' he said. 'I've got to drive home. And I can't sleep if I drink.'

Celia put her head on one side and looked at him; she realized Gabriele hadn't ever really talked about himself to her before and she felt obscurely guilty. 'Tea, then?' she said, realizing she probably shouldn't have another glass herself, either.

Gabriele nodded, and she put the kettle on to boil. Gabriele leaned against the sofa and undid one button of his jacket; as she saw him looking at her, for the first time she wondered why he'd come. She thought of the wave he'd given her as he'd driven off with Emma and Lucas Marsh, then thought of Emma, pale on the back seat of Gabriele's car.

'Well,' she said, 'what did you think of them? Lucas and Emma?' Gabriele would be interested, she knew it; he was curious, and a gossip.

'She's pretty,' he said, and Celia smiled. 'Typical,' she said, and he shot her a glance she didn't understand. 'Not as pretty as you, though,' he said seriously, and Celia gave him a little push, laughing. The kettle whistled and she turned away, set out cups, brought the milk out of the fridge.

'And what about him?' Celia said, sitting down on the sofa, her tea warm between her hands. She'd made room for Gabriele but he was still leaning on the sofa's arm. He shrugged.

'Very – stiff,' he said. 'Very English. Repressed.'

'We're not all like that,' said Celia, absently pretending to be offended while she thought about Lucas Marsh. 'She's pregnant, did you realize? That's why she fainted, I suppose.'

'Really?' said Gabriele, sounding surprised. 'They didn't seem very happy. More like they'd had bad news, than good.'

'Yes,' said Celia. 'You're right. He seems distracted to me, not just uptight. Worried.'

'Well,' said Gabriele, 'it's a serious business, a new baby. Expensive, to start with, then I suppose there's plenty of other things to worry about, the development of the baby, all that.' He sounded earnest, as though it was a subject he'd thought about, and idly Celia wondered if he had a family pressurizing him to settle down, too.

'Yes, well,' she said, 'I don't think the money's a problem for Lucas Marsh, do you?'

Gabriele shook his head, draining his cup. 'No,' he said. 'But I suppose money's not everything, is it?'

'No,' Celia agreed. 'They're tricky, rich people. I'm beginning to think I'd rather have a coachload of package tourists.'

'Well,' said Gabriele seriously, 'I hope you're not going to need me in the morning, I'm picking up from the airport. Where did you say you'd be in the afternoon? The Cappelle Medicee?'

'Yes,' said Celia, touched that he'd remembered, a little taken aback that he was taking his responsibilities so seriously. 'But you don't have to worry, really, you've done enough. Give yourself a break tomorrow afternoon.'

'No, no,' said Gabriele, lightly now. 'It's no problem.' He paused. 'When do they leave, anyway?'

'Sunday,' said Celia, 'but I finish tomorrow night.' Only another day, thirty-six hours maybe, but suddenly she had the feeling it was going to seem much longer. Gabriele pushed himself up from the arm of the sofa and set his cap carefully on the side.

'What are you doing next week?' he asked casually. 'When they've gone?' Celia shook her head a little, trying to remember; she was still finding it hard to think ahead, to get past this weekend. Something was making her uneasy; was it Emma's pregnancy? Medical complications always made her feel jittery, an extra responsibility to the job. But that wasn't all; there was a precariousness about the Marshes' relationship, an edginess that unsettled her.

'I don't think I'm doing anything,' she said, not really applying her mind to the question.

Gabriele put his cap on and stood square and solid in front of her. 'I – well,' he said, 'I think you need a break. You're looking worn out yourself.' *Maybe I am*, thought Celia, feeling the effects of the wine wear off, wanting her bed.

Gabriele went on, 'Why don't you come down to Rome with me for a day or two? My mum could feed you up.' Despite herself Celia laughed.

'I don't need feeding up,' she said. 'I'd love to meet your family, though, that would be great. Sometime.' Impulsively she leaned up and gave him a kiss on the cheek; he stood there, serious. 'Thank you, Gabri,' she said, 'thanks for everything.' Still he didn't move, looking at her as though there was something else he wanted to say, but Celia was too tired, suddenly, to think about what it might be. 'I'll talk to you tomorrow, sweetheart,' she said, and then he did turn for the door at last.

As she leaned her back against the door and listened to Gabriele's steps recede Celia thought, *I'm lucky, to have friends like Gabriele. And Beate, and even Jo Starling, out there in the dark somewhere. But I'm lucky to have my own place, too, somewhere all to myself.* And then she thought only of her bed.

Chapter Fourteen

Sandro was gone when she opened her eyes. It was late, too: she'd left the shutters open and without the nets the pale winter light flooded the bedroom. The same room they'd slept in since they were married – slippery satin bedcover, glass ornaments on the shelf, veneer dressing table polished to a high shine – but it looked different. Registering the time, with an exclamation Luisa leaped out of bed.

It was cold in the kitchen. In the sink stood the small aluminium pot Sandro had used to make himself coffee – the one he always used. Luisa remembered that only yesterday, after that lunch and a peaceful afternoon idly dreaming in the shop, she had even begun to think they might be getting up together now and again. Standing side by side in the kitchen, half asleep in the early morning. She stared at the little coffee pot, the single tiny cup with its dregs.

It had been Sandro, of course, who else at one in the morning opening the door with his own key? But in the space of a short winter afternoon, it seemed, the tiny budding growth of possibility she had felt – no more than that, not even hope, not yet – was frost-blasted, over before it had begun. Sitting up in bed, Luisa had heard him sigh in the narrow confines of the hall, hanging up his coat, and he walked slowly into the kitchen as though he was dragging something with him. She heard him pour a glass of something. She waited.

He started as he came into the room, his face white in the moonlight as though she was a ghost sitting there in the bed. She could hear her own heart beating as he stared at her.

'What is it?' she'd said, faltering, a hand up to her hair that stood out madly around her head.

In the kitchen now Luisa pulled the robe around her, and involuntarily she closed her eyes. She felt a heaviness in her chest, a weight of blame she shared with Sandro for never having talked to him about it. She should have asked him, begged him if need be, to tell her what was on his mind, what he had seen. All these years, that was what he had needed, and she had said nothing. Mechanically she stood up and walked back into the bedroom. She began to take down the clothes she would need. Saturday; it would be busy so close to Christmas.

Sandro had crossed to his side of the bed, sat down heavily and put his face in his hands.

'What?' Luisa had repeated, gingerly putting a hand to his shoulder. 'It's the suicide, isn't it? You're blaming yourself—' But he interrupted her. His voice, when it came, was muffled.

'It's worse than that,' he said. 'I wouldn't have lost sleep over that.'

'Then what?'

'He didn't kill himself,' said Sandro, lowering his hands. His face was white, drained. 'Bartolo was murdered.' He took his hands away from his face and stared at her. 'Do you know what that means?'

Bewildered, Luisa had shaken her head.

'It's down to me,' said Sandro. 'Ever since – these last fifteen years, I've been passing on information. What we know, things we found at the scene, the condition of the body, telling him about Bartolo's form, his whereabouts. Things no one outside the force was supposed to know. And now he's dead.'

'Who?' said Luisa. 'Telling who?'

He looked at her. 'The father, of course. The girl's father.' Luisa stared. Sandro went on, talking quickly, insistently in the dark as though he was in a confessional, mumbling to a priest.

'They changed their name, did you know that? The girl's parents. That's why no one ever heard anything more about them. They wouldn't talk to anyone, no press, no counselling service.' Sandro looked up at her at that, and made a small, gruff sound. 'A bit like us, hey?' He looked down again. 'It was as if they were ashamed, as if they'd done something wrong, not him. Not Bartolo.' Luisa nodded, remembering their faces, heads down as the television camera watched them emerge from the police station.

Oblivious, Sandro went on. 'I had the new identity, the new address, of course. So I wrote, one day I just sat down and wrote, all the things I knew. Every time I got a piece of evidence, I passed it on. And he wrote back sometimes. He wrote when his wife died. She killed herself with an overdose, a year after. Exactly a year.' Sandro paused, musing. 'He wasn't asking for sympathy. Just the facts, this has happened, on this day, like this. A bit like a policeman.'

Luisa felt sick. 'And – the DNA test?'

Sandro nodded. 'Yes,' he said. 'I sent him a photocopy of

131

the result, about a month ago. *Inconclusive.*' His voice was as savage as it had been in the Bar La Posta, the last time he'd spat that word. 'I'd let him hope. And it came back, inconclusive.'

Luisa thought of those letters, letters full of dangerous information, like bombs, passing across the continent. Where were they sent? Not to the station, surely, where anyone might have opened them. Not here, either. If Luisa had seen foreign postmarks, a stranger's writing, she would have suspected something. Suspected what? An affair, a betrayal? Or would she? She saw herself, wound up tight for fifteen years in a kind of shroud, not seeing, not wanting to see, only thinking about the shop, stock, window displays, the right shoes to wear to work.

Seeing her face, Sandro said softly, 'I had a box number. At the post office.' Helplessly he shrugged. 'Would you have wanted to know?' Luisa just shook her head, not to agree, but to shake something loose in there, to understand.

Sandro went on. It seemed so intolerable that we couldn't pin it on him, that no one could get to him. That you should lose a child like that, broken and thrown away like rubbish, and nothing to be done. Everyone in Galluzzo knew, but Bartolo didn't care.'

'So when they said Bartolo had committed suicide,' Luisa said slowly, closing her ears to the sound of Sandro's voice cracking at the mention of the child, 'you didn't believe it, not even at the beginning?'

'No,' said Sandro, 'I knew he'd never kill himself, never.' He looked down at his hands. 'I persuaded myself it might have happened. We were all doing that. It's still the official line. But they know now, you see. He was bound, ligature marks on hands and wrists. Angle of the cut all wrong, too, he couldn't

132

have reached that far around. No tentative marks – you know, almost no one can just slash their own throat like that, one decisive cut. Whoever did it left the knife, cut-throat razor it was, but the trajectory was wrong, it couldn't have fallen from his hand where they found it.' He spoke mechanically, as though he was in the witness box, rehearsing evidence for the jury.

'It might have been anyone, though,' said Luisa, trying to sound reasonable. 'He wasn't exactly popular, was he? Like you said, everyone knew.'

Sandro shook his head slowly. 'What if they find out?' he said, and there was something in the way he spoke that made Luisa's heart sink. She took his hand, and he looked up at her and said, 'It was like putting a loaded gun in his hands, wasn't it? I wanted him to act. I wanted him to do something. And now he has.'

At her dressing table in the cold light of morning Luisa brushed her thick dark hair, twenty strokes. She buttoned her coat; it was going to be another cold day.

'Let's start with coffee,' said Emma, putting an arm through Celia's. She looked a different person this morning, her cheeks bright with colour. She was wearing a cherry-red coat and stood out in the Regale's expensively neutral lobby like a dancing girl. 'Not here, though.' She looked around the pale, tasteful space with ambivalence.

'Isn't it what you wanted?' said Celia, her heart sinking. It was difficult to relax, even when a client had her arm through yours. Was this going to be a complaint?

'No, no, it's lovely,' said Emma. 'Wonderful. It's just that sometimes – don't you find these places feel rather – confining?

Lucas is used to it, I suppose. His office is rather like this.' She laughed, not entirely happily.

'Where is his office?' asked Celia, by way of polite conversation. She wondered where Lucas Marsh was now, and what his plans for the morning might involve.

'Oh, in the City,' said Emma vaguely. 'I've only been there once; I don't think he was quite comfortable with me there.' Celia could imagine it, the brightness of her, Lucas Marsh frowning at a desk. They turned for the door and she saw the dark, serious-looking concierge look over at them and raise a hand as if to attract Emma's attention, and Celia stopped.

'He works all the time, you know,' Emma was saying, almost as though she was talking to herself. 'Don't you sometimes wonder what they do, those men in offices, sitting behind their desks? It's not as if we need the money. Taking calls at midnight, meeting people at all hours. He's up there working now.' Then she stopped. 'What is it?'

'The concierge,' said Celia, nodding towards the desk.

'Signora Marsh?' the man asked. 'There is a letter for your husband. A small package. He is in your suite still?'

Automatically Emma put out a hand to take the package the concierge pulled from a rack of wooden pigeon holes. Celia registered a cheap, flimsy envelope addressed in very un-English rounded, curling letters, and without a stamp, loose inside it something roughly the size and shape of a fat chocolate bar, or a mobile phone. Hand-delivered. Emma Marsh's hand paused in mid-air, then she put it to her mouth.

'Yes,' she said. 'He's working. Perhaps you might take it up to him? I'm just on my way out, you see.' She smiled her charming, well-bred smile, but Celia saw that her eyes were frightened and she looked away, feeling suddenly like a spy.

'Shall we go now?' said Emma, a little breathlessly. Her arm was no longer through Celia's and without waiting for an answer she made for the wide glass doors. *Is he betraying her,* wondered Celia. Emma Marsh seemed wounded, somehow, by the arrival of the letter. *Is he one of those men who has mistresses all over the world?* She couldn't imagine it somehow, and the crumpled envelope had not looked like a love letter.

They were shown to a window table in the warm, wood-panelled tea room of the Caffè Gilli on the square. Emma Marsh spent some time settling herself in the padded leather, looking in her handbag for lipstick, a wallet, smoothing her hair. Celia waited, and the movements became less flustered, the agitation subsided and finally Emma Marsh gave a little sigh and smiled. She looked more at home here; she suited the old-fashioned prettiness of the tea room. The waiter who appeared at her elbow within seconds seemed to agree, eyeing her with undisguised approval. Celia ordered a caffè latte, thinking for a second of Beate, sitting in the Maoli and treating the drink as though it were medicine. Emma Marsh ordered hot chocolate with whipped cream.

'And a pastry,' she added with certainty. 'Could you choose for me?' She gazed up at the waiter and he nodded, mute with admiration. As he left, Emma unbuttoned her cherry-coloured coat, and Celia couldn't help gazing at it, a narrow edging of velvet on the collar, the heavy, deep-dyed wool, big pearly buttons. She felt an unfamiliar and frivolous urge, a longing to wear something bright and impossibly expensive, to gleam like this, to abandon her plain, dark, carefully maintained uniform. She looked up and saw that Emma was watching her, and laughed.

'Nice, isn't it?' Emma said, stroking the scarlet wool with

satisfaction. 'Lucas bought it for me.' She hesitated, then went on with a carelessness Celia wasn't quite convinced by, 'Oh, yes, I meant to say straight away. I'd – we'd like you to stop with us for a drink, at least, this evening. At the Palazzo Ferrigno? As our guest, not – not as a job.'

'Oh,' said Celia, touched. *Yes, please*, was her first thought. That would be – that's very sweet of you.' Then, imagining the brazier-lit terrace of the Palazzo Ferrigno, the sombre staterooms, *What shall I wear?* Emma Marsh smiled at her gaily. 'Perhaps we can find you a cocktail dress this morning? On our shopping expedition?'

Despite herself, Celia laughed. 'Maybe,' she said, wondering if Emma Marsh had the slightest idea where Celia usually bought her clothes.

'That's settled then,' said Emma, and she took off her coat. Underneath it she was wearing a dress of the same red with a low neck and a wide skirt. It was close-fitting and narrow at the waist, and as she admired it Celia remembered with a start that Emma Marsh was pregnant.

'Not quite three months,' said Emma, watching her, and it occurred to Celia that not for the first time Emma was answering a question she had not asked, only thought. The thought passed through Celia's mind that her client was a clever woman. An observant woman. 'I don't feel any different at all,' Emma said carelessly. 'Isn't that funny?'

'It's probably quite normal,' said Celia, thinking of Kate fussing over cravings and swollen ankles before she was two months pregnant. 'With your first baby. I mean, some people don't realize for months, do they?'

'Perhaps I'm in denial,' Emma said, shrugging. 'But sooner or later, I suppose I will get fatter. I can go shopping for a few

136

things to grow into, can't I? But no maternity clothes, not yet. Awful.' She made a face, then her expression grew serious. 'And I don't think Lucas would like it, somehow.'

'But surely – he must be pleased?' Celia regretted the question straight away. What if he wasn't?

Emma looked down, circling the lace on the tablecloth with a neat fingernail. 'Mm,' she said uncertainly. 'Well,' she flushed now, 'it wasn't planned exactly. I think he's pleased, I mean, I've hardly had time—' She broke off and with sudden clarity Celia realized that Emma Marsh had waited to tell him until they were here, in this romantic city. No wonder he had seemed distracted that first morning, in the hotel room.

The waiter appeared with a silver tray and with elaborate ceremony laid down cups, pastries, napkins, a jug of iced water. When he had gone Emma looked straight at Celia. 'I only told him yesterday morning,' she said. 'It was – difficult. He's older and – I'm not his first wife, you see, perhaps you could tell.' She darted a glance at Celia.

'No,' said Celia truthfully. 'Actually, it didn't occur to me.' Although in retrospect it was obvious.

'But he likes children,' Emma said. 'I know maybe he doesn't look much like that kind of man, but he's got god-children. A god-daughter at least, he's got a soft spot for her. He keeps her picture in his desk.' She looked at Celia as if admitting that this wasn't much in the way of evidence. Her confidence seemed all gone, her brightness. She went on, 'He had a hard time with his first wife, I'm not quite sure what happened, you see, but I can tell it was unhappy.' She tailed off and looked down at her chocolate cup with a perplexed expression, like a child unable to explain some new and troubling fact about the adult world.

'You don't know?' said Celia, unable to disguise her incredulity. It seemed hardly believable that a clever woman should know so little about her own husband. After all, he might be Bluebeard. Celia knew it was not quite rational, nor even practical at her age, but she distrusted men on their second marriage. How hard could it be, to make a marriage work?

Emma shrugged uncomfortably. 'He's a very private person,' she said stubbornly. 'I didn't want to – upset him.' She looked at Celia. 'It's not as if – they didn't divorce, or anything,' she said patiently. 'Nothing like that.'

Celia frowned. 'So . . . ?' She didn't understand.

'She died,' said Emma. 'Lucas was a widower when I met him.' And she picked up the long silver spoon and poked it into the tower of whipped cream. 'He'll come round,' she said decisively, retrieving a spoon of the dark, glossy chocolate from underneath, then another. 'Lovely,' she said, licking the spoon, and Celia could see that the subject was closed.

From the window of her office over the gatehouse of the Palazzo Ferrigno Paola Caprese looked down into the narrow, cobbled street outside. On the corner a couple of men muffled up in hats and layers of coats had set up a brazier, raking coals in an old oil drum, a half-full sack of chestnuts leaning against the wall beside them. It was a pretty scene, but Paola, who was not susceptible to prettiness, only wondered if they had a permit; this wasn't a regular patch for chestnuts, too far off the beaten track. She thought they must be cold out there; the street was still in deep shadow and the cobbles were steely with frost. Further along, though, where the road widened to meet the bridge, the winter sun shone yellow on the façades of the Piazza Goldoni. It was a beautiful day.

Paola was thinking about the week's bookings, a reception in the gallery, a conference and on Friday a charity cocktail party for 500 thrown by some English duchess. Paola couldn't imagine where they got their money, these English aristocrats. Their Italian counterparts had crumbling frescoed palaces to spare, but no cash; they were the charity cases themselves, to hear them complain. But the English – what did they make there, after all? Paola herself was from a peaceful, industrious town in the Po valley where every household had heavy machinery in the garage, churning out knitwear or lace or handbags on piecework. In England, as far as she could tell, there was no art, no fashion, no leather, no glass, no steel; they didn't make refrigerators or cars or precision instruments. Only some anonymous, murmured business in a grey skyscraper, columns of figures on a computer screen that translated into vast sums in their bank accounts and wads of cash handed over on the Via Tornabuoni.

This evening's private dinner in the Titian room was nothing, of course, she told herself, not by comparison with sorting out canapés for 500 assorted dignitaries, but still, it was weighing on the administrator's mind. Paola Caprese had been in the business thirty years, and she had a nose. That English girl, the guide who'd set the dinner up, had looked out of her depth, rather, trying to keep her end up but clearly floundering a bit, nervous. They were obviously a power couple these two, Mr and Mrs Lucas Marsh. *Five thousand euros on a dinner for two, well*, Paola inclined her head, thinking of the Titian behind its protective curtain. She supposed, grudgingly, that that was class.

Paola turned to the side, looking along the building beyond the Piazza Goldoni. The men with their chestnut burner had stoked up quite a glow now. A gaunt woman, skeletal under a heavy, shabby coat, edged towards them along the wall to keep warm; that was the trouble, Paola thought vaguely, on a day like this they could attract the wrong sort, winos, junkies with their peripheral nervous systems shot, desperate for warmth. The thin woman looked up, almost straight into Paola's window, and her starved face seemed lost, adrift in the busy street. Paola shifted her gaze away from those eyes; if she set her cheek against the glass she could see down along the river to where the skeleton trees of Le Cascine stood out against the pale blue sky.

Of course dead bodies found with their throats cut in swimming pools didn't help the city's image, did they? The administrator was not a superstitious person but as she looked at the dark trees she felt a prickle at the back of her neck. It was a bit close for comfort; she thought of the drained pool at Le Pavoniere, enclosed by trees grown tall over a hundred years, like Sleeping Beauty's castle. Reproaching herself for an overactive imagination, Paola looked away. All the same, she decided, perhaps it wouldn't do any harm to go down and give the Titian room the once-over.

The panelled room was cold, the temperature kept deliberately low of course to protect the paintings, but this was *esaggerato*. Too much. Paola made a mental note to adjust the temperature in good time and pulled back one of the heavy damask curtains at the window to let in a shard of thin, wintry sun. On the terrace she could see that the heaters were ready, and a heavy iron fire-basket stood stacked with wood between padded chairs.

Leaving the window, Paola went to inspect the table. It was already laid, pewter candelabra, lilies, silver and glass, and Paola turned a knife over in her hand. Each piece of 300-year-old crystal and porcelain had to be washed by hand, dried with clean, dry linen, handled thereafter only with cotton-gloved, careful hands, but you couldn't get the staff these days, and mistakes were made. So many *extracommunitari*, cutting corners. The knife was clean and she laid it back down. She stood back, surveying the scene; chairs, candles, light, imagining where fault might be found. Of course, she needed to see the painting. Carefully Paola leaned up and detached the curtain that covered it from the tiny hooks in the panelling and stepped back into the middle of the room, the faded red linen in her hands.

The room was dim, as Paola had not drawn the curtains at the window back more than a crack, but it was enough. The painting glowed, red and gold, and Paola stepped closer. She saw the figure of the maidservant bending over a linen chest in a corner of the noblewoman's bedchamber, coiffed and humbly dressed. That's me, thought Paola, but without rancour. She saw the embroidered damask on the chaise where the mother sat, saw the lovely tilted oval of her face and the gleaming black head. The child's fine, curly hair brushed the mother's neck. To her surprise and annoyance, for she was a woman who had brought up her own children without sentiment, Paola felt a knot in her chest at the thought of the child's death, only months after the painting was finished. With a frown she turned from the picture and behind her she heard someone outside the door.

'Yes?' she said, unaccountably annoyed. The door opened and she could see that it was one of the porters, or at least she supposed so in the dim light, a man in a worker's long brown overall. 'Have you come to do something about the heating?'

she said, before she realized that of course she had not yet issued that instruction. 'Who's sent you?' she asked then, imagining that he must be in the wrong room, dressed as he was for furniture removal or some heavy work. He said nothing, but his eyes darted around the room, appraising, scrutinizing. For a moment Paola had the impression he was registering every detail of the room, the size of the windows, the angle of the dining table, for some obscure purpose, but then his gaze settled on her, mild, apologetic.

'Yes?' said Paola again, irritated. 'Is it the telephone? Am I needed?' The man took a step towards her into the pale light that fell through the half-curtained window and she saw that she did not recognize him at all. He was fair-haired, with pale blue eyes, but his skin was red with exposure to the cold and his chin was coarse with stubble. She thought, a casual worker, Polish perhaps. All at once she became aware of the crumpled curtain in her hands, the painting exposed on the wall behind her, and protectively she stepped back.

'Yes,' he said. 'The heating.' She saw that he held a tool bag; she searched his face again but still it was bland, empty, harmless. *Pull yourself together,* she thought.

The radiators need . . . ' he frowned. 'To be . . .' He used a foreign word.

'They need bleeding,' said Paola briskly, turning away to disguise her lapse, her unaccountable nervousness in his presence. He was nothing, just a workman; what was this idiotic jittery behaviour – the change? She felt her cheeks burn at the thought and she gestured towards the door.

'Yes, well,' she said, 'I can't leave you in here, you know, not with the painting. It's rules. You can start along the landing.' Drawing herself up, she walked past him and held the door open; with a servile half-smile he turned and left the room. He stationed himself at the end of the long landing, illuminated by the cold wintry light that fell through the glass cupola, and knelt beside the heavy iron radiator. Paola locked the door twice, three times with the heavy key and walked slowly down the stairs.

The concierge, curious about the package left for Mr Marsh by a man in a cheap suit at seven that morning, had asked for five minutes away from the front desk and taken it up to the honeymoon suite himself. He felt the small, heavy object through the cheap paper; he didn't need to open it to know what it was, although it beat him why anyone that rich would buy a dodgy mobile off a Ukrainian. Marsh had been there on the threshold almost before the concierge had knocked, as though he had been waiting behind the door. In the couple of seconds it took Marsh to take the envelope and with brusque thanks hand a folded five-euro note in exchange through the barely opened door, the concierge had the impression of a man somehow caged, holed up, waiting for something or someone to release him. He was a pale man, Lucas Marsh, narrow, dressed with expensive, anonymous neatness, not what you would call muscular or powerfully built. But as the concierge took the money with a polite smile and for a brief fraction of a second they were connected through the door, he felt something, he could have sworn it, something like an electrical jolt from the pale, manicured fingers.

Half an hour later, back at the front desk, the concierge called up to the honeymoon suite to announce a visitor for Lucas Marsh, and was instructed in meticulously polite Italian to send the man up. The concierge watched the visitor into the lift, wondering where he'd seen the man before. He was stocky, leather-jacketed, Italian through and through, nothing like the early-morning messenger, who had obviously been from Eastern Europe. You wouldn't have put them on the same planet; there was a world of difference between a cheap-suited, shaven-headed thug probably living rough out by the motorway and a solid, middle-class citizen. He had the air of authority, of officialdom, a lawyer perhaps, a bureaucrat. A policeman. The concierge thought of the man upstairs, waiting for his visitor. Not the usual sort of honeymoon suite visitors, he thought. Something funny going on there.

Chapter Fifteen

It was fifteen years ago, near enough, but as Luisa stood in the bar and stared at the picture of the little girl in the morning's paper, it all came back, as sharp and clear as if it had happened yesterday. For almost all of those fifteen years, it seemed to Luisa now, she had persuaded herself it was over, gone, forgotten. What was the point in dwelling on frightful things, that was what she'd always thought, how could good come out of it? What lesson could you learn from the random murder of a child? That the world is a terrible place. The coffee came and Luisa drank it in a single mouthful, folded the paper small so that the girl's chip-toothed smile was hidden, and headed back to the shop.

The first thing that came back, she thought as she stepped into the busy street, was how the city had felt for that terrible, sweltering week. The August silence in the narrow streets that Luisa had once loved was changed, turned sour and heavy with foreboding. People crept out of their houses at dusk, when the temperature dropped a degree or two, to talk it over. But we all knew, thought Luisa, we knew how it would end. And she knew particularly, because she lived with Sandro.

'The first twenty-four hours are crucial,' he'd said at the kitchen table, in a dead voice on the morning of the second day. In the days when she dragged herself out of bed to be with him before he left for work. 'After that, there's almost no possibility the child is still alive.'

Luisa had thought about how he came to know these things. Case conferences, statistics. Photographs of dead and abused children. She felt herself turn to stone, hardly able to reach out a hand to him at the table for fear of what he knew.

Every one of the nights of that long week before the girl's body had been found Sandro had returned home with a greater burden, Luisa could see that now. The first night, when he'd come home at two in the morning, there had been hope. A sighting of a girl wrapped in a towel, chatting to an old lady in the street, the fantasy of a babe in the woods, kept warm by forest creatures, which they allowed themselves to believe in for one night. The following morning she would stumble out of some bamboo thicket or vineyard on the edge of Galluzzo with leaves in her hair. But the sighting turned out to have been invented by a pathological hoaxer, a misfit who wanted to get his name in the papers.

Then they had a suspect, a definite. Bartolo, who was always hanging around at the perimeter fence, sometimes calling things to girls, asking them where they went to school. Nothing you could charge him with, but he made people uneasy. They got a warrant and searched his house, hyped on adrenaline as they battered at his front door. Sandro came home with a face black and set with rage, and told her. They had combed the house for evidence and found nothing, no clothing fibres, no bodily fluids, no photographs. There was the girl who worked in the changing rooms, but she was still refusing to alter her story. 'I don't know if she's crazy, or stupid, or just stubborn,' Sandro had said, white-lipped with fury. 'I can't get through to her.' And Bartolo's old fool of a mother just kept repeating, over and over again, that her son had been with her all afternoon, helping her scald tomatoes in the kitchen.

'He's such a good boy,' she said, beaming at them apparently without comprehension, asking them to agree. And at her side Bartolo had grinned like a simpleton. They even brought her in and made her give a statement but they couldn't fault her, she was sharp as a whip underneath the veneer of senility.

'I'll bet she's trained herself up to this,' Sandro had said, his voice ragged. 'He's done it before, maybe not killed anyone but pestered kids, messed about with them, and she protects him.' Sandro's helplessness and frustration turned him savage, and Luisa had stayed back, unable to think of the right thing to say. She thought of the old mother gazing at her terrible child and believing no ill of him, and her stomach churned.

After four days they knew it was over, it was just a matter of time. They asked the parents, who had moved into a dive of a hotel by the station as though burying themselves, to give a press conference. 'How – how are they?' asked Luisa, terrified of the answer.

Sandro had averted his eyes. They won't do a press conference,' he said. The mother's finished.' His voice was flat, emotionless. 'She might as well be dead.' He looked up at Luisa. 'I can't stand to look in her eyes,' he said, and Luisa thought of the baby, of how she'd been after the baby. She felt stiff and cold with the horror of it but she just nodded.

'And the father?'

Sandro's expression changed. 'Can't make him out,' he said slowly. 'Perhaps it's because he's English.' He paused, and Luisa tried to picture the man; there'd been a snatched shot of the couple leaving the police station, their faces drained and hollow. 'He just stares,' said Sandro, 'stares straight ahead, like he's fixing on something far away. He hardly talks, doesn't cry, doesn't break down. His wife sits there next to him falling apart, really, she can't control anything, can hardly answer a question, and he's nodding to himself. Sometimes he asks questions, in this cold, dry little voice. He's . . . frightening, that's what he is.'

'Perhaps it's not because he's English. Perhaps it's because he's a man,' Luisa had said then, before she could stop herself, and Sandro glanced at her quickly, then looked away.

'Yes,' he said hoarsely. 'Perhaps.' He hesitated, his eyes distant. 'He thinks it's his fault. Something he said at the beginning, before he clammed up, when his wife was saying it was her fault, crying that she shouldn't have let the girl go on her own. He said no, that it was his fault they had to go to the public pool. It was his fault they couldn't afford a decent villa where things didn't go wrong.' Sandro paused. 'He didn't provide for them, didn't protect them, and now he's thinking he should have been able to protect them, because that's what fathers are for.' He'd stood up with a start as though made self-conscious by what he'd said, and the chair grated against the tile of the floor with a hard, ugly sound.

Luisa stopped short in the cold street as she remembered Sandro, all that time ago, turning away to hide his face as he spoke. A couple forced to separate to come around her as she stood there gave Luisa a funny look, but she was oblivious.

She could see now why Sandro had fed the man information, had passed every scrap and clue and hint they'd found across Europe to him and closed his eyes to the consequences. That's what he'd have wanted, if it had been him. There in the street she allowed herself to think, just for a second, of that maternity ward where she'd sat, her arms empty and her future gone, and Sandro incapable even of looking at her. There'd been nothing he'd been able to do to protect them.

Luisa became aware of the bleep and flashing light of an approaching refuse truck and realized she was standing in the middle of the street. Shaking herself back to life, she pushed open the door of the shop and stashed her bag with the newspaper folded inside it behind the till. She felt Gianna's eyes on her and carefully took off her coat. Her face felt as though it was frozen, inanimate, and she rubbed her cheeks to bring some life back.

'Was I too long?' she said, trying to seem normal, though she couldn't remember what normal was for her just at the moment.

'No,' said Gianna, peering at her curiously. 'It's just – oh, nothing.'

'Cold out there,' said Luisa by way of explanation. Last night seemed a long time ago, wandering through the arcades arm in arm with Beppe and Gianna. Had it been one big mistake? 'Bitter. And they say it's going to snow.'

Gianna frowned a little, then shrugged and picked up the dog-eared copy of *Gente* she kept under the cash-desk. Luisa stepped back on to the shop floor.

They'd asked for coffee to be brought up. By some instinct the waiter with his tray hesitated before knocking; perhaps it was the tone of the voice, level but furious, coming from behind the door. It was an English voice, but speaking Italian, so he understood everything.

'This wasn't supposed to happen,' it said, each word emphasized with quiet force.

The murmur that responded was harder to pick up, but the waiter heard it all the same; he was listening now.

'It's not safe,' said the Italian. 'Do you understand? You can't mess about with these people, it's not like some civilized conference in Geneva with a bunch of lawyers, this is the sharp end. This is a dangerous game, and if you don't pay them what they're owed they'll come after you until they get it.'

The waiter didn't understand what the Englishman said next, although he spoke in Italian. It sounded technical, something you'd hear in a court of law. 'I won't be a party to it,' he said, and turned away. 'I'm not—' And then the telephone began to ring. It rang and rang, but no one answered and eventually it stopped.

The room-service waiter had been in the business of discretion for long enough to know he didn't want to get involved. Briskly he knocked at the door, and when the Italian opened it, Lucas Marsh seated behind him and shielded by his bulk, he averted his eyes so the lawyer wouldn't know he'd been listening. He didn't wait for a tip.

They'd started in the Via Tornabuoni, of course, the lovely, curving street where all the big names were, sleek black and silver windows set in the ancient, forbidding stone façades. Emma Marsh crossed each imposing threshold without a qualm, as though she owned the place, and the black-suited heavies behind the doors whisked them open in front of her, knowing money when they saw it. Together Celia and Emma Marsh wandered through the showrooms and corridors, up cantilevered staircases and through stone arches, their footsteps muffled by pale, close-cropped carpets. They looked into glass cases filled with handbags in exotic colours: dark red, magenta, green; passed rows of dresses, pressed and gleaming with newness, each hanging a regulation centimetre apart and each minutely adjusted outwards, to greet the browsing customer. The saleswomen, who usually in Celia's experience were unable to resist close and suspicious questioning of each customer disguised as solicitude – 'Are you looking for something in particular? If there's anything I can help you with' – hung back when Emma came through.

Emma was very thorough. She tried nothing on, but she touched and stroked and examined anything she liked and politely, charmingly, she asked detailed questions of the showroom assistants about the weight of fabric, techniques and provenance. Then she listened attentively to their answers and judiciously expressed appreciation and approval, and Celia watched how well this worked. Also she spent, which, Celia had to admit, was probably the key. A jewelled sweater with a crew neck, two handbags, one plum-coloured, one dark mossy-green, a pair of shoes in a silver shot-silk velvet that looked as though they might have been made for a geisha, so teeteringly high and delicately strapped were they. Emma chatted to the assistants as they wrapped things for her and Celia saw the severe, black-suited women soften and respond.

It wasn't just that she was wealthy, nor even that she had good taste. Celia had been shopping with rich women before, after all, and many of them richer and sleeker than Emma Marsh. She had spent long mornings standing back and trying to conceal her discomfort as they found fault in loud English without caring who understood, left boxes of shoes or underwear strewn and discarded in their wake, pinched pennies or spent with stupid extravagance. It was, Celia realized as she watched the shoes reverently packed away in their tissue-lined box, that Emma Marsh really might have been a kind of Western geisha, bred and raised for softness, charm, appreciation. Had she married Lucas Marsh for his money? The question was an uncomfortable one. Would she be the same if she was married to a poor man? How would she deal with adversity, deprivation, violence? Celia frowned, wondering why such a question should occur to her here, in this padded and luxurious sanctuary where the thought of violence could not have been more incongruous.

Lifting her bags lightly from the counter, Emma turned to her and smiled. 'Where next?' It was almost midday.

'You haven't had enough yet, then?' said Celia, laughing, as they came out on to the street. It was, if possible, even colder than it had been first thing, and as Celia glanced into the sky she could see that a skein of white cloud was moving across the wintry blue from the north. She wondered if it would snow; it almost never snowed in the city.

'Oh, no,' said Emma in mock horror. 'Never!' There was no trace of yesterday's pallor; her cheeks shone pink in the cold, her breath clouding in the air. Then a tiny frown appeared, drawing her brows together. 'I should phone Lucas,' she said. 'He said he might come out and meet us.' She fished in her pocket, her catch a tiny silver mobile she peered at as though it was unfamiliar to her. Celia, who didn't like listening to other people's telephone conversations, feeling it was not quite polite, turned away as Emma dialled. She looked down the street towards the towering bulk of the Palazzo Spini-Ferroni, the seat of the Ferragamo, a rusticated fortress on the river turned shrine to expensive shoes. Behind her, despite herself, she could hear Emma Marsh's voice, soft and somehow sad, and she tried not to listen.

As Celia concentrated on the view, from the far end of the Via Tornabuoni a figure walking up towards her grew distinct, and familiar. It was Beate, in a long red fur-trimmed coat, silver-ringleted and bareheaded despite the cold, something slung across her back.

'All right,' Celia heard Emma say. Would you mind leaving that message for him?' There was a tiny click as she closed up the phone, and Celia turned back to look at her. She was frowning at the phone as though absorbed in some private worry.

'Is everything okay?' Celia asked.

'I don't know,' said Emma slowly. 'There's no answer from his room.'

'So he's gone out?' said Celia, not understanding.

'Well, they – yes, I suppose that's what they meant. Yes.' Her voice grew firmer. 'Anyway, I left a message, in case he wants to come out and meet us. I said we'd be in that shop, there's a shop on the corner that looks nice, near the hotel. Do you know it? There's a green dress in the window.' There was still a wistful, preoccupied edge to her voice.

'Why are you worried about him?' asked Celia on impulse. She couldn't quite make it out, this relationship. 'I haven't been shopping with many women who wanted their husbands along. Mostly they try to get rid of them.'

Emma looked at her. 'I don't like being apart from Lucas,' she said. Celia looked at her and realized that she loved him. She felt

153

faintly embarrassed that she had, as she supposed many people would, assumed that when it came down to it Emma Marsh had married Lucas for money, or at least for everything that money brought. Security, luxury, beauty. 'Yes,' she said. 'Of course.'

Emma, who didn't seem embarrassed by either her declaration or the need for her to have made it, just smiled.

'Is this a friend of yours?' she said, looking over Celia's shoulder. Celia turned and there was Beate behind them on the pavement, rubbing her hands together and smiling, the fine skin around her eyes crinkling. She still seemed tired but her cheeks were pink with the cold and she was buoyant.

'Yes,' Celia said, hugging Beate impulsively, suddenly full of pride. 'A very old friend.' Emma Marsh looked interested; even without make-up and looking her age, Beate attracted attention.

'Beate Lilja. Beate, this is Emma Marsh. Do you remember, I mentioned ...' She tailed off, colouring, as she herself remembered that evening in the Scarlatti, in more detail, when they'd gossiped about Lucas. What had Beate said about Marco, and Lucas Marsh? *What do they do, these businessmen?* And of course, having met Lucas, Celia was none the wiser.

But if Beate remembered what she had said she showed no sign of it now. 'Oh yes,' she said warmly, and Celia was grateful for her perpetual charm, her perfect manners. She held out a hand. 'I am delighted.' Emma took the hand and shook it; she seemed reluctant to let it go.

'We should be going,' said Celia apologetically, looking from Beate to Emma. She turned to Beate and said quickly, 'You're all right, Beate? We didn't get to talk properly, did we, at the Scarlatti? I'm sorry. And you've been looking so ... worn out lately.'

154

Beate took Celia's hands in hers, looking at her for a moment. 'Well,' she said, 'yes. I've been thinking, I've decided I really am getting too old for this. Walking the streets all day like some nomad.' She winked at Emma, smiling. 'It's all right for a little girl like Celia, but I'll be sixty next month.'

Celia goggled, speechless, taken aback by Beate's sudden, cheerful declamation. Sixty. Beate's age had always been a glamorous mystery that they all conspired to preserve, and suddenly it was out in the open. Celia felt obscurely heartened by the announcement, which seemed to say, sixty's nothing.

'No!' said Emma Marsh, delighted. 'Really?'

Beate beamed back at them both. 'So, time to branch out,' she said. 'I'm on my way to pick up some colours. I thought I might do some drawing today.' And she pulled the portfolio around from where it was slung across her back, as proof. She looked around with an air of determined optimism. 'It's not so cold, really.' They all laughed then, united in the face of the statement's absurdity. It was freezing. 'And it's so long since I've done any. I'll go down to the river and have a bit of time to myself.'

Celia remembered that Beate had come to Florence to paint and it came to her that this was what it had been all about, Beate's tiredness, her preoccupation. She'd been working on the next phase of her life, the work in progress, and Celia found herself nodding in admiration. 'You will keep warm,' she said sternly, to cover her affection, 'won't you? Don't forget the time and freeze.'

'Don't worry about me,' said Beate, laughing and shouldering her portfolio, her tapestry bag, her shawl. 'You girls enjoy your shopping.' And lifting a hand to wave goodbye, in a gust of scent, a cloud of silver curls, she was off.

'Isn't she beautiful?' said Emma Marsh, looking after Beate with an indefinable look in her eye. Celia wondered what she was thinking, and remembered what she had said that first morning in the honeymoon suite of the Regale. *I love beautiful things.* Were they alike, Emma and Beate, with their perpetual optimism? And Celia felt that she was the odd one out, tentative, unsure, that somewhere here, between Emma's pregnancy and Beate's drawing, there should be a lesson for her, but she wasn't sure what it was.

They walked briskly towards Frollini, both of them suddenly feeling the cold after standing still. A raw wind had started up, pushing the cloud across the city, and the sun had gone.

They turned into the arcades along the Piazza della Repubblica to get out of the wind and Celia, feeling it her duty, was telling Emma about the construction of the square and the nineteenth-century attempt to remodel the ancient city when suddenly Emma said, 'Let's stop in here.'

Taken aback, Celia stopped; Emma Marsh was pointing at a modest corner bar. 'Okay,' she said. 'Of course. Are you all right?' She looked at Emma more closely; in spite of the cold she was pale against the red of her coat, and seemed breathless. 'I'm sorry,' she said, reproaching herself. 'You're tired. I've been walking too quickly.' She pushed open the door and felt a gust of warm air embrace them. It was loaded with lunchtime scents – coffee, wine, salt ham and fennel.

'It's all right,' said Emma as they went inside, and as Celia scrutinized her worriedly she saw the colour begin to return. 'Stupid of me. I should have worn something warmer.' She looked down, holding out her foot in the thin, expensive shoe and fine tights for inspection, like a ballerina. 'I expect your

clients are always coming here expecting it to be summer all
year round. Or at least not this cold.' They ordered chocolate.

'I liked your friend,' Emma said, sipping hers. 'She looked
interesting.' Celia nodded, smiling: she did that, Beate. Look
interesting. Emma went on, 'I must admit, it's nice to hear
other people's secrets. Their dramas. Don't you think?' She
smiled with an innocence that didn't quite convince Celia.
'Makes one's own life seem quite tame.' Celia must have
looked disbelieving.

'Oh,' said Emma, 'my life's very tame. I like it that way.'

Something about the way she said it made Celia curious.

'How did you meet your husband?' she asked.

'Lucas? Oh, at work. I was working at the Royal Academy.'
Seeing Celia's expression, she said quickly, 'Not what you
think, perhaps. I was working in the shop.' She set her cup
down. 'And before that, I worked in a restaurant. You see, I
wasn't born to all this.' She spread an arm out to include the
city around them, the austere, exclusive façade of the Regale
across the square, her stacked carrier bags. 'I was born in Essex.
Near Southend,' she said cheerfully. 'Mum – my mother – was
on her own; my father left us before I was born. She was beautiful – but it wore her down, being alone. She had good taste.
That's what she taught me, make sure you have good shoes
and a good coat, learn to speak properly and go where the nice
people are. If you've got to work in a shop, make sure it's on
Bond Street.' There was some defiance in Emma's voice, and
her cheeks were pink now.

Celia nodded; she couldn't feel censorious, somehow, only
sympathetic. After all, she realized belatedly, it was what she'd
done, coming to Florence. *Go where the nice people are.* Was that
such an immoral strategy?

'And Lucas – your husband came along?' She said it tentatively, not wanting to sound prurient.

Emma nodded. 'They were sponsoring some exhibition. His company. They were short of waiting staff so I did some handing round of canapés. And he just – chose me.' She shrugged, and tried to laugh, but Celia could tell something was puzzling her.

'It sounds romantic to me,' she tried.

'Yes,' said Emma slowly. 'It was. That was what I thought at the time. He didn't seem to care what people thought, that he wanted to talk to the waitress and ignored all the Academicians and the painters and all that.'

'Yes,' said Celia, thinking with a tug of some emotion she didn't care to define of Dan, and the British Council and those parties.

'But now,' said Emma, looking lost suddenly, 'I'm not sure. There's something – it's odd, since we've been here I get this awful feeling that he's – I don't know how to describe it – that he's got a whole other life I don't know about. I mean . . . ' She paused, looking away, out through the door. Her face averted, she said, 'Well, he did, didn't he? Have a life before me, one I'm not supposed to know about.' Something about this struck Celia as contradictory, evasive. Emma looked back at Celia, and her face was sad. 'And it makes me wonder if he didn't choose me because I sort of, you know, shone, he just chose me because I was easy, and that's all. Do you know what I mean?'

Celia hesitated; she did, suddenly, know what Emma meant, but she didn't want to be party to this. She could see that bright confidence crumbling in front of her, and her only thought was to restore it.

'He's – it's probably some business thing, isn't it? You said he had to work this morning. Some deal he's caught up in?' Emma didn't reply; she was looking down at her hands, small in red leather gloves, as if wondering whether her mother's advice had been enough, after all.

Fishing in her pocket for a few coins which she handed to the cashier, Celia watched for a moment, then gently took Emma by the arm. It wasn't the kind of gesture she was accustomed to with her clients, but suddenly it didn't feel any longer as though Emma was just a client. Emma did not object, and momentarily Celia felt her lean in against her shoulder.

'We can go straight back to the hotel, if you'd like?' Celia said, but Emma shook her head.

'No, no,' she said. 'I left him a message. He doesn't like plans to be changed.' And squaring her narrow shoulders in the bright coat, she walked out through the door.

Chapter Sixteen

Luisa saw the light change over the morning; it grew darker when it should have got brighter, and she knew it would snow. There was a wind, too; you could see it in the set faces of the passers-by, their noses sharp and red, cheeks burned raw, and even though it was close to Christmas there was barely a single customer tempted in by their display, bare-shouldered mannequins freezing in their party dresses.

Crossing to the glass cabinet at the centre of the showroom, Luisa began to fold sweaters, all cashmere these days, no one seemed interested in lambswool any more, nor even the beautiful fine-gauge merino that used to sell so well, more fool them. She ordered them by colour: lavender, purple, damson, grey, stacked them below the glass. Across the room something caught her eye outside; it was snowing.

Slowly the big white flakes drifted down, insidious, ghostly; you could see how you might get caught in it, although no one in the street had noticed yet. Luisa thought of a bend in the river shadowed by hills, where reeds clogged the bank and the girl's body had been found. For a terrible moment she was seized by the thought that the child was still out there in the cold. She bent and took out another stack of sweaters, briefly holding the soft, thick wool against her face as if to suppress the thought of that steep, wooded valley, where the snow was falling silently into the dark water.

It seemed very quiet suddenly, as though the snow was already muffling everything out on the street; the spotlights on the shop floor seemed brighter as it grew dark outside. Luisa shivered, although it wasn't cold, feeling suddenly jittery and as she turned to look at the door, to see if it was letting in a draught, the outline of a stocky figure appeared against the window, pressing his face against the glass with a hand cupped either side so he could see in. It was Sandro.

Made suddenly ungainly by surprise, Luisa started across the room towards him and Gianna looked up.

'Come in,' said Luisa at the door, 'you're frozen,' but Sandro hung back. The snow fell on his shoulders in the leather jacket he was wearing over his uniform; the collar was turned up high and she could hardly see his face. 'Can you come out?' he said bluntly, no time or emotion to spare for pleasantries, and Luisa bit her lip. She didn't know how to deal with this; she wanted to help him, but she felt all her old certainties, the ground under her feet even, shifting. The shop had always been where she felt safe, and comfortable, and in charge, and here was Sandro at the door, wanting her to leave it behind.

'Not on a Saturday,' she said uncomfortably. 'We can only take ten minutes at a time, and I've not long come back from my morning break. Come inside, you're letting all the cold air in.' She tried to scold him into it, but he wasn't having any. He backed off.

'Go on, Luisa,' said Gianna, who had been listening. 'Just ten minutes, there's no one in.' Luisa looked at her with surprise; Gianna was usually the one insisting on her rights and others' obligations. Gianna reached behind her for Luisa's coat and held it out. 'Bag?' she said. Gratefully Luisa took the coat and pointed behind the till; wordlessly Gianna passed the bag across, pushing down the newspaper that threatened to fall out as she handed it over.

'Ten minutes,' said Luisa, and pushed Sandro ahead of her into the street, holding her coat together in the wind. Out of the corner of her eye something scarlet approached; two women huddled together arm in arm in the cold, one in a red coat. She knew them, they chimed somewhere in that clever memory of hers, former customers, prospective customers, but today her memory was working too hard elsewhere and she let it drop. No time. Sandro's hand was firmly on her arm and he steered her around the corner, down an alley, into a bar she didn't know.

'Why . . . ?' she began, wanting to ask him, *Why here?*, but then he led her into a back room with a row of booths in dark wood, narrow marble tables, and she could see why. It was quiet in here, and warm; perhaps this was where Sandro always came when he didn't want to be overheard.

Her stomach churned; she wanted to know what kind of trouble to expect, but at the same time she desperately didn't want to know. Did he bring people here? Informers? Luisa felt stupid, realizing that after twenty-five years married to a policeman all she knew of his work was gleaned from the television. She felt unaccountably nervous, and Sandro seemed to realize it; he slid the coffee across to her and put a hand on hers. His hand was warm, his police-issue leather gauntlets resting on the table beside the coffee cups. She wondered why he wasn't wearing his uniform ski-jacket in weather like this, and tried to stop her mind wandering to such things, petty detail, food and clothes. She stared at his hand over hers on the marble.

'I haven't got much time,' said Sandro. 'I'm supposed to be back at the station already, we were on our way back.' He turned her hand over in his. 'I just wanted to see you.'

'Why?' whispered Luisa, and her heart contracted in her chest. 'They're not – you're not . . . ?' She didn't even know what she was going to ask, all she could think of was that Sandro was saying goodbye to her.

'I just wanted to see you,' he said, and put out a hand to stroke her cheek. 'Don't worry.'

Luisa looked down at her hands and swallowed. She closed her eyes and willed herself back to calm; he needed her to be calm, didn't he? 'So where . . . ?' Her voice croaked. 'Where had you been? This morning?' Sandro compressed his lips, looking away; the barman came over to the table with two more little cups of coffee and Sandro gave him a tiny nod, waiting until he had gone.

'We went to Bartolo's house,' he said briefly. He put his head in his hands. 'I don't know what we were expecting, I don't know. Some sign of a struggle, perhaps, or a suicide note, that's what they were looking for.'

'And you?' said Luisa gently. 'What were you looking for?' He looked up at her, and there were tears from the cold in his eyes.

'It wasn't there,' he said. 'Whatever I thought I might find,

163

it wasn't there. Something concrete, pictures, a computer with porn on it, children's toys – you don't want to know what. You don't want to know what they have, how we know what they do. They take trophies, some of them, make the children write things for them . . . ' His voice was clogged with loathing, and he stopped. Luisa held on to his hand. He was right, she didn't want to know, but the thought of all this locked inside him frightened her more.

'But it wasn't there.'

He shook his head. 'Funny thing,' he said grimly. 'The old place is a dump from the outside, no plaster left on the bricks, paint all gone from the window frames. But you go through the door, and it's clean as a whistle. As though his mother had been in and cleaned for him that very morning, everything vacuumed, bins emptied, surfaces empty. Door locked.'

'She's . . . ' Luisa frowned, trying to calculate the time passed.

'Just – a figure of speech. She's dead, oh, a year since.' He paused, and Luisa wondered how he knew, and she realized that the man Bartolo had not been out of his thoughts for fifteen years. It was almost as though the man and his mother were some terrible, shameful family members Sandro kept hidden, family he visited in secret.

'I guess she taught him to tidy up after himself though,' Sandro went on. His face was grim. 'It was terrible, being back there.'

'You were there all that time.' Luisa thought of Sandro slipping out of the house before dawn to go to Galluzzo in the bitter cold, to the dead man's decaying farmhouse, its kitchen gardens untended, stranded on waste ground between the river and the motorway and the housing blocks.

Sandro looked into her eyes and she thought he was going

to say something else, but then he looked away, and following the movement of his head she saw the time on the clock above the bar. 'I've got to go,' she said reluctantly, and he nodded. 'I'll see you tonight?' She heard the tenderness in her own voice with a kind of alarm. 'When will you be back?'

'As early as I can,' Sandro said, but his voice was dull. 'God knows, I hope this is over soon. There's nothing I want more.'

Beate had wandered up to an artists' supplies shop in the shadow of the cathedral, down an alley. It had been here for ever; it had certainly been here when she arrived in Florence as a nineteen-year-old, to study painting at the Accademia. She directed those of her clients who liked to dabble in art to this shop, telling them it was the best, although she hadn't bought anything here for herself in twenty years or more. The window was unchanged, though, still pleasantly cluttered with easels and canvases, jointed wooden models and boxes of watercolours.

Inside, the smell was still of new wood and oil paints. A row of old glass jars filled with powdered colours and labelled in gold script – cobalt, umber, Naples yellow – were still ranged over the counter, and behind it the shop's owner stood in his eternal grubby white cotton overall, only a little more wizened. He peered at her over his glasses and nodded. '*Ben tornata*,' he said mildly. Welcome back, after twenty years; Beate had had to smile.

On the Lungarno between the Ponte Vecchio and the Ponte Santa Trinità a broad stone buttress jutted on to the pavement, the perfect vantage point. In the summer it invariably held half a dozen art students sketching the Ponte Vecchio but today, with the white sky heavy with snow and a bitter wind coming off the river, it was empty. Beate sat down and unpacked her modest purchases – a ring-bound sketchbook, pencils, a box of charcoal – and muffled in her velvet coat, with a board propped on her knee, she began to draw.

Beate began with the bones of her beloved city; the architecture. She drew the shallow curves of the Ponte Santa Trinita and the patchwork rear of San Jacopo sull'Arno, the neat dome of the Cestello and the parapets of the Palazzo Corsini in the distance. She tried the skyline next, a ridge of cypress out to the east in San Niccolò, a distant bell-tower, and then an old woman came to rest on the parapet opposite her and fished out a bag of stale bread and she had a new subject. A knotted scarf and a bulky coat, a kindly, wattled chin, and the woman was there on the page; Beate began to enjoy herself. Two middle-aged women arm in arm, in padded coats, stopped to look down at something in the water. Her cheeks pink with the cold, on her face an expression of peaceful concentration, Beate drew, and drew, and drew.

When Lucas Marsh came down the receptionist handed him the message Mrs Marsh had left for him, looked down at the ledger in front of him to make a note, and when he looked back up the man had disappeared.

One of the reasons Lucas had got on in life – aside from the thing so many people lack, the clarity of purpose sometimes called a killer instinct – was this self-effacing quality, a kind of camouflage. Although in business he could make his presence felt in a second if he chose, a moment before you might not have given him a second look. Not dangerous, not powerful, neither dark nor fair, a man from nowhere. Lucas Marsh had made most of his money, although very few people were aware of it, buying property in Europe on behalf of a syndicate of Russian businessmen who wanted to settle their funds outside the former Soviet Union, to spread their risks. They liked the fact that he was quiet; they distrusted the flashy types, property developers with signet rings and shiny brochures. There was an oil billionaire, a couple of steel magnates and another the source of whose funds remained obscure even to Lucas Marsh. He worked hard for them.

As he slipped back out through the lobby of the Regale, the great glass doors eased open in front of Lucas Marsh and he stepped into the icy, gusting air. His face was drawn above the dark coat, its collar blown up against his pale cheek. He crossed the piazza in the cold; it was grey and almost empty, and there was something desolate about the cheap handbags and model domes swinging on the handful of souvenir stalls. Without a glance Lucas Marsh walked past the pink, blue and gold carousel that was deposited in the piazza for excited children in the runup to Christmas. It stood there silent and still, the owner huddled in his booth reading a newspaper.

Lucas left the square and was swallowed up in the gloom beneath the Victorian arcades, his steps measured and purposeful, heavy leather on polished marble. Beggar-women sat here, out of the wind, panhandlers, a man abased himself, face to the marble, with only a handprinted sign on cardboard asking for pity, and coppers. A woman emaciated to the point of extinction drew her bony knees up as he passed; she might have been any age, her skin furred with malnutrition. She looked up at him, but Lucas didn't look down. If he had he might have recognized her, but then again he might not. Fifteen years was a long time.

Lucas Marsh walked not towards the shop where his wife

had told him she and Celia would be but instead wound his way back into the medieval alleys that led down to the river. He walked past tiny, secret churches and subterranean bars, slipping between trash cans and tradesmen's entrances as though he knew the place like the back of his hand. At last he emerged from a narrow passage barely wider than his shoulders on to the river front, crossed through the traffic with barely a glance and stopped there, leaning on the parapet. He was breathing hard, and his hands in the dark, costly leather gloves trembled as they rested on the stone, palm down. The river flowed fast beneath him, swirling and eddying, brown and choked with debris washed down in the winter rains. For a long time he stood there in the freezing wind, looking over into the cloudy water; even after it began to snow he stayed there, and looked.

Eventually, at the far end of the embankment, a huddle of figures hunched in cheap jackets appeared, Eastern European tourists, perhaps, or something lower down the food chain, ill-dressed for the cold. There were three of them and they moved down along the river; when they reached Lucas Marsh they stopped, one on either side and one behind him.

Lucas looked at them, his face impassive in the wind and very white against the dark coat. The tallest of the men, broad-shouldered and with a shaven head under his woollen cap, faced him, holding out a huge, raw-knuckled hand. 'Mr Marsh,' he said. His voice was so thick and guttural that the syllables sounded brutal, like an insult. The snow fell thick around them, and for a long moment no one moved, no one spoke.

Emma and Celia paused in the cold, looking up at the mannequins, haughty and white-shouldered in tulle and satin and staring down into the street through their sightless eyes. At the mannequins' feet shoes were scattered in a froth of pale silk as though discarded after a riotous night's partying; jewelled shoes, velvet saturated with colour, steel-blue, silver, a glitter of green. At Celia's side Emma Marsh was silent, looking in at the display, and Celia wondered what she was thinking, wondered what it must be like to be pregnant. All that future no longer vague and delicious with possibilities, with the prospect of parties and skiing trips and summer holidays, but filling up instead with pressing and unfamiliar detail. Prams and sleepless nights and nappies, the weight of a child on your shoulder wherever you go.

Emma looked at her. 'Shoes,' she said, and smiled palely, the smile firming with an effort. 'I can always wear shoes.' And then she nodded up at the green silk dress, the same one that had made Celia stop to look in the window two days earlier. 'And I'd like to see you in that. With your colouring.' Celia felt her cheeks burn. 'Look upon it as part of the job,' said Emma kindly. 'If I'm going to squeeze into anything myself, I'll need moral support.'

It was very quiet inside, and they hesitated. A woman sat behind the cash-desk reading a magazine, stiff-haired and lip-lined, but when she raised her head to greet them her smile seemed genuine enough under the make-up. She put her magazine aside but then there was a small commotion at the door and the saleswoman Celia recognized, the one she'd seen in the bar yesterday morning – *What was her name?* Celia knew it, had heard it called across the shop, *Lucia? Sofia?* – came in, rubbing her arms and stamping her feet. She looked up at them apologetically, swiftly extracting herself from her coat, sliding it on to a hook behind the cash-desk and transforming herself suddenly into a figure of authority, ready to serve them. *Luisa*.

Celia held out her hand; it seemed only polite. 'It's Luisa, isn't it? I have been in so many times, I should know. Celia Donnelly.'

Luisa took her hand and shook it. 'Of course, yes. Luisa.' Her hand felt icy to Celia's warm one.

Beside them Emma pulled off her leather gloves and sat down on a dark leather cube. She stretched out a foot, her calf curved, the ankle narrow.

I'd like to try everything you have in my size,' she said, smiling engagingly. She spoke in slow, careful Italian, schoolgirl-accented although, Celia reminded herself with dawning respect, she was not likely to have learned it in school, so must have applied herself to a phrase book in preparation for this trip. As though Emma's was an entirely usual request, Luisa inclined her head with a half-smile.

'Thirty-six?' said Luisa, assessing the small, white foot with a professional eye, and Emma nodded, dimpling. They were two of a kind, Emma and Luisa, thought Celia out of the blue as she saw the look of shared appreciation pass between them. And there was something different about the saleswoman, Celia thought, something that drew out the comparison with Emma. When Celia had seen Luisa yesterday in the bar she had been pale, as though the life had been drained from her by something, a bad night, perhaps; this morning she had a flush, a warmth to her.

Luisa seemed to catch Celia's eye on her, and turned away quickly. 'Everything in a thirty-six,' she said, and disappeared down a narrow, padded stairwell in the corner of the room. At the cash-desk the other woman was absorbed once again in her magazine, and a quiet fell in the pale room. Emma looked down at her small hands, her stockinged feet stretched out in front of her and turned inwards, a child's feet.

'Don't say, will you?' she said quickly. 'Don't tell Lucas I told you all that. About how we met. And about him having another life? I'm just being silly.'

'No, no,' said Celia. 'I mean, I don't know why I would.' *You're going home tomorrow, aren't you?* she thought with an odd kind of pang; she'd almost forgotten – for a moment she'd somehow imagined Emma Marsh would still be there. There was a tug she sometimes felt at the thought that her clients came and went, some she liked and never saw again, some she never wanted to see again, but they were all there one day, gone the next, as if they'd never been. It wasn't that this time, though, it was not for herself but for Emma she felt the pang, the thought of her going back to grey London and some big white stucco house full of expensive furnishings, Persian rugs, cherrywood floors, pregnant and, Celia suddenly saw, alone. Lucas Marsh was barely there, was he? She tried to erase any trace of pity from her returning smile.

'No,' she said again, more briskly. 'Of course not.'

Emma nodded, as though the subject was closed. 'What about that dress, then?' she said with sudden gaiety, a change of mood, nodding towards the window display.

'Oh, I don't know,' said Celia in dismay, feeling exposed, the spotlit room chilly suddenly at the prospect of removing any of her clothes. Her coat, she realized, was still buttoned to the neck.

'Let me have my fun,' said Emma, chiding. 'Go on.' Behind her Luisa appeared, a stack of shoeboxes in her arms.

'My friend would like to try the dress in the window,' Emma enunciated carefully, and Celia thought, *My friend.*

And then her heart sank; once the dress was on, how would she manage not to buy it? She thought of the dismal condition of her bank account and tried to calculate, rent out after Christmas, presents still to buy and send for Kate's two. Gas, electricity, water. She tried to remember how much the dress had cost, knowing it was too much.

'No, no,' she said, protesting, hunching her shoulders in the coat.

Luisa looked up at the two women from the soft pale carpet where she was extracting a pair of bronze sequinned slippers from a tissue-lined box, and saw the balance between them. One with money, one without, of course, but underneath the brightness, the cherry-red coat, the shiny black hair, she thought the well-heeled one was somehow lost, adrift. Luisa transferred her scrutiny to the other, the one she knew, sort of, Celia Donnelly who she'd seen stealing a glance at this very dress two days ago. Luisa knew the whole story there, and it reminded her of herself, looking in at that emerald necklace on the Ponte Vecchio; a girl with more taste than money and a secret longing for a knight in shining armour. You never thought the knight might turn out to look like Sandro, did you? Short, bad-tempered, loving. When you gave him the chance.

Luisa laid the bronze slipper at her customer's little foot. She looked quickly across at Celia and saw that her coat was still fastened up to her chin.

'No harm in trying it on, Signorina,' she said quietly, addressing herself not to the pretty little Biancaneve with her foot extended for the slipper, but to her companion. 'We're hardly rushed off our feet, are we?' She gestured at the empty shop. 'Just for fun, eh?'

The girl's inward look refocused then, from whatever it was that was preoccupying her, the cost of Christmas maybe, and looked across at Luisa with a look half of reluctance, half of gratitude.

'Just one moment,' said Luisa, getting to her feet with care, smoothing her skirt where it had creased. 'I think I can guess your size.'

By the time she returned Celia's coat was off and she was watching as her companion walked up and down in front of the long mirrored wall of the shop in her little red dress, looking down to admire her feet. She walked like a model, a trained walk, the bell-skirt swinging around her hips. Luisa could see the dress was made to measure, could see the tiny hand-stitching at the cuff, the darts at the breast to fit the bodice like a second skin; she could also see that it was just beginning to get tight at the waist, a hook and eye left undone, a seam straining. A little curve of stomach pushing out the fine wool of the skirt.

Luisa averted her eyes, not wanting to bring bad luck; how did she know, anyway? And was it her business? She busied herself removing the protective polythene and layered tissue from the green dress, stroking the emerald-green silk, separating the layers of fine tulle underneath. She held it out across her arm for Celia Donnelly to see and watched as, unable to stop herself, the girl reached for the garment.

'It was the green?' Luisa said, not sure if they'd specified. The red, she realized belatedly, would have been the more obvious choice; she'd just taken the green because she liked it better.

'Oh yes, the green,' said Celia, holding the silk between both hands.

173

'Come with me,' said Luisa, and she had to stop herself taking Celia Donnelly by the hand. 'No hurry.' She pulled the heavy velvet curtain across the changing booth and turned back into the room to attend to her other customer.

'These, and these, and these,' said the woman Luisa could only think of as Biancaneve, Snow White, setting three pairs of shoes side by side on the suede bench. The glittering bronze slippers lined with rose-pink leather; slender-heeled, bottle-green boots, and the last pair pointed and embroidered, silver thread on red velvet and a tiny curved heel like something that might have been made for an eighteenth-century French courtesan.

'Ah, these are wonderful,' said Luisa impulsively, her approval for once unrestrained. 'Perfect.' She took each pair and repacked them in their rustling paper nests, a felt bag laid across the top. Little Snow White, easing her arms back into the scarlet coat, paused.

'My husband will be here in a moment,' she said. She seemed nervous. 'I'll just wait, to show them to him.'

Inside the narrow cubicle Celia carefully removed boots and socks, reluctantly peeling away the soft warmth of trousers and sweater. She felt chilly and vulnerable; she was very pale. It was down to a summer's constant work, days on coaches with no time at the beach this year, but she was hardly a sun-worshipper at the best of times, had that annoying northern skin that only burned and peeled, much better left marble-white. With apprehension she pulled the layered dress over her head and for a moment was blinded by a cloud of silk and net, in her nostrils the elusive, delicious scent of the loom, the workshop, the dressmaker finishing the last hem and ribbon by hand. The smell of something new and

174

precious. It slid over her ribs, settled at her waist as though it had been made for her.

'How are you doing?' She heard Emma Marsh's voice through the curtain.

'Mm,' Celia said uncertainly, looking around for a mirror in the cubicle but finding none, and she realized with a sinking heart that she would have to come out. She looked down at herself. The brilliant green, as clear and bright as moss under water, made her pale skin look strangely luminous. She pulled back the curtain.

They turned to look at her, Luisa at the cash-desk and Emma pensive on the leather bench with a pile of shoe-boxes beside her. Luisa opened her mouth but said nothing, a wistful expression on her face. Emma looked up and smiled with such unforced pleasure that Celia wondered whether that anxious look might have been a figment of her imagination. Celia stood there awkwardly, embarrassed. Luisa came over and Celia felt the saleswoman's cool hands on her shoulders, adjusting a strap, pulling gently at the satin ribbon around Celia's waist, smoothing something she couldn't see at the small of her back. Then gently she turned Celia towards the mirror that covered one wall.

'Look,' she said. '*Guarda che bella che sei*. Look, how beautiful.'

Celia looked. She barely recognized herself; she seemed so naked, her pale shoulders gleaming under the spotlights. She turned a little in front of the glass, looking at herself as though she was someone else; she felt buoyed up, breathless.

'It's not me,' she repeated to herself. 'Is it?' And she saw Emma Marsh smile at her.

'It is,' she said. 'You must have it.'

Celia was about to remonstrate – the cost, the impracticality – when she felt a draught. The door opened inward to admit a customer; he stood in the corner, a tall, dark figure, a shadow Celia couldn't quite make out immediately. She raised a hand to shield her eyes from the spotlights, and seeing the gesture Emma turned to follow her gaze. Lucas Marsh stood in the doorway. His face was pale and set, and there was a dark glitter in his eyes, something indefinably wild about his appearance. Instinctively Celia took a step back, wanting to cover herself.

'Darling,' said Emma, and she got to her feet; he stood still, but allowed her into his side, a small, bright figure against his sombre height, leaning up to press a kiss into his cheek. Beside her Celia detected some subtle shift in the atmosphere and turned slightly to see Luisa scrutinizing Lucas Marsh with a puzzled expression. She frowned as though she was trying to place him, shook her head a little as if to reproach herself for some mistake. She had turned quite pale, and if she'd known Luisa better Celia might have asked her, laughing, if she'd seen a ghost, rather than Lucas Marsh, standing there with his arm around his wife.

At the Palazzo Ferrigno everything was going exceptionally smoothly; in the kitchens not only had the dinner for Mr and Mrs Lucas Marsh been largely prepared, but in anticipation of the following week a thousand tiny canapés – quails' eggs in aspic, miniature rolls of vitello tonnato, beef carpaccio – were ready and waiting in the cavernous cold-store below the kitchens. The ancient staterooms had been aired and dusted and the staff had gathered in the kitchen for their own early lunch of pasta, meat, and a salad of winter puntarelle lightly dressed.

At one end of the long table, the chef, sous-chef, house-keeper and two maids sat at the oilcloth, eating fastidiously; at the other, the four handymen in their brown overalls were methodically putting away penne in meat sauce. Three of the handymen and the maids would now depart for the weekend, and two waiters would arrive at six for the evening's service. The place ran as smoothly as clockwork; everyone knew the tasks that awaited them, down to the last fruit-knife to be polished.

The administrator stood and served herself, surveying her table, thinking of this evening. She would stay to meet and greet these two, Mr and Mrs Lucas Marsh; she was intrigued by them. She wanted to know what they were like, to witness their appreciation of the Madonna, to tell them its history. She didn't think any more of the overalled workman she had encountered in the Titian room; she'd long since decided he was just curious, admiring the proportions of the room, and why not? She told herself she had to relax about the foreign workers they had to employ these days – they worked hard, they were cheap, and she must stop thinking of them all as potential burglars, casing the joint. She didn't notice that he was not at the table, but his absence should have been sur-prising, certainly to the housekeeper who was responsible for taking on casual labour. Even foreign help was entitled to sit down for lunch, they were all workers together, but if the man had appeared none of them would have recognized him, for the simple reason that he was not, nor had he ever been, on the payroll at the Palazzo Ferrigno.

Chapter Seventeen

After they'd gone Luisa tidied away the shoes in a kind of trance, repacking the toes with tissue and putting the right pair in the right box, then taking them carefully downstairs to the storeroom, each box in its proper place. All the time the two of them danced a kind of slow waltz in her head, the pretty little dark-haired wife, the tall, pale, handsome husband. Little Snow White, *Emma* he'd called her, kissing the top of her head absently, as though she were a child. *Too young, must be the second wife, Sandro said she was finished, the first one, hadn't he?* He'd paid with a platinum card, his signature small, neat and definite. *Lucas Marsh.*

'What was all that about?' said Gianna as the door closed behind them.

'Nothing,' said Luisa, straightening the dress rail where the green silk had hung, trailing its ribbons to the floor. 'Nothing. I – I thought I recognized him, that's all. One of those faces.' Could she be sure, after all this time? The answer was no, of course. But it couldn't be just coincidence, either. The day after Bartolo's murder. And in the pit of her stomach she knew this wasn't good for Sandro, this was as bad as it could be.

I have to speak to him. She turned to reach for the phone, but behind her the door opened and a couple came in, a young woman with a curtain of shiny black hair, her older boyfriend. They went upstairs to menswear, and she knew without even applying herself consciously to them that he would be looking for something short and tight and glittering so that some of her youth might reflect on him. She calculated, watching them ascend.

'Listen,' she said carelessly to Gianna, 'they'll be a while up there, won't they? You'd better go for lunch now. You haven't had a bite since you arrived.' And overtaken by an access of fondness as she saw Gianna's expression, a mixture of exasperation and bemusement, she patted the younger woman on the arm. 'Go on.'

She waited until Gianna was buttoned up and out of the door, then waited a little longer as she came back for a pack of tissues and her cigarettes. Then she was out again, around the corner in the whirling snow and out of sight to her usual haunt, an awful place that did novelty low-calorie salads for tourists, bean sprouts and passion fruit, and a hit of espresso to take the taste away afterwards. Gianna needed to keep her figure.

Listening to be sure they were busy upstairs – the conversation had entered an earnest phase – Luisa slipped behind the till and dialled Sandro's number. As she listened to it ring she gazed, unseeing, out through the plate glass at the dark figures moving to and fro in the snow. When at last Sandro answered she could hear the crackle of a police radio in the background; he must be out in the squad car.

179

'Where are you now?' she said. 'Are you alone?'

'Sort of,' said Sandro, and she could hear wariness in his voice. 'I'm with Pietro, out near the airport, but he's not in here with me. We're on a tip-off. There's some guys, a gang of Ukrainians we've been monitoring. They were seen in Le Cascine – oh, I'll tell you later. What is it?' He sounded nervous, and Luisa pictured him out there in the city's bleak hinterland, the light industrial units and trailer parks, and for a heartbeat she wondered if he was safe.

She swallowed. 'It's him,' she said, and suddenly she felt as though she couldn't get enough breath to say the words, now that she'd got this far. 'I've seen him. The girl's father is here.'

There was a long silence, an urgent crackle in the background. 'What?' said Sandro urgently. 'What did you say?' Luisa couldn't speak, her breath had all gone. *Could I be making a mistake?* She thought of the father of the murdered girl as she had seen him all those years ago, his wife beside him with her face in her hands, his face preserved for ever in the single snatched newspaper shot, pale and gaunt with loss. He had hardly changed. Every line and shadow in his face etched there by that week of waiting had been preserved, had deepened over the fifteen years that had passed. *No.*

'I know it was him. He calls himself Lucas Marsh, but it's him, and he's staying at the Regale, I heard them talking.' The words were tripping over themselves now but still Sandro was silent.

'Sandro? I'm not imagining it.' Her voice was firm. 'Are you there?'

'Yes,' said Sandro, and he sounded defeated. 'I know. I know he's here.'

*

They hurried north in the snow; it whirled and danced in the sombre streets, white against the towering dark façades. Celia had her umbrella up in an effort to protect her clients but it was little use; the soft, insinuating flakes found their way underneath it, settling on her collar, tickling, damp and cold. It lifted her spirits, all the same, there was something exhilarating about all that motion in the still air, all that bright white in the winter grey.

'It's rather late,' said Lucas Marsh; he seemed distracted, and he was walking very fast, tilted into the snow with his hand tight on his wife's arm. 'Can we just press on, go straight there?'

'You don't need to eat?' Celia looked at Emma Marsh's pale face. 'I think ...' She hesitated, and abruptly he came to a halt, stepping back into a doorway and drawing his wife into his side and out of the snow.

'What?' he said, but Celia had the impression he was hardly listening; he seemed to be looking around them, over Celia's shoulder, searching for something. Had he seen someone he knew? The streets were almost empty; it was after one and the shops were closing, the restaurants filling up. And the visibility was poor – the movement of the snow, thicker than ever now, confused everything. She thought she saw a figure standing across the road, a man with his hands in his pockets in a dark coat, but when she blinked to see more clearly there was no one.

'Emma – Mrs Marsh, she ...' She hesitated again, not wanting to offend him by pointing out his responsibilities to a cold, tired, pregnant wife.

'Oh,' he said, refocusing, deflated. 'Yes, of course.' He rubbed her shoulder distractedly. 'I'm sorry. Do you know somewhere – where we could eat quickly? Nowhere ... ' He put a gloved hand to his forehead as though to help himself formulate a plan, and he looked almost in pain with the effort. 'Nowhere grand, a quiet place, something out of the way.' He looked into his wife's face, his head tilted a little, anxiously regarding her. 'Sorry, darling. I thought – I thought we could just get on, then get back to the hotel early, you could have a rest then? Before dinner?' Celia saw Emma Marsh struggling to regain her spirits, her lip trembling a fraction.

'Yes,' she managed. 'Yes, of course. I don't want to spoil my appetite. But maybe just, just a little, you know, something hot. Sit down for a minute.'

'I know somewhere,' said Celia quickly, wanting to stop this, feeling a stir of anger with Lucas Marsh for not being able to see how desperately tired his wife was. What was wrong with him? She had to get Emma Marsh into the warm. 'Down here,' she said, and tugging them after her she turned left, then right into the Via dei Tavolini and the Cantinetta di Verrazzano.

Half baker's, half wine bar, the Cantinetta was Celia's standby; she knew every café, every corner bar where you could sit down at no extra cost, where the rest-rooms were clean, and this was one of the best. Comfortable booths, good coffee, a wood oven at one end that could cook you alive in the summer but on a day like this ... as long as it wasn't too crowded. They pushed the heavy glass door and a gust of warm, yeasty air, the smell of new bread and wood smoke and wine, enveloped them. It was very full.

Along one mirrored side opposite the baker's counter stood wooden benches, each one fully occupied by elderly locals. They were sitting bundled in their winter coats and drinking wine or caffè latte, eating pastries or slices of *schiacciata*, the hard Tuscan flatbread, with unhurried gusto. Celia edged past them, her charges in tow, to the back of the long, narrow shop where it widened to accommodate six or seven marble tables in a cramped, wood-panelled tea room. As they arrived a couple stood up to leave, a pair of women in swinging furs, leaving behind them discarded coffee-cups that looked to have sat there empty for some time. It was an old-fashioned place, somewhere the locals could serve themselves then sit and gossip at leisure without fear of being chivvied for their table.

'Will this do?' asked Celia anxiously; it was difficult to read Lucas Marsh, to know if this was what he had wanted.

'This is fine,' he said with a hint of weary gratitude she hadn't heard in him before, as though he'd let down some kind of defence, as though at last they needed her. 'Just the kind of thing I meant.' He looked around the tables quickly, then down the length of the baker's counter to the window, across the sea of green loden and felt hats, the stiffly permed, spun-gold hair and furs of the women. What he saw seemed to satisfy him. With a little sigh of relief Emma subsided on to the wooden bench and pulled off her gloves.

'I'm starved,' she said, but she smiled, and Celia saw the colour was returning to her cheeks in the warm.

'I'll get us something,' said Celia briskly. 'Is that all right?'

Lucas Marsh sat beside his wife. He looked tired. 'Oh, yes,' he said. 'Fine, anything.' His hand went an inch across the table and rested against his wife's; it was as though he didn't want the gesture to be noticed. Not a demonstrative man. Celia found it hard to read him; he seemed so tense, and she wondered if he was always like this. Perhaps it was the baby, or

183

maybe the meeting had gone badly this morning. 'A bit of local colour,' he said to Emma. 'Sorry it's not a proper restaurant. I just—' He stopped.

'It's lovely,' said Emma quickly. 'I'm glad we came. You choose for us, Celia, yes.' She threaded her fingers through his and he looked away. Suddenly feeling superfluous, Celia crossed to the counter by the wood oven where a queue had formed. It was busy. The burly baker, his forehead beaded with sweat, was scattering olives, shards of artichoke heart and pork fat and little bitter salad leaves on to the rounds of dough, shovelling them in and out of the blazing oven as fast as he could. Celia glanced back at Lucas and Emma Marsh; their hands were still folded tight across each other's on the table but they were not talking, and Lucas Marsh was still looking away from his wife, his face set and pale.

Celia thought, not for the first time, how odd marriages could turn out to be, how mysterious, and how apparently lacking. Why, if Lucas Marsh was not a voluble man, didn't Emma at least fill the silence now they were alone together, talk to him until she got something out of him? With Celia she had turned out to be so open and spontaneous; certainly, compared to many of her wealthy clients, Emma had appeared impulsive and ready to confide. But with her husband it was as though she felt she had to be circumspect, as though she had to restrain her own natural interest in him. Was there something even Emma was afraid to discover about Lucas Marsh? It wasn't Celia's idea of a marriage, but then, perhaps that was why she was still single. The queue shuffled forward and as Celia moved on automatically, deep in thought, she felt a hand on her shoulder and looked up: there was Beate, her face flushed and bright. Behind Celia in the queue someone grumbled.

I'm so sorry.' Beate turned to him immediately, an old man in a hat, apologizing profusely and charming permission from him. 'I'm not stopping, just saying hello, just a word with my friend.' And she turned back to Celia, alive with a kind of exuberance Celia hadn't seen in her for a long time. 'My dear friend.'

'Had a good morning?' said Celia, laughing.

'Oh, heavenly,' said Beate, holding a hand to Celia's cheek. 'Feel!' Her fingers were icy. 'I've been drawing all morning,' she said. 'It's wonderful. I can't understand why I stopped, such laziness.'

The ring-binder of a small sketchbook stuck out of Beate's overstuffed tapestry bag, and Celia pulled it out. 'Can I look?' she asked.

Beate pulled a face. 'Oh, well – go on,' she said. 'As long as you don't look too hard. I'm a bit rusty.'

Celia opened the little book, saw a bell-tower that looked like the one she was beginning to think of as hers. 'Lunch break?' asked Beate, looking around the crowded bar.

'Actually,' said Celia absently, turning a page, 'I'm here with my clients. Lucas and Emma. Over there.' She nodded vaguely towards their table, without looking. 'These are really good, Beate. *Really* good.'

'You are kind,' said Beate. 'Oh, I see her, that red coat. Very pretty. I liked her, and I meant to say, although of course I couldn't with her there. Sorry, I meant to say sorry properly. All that ranting about him, rich men, you know. I'd had too much to drink, this birthday of mine to deal with, you got me at a cross moment. I'm sure Lucas Marsh is perfectly – he's – but where – oh!'

Celia looked up then at the surprise in Beate's voice. 'It's him,' said Beate, turning from Lucas, who was looking across at them over Emma's shoulder, back to Celia.

'You do know him, then?' asked Celia.

'No,' said Beate, and she leaned across and turned another page of the sketchbook. 'But I saw him this morning. I drew him.' She lifted the book and there was Lucas leaning on a parapet beside the river, unmistakable, the fine hair high on his forehead, the sharp-shouldered, expensive coat, even the clouded, distant eyes.

There was someone else in the drawing too, although he was turned obliquely away from view. 'I thought they made an interesting composition,' said Beate thoughtfully, studying her drawing. 'An unlikely pair.'

'Yes,' said Celia, uneasy. The other man Beate had drawn leaning on the parapet and turned away from Lucas reminded her of someone, or something, she'd seen not long ago. He had a knitted cap pulled down, and an earring; his shoulders had the hulking breadth of a manual labourer's and the ungloved hand she could see resting on the wall was big-knuckled.

'I don't know what they were talking about,' said Beate, 'I didn't hear. Perhaps he was being panhandled.'

Celia nodded. 'Perhaps,' she said. Slowly she turned the page, caught a glimpse of the same broad-shouldered man but with a woman this time, towering over her.

'Signorina?' The baker's voice broke in on them, and Celia realized with a start that she had come to the head of the queue. She closed the book hurriedly and thrust it back into Beate's bag, feeling oddly as though she'd been spying.

'I'll run, darling,' said Beate. 'You're working. And I don't want to look like a queue-jumper.' She bestowed her sweetest smile on the old man in his hat, and squeezed Celia's hand.

'I'm meeting Marco off the plane,' she said. 'I'll call you in the morning.'

The baker's voice was impatient now. 'Please, Signorina. I haven't got all day.' And Beate waved, and was gone. Thoughtfully Celia ordered slices of pizza with buffalo mozzarella and slices of ham, two more slices with capers and anchovies. Emma had looked very hungry. She stacked them on a tray and collected bottles of water, glasses, a half-bottle of the Cantinetta's own wine.

'Oh, oh,' said Emma when she saw the food. 'That looks good.' Her cheeks blazed with colour now in the heat from the oven and the massed bodies and she had taken off her coat. Celia set down the food. Lucas Marsh took one slice, and when he'd eaten that sat and watched his wife; she seemed ravenous, eating quickly and neatly, trying everything.

'Wine?' asked Celia.

'Not me,' said Emma with wry regret. 'Better be good. Save myself for tonight.' Celia held the bottle out to Lucas Marsh, and he frowned at it.

'No, I – oh, well, why not?' he said, pouring himself a tumblerful.

'Darling,' said Emma, surprised. 'Not like you, a drink at lunchtime. Has it been so stressful?'

Celia studied him. He looked pale, but no paler than usual; distracted, perhaps, but then he'd been like that since that first morning in the Regale. Had the man in Beate's drawing been panhandling him, hassling him? An occupational hazard for the tourist, and it might well have annoyed Lucas. It struck Celia that the river was not on Lucas's route from the Regale to meet them at Frollini; in fact it was in quite the other direction.

187

'No,' he said quickly in answer, 'not at all. Just – why not? We're on holiday.'

'You wouldn't believe how hard it is to get Lucas to relax,' said Emma, emboldened by the smile he gave her, even though to Celia it looked somehow stiff, anxious. *Actually*, thought Celia, *I would believe*. 'We really almost never go on holiday, not really. There's always a business meeting, Lucas has to go and see some development or other for clients – do you remember that time in Nice?'

Lucas nodded, looking down into his tumbler. It was already empty, and he refilled it with a kind of determination as though taking medicine. *Dutch courage*, Celia found herself thinking absently. A spot of colour had appeared on each of his pale cheeks. 'Excuse me a moment,' he said abruptly, and stood up. He took a few steps away from them and stopped, looking down the bar and into the street outside, his glass in his hand.

Emma seemed not to notice. 'Of course,' she said, confiding, 'I shouldn't have been here, on this trip. But I've always wanted to see Florence.' Her voice was dreamy. 'It's even lovelier than I expected.' She transferred her gaze to Celia but it was distant. 'You're very lucky to live here all the time. Or perhaps you just get used to it, you take it for granted?'

'No,' said Celia, 'it's always beautiful.' Without thinking she said, 'What do you mean, you shouldn't have been here?'

'Oh – I . . .' Emma seemed flustered suddenly. 'Nothing, not really.' She darted a glance at her husband; he was within earshot, just about, but he didn't appear to be listening. She lowered her voice. 'It was a business trip, Lucas didn't even tell me about it.' Her voice grew quiet, became indistinct. 'I think he'd even forgotten it was my birthday. He – he was busy, it was understandable.' Emma looked up. 'But they sent the

188

ticket to the house by mistake, not the office, and I opened the envelope.' Celia imagined Emma's downcast face as she looked at the ticket, and she wondered if that was when Lucas Marsh had decided to phone Celia. *Thousands of pounds on a weekend for his wife's birthday, the full works; how much in love he must be.* That was what she'd thought; now she realized that the older she grew the more ignorant she felt about it. Love. She watched Emma now; she had her head on one side, a distant smile on her face, but she seemed to grow uncomfortable as she spoke. 'Lucas said he didn't think I'd be interested!'

Her voice was louder now, and artificially bright; she tried a laugh, and at the sound Lucas Marsh turned, and in two steps he was back at the table, offering no explanation for either his departure or his return. 'But then he laid on all this,' Emma said, sweeping a hand around the crowded room, then, realizing that perhaps a packed and steamy baker's was not what Lucas had had in mind, went on, 'What I mean is, arranging for you, and the dinner this evening, and the hotel – oh, everything. He's made it wonderful, something for me to do every minute!' She smiled radiantly, but at the corner of each eye Celia saw the gleam of a tear squeezed back and heard a kind of despair in her voice. Emma must have wanted something else from this holiday, Celia thought, and glanced surreptitiously at Lucas. His face was softened, made defence-less by the wine, and he was looking at his wife with an odd, conflicted expression, a mixture of longing and impatience and almost, she thought, of desperation. Then he turned to Celia, and the look was gone.

'So,' he said abruptly. 'This afternoon. Will we be able to get into the chapel early? I'm sorry to mess the schedule about.' He stopped abruptly, as though unused to apologizing, and

Celia found herself wondering for the first time if there was some strategy behind all this, some reason for Lucas Marsh's behaviour, ducking into doorways, hiding in crowds, changing plans at a moment's notice.

'Yes,' she said mildly, deciding that getting them where they wanted to go was her business, not where Lucas chose to go for a solitary walk, or who he stopped to talk to on the way. 'There shouldn't be any difficulty.' Early afternoon was never the busiest time at the Medici Chapel, tourists prizing their lunch-hour above all things, and besides, it was very quiet. She took a sip of her wine and felt it warm her stomach, thought with wonder of the cold, snowy streets, the sudden hush and emptiness of the city outside. 'And we can always go to the library first, the Michelangelo staircase . . . ' She tailed off as the image of the great library was summoned up, the deep and forbidding gloom of its vestibule, and suddenly she wondered if it was a good idea after all. But it was too late.

'All right, then,' said Lucas Marsh, on his feet and pulling on gloves. 'Let's go.'

Out on the plain towards the sea the snow had fallen thick and silent for hours on to frozen ground, and there were drifts along the riverbank, up against the shanty towns and trailer parks, the rows of blank white factory units. The police car was parked outside a broken wooden fence; inside the snow was trodden into dirty mush between the caravans and corrugated iron lean-tos. The two policemen were standing behind a camper out of sight of the dirt road with a third man, one with three-day stubble and bundled in layers of greasy coats. Otherwise the place seemed deserted, a plastic chair thickly furred with the morning's snowfall sat out under the blank, louring sky, and the caravans looked dark and empty.

Of course during the day their occupants would be working, if you could call it that – selling drugs at the station, begging outside the cathedral, picking pockets in the market – but still the place looked abandoned. Not much of a place to call home; you could see that in the policeman's eyes as he kicked at a patch of frozen snow, his expression an uncomfortable mixture of disgust and pity.

'You haven't seen them – for two days, then?' The man's hands were jammed into his pockets – *They never had gloves,* thought Sandro with disbelief, *do they think they've come to the Promised Land, perpetual summer? You would have thought they could lift a pair of gloves if they can steal handbags, silver, sunglasses –* and, hunched against the cold, he shrugged his shoulders even higher. The man frowned, his stubbled double chin wrinkling as he buried it in his mangy scarf.

'Yeah, whatever,' he said in his guttural, alien Italian. 'Packed up, off and out of it, Friday morning early, three, four. Pots, pans, girlfriend and all.'

'And that's all you know?' The man shrugged again.

'Where you from?' asked Pietro with mild curiosity. The man looked alarmed.

'Romania,' he muttered, his voice hoarse as he pronounced it. Pietro nodded, kicked out idly at the plastic chair, and a chunk of snow slid off the arm, revealing the dirty plastic underneath. 'Refugee, is it?' he said.

'That's it,' said the man hopefully.

'Wouldn't do you any harm to be a bit more cooperative, would it?' said Pietro, his tone still mild. Then he kicked the chair again, hard this time, and it skittered across the frozen ground, one leg hanging off. The Romanian's face set hard with anger and fear.

'Where are they from?' said Sandro. 'Ukraine?'

'Yeah,' said the Romanian, sneering. 'Chernobyl country. That's Russia, isn't it?'

'Not any more,' said Sandro, his head on one side.

'I'd have called them Russians. Sounded like Russians, acted like 'em. Nasty. Kicked the girl about.'

'What game were they in?' asked Sandro, thinking of the girlfriend. 'Whores? Drugs?' As he waited for an answer he leaned down and picked up something from the ground where the chair had been, a wedge of paper used maybe to prop a table, folded tight. Idly he began to unfold it: a typed sheet, times, places blurred by damp, in a corner a photocopied face, some kind of certification. A woman's face, the city's official stamp beside it, *Guida di Firenze*. He frowned down at it for a moment, then slowly he folded it back up and put it into his pocket. Watching him, the Romanian shifted from one foot to another uncomfortably; it wasn't just the cold, either, the look on his face wished him out of there, wished he'd been somewhere else when the police car had bumped slowly along the dirt track by the river. He pulled a crumpled pack of *nazionali* from his pocket, pulled one out and lit it; it took him some time in the icy wind, hiding his face in his cupped hands.

'Don't know, really,' he said slowly once he'd got the cigarette lit, pulling on it hard. The tobacco reeked acrid and sour, dirtying the clean smell of snow. 'Not whores; they wouldn't have got much for that piece. Drugs, mostly, but whatever they could get. A bit of burglary ...' He darted a glance at them, not wanting to give the impression that he

192

himself could be considered an associate. 'Hired muscle, bully boys. Drifters. Came down about a month ago. I thought they had to be a building crew, site labour, but they had no kit, no tools, no overalls. And they never went anywhere for more than an hour or so, just hung about. Like they were waiting for something.' He looked around after this uncharacteristically long speech as though to see if he might have been overheard. 'Can I go now? I've – I've got my shift starting in half an hour.'

Sandro ignored him. He looked at Pietro, his face impassive. 'The guy was found Thursday morning.' He turned back to the Romanian.

'Shift work?' he said.

'In a bakery,' said the Romanian. 'Pays pennies, not worth your while. Someone's got to do it, haven't they?' His face was sullen.

Sandro nodded noncommittally, not letting him off the hook. 'Before they disappeared,' he said slowly, 'just before, say Wednesday, Thursday. Was there anything different? You know what I mean?'

The Romanian looked up at the sky and in the blank grey light Sandro saw that his eyes were a funny colour, blue-green. He stayed like that for a while, looking up at the sky with his luminous eyes and thinking, the snow falling on his unshaven cheeks. For a mad moment Sandro wondered if he was looking for heaven up there, like you do when you're a child.

'Yeah,' he said eventually. 'They had a fight, early Thursday morning. A lot of noise. Might have been about the girl, that was what I thought at the time, screaming like dogs fighting over a bitch. I went out – to the baker's ...' He glanced at them for a reaction but there was none. 'By the time I got back, eight or nine that night, they'd calmed down, you'd never have known there'd been any trouble, the place was neat.' He frowned. 'I guess they'd packed everything up ready to go, though I didn't know that then. And then they sat up all night, playing cards and watching the planes land, one after the other. Every time one landed they'd stop, and look up.'

'You don't know their names, do you?' said Sandro, without much hope. 'Of course you don't.'

The Romanian shrugged. 'No surnames, no. The main man, the boss, they called him Jonas. Big bloke, shaved his head. Don't know about the others. Not the kind of guys you'd want to be caught eavesdropping on.'

'The girl?'

The Romanian gave a sour laugh. 'They don't have names, girls like that. A stray dog. You don't give a stray a name, do you? She looked sick.'

'And you've no idea where they've gone,' said Pietro.

The man shook his head. 'No. The car's a heap of junk, though, wouldn't get them to Sesto Fiorentino, let alone back to Russia.' Pietro looked at him, head on one side.

'An Opel coupé about fifteen years old, bronze, Modena plates, dented offside wing, no rear fender,' muttered the Romanian quickly, looking away, as though he might be overheard. He turned back. 'If they wanted to go back to Russia, which I doubt. Ask me, they still had business around here, don't know why, just a feeling. Something going on in the city, something to do with one of those planes landing.' He eyed the policemen with sudden recklessness, then ground the stub of his cheap cigarette on the ground. 'I'm going,' he said.

The two policemen just nodded as if they were no longer even thinking about him, and unable to believe his luck, the Romanian turned and headed for the gate.

'Hold up,' called Sandro. 'Just a minute.' The man stopped.

'Just the one woman?' he said. 'Between them?'

The man shrugged. 'She didn't arrive with them,' he said. 'Just turned up one day, hung around. They ignored her; she cooked for them, that was about it.'

Sandro nodded, frowning. 'So she wasn't Russian?'

The Romanian shook his head. 'Italian,' he said. 'Skinny as hell. Drugs, maybe.' He waited a bit, but they seemed to have forgotten about him, and he took his chance. This time no one called after him; as he pulled his coat up around his ears and hurried past the police car towards the main road and the bus stop he risked a glance back at them. There they stood, saying nothing. He thought of the Russians, and his next thought was, *I'm gone.*

'Better find that car,' said Sandro to Pietro. 'Hadn't we?'

Pietro nodded. 'I'll call in the details,' he said. 'You never know, that expensive computer might earn its keep for once.'

Sandro snorted. 'You try the computer,' he said. 'I'll stick to the old methods. He turned away a little, gazing out over the frozen landscape, and dialled a number on his mobile.

'Fausto?' he said. 'I want you to find a car for me.' Without even needing to look at his notebook he reeled off every detail the Romanian had given them. 'Bronze Opel coupé with Modena plates, dented offside wing, no rear fender. Fifteen years old or so.' He listened a moment, then snorted. 'Yeah, yeah. A piece of cake for a lad like you. But do us a favour and make it quick, I don't think it'll be around long.' His face was grim as he folded the mobile closed and turned back to Pietro.

Chapter Eighteen

They walked through the market on their way. The Chapels of the Princes stood proud and calm at the centre of all the tourist tat, the stacked layers of cloisters, library, loggia all surmounted by the dark red dome of the Chapel, the noisy commerce moving ceaselessly around it. When Celia had first lived in the city, she had often come here; now she found it hard to believe that she had once found the stalls exotic. She had bought a leather satchel long since disintegrated, a string of scarlet corals too bright to be real that she still wore. She still had a residual fondness for the place, but today in the grey light it all looked flimsy and cheap, a pedlar's cardboard suitcase full of tin and glass. The stall-holders stamped their feet, listless and cold in the wind. On a corner there was a news-stand, thin European editions of the English papers already tattered from the snow, but Emma seized on them.

'That's what I've been missing,' she said eagerly. 'A news-paper. Why didn't we think to ask for the papers at the hotel?'

Lucas shrugged a little. 'Time enough for that when we get back, don't you think?' he said mildly. His indifference seemed unusual to Celia – in her experience men were always obsessed with the latest edition of their usual paper, as though they had to keep in touch with world events at all times. Perhaps Lucas Marsh was above all that.

'Oh, that's not like you,' said Emma. 'Come on, I'm getting one.' She took two, and then had nowhere to put them.

'Let me,' said Celia; as she folded them inside her bag a small paragraph caught her eye at the bottom of the front page, the photograph of a child she recognized from long ago. She glanced up and saw that Lucas Marsh was looking away, his face even paler than usual.

Some of the stalls had already packed up in the snow, their stock boxed and locked in wooden compartments. But it was still busy enough: handbags dangled over their heads as they walked; the trestles were piled with cheap, bright knitwear and stacks of fake jeans. Tunisians and Algerians bantered across the passing trade, occasionally pausing to ensnare a customer, thrusting the cheap leather jackets at the susceptible. None of them approached Lucas and Emma Marsh; they walked through the crowded street untouched, as though they had arrived from a different planet and had to be treated with caution. Lucas Marsh looked around curiously, eyeing not the produce but the merchants; they seemed to be what interested him. Chinese girls folding locusts and peacocks out of rushes or holding up beaded vests, a Neapolitan selling gilt and marble chess-sets, an Algerian shivering in his ill-fitting leather coat, his skin bleached sallow in the cold. Then they passed a stall selling tiny sheepskin boots for babies, and Emma stopped.

'Oh,' she said. 'Look at these.' She pulled off a glove and reached out to touch a pair. The stall-holder eyed her judiciously, smiling and nodding, keeping his distance. Emma unhooked the boots and held them to her cheek.

They're so soft,' she murmured, looking up at her husband. Celia followed her look; she couldn't read Lucas's expression at all, and she felt impatient suddenly.

'Have them,' she said impulsively, and she fumbled in her bag, pulled out a note and handed it to the stall-holder. Gently he took the little boots from Emma. 'These?' he said, looking curiously into her pensive face.

'Isn't it—' Emma darted another look at her husband. 'Isn't it bad luck?' She turned back to Celia, who felt a pang of guilt, then a stab almost of anger, once more obscurely directed towards Lucas Marsh. She felt sure that somehow he had made Emma like this, so fearful.

'No,' she said slowly, looking at him. 'You can't think like that, surely? They're a present, from me.'

Lucas Marsh looked back at Celia and she thought that, for the first time, he was curious, that she had said something to make him think.

'She's right,' he said almost angrily, taking her by the shoulder. 'Listen. She's right, you can't think like that. A pair of little shoes – that's nothing, how can they make a difference to anything? Have them.' His voice caught, but Emma didn't seem to hear, she just gazed back at him. At last he let her go; she looked at Celia and then at the stall-holder with a dazed expression. She took the little paper bag he held out to her. He watched them go with mild incomprehension; the purchase of a pair of baby boots had never seemed so weighty a matter.

They moved quickly through the chapel; it was gloomy

today, dark and almost empty. Emma seemed unfocused, exclaiming over the inlays, the blood-red marble of the high octagon, the jasper and agate of the great sarcophagi, but her mind seemed to be somewhere else and she had a self-absorbed, inward look. She wandered off, standing in the light that fell through the doorway and examining some small piece of carving, dreamily absorbed. It was the kind of look Celia had always imagined pregnant women to have, a look of secret knowledge, private satisfaction; she felt sad for Emma, if all it had taken were those few words of support from Lucas. Her mood seemed precarious, one moment on the verge of tears, the next brimming with excitement and delight. Perhaps it was just hormonal. Celia tried to think how she might feel, pregnant; she found she couldn't think about it, there was something dangerous even in imagining it.

Lucas Marsh was the one who seemed really to like it in the chapel, from the moment they stepped inside and the thick stone walls of the octagon folded around them. He seemed quite at ease in the strange, cold atmosphere among the gleaming tombs, where the peculiar light was diffused from some indistinct source high over their heads. He asked Celia a number of rather interesting questions about the Medici; she had expected him to want to know about their power and their wealth – many rich people did. But he seemed to be as curious about their kindness, their involvement with the lives of the city's ordinary citizens, their benefaction. Their bid for eternal life. The tombs themselves seemed to move him to silence, and he stood and stared at their great cold bulk. Celia wondered what he was thinking. She thought she might even ask; she had rather surprised herself by enjoying her discussion with him. But just as she turned towards him to break the silence,

Emma, who had detached herself from them as they talked in order to wander rather aimlessly at the other side of the chapel, hurried across the inlaid floor towards them, almost as if to forestall Celia's question. Her heels rang out on the marble, a neat, sharp sound.

'It's rather gloomy in here, isn't it?' she said cheerfully as she approached. Her voice was bright and loud in the hushed atmosphere. 'I don't know if I'd like all this when I go.' She swept a hand around the space with its great burden of marble memorial. 'A nice windswept hillside, that's what I'd like. An estuary view.' Lucas looked at her, frowning, as though trying to make sense of what she'd said. And it did seem an odd remark; she stood there in front of them more alive than anything in the place.

'It's still quite current, in Italy,' said Celia. 'The mausoleum.' She thought of the miniature mansions the Sicilians constructed for the dead, pink and white and gold, the cult of death. The cemetery up behind San Miniato where Lucas Marsh had wandered off among the crowded tombs to talk in private on his phone. 'It's more . . . a part of life here than it is in England.' She realized that she might once have said, *at home* and meant England; instead it seemed a place quite distant and unimaginable, like something she'd read about long ago. 'Death is still more . . . present here. In the middle of everything. Not something hidden.' She shrugged. 'There's probably a reason for that, an anthropological reason, a historical reason. It's hard to say if it's healthy, or not, isn't it?'

'I don't mind all this,' said Lucas, looking around him, his voice a little rusty with silence. 'Odd, isn't it? I find it . . . comforting. Hard to erase, all this marble and stone. Why not make your mark?'

'Perhaps it's a man thing,' said Emma with deliberate carelessness. 'But it makes me feel cold.'

At the door there was some kind of commotion; where the light fell through glass screens there was movement. Celia heard the voice of the attendant raised as he told some invisible interlocutor he couldn't come in, not without a booking; at first he sounded reasonable but firm, but then his tone hardened, turning to anger. She imagined an indignant foreign tourist party, unable to believe they couldn't simply walk in, ill-equipped for the delicate negotiation and elaborate courtesy that had gained Celia entry an hour early. She listened, but what struck her as odd was that there was no strident American or French voice raised in outrage; she could only hear a kind of low, threatening mutter. She detected a movement at her side and saw that Lucas had stepped back out of the light. Emma, meanwhile, took a step towards the door, leaning out to see what was going on.

'He was looking at me,' she said thoughtfully.

'Who?' said Lucas sharply from the shadows.

'The man there they don't want to let in.' She nodded towards the far side of the crypt. 'When I was over there on my own. He was just standing inside the door, like he had come in out of the snow, but he was staring at me.' She shrugged.

'What did he look like?' said Lucas.

Emma frowned, concentrating. 'Tall,' she said. 'Scruffy. He had a ski hat pulled down but he had no gloves on, had his hands like this,' she gestured, 'under his arms, to keep them warm. But I couldn't really see his face. The light was behind him.'

'Look . . .' Celia frowned at the familiar details. Could it be the man Beate had drawn, hoping for a handout from a rich man? She couldn't help thinking what Marco had said about Lucas Marsh, that he was the kind of man that attracted attention. She had no experience with this kind of thing. 'I'm sure he's just a beggar, they're all over the place, this is the worst area for them, too close to the station. Are you worried? Would you like . . . security?' Not that she would have had the first idea of how to arrange a minder, but there was always Gabriele. Celia wondered if he was back from the airport, wished he was here.

'Darling?' said Emma, looking confused. Lucas Marsh shook his head, looking away from them.

'No, no,' he said, tight-lipped. 'Nothing like that. For God's sake, it's just a holiday.'

'Shall we go, then?' said Emma, and Celia had the impression she was changing the subject, trying to be obedient. 'See the library quickly, then back to the hotel?'

'Can we get to the library through the chapel?' asked Lucas, looking at the entrance. 'Do we have to go back the way we came in?' Celia could see the attendant standing square in the light to block the way, feet apart and gesticulating angrily.

'Yes,' she said.

They came out into the cloister through a tiny side door. Celia had only known of the door's existence because once a young American girl had suddenly felt sick in the chapel. It was the smell, she'd said, she thought she could smell dead bodies, and the sweet, heavy scent of old incense hadn't helped. They had had to be ushered out into the fresh air by the quickest route available.

She stood there now with Lucas and Emma Marsh, blinking in the white light; the courtyard whirled with snow. The cloister was the perfect antidote to the chapel's heavy gloom; pale, golden vaulting surrounded a green square planted with box and turning white now, at its centre an orange tree almost forty feet tall, the snow beginning to settle on the stiff, glossy leaves.

'Oranges,' exclaimed Emma, delighted, peering to glimpse the waxy fruit under the snow. 'Are they real?' She turned to Celia in amazement.

'Of course they are,' said Celia, laughing. 'Can't you smell them?' The sweet orange-blossom scent was faint but distinct. They *were* almost miraculous, she realized, oranges in winter.

Emma perched on the low wall that surrounded the garden, leaned in to get a view of the layered terracotta roofs where the snow was beginning to settle, the loggia, the dome, that all looked in on the green square.

'Shouldn't we go into the library?' said Lucas, looking around them, and for a moment Celia had the impression he was afraid. In one corner of the courtyard was the gate that allowed the public to enter the cloister and his gaze stopped there. The gate stood open; you could see half a market stall hung with football shirts, and people hurrying past in what was becoming a blizzard.

'Oh,' said Emma. 'Can't we just sit, a bit? We don't have to do the library, do we? A load of old books.' She looked at Celia beseechingly. Celia looked from one of them to the other; she was used to this, at least.

'We could leave the library, just see the vestibule,' she said, momentarily forgetting her qualm about the place in her eagerness to find a compromise.

'The what?' said Emma, laughing.

'It's a kind of lobby,' said Celia. 'An enclosed foyer, leading you to the library. It's by Michelangelo. It's just here, in the corner.' She pointed along the cloister.

'All right then,' said Emma. Celia noticed that she was looking pale again. 'How long can a vestibule take?' And she slid awkwardly off the wall, brushing a chalky trace of plaster dust from her red coat. Lucas took his wife's arm with what Celia took at first to be solicitude but seemed also to be a kind of nervous haste. She began on a simple explanation of the origins and significance of the vestibule, the birth of mannerism, the unusual proportions, but she had the impression neither of them was paying much attention.

There was no attendant beside the sign to the library that stated it was open; the place seemed deserted. It was a quiet time, Celia supposed, and perhaps he had been called into the chapel to deal with whatever was going on in there. Certainly there was no indication here of any disturbance; it was preternaturally quiet. They pushed the door open; it swung to behind them, and suddenly, abruptly, all the light and movement, all the whirling snow, the brilliant white sky, the scent of oranges, turned to stillness.

The lobby to the library, which Celia had seen and admired and explained so many times – the sweeping, liquid staircase, the blind, internal windows, the impossible towering proportions – had never before struck her so forcibly as sinister. Perhaps it was because they had all fallen silent at once, and so there was no commentary to distract them; perhaps it was the unexplained disappearance of the attendant, leaving them alone there. Or that each one of them had been trying to keep a certain, secret anxiety at bay before they even entered. It was something to do with the man shouting at the entrance to the chapel, the man who had effectively trapped them in here.

'I don't like this,' said Lucas Marsh suddenly, turning his

head sharply, as if to catch someone behind the blind stone windows staring back at him. 'I – I—' His voice was oddly stifled, strangulated; he seemed to have run out of breath. As Celia stepped forward to ask if he was all right she heard hoarse shouting outside, and the brisk approach of footsteps on the flagstones.

One of Luisa's regulars came in wanting an evening dress for Christmas, and gossiped on and on as Luisa brought out what she had, only pausing to dismiss each one – not tight enough, not sexy enough, *too dreary*. She wanted a miracle, as usual, but for once Luisa didn't feel it in her to work it; her mind was worrying over something far away from party dresses. Sandro, out there in the snow. In trouble. The woman was talking about her husband, too.

'He'll complain, if I don't look sexy enough, you see. You can't let yourself go, not for a minute. He hates me all covered up. What about this?'

She seized a corseted, strapless creation in zebra stripes; even Gianna, across the room, raised her eyebrows.

'Not in your size,' said Luisa, pretending regret, lying mechanically. Her hair dyed flaming red, the customer was too old for bare shoulders but she was the kind of woman who didn't notice, who saw herself through a twenty-year-old lens. *Why not?* thought Luisa, almost too weary to judge, or perhaps she was losing her critical edge; it was no more than a learned reflex now: don't let them walk out looking ridiculous. She brought out something in silver-grey satin, nicely cut and clinging enough, but the straps were too long. Luisa got out the little pincushion, fastened it to her waist and began to pin them up. Narrowing her eyes to admire herself, the woman went on, 'Well, he's a very important man, you see, temptation comes his way all the time.'

Luisa didn't want even to listen to this drivel, but she couldn't help it. Had she let herself go? The awful thing was, she couldn't imagine Sandro being tempted, ever, as if there was something inside him that had died off, through neglect. She fumbled with the pins, her fingers stiff and cold, and the woman standing in front of her in the grey satin let out a cry of pain.

'What are you doing?' she snapped, outraged, and Luisa began to apologize.

'Almost done, Signora,' she said. 'I'm so sorry, the light – it's the light. There.' She stood back. Mollified, the woman looked at herself in the mirror with grudging approval. As Luisa had said, the shorter straps made all the difference, a little more coverage over the bosom; she turned this way and that.

Although it was no later than four the lights had come on outside, blurred and twinkling in the snow that still fell, soft as feathers, in the grey street. Luisa gazed out over the woman's shoulder, trying to make herself focus; she felt a leaden tiredness as though she hadn't slept for days. She'd been having the dreams again, of course, although when she woke all she knew was that she still felt tired. She'd get started straight away, register, *Sandro's gone to work*, make the coffee, getting on with the real world, but the dreams were there. They glided under her daytime consciousness like fish, darting away when she tried to fix on them. She dreamed she was pregnant, she walked through the streets and people stared and whispered, *Unnatural, at her age*. Or she'd had a baby and someone had taken it and drowned it, like a kitten. It'd be all this business stirred up again, that would be it; like Sandro she thought, *I'll be glad when it's all over*. That was what he'd said.

Carefully Luisa pressed the pins back into the pad at her waist, and waited for the customer's instruction. She thought of the flat misery in Sandro's voice; she heard despair. With a shock she realized he was almost at the end of his tether, that sometimes all he wanted was to lie down and never wake up again. She thought of Lucas Marsh with a kind of bitterness: *Why is he here?* But of course she knew why he was here. It couldn't be a coincidence.

'Yes,' said the customer without turning around, without looking at Luisa, only at herself. 'By Monday, please, I have the opera on Tuesday, that charity thing on Thursday.'

She spoke as though Luisa should know her diary inside out, but today Luisa didn't care about this woman one bit, didn't want to advise her on shoes, on her hair, on how to keep her shoulders warm and her dignity intact between the car and the opera terrace.

'Of course,' was all Luisa said. She took the slippery handful of fabric the customer handed out to her from the changing room and with automatic respect for the garment if not the customer she shook out the creases. It was only as she was packing it for the dressmaker that she remembered the boxes she had to take over to the Regale by six. Mrs Emma Marsh, the honeymoon suite. The note was there, in his neat handwriting; they had been very polite, apologetic about it.

'We have some walking to do,' the girl had explained, the guide, Celia. A pretty name, a modest girl, the way she had pulled the dress off in a rush of embarrassment at being caught in the dressing-up box, desperate to be back in her sober clothes. So they were here just for an innocent weekend, the wife's birthday; she'd heard him say, 'Happy birthday, darling.'

The man had looked uncomfortable, to do him justice.

Why had he brought her here, now, for her birthday? What had possessed him? All she could think was, it must have been a mistake; Luisa had looked at his wife, and felt a hard, wrenching pity for her. Hard enough to be a second wife, but in such circumstances – how could it work? And all at once Luisa realized Emma Marsh didn't know, had never been told, what had happened to her predecessor, Lucas Marsh's first wife. She didn't know what had happened to his child. So had he brought her here as cover, and pregnant, too? What kind of man would do that? She thought of what Sandro had said on the phone, the wind hissing behind him out there on the plains.

'I didn't know he was coming,' he'd said down the line, pleading with her, and she knew he was rehearsing for what they'd say when they found out. How bad would it look, for him, if he had known Lucas Marsh was coming? He'd spent fifteen years feeding the man's grief, passing on privileged information, unconfirmed material, rumour from unnamed sources. Never letting him forget. And now it would look as though he'd been Lucas Marsh's hit man, a cat that catches a mouse and lays it on his master's pillow. The way Sandro had been these past few years, no one got close enough to him to be able to say, *Never him. Straight as a die. Not Sandro.* Not even Luisa could swear to that.

Sandro had sighed, the sound swallowed by the wind. 'He only called me yesterday, soon after he arrived but we didn't talk, not more than the minimum. He was with his wife, can you believe it? On some little guided tour. Had to ring off.' He paused. 'I went to find him today. At the hotel.

'He's got himself in a lot of trouble, Lucas Marsh. Somewhere, through his work, I don't know how, he's got himself a bunch of Ukrainian hardmen who'll do anything for a couple of thousand euros, who would cut a paedophile's throat without stopping to take a breath. And they'll say anything, tried telling him they didn't kill him, the guy must have cut his own throat, but Marsh knows better, because he's seen the papers. He's talked to me; he knows Bartolo was murdered. And that's not what he wanted.' And there was a grunt that had something of respect, Luisa thought, and something of disbelief.

'He didn't want Bartolo dead?' She had looked around her as she said that, hearing herself sounding like a Mafia wife, shocked at the words coming from her mouth. And what, wondered Luisa, had he wanted with the man if he didn't want him dead? The alternatives, somehow, frightened her more.

'God knows what he wanted,' Sandro said. 'God knows. When that happens to you—' And he stopped short, his voice turning ragged. Luisa thought of what she'd want to do to the man who'd killed her child and found herself without words. Sandro spoke for her. 'What could make it better?'

There had been a pause, then Sandro sighed. 'He tried to explain it to me. He said, he just wanted to have the man in front of him, and he knew we'd never have allowed that. A moment alone with him.'

'Yes,' said Luisa. *I can understand that.*

Sandro went on, 'He said, the worst thing was not knowing. He said, you spend years imagining. Was she afraid? You want to stop imagining, you want to know, and if he had Bartolo there in front of him, just the two of them, then he'd know. So he got this guy, Jonas, to track Bartolo down, so that it could be over.'

Luisa thought of the new beginning Lucas Marsh might have if it was allowed him, that baby growing in his new wife's belly. And fervently, she hoped that all he wanted was to start all over again, that it wasn't that he had paid for the man to be killed and now he was having second thoughts. And it occurred to her that sooner or later the police would have to know Marsh was here, sooner or later they'd have to talk to him, and what would happen to Sandro then?

Sandro went on, 'To be honest, I don't think he had any idea what these guys are capable of. I told him how we'd found Bartolo, bound, gagged, his throat cut in a swimming pool. He looked like I'd hit him, like he couldn't breathe.' Sandro sounded in despair, and he sighed again.

'So I went to see him this morning. I had to; he doesn't know it, but he needs help. But of course, there's nothing I can do, not any more. All I could do was to tell him, just pay them, this guy Jonas, and he'll go away. Because if you don't – I tried to tell him what happened if you don't pay these people, that there's no one can help you, not the police, not anyone. But he wouldn't listen, would he? He went all English on me, his face – he went all cold, he stood up straight like he was in court or something and looked out of the window, he wouldn't look at me.'

Sandro sounded almost grief-stricken and Luisa wondered what they could possibly have made of each other, Sandro and this stiff Englishman, face to face after fifteen years of terrible intimacy a thousand miles apart.

She murmured something automatically, something meaningless like, 'I'm sorry.' Sandro didn't seem to have even heard it.

'He said, "I'm not a murderer."' And Sandro had sighed again, and he sounded so tired, so shamed, so hopeless that Luisa didn't know what to say any more. '"I won't be a party to it. I'm not a murderer."'

And now in the fading light Luisa had to wipe her eyes to see, as she sealed up the package for the dressmaker's and carefully wrote out instructions while the woman beside her nattered on to Gianna about her husband, how much he earned, how he took her to the theatre at least once a week, she never had to lift a finger at home, treated her like a queen. And as Luisa tried not to listen, as she followed the neat and tidy course that had kept her going all her life, through everything, she felt rage rising up in her against the indolent complacency of the woman standing there, no more trouble in her life than in a baby's. She raged against the unfairness of it all, and with a sense of revelation saw that what it was, was a mess. She saw how something that by sheer chance had gone so badly wrong fifteen years ago – in her life, as well as in Lucas Marsh's – had gone on going wrong since. Like cancer, like some toxic chemical that ran its unstoppable course through the system, mutating and disfiguring and distorting until every cell was damaged. He couldn't help himself. How far might he have gone? Luisa thought of that fixed, distant look on Lucas Marsh's face and she knew if it was her, she would be capable of anything. What a mess.

'I'm off,' she said to Gianna, making her mind up there and then. 'I'll take this along to the dressmaker, and I've those bags to deliver to the hotel. To the Regale.' Gianna stopped talking and stared at her, mouth open, but Luisa looked away, leaning behind her for her coat and the ribboned bags. She turned back, reached across Gianna and opened the till, easing out the cotton sack with the day's cash takings they kept stashed at the back.

'I'll bank these, too, while I'm at it,' she said, feeling the bag's bulk; not such a bad day after all. 'Just remember to set

211

the alarm.' She turned back at the door. Thanks, sweetheart,' she said, and that did it, she saw Gianna almost recoil at the word. *She thinks I'm crazy*, Luisa realized. But she didn't feel crazy; she felt alive.

Chapter Nineteen

For a moment even the light in the vestibule seemed to change and darken, and the situation seemed to be about to turn into a nightmare of a kind even Celia had never imagined. She'd sat in casualty with clients with ear infections and sprained ankles, dealt with sudden vertigo in bell-towers, food poisoning; she'd been harangued for bad choices, interrogated about her qualifications, argued with; she had been ignored by bad-tempered teenagers and treated as invisible by their parents. But through it all she had always been able to fix her eyes on something beyond them, the detail of a painting or a piece of stone worn soft by centuries, and tell herself, *Well, they'll be gone in the morning, and this will all still be here. I'll still be here.* Now she looked at Emma and Lucas Marsh and was overcome by the sudden thought that she was bound to them, somehow, that this was all going to get worse before it got better. A lot worse.

There was an astounded expression on Lucas Marsh's face,

a look of profound and private astonishment, as though something quite extraordinary and unexpected was happening to him. And as the three of them stood there in a space becoming more intolerably claustrophobic by the minute and stared at one another, for a hallucinatory, panic-filled moment Celia thought he was going to have a heart attack. He was going to die in front of her, and in front of his wife. He would never see his child. Celia was startled by how much, in that moment in extremis, she felt she knew about these two. And then the colour began to come back.

'Darling?' said Emma, and Celia was surprised by the gentleness in her voice. She realized she would have expected Emma Marsh to panic. Lucas Marsh turned to his wife, his eyes unfocused, as though he had been looking at something far away, was returning from a distant place.

'Yes?' he said, and he frowned a little, politely, as though trying to remember a name at a party. She put a hand on his arm and suddenly he was himself again.

'Sorry, darling,' he said. 'I don't know what – the windows ...' He looked around at them, walled-up, blind and dark, and back at Emma. 'Take a deep breath,' she said, looking into his face. The door opened, and Celia felt her heart thump in her chest.

It was the attendant, blustering and gesticulating with outrage. He seemed very annoyed, but all Celia could feel was a kind of hysterical relief at his arrival and the sight through the open door of the world outside, the orange tree and the bright snow. Immediately she began to apologize for their unauthorized entry.

'Yes, yes,' the attendant said impatiently when she began to explain that there had been no one at the door. 'I was called

214

away, I was needed in the *cappella*, at this time of year there's only one—'

At the mention of the chapel Celia leaped in. 'There was someone trying to get in?' she said. 'We heard something—' She saw Lucas Marsh look up, and she remembered he spoke Italian.

'Yes, some Albanese.' Celia assumed the attendant was using the term loosely, as was common, to indicate an Eastern European. 'Some idiot.' He was trying to sound dismissive but Celia heard puzzlement in his voice, too. 'Trying it on.' He glanced at her, assessing her; to the curators and museum attendants the guides could be looked upon as troublesome, foreign interlopers, but if they were lucky they might be counted as one of them, fellow professionals, guardians of the artistic legacy. The attendant seemed to come down on Celia's side. He shrugged. 'They say, it's a place of God, they should be allowed free entry.' He shook his head. 'Crying sanctuary, so they can come in and pick a few pockets in the dark.'

'Has he gone now?' said Celia.

'Yes,' said the man slowly, musing. 'We got rid of him. Suddenly seemed to lose interest.' He paused, frowning as he mulled it over. 'They're usually women, though, the ones that try it on like that. And they don't usually come to the chapel – it's a mausoleum, really, they don't like that, it's hard to pull the place of worship card. Plus, they're a superstitious bunch.' He seemed to recollect himself then, and drew himself up.

'So,' he said, switching to a more official tone. 'Will you be wanting to see the library? It's not open at the moment, but I can allow you a look.'

'I don't think ...' Celia hesitated, looking over at Lucas Marsh; the attendant followed her gaze.

'Is he all right?' he asked curiously, nodding in Marsh's direction. It hadn't just been her imagination then; although the colour had begun to return his eyes still held something of the astonishment she'd seen in them earlier. A kind of curiosity, the look a man not used to being afraid might have, when he thinks his time has come.

Emma seemed to bridle a little at their discussing Lucas without addressing him. 'Fine, thank you,' she said, but she looked anxious to Celia. 'Just a – I don't know, claustrophobia. He's been having—'

Lucas Marsh interrupted her. 'Mild claustrophobic reaction, that was what the doctor said. Time of life, or something.' He spoke casually but he seemed uncomfortable, looking away from both of them towards the open door. 'Perhaps I should have warned you.'

'It's quite common, in fact,' said the attendant earnestly, his irritation evaporating. He gestured around at the over-sized architectural detailing, the slippery grey stone of the great serpentine staircase. Even with the door now open to the courtyard and the fresh, cold air that smelled of snow, the heavy grandeur of the space felt vaguely threatening. 'In here, it can have that effect. And of course, you should never go to the top of the *cupola*.' He shook his head at the thought, and with a qualm Celia imagined the cramped, tilting space between the inner and outer skins of the dome. Why *hadn't* he warned her? Something about Lucas Marsh's explanation didn't strike her as convincing.

'I think we should be going now,' she said apologetically to the attendant who had had his dignity restored now that he had been of use, and was smiling and affable. She turned to Lucas and Emma; it was barely ten minutes' walk to the Regale from here but they looked drained. 'Shouldn't you . . . ?' she began, wondering whether she should suggest she take Lucas Marsh to the hospital, but something in his expression stopped her. *Don't be silly*, it said. *She'll only worry.* And thinking of the wait in casualty, she weakened, and conspired with him in silence. In her pocket Celia's mobile bleeped cheerfully.

It was a text message from Gabriele. '*Tutto ok?*' She smiled, wondering if he could read her mind; she couldn't remember what she'd said about her timetable today.

'I'll sort us out a lift,' she said, turning to Lucas and Emma, and they just nodded. They seemed exhausted into silence, docile as children.

Gabriele answered in two rings. 'I'm on my way,' he said immediately. Ten minutes.' He had just got home, he said; Celia realized that she'd never seen his apartment, down in the suburbs. And as she visualized him there, his parking space, his neat apartment block somewhere in Galluzzo, she realized that the suburbs no longer seemed like home to her, they seemed strange, alien. The dirty, noisy city, the child that cried at night, the man who cleaned the courtyard at two in the morning: that was home now.

They waited for him in the cloister, behind the gate, Celia watching out for the car through the bars. The attendant had closed it, presumably for security. Emma had her arm through Lucas's; he stood stiffly beside her, watchful. It was still snowing heavily, the air thick with it, and the broad stone pavement that skirted the church had a covering of virgin snow already a couple of inches deep. Immediately outside the gate, though, it was trodden into dirty slush, and the marks of several footprints were visible.

'*Were* you worried about that man?' said Emma to Lucas

suddenly, as though Celia wasn't there. Lucas glanced over at her, and Celia realized Emma somehow wanted her as a witness to his reply. Like a woman worn out with convincing herself her husband is telling her the truth when he denies an affair; they want someone to watch and say, *Yes, he's lying.*

'Yes,' said Lucas, and his voice was weary. 'Yes, I was.' He hesitated, looked away, fixed his gaze on the dome of the chapel that looked down into the cloister. 'He was Russian – Ukrainian actually. I heard his voice.' He fell silent, as if that was enough of an explanation. Emma looked at him, waiting; her eyes were round. When he turned back to her and spoke again his tone was lighter, and to Celia, evasive. 'If you deal with the Russians,' he shrugged, 'you have a certain reaction to that tone. Towns like Moscow, Kiev ... they're not like Florence. They're ... like frontier towns.' He smiled a little, distant.

'Lucas does a lot of work for the Russians,' Emma said slowly, and Celia saw a little frown, saw her begin to wonder about her husband. Had this kind of thing happened before, perhaps on their trip to Milan, had he shut himself away there? It seemed to Celia that this was new to Emma, that she'd been happy with Lucas until they came here, to Florence. Was it the pregnancy that had changed things? Or was there something else? From the street outside there came the sound of a discreet touch on a car's horn, and Celia turned to see the low, dark shape of Gabriele's Mercedes.

The traffic crawled in the snow; the Via Nazionale was at a standstill and Gabriele took a meandering route the half-mile back to the hotel. Around them the streets were filling up again; on the soft white pavements people slid and laughed, leaning against one another for support.

They hardly spoke in the car. Once Lucas leaned forward and said, 'The Palazzo Ferrigno. It's – very private, is it? Secure?'

'Oh, yes,' said Celia, aware that he'd already asked her this. She wondered what it would take to make Lucas Marsh, with all his money, feel safe. 'They're used to conferences, politicians, even royalty, I think.' Although of course tonight, as far as they knew, they were simply entertaining a wealthy lawyer and his wife; would they have any security to speak of? She could tell Gabriele was listening beside her, although he was looking straight ahead, and suddenly she wanted to be away from the Marshes, to sit and talk to Gabriele about it all. What had Lucas Marsh been afraid of in the library? It came to her that they'd been hiding in there, that since he met them in Frollini Lucas had wanted to keep them out of sight. Her neck was stiff with tension from the day, and her back ached, and she had a feeling she couldn't ignore that something here was wrong.

'Are you sure you're up to it, this evening?' she ventured cautiously. She knew how much the dinner had cost them but it seemed to her the Marshes were rich enough for that not to matter. She turned to look at them in the back of the car.

'Of course,' said Lucas Marsh, but he seemed distracted, looking out of the window, scrutinizing the passers-by from below.

'I've been looking forward to it for ages,' said Emma, squeezing his arm.

'When shall I ask Gabriele to collect you?' Celia said. 'A quarter to?'

'No,' said Lucas quickly. 'I can arrange something. Or perhaps we'll walk. In the snow.'

'But perhaps you'd like to be on your own, at least,' Celia said, hearing that edginess in his voice she'd noticed, on and off, since they'd arrived. It suddenly seemed to her that it would be so much easier if she could just say goodbye to them now, put them behind her. They came out into the piazza, where the snow was settling as the temperature dropped, and Celia peered out through the window in wonder at the transformation. The little green and gold carousel was turning slowly with its load of booted and mittened children, and the grandiose, nineteenth-century façades were softened by the falling white. The car glided to a halt at the front of the Regale, and a green-frogged doorman was there, leaning down to Emma's door; Celia saw his face peering in, a brief flare of curiosity quickly erased.

'No, no!' Emma's protest was robust. 'We can't say goodbye yet! And besides, there's something – no, you must come.' There was even a hint of pleading in her voice.

'Please come,' said Lucas Marsh from the dark corner where he sat, and for a moment, before his face came into the light, Celia was reminded of their first conversation, the effect on her of the voice that seemed to reveal so much more of him than his face. He leaned forward and now his tone was formal. 'Please.' He opened his own door, climbing out without waiting for an answer.

'That's settled,' said Emma, taking the hand the doorman offered her. 'Lucas never asks twice.' She leaned to climb out then, and momentarily all Celia could see was the curve of her waist in the red woollen coat and the slender, stretched tendon of her ankle, stockinged pale. 'Just a minute,' Emma said, and Celia saw her run into the foyer of the hotel, saw her leaning across the reception desk to ask something. She saw the receptionist shake her head, and Emma ran back out, her shiny dark hair falling back from her bright face. Celia heard her say something like, 'I'll have to send it over,' to Lucas, and then she leaned back in. 'Are you going home now?' she asked, her eyes bright and inquisitive. 'Or are you two off for a drink?'

'I'm going home,' said Celia, wondering if Emma thought they were a couple, darting a glance over at Gabriele to see if he'd picked up on it. If he had, he showed no sign, gazing through his windscreen at the snow.

'Thank you,' said Emma, pulling off a glove and holding out a hand across her to Gabriele; Celia saw him look up at her in surprise, charmed.

'It's nothing,' he said, shaking the small white fingers. Celia was aware of Lucas behind his wife, standing stiff and silent with his hands in his pockets.

'We'll see you there at seven, then,' said Emma, and straightened, disappearing. Celia could see her hand reach out for Lucas, but he turned and she couldn't see whether he took it or not. They walked through the door side by side, silhouetted against the luxurious golden light of the lobby.

Celia leaned back for a moment on the soft leather of Gabriele's passenger seat and closed her eyes, and for a moment she felt blissfully, perfectly at ease, cosseted, protected, warm and safe. She was aware of him at her side, saying nothing, and aware too of not having felt like this for a long time. She opened her eyes, and there was Gabriele, looking at her.

'Sorry,' she said, 'Just tired out, somehow. Now they've gone. Give me a minute.'

'Let me give you a lift home,' he said, serious suddenly, and intent.

She sighed, looked out at the snow. 'I think I should walk,' she said. 'My head needs clearing, if I'm going out again later. A bit of exercise. And it's so pretty, isn't it?' Gabriele shrugged, eyeing the snow sceptically. 'Whoever said Italian men were romantic?' said Celia, laughing as she began to button her coat; out of the corner of her eye she saw Gabriele frown a little at what she'd said. Then he leaned towards her, put his hand on the back of her neck and pulled her mouth against his.

'Romantic enough for you?' he said, letting her go abruptly and still frowning. Celia felt her cheeks burn, not sure whether to be shocked or delighted, her heart pounding. 'Gabri—' she began, holding out a hand to him, but she realized she didn't know what she wanted to say. 'I'd better go.' She pressed her cheek against his, feeling the tiny prickle of stubble, smelling his aftershave, breathless. 'Thank you.' She hesitated, feeling stupid that she could think of nothing else to say. 'Thank you.'

'I'll call you later,' said Gabriele. She thought she saw amusement in his eyes, and felt foolish. 'Yes,' she said. 'I'm at the Ferrigno from seven till, oh, I don't know, about nine.' She realized she was gabbling, realized he didn't need to know any of this, and to cover her confusion stepped out of the car quickly, slamming the door; she saw him looking up at her through the glass. Celia lifted a hand, and slowly the car moved off; she stood there for a while, dazed. She was still half in a daze as she walked away, out of the bright square and down the nearest side street, pulling on her gloves, absently feeling for her bag, purse, mobile, the snow falling soft and cold on her cheeks. She was thinking about Gabriele, thinking, as it all fell into place, about his visit late last night, the looks he'd given her, how slow on the uptake she'd been. She only became aware quite suddenly that it had grown dark and she had taken a wrong turning when she felt her arms seized, both of them at once, from behind.

It had taken Luisa longer than she would have liked at the dressmaker's, and there was a queue at the bank; the longer it was postponed, the more she wanted to see Lucas Marsh again. As she waited it began to seem to Luisa that he held the answer to something, to everything that had gone wrong in her life; he was bound up in the loss of their child as well as his. After half an hour in the queue – an argument about documentation at one of the cash-desks – her impatience got the better of her; she stowed the takings at the bottom of her bag and left. *I could run away with this kind of money*, she thought absently as she waited for the security airlock to open. When the door opened she pushed her way out in a hurry, in her mind some confused desire to have it out with them.

Have what out? *My husband*, she wanted to say to Lucas Marsh, *look what you've got him into*. And what about his wife? She'd have to say this in front of the young wife who knew nothing. Luisa didn't want to think about his wife. She hurried past the Venetian façade of the Orsanmichele, lovely in the snow, but she was heedless; the stiff bags swung against her legs as she hurried, their sharp corners bumping her calves, but she hardly felt it. The piazza opened in front of her, the grand frontage of the Regale came into view and she slowed, straightened, tidied her collar. You had to look decent before they'd even let you through the door; as she approached, Luisa saw the doorman shaking his head as he looked down into the face of an old woman all bundled up against the cold. Under the coats you could tell she was poor, and thin as a rail, her hair hennaed and thin. He'd never let her past him.

The doorman nodded Luisa through as he stood, impassive, blocking the beggar's path; Luisa glanced back as she passed through the door, and looked into the woman's face. She wasn't even that old, just ill-fed, her skin coarse and grey from poverty or drugs, her eyes too big, glazed and sunken, and her cheeks startlingly hollow. Their eyes met for a moment and Luisa thought, with horror, *Do I know her?* She looked away, moved on towards the bright, warm interior of the hotel's foyer, but behind her she heard the beggar pleading, obsequious, '*La pregho.* I implore you. You don't understand, he will speak to me.' The doorman murmured in response, soothing but giving no ground, then the revolving door turned with a soft shush and shut them out.

Inside it was hushed and warm. Luisa hurried to the reception desk, thinking with a kind of relief, *Of course I shan't even see them, I'll leave the bags here.* She raised them to the desk and the receptionist nodded straight away in recognition. 'Ah, what a shame, yes. For Signora Marsh?'

'Yes,' said Luisa, not quite understanding.

'Mr and Mrs Marsh have just returned,' said the receptionist. 'She was asking for the bags.'

'Mrs Marsh said by six,' said Luisa in alarm, looking at her watch. It was just after five.

'I'm sure, Signora Luisa,' said the receptionist, politely reassuring. Luisa knew the girl, she shopped at Frollini, often asked for advice. They had to be smart, working in this place; a cheap chain-store suit would be noticed. Luisa felt tired, a little relieved that all she had to do was leave the boxes and walk away. She turned to go.

'Just a moment, Signora,' said the receptionist, lifting the telephone receiver. 'I'll tell them you're here.'

224

Luisa felt a prickle of alarm. She waited, looking away, keeping her coat buttoned. *I'll go*, she thought. Outside the door she could see the thin woman pleading with the doorman in the dark; the woman put her hands to her temples in a gesture of desperation, the tendons in their backs strung like wire, and her mouth was moving but Luisa could hear nothing. The receptionist spoke into the receiver.

'Would you mind?' Replacing the phone, the receptionist was respectful, and Luisa felt her face frozen, unable to respond. 'They would like you to take the bags straight up. I'm sorry.'

Emma Marsh opened the door for her, smiling. She was still wearing the red dress but had unbuttoned it a little way at the side; Emma saw her looking and lowered her eyes, a flush on her cheeks. She looked pretty, like a painting Luisa remembered from somewhere. 'Come in,' she said eagerly, and with some reluctance Luisa obeyed. The honeymoon suite, the receptionist had said meaningfully; something about that shocked Luisa, the privateness of it. She and Sandro had gone to his mother's in the Abruzzo for their honeymoon, two days by the sea in Pescara. She remembered the view from their room; there had been an ancient *matrimoniale*, a double bed piled with mattresses that looked out to sea. It had been the first time she'd slept in a double bed.

Slowly Luisa lowered the bags to the shiny parquet and stood and looked around the room. It was as big as a ballroom, the ceilings as high and ornate, and the long windows hung with net gave out on to the Orsanmichele, rooftops and a great dark skyful of snow. Three dresses were hanging from what Luisa took to be the bedroom door; it was ajar but she couldn't see more than the corner of a dressing table and a spillage of cosmetics boxes and bottles. The dresses were all beautiful, she could see that even on the hangers – money and taste, Emma Marsh had them both. There was a red one, with chiffon at the neck, a flowered silk in green and blue, and a black dress that stood out, austere and grown-up in a way she hadn't associated with Emma Marsh, the kind of dress a beautiful widow might wear in a film.

At the centre of the room Lucas Marsh was sitting at a large mahogany table in shirtsleeves with a newspaper spread out in front of him, although something struck her as odd about the fixed way he was looking down at it. Beside it his hand rested on a mobile phone, as though he was about to make a call or had just received one. He was a handsome man, thought Luisa, there was a combination of strength and nerves about him that drew her, and she realized that all the anger she had felt as she walked up from the shop, all that wild resolution to challenge him, had quite evaporated. She just felt a kind of heartsinking, miserable pity for him, him and Sandro both. Where would it end?

Emma Marsh crossed to the table and leaned over her husband from behind, pressing her cheek against his. 'Look at him,' she said. 'Always working.'

Luisa saw his hand move across the newspaper, and it seemed to her he was as tense as a stalking animal sitting there. *For God's sake*, she thought, imagining the humiliation of being kept in the dark about this, *the story's in the newspaper, it must be. He has to tell her.* Would there be a picture of the child? Luisa wondered if he kept one hidden away, just to have it there, you didn't have to look at it. Should she have done that, taken a photograph of that tiny, wrinkled face? Emma frowned down at something over her husband's shoulder and

226

he shifted suddenly, dislodging her. It was an unmistakable gesture of rejection and Luisa saw the confusion in Emma's eyes as she turned away. Luisa held up the bag of shoeboxes, pretending she'd noticed nothing.

'You are kind to bring them up,' said Emma, and slowly she pulled at the ribbon tying the bag. 'I'm trying to work out if I should wear the red ones tonight.'

'It's my pleasure,' Luisa said carefully. She saw that Lucas Marsh's hand, held up to the side of his face at the table and shielding it, was trembling.

'I'm sorry, would you like a cup of – tea, or something?' Emma said, stopping midway through opening the bag, eager. 'It's so cold outside.'

'Tea?' Now Luisa had seen them together, she wanted to go more than ever. 'I – no, no tea, thank you.' Emma Marsh looked downcast. 'Perhaps a glass of water?' said Luisa, relenting, and Emma brightened. 'Sit down,' she said, 'please.' There were too many places to sit in the room, two great sofas, a leather armchair, an upholstered *bergère*; at random Luisa lowered herself gingerly on to a corner of the nearest sofa. Emma Marsh brought her a glass of water with some ice in it, and stood beside her as she sipped at it. She folded her arms tight against her waist as she sat there.

'Lucas has arranged a dinner for me,' she said, sweet and animated, smiling into Luisa's face. 'Just for me! I'm trying to decide what to wear.' She nodded at the hanging dresses, and Luisa thought there was something not quite innocent in her gaiety, something forced. It was perhaps the contrast with her husband's fixed silence at the table, the muscle in his jaw clenching as Luisa stole a glance.

Emma Marsh went on determinedly. 'I think you always

227

need something new, don't you, for a party? And it is my birthday.'

Luisa smiled, remembering what that had felt like, Saturday for shopping, a new dress and a party in the evening. Emma crouched suddenly at Luisa's feet and took out the shoeboxes; it felt curious to Luisa to have the roles reversed, however briefly. The shoes came out and Emma laid them side by side. She picked up the embroidered one with its tiny curved heel.

'The red ones,' she said slowly as she looked down at the ornate object in her hands. 'Isn't there something about red shoes?' *There is*, thought Luisa, some distant memory of a children's story slipping into her mind. What had happened to the girl in the red shoes? She couldn't remember. Emma slipped her feet into them, stood up and executed a little spin on the spot, poised and graceful. She held out her fine white arms for balance and the sliver of pale skin was revealed where she had undone the buttons, the thickening at her waist emphasized. At the table Lucas Marsh lifted his head and Luisa turned, detecting the movement, to see him gazing across the room at them. For a moment it seemed to her that he was looking at his wife as though she was a stranger.

As Luisa watched, Emma completed her turn and she saw that as she came around to face him, Lucas had managed a smile, a fond look. 'What do you think?' said Emma, smiling back; her eyes, though, were anxious.

'You're lovely,' he said gravely, and suddenly, radiantly, Emma beamed. She sank to the sofa, pulling off the shoes. Leaning down, she saw the second bag. 'Oh, yes,' she said, frowning momentarily. 'Maybe . . .' She looked up earnestly at Luisa, who sat there still with her half-empty water glass on her knee. 'Can you do me a favour? Darling,' she said, turning to look over her shoulder at Lucas, 'have you got her address? Celia's address?' She leaned back towards Luisa and said, 'It'll be such a surprise for her.' Behind them Lucas Marsh got to his feet and went into the bedroom. Seeing Luisa's face, which revealed her confusion, Emma said eagerly, 'The dress, you know, the green dress. If I can only have new shoes,' she glanced deprecatingly at her waist, 'at least someone can dress up.'

'When is the baby due?' asked Luisa before she could stop herself. Her voice sounded hoarse and unpractised, she could hear it, as though the words were so weighted with fear and longing that she could hardly pronounce them. Emma heard it; she gazed at Luisa and suddenly all the animation, the vivacious chatter evaporated. 'June,' she whispered, and Luisa thought of the hospital in the heat when her baby had been born, the hair sticking to her forehead as she laboured; she took Emma's hand. 'It's wonderful,' she said, clearing her throat to disguise her emotion. Emma's head tilted to one side and she looked into Luisa's face as if trying to understand something. She straightened, nodding a little. 'Yes,' she said hesitantly, 'I – yes. It is, isn't it?' Behind them Lucas Marsh emerged from the bedroom holding a piece of paper.

'Can you have it sent over to her?' said Emma, taking the paper from Lucas and handing it to Luisa. 'I hadn't thought, really. Could you put it in a taxi or something?'

'A taxi, yes,' Luisa murmured, taking the paper, hardly glancing at the printed lines, only taking in a telephone number and an address. She stood up hastily, feeling awkward at the way she'd spoken to Emma Marsh, feeling she might have gone too far. She found herself face to face with Lucas Marsh, saw his face blank with a lifetime of hiding and covering up, and suddenly she felt a surge of anger. *He has to tell her*, she thought, *or what kind of life can they have? The same kind Sandro and I have had, for fifteen years.*

'I think you know my husband,' she said to Lucas Marsh, before she could think about it. 'Sandro Cellini? He's a policeman.' And Marsh turned pale, before her eyes, and she knew he understood that if he didn't tell his wife, she would. She saw Emma look from Luisa to her husband, and back again.

'Really?' she said, startled. 'How's that, darling? Italian policemen?'

'Oh, it's – I met Sandro a long time ago,' said Lucas slowly. 'It's a long story, isn't it, Signora Cellini?'

'Yes,' said Luisa, looking at Emma. 'I think I should leave your husband to tell it to you, don't you? I have a delivery to make, after all.' And she put a hand to Emma's cheek. 'Good luck,' she said.

And as she pulled the door shut behind her, the last thing Luisa saw was the look on Emma's face as she turned towards her husband. *She's young*, she told herself. *She's strong.* She stood a moment outside the door, unable to move; at the end of the corridor she heard the hiss of lift doors opening and hurriedly she stepped away from the door and began to walk away. Before she had gone far, though, she heard Emma Marsh say, 'What?' on a note of rising disbelief that made Luisa close her eyes briefly in an attempt to blot it out as she wondered, *What have I done?*

Chapter Twenty

The hands that held her upper arms behind her were not rough but they were strong, a man's, she was sure, and for a second, twisting in his grip, Celia panicked. In the dark it crossed her mind that surely this was a crazy place to mug someone. Even if she wasn't exactly sure where she was it was no more than a stone's throw from the Via del Gorso, and she didn't look a natural victim, always took care to carry no expensive handbag, no jewellery – didn't even have any jewellery, she thought savagely in a moment's self-pity. *Oh no, no*, she raged in that same instant, thinking of all the things she'd have to replace, driving licence, *permesso di soggiorno*, and the money, the money, *damn it*, and around her the dark façades gazed down, unmoved.

Then at once Celia became aware both that her assailant was speaking her name and, quite distinctly, that she knew him, even in the dark, she knew him, knew the hands, knew his smell. 'Celie,' he said urgently, 'Celie, it's me.' And as she twisted to face him, he slackened his grip. It was Dan.

231

'Bloody hell,' she said, furious. 'Bloody hell, Dan, what d'you think you're doing?' He had his arms around her in what would probably have seemed a lover's embrace to a passer-by and he let them drop. He backed off.

'I'm sorry,' he said, not sounding it; his voice was ragged with something more like rage. Celia felt shaken, in a sweat from the struggle and the proximity of his body.

'I should hope so,' she said, peering at him in the poor light. 'What is it? What's wrong?'

'Are you seeing him?' he said furiously. 'That guy?' Suddenly Celia felt anger boil up inside her.

'What guy?' she said, knowing he meant Gabriele. 'And anyway, what business is it of yours?' she went on, almost shouting. She saw his face, unhappy, ashamed. 'Dan, you're not – are you jealous?' He looked down, and she saw that he was. Dan, jealous. She was stunned. 'I – I'm not going to talk to you about this,' she said, still angry, but not frightened any more. 'Not here.'

At the end of the alley she saw the glimmer of a streetlight and turned towards it, setting her back to Dan. It seemed unfair, this ambush; had he followed her down this alley, had he waited until she was alone? She stopped abruptly and felt him at her back; she remembered the man she thought she'd seen that afternoon in the snow, as she talked to the Marshes in a doorway. She turned to face him; she could see him now in the distant glimmer of the streetlight. 'How long have you been following me? This is creepy, Dan. Really.' She said it to hurt him, but she was confused; it *was* creepy.

'I – I – It's—' Dan stammered, looking around him, and as she looked into his face Celia felt the tension ebbing. *This is Dan*, she thought. *Come on.*

'Well?' she said, more gently. He looked down.

'Are you seeing him, though?' he muttered.

'No,' said Celia immediately. 'No. I mean, I don't think – no.' *None of your business anyway*, was what she thought. Dan nodded sheepishly.

'Was that why you were following me? To find out who I might be seeing?' It was extraordinary; he'd never been the jealous type even when they were together. There'd been nothing he couldn't shrug off with some light irony or a joke; she'd never seen him angry, only ever witty in the face of failure, or adversity, or pain. His own, or other people's. Had Allegra dumping him affected him so badly? For a moment Celia felt a spasm of jealousy that Allegra had managed it where she had failed, quickly succeeded by remorse. She had a brief and sudden vision of Dan metamorphosed into an ageing depressive, one of the city's great diaspora of rootless, maudlin expatriates, drinking too much, moving from one seedy bedsit to the next, sponging off friends, unable to return home a failure.

But something in Dan's look gave her pause; it was sad but not self-pitying, wary, a little calculating; it told her, this was more complicated than being dumped by Allegra. He looked at her for a long moment in the dark street and then he shook his head. 'You're right,' he said. 'We shouldn't talk about this here.'

The nearest bar turned out to be the Cantinetta where only hours earlier she'd sat with the Marshes; the evening rush was on, the little marble tables in the wine bar filling up with tourists, locals at the bar sipping contentedly and gossiping, but by some fluke the back room was half empty.

Dan got them each a glass of wine; Celia stared at hers but she wanted a clear head and only took a sip. Dan stared into his, his expression gloomy.

233

'Sorry,' he said again. 'I – I don't know why I grabbed you like that. I just – when I saw you kissing him—'

'I wasn't kissing him!' said Celia indignantly. 'Well, I was, but – he – I – look, he's just a friend.' She felt guilty on several counts; for being evasive like this with Dan, for using Gabriele, for not knowing any more how she felt about either of them. Gabriele *was* just a friend, but suddenly Celia felt she couldn't have managed without him these past couple of days.

Dan took a slug of his wine and sighed. 'You're right,' he said, 'it's none of my business.' He turned the glass in his hands, frowning. 'It didn't start out like this,' he said slowly. 'I wasn't following you. I was following him.'

'Following Gabriele?' Celia was bemused. This *was* weird.

'Is that his name? Your *chauffeur*?' He allowed a hint of bitterness into his voice but seemed to regret it immediately. 'Sorry.' He looked up at her. 'No, not him. I was following your client. And his new wife.' His voice wasn't bitter any more, but dark and determined.

'Lucas Marsh?' This should, she realized, have struck her as weird too, but somehow she was not surprised. 'How do you know him? How do you know she's his new wife?'

'Well,' said Dan slowly, a little defensively, 'I think anyone could tell she was a – what d'you call it? – a trophy wife, couldn't they? Twenty years younger, gorgeous, full of life. Young blood.'

'You're making him sound like Dracula,' said Celia, meaning it as a joke, but then she thought of Lucas Marsh's pallor, that strange coldness, and she was chilled, afraid for Emma. 'She's not like that, anyway,' she said quickly, defensively. 'She's . . . ' She searched for the right word, to show him. 'She's clever. And good. She's a good person.'

Dan nodded. 'Well, maybe. Whatever you say. You were always kind, Celie. Kinder than me.' The unfamiliar softness in his voice as he pronounced her name seduced her; it brought back those long evenings they'd spent in his flat among the piles of books as the light faded, and she wondered if that was his intention. She steeled herself. 'But it wasn't a guess, was it?' She searched his face. 'What do you know about Lucas Marsh?'

Down by the river Jonas stamped his feet in the snow and edged closer to the brazier. He liked the snow, didn't mind the cold. He looked at his hands, red-knuckled and swollen like a cheap cut of meat, and felt nothing but contempt for the passers-by in their furs, picking their way through the slush and complaining. If he half-closed his eyes he might be at home, roofs loaded with snow like sugar on gingerbread. With grim pride he thought of the housing project where he'd grown up, rows of decaying concrete blocks on a windswept plain, not a tree to soften them, snow on the ground for six months of the year. *Don't know they're born. I'm never going back.*

Hesitantly a beefy kid in a ski-jacket stopped and held out a euro for some chestnuts; not a bad game this, money for old rope, and idly Jonas thought perhaps he shouldn't dump the brazier back in the lock-up in Galluzzo he'd stolen it from along with the sack of chestnuts, it'd be a living, wouldn't it? Carelessly he scooped a handful into a cone of newspaper and turned his back on the kid. He looked up at the big windows of the Palazzo Ferrigno with satisfaction; *he doesn't know*, he thought. *He thinks he's safe.* Lucas Marsh had been very careful not to tell them his plans, where he'd be when, but he hadn't counted on Jonas covering every eventuality, had he? Trace the guide, get hold of the schedule. And after twelve hours covering this place Jonas prided himself that he knew it inside and out, knew he could walk straight in, even knew where to get out again in a hurry. *And since that plane came down we've known where he is, every minute.* A nice weekend away with the wife, make the drop and back to his plush hotel with no one any the wiser. Only Lucas Marsh didn't make the drop, did he? Didn't pay up. He thought of Lucas's face beside the river, staring into the water as though he might jump in himself.

A figure walked from window to window above Jonas's head, a small, upright figure silhouetted against the light. Jonas wondered if she'd know him again out of the brown overalls, if that was why she was looking down at him now. The boss. Jonas didn't like bosses, he was a free spirit, and that was why this kind of thing suited him. He was glad he was out on his own now; when the others had got impatient he had just shrugged and let them go, drifting off their separate ways. He'd promised them they'd get paid and they were too scared of him to argue, he'd made sure of that. He'd get the money, would meet them in some truck stop a couple of weeks on, give out the cash and the whole business would be done with.

Jonas stamped his feet and turned away, looking down towards Le Cascine, the park a great dark shape lying like some soft, dangerous, sleeping animal along the bank of the river. He thought about that empty swimming pool in the rain and ground his teeth; it should have been so simple. But what the hell; so what if he's dead? *Just give me the money.* The thought of it made Jonas twitchy, and he moved his body from side to side, his jaw clenching and unclenching. He couldn't suppress the feeling that they should never have got into it, the guy doesn't know what he's got himself into, doesn't know the rules of this kind of game. *Jesus.* He ground his teeth with frustration, felt

236

the pressure build in his head at the thought of business badly done. Why should he be waiting around like this? Jonas wasn't a drone, a worker, a slave, he wasn't born to put on an overall and doff his cap to a boss, not like the old days.

He glanced up again and saw she hadn't moved, standing up there quite still in outline. Jonas mulled over the way she'd looked at him in that grand room; suspicious, arrogant, as if he was no more than an animal. He could feel her eyes on him now and he looked away down the street with the cap pulled over his eyes, slumped his shoulders to give himself that useless, defeated look that could make anyone invisible. It had been a mistake, he was willing to admit that, but he'd got away with it, hadn't he, bleeding the radiators right there in front of her? He felt a bubble of triumph swell his chest.

She moved away from the window and Jonas thought, *Well, wouldn't do any harm, would it? Make sure she can't identify me. Just to be on the safe side.* He felt something at his side, a soft, shuffling presence, and he started, his hand going automatically to his pocket and the blade he kept there. *Jesus, don't do that*; he rounded on the newcomer and glared, furious at being taken unawares. *Oh, Christ, she's back.* His rage kindled and caught; *it's all your fault. Bitch.*

With weary relief Celia set her bags down on the top step, the timed landing light ticking away in her ear, urging her on. Patiently she teased the recalcitrant lock, pushed open the door, flicked the light switch, and the rough, soft terracotta floor and clean white walls emerged from the warm darkness. Home.

She could still hardly believe what Dan had told her. You didn't expect a news story to come to life like that; you didn't

237

expect to wake up and find yourself a part of it. And this was a story that had, intermittently, haunted Celia for fifteen years; it was embedded in how she felt about the city, it appeared in her dreams. She thought of the assumptions you have about people, the things you believe them capable of, the past you attribute to them; she thought about Lucas Marsh and her insides coiled and tightened at the horror of what had happened to him.

Celia's hands were stiff and cold from the walk home; outside the snow was still falling, soft and silent, and it had added an extra air of unreality to her dazed passage through the streets. Dan had wanted to walk her home but she had been quite sharp with him, in retrospect; it wasn't his fault, after all, but he had given her a shock and she wanted to be alone. With a sigh she set her bags on the kitchen table, put away the water and milk she had picked up from the baker's, on autopilot it seemed, put the kettle on. *At times like this*, she thought wryly, *what you need is a nice cup of tea*, and just as, by association, Kate's worried smile sprang into her mind, the phone rang.

'Are you all right?' Kate's voice was sharp with concern, and Celia sat down abruptly on the sofa by the phone, suddenly feeling quite overwhelmed with gratitude for Kate's persistence, her motherliness, her very existence all that way away with her immaculate kitchen and her noisy children and her bloody dog. Celia wiped an idiotic tear from her eye.

'Fine,' she croaked, turning the sound into a laugh. 'Well, actually, not so fine, it's a bit – it's all a bit weird out here.'

'Weird?'

Celia sighed. 'Tell me,' said Kate kindly, and Celia told her. She told her everything; everything Dan had told her about the murder of Lucas Marsh's child, the discovery of Bartolo's body, told her sister everything she herself had speculated about the Marshes since their arrival. As she talked a kind of sense began to emerge from what had, when Dan first told her, seemed unbelievable. Lucas Marsh's coldness, his more-than-ambivalence about the baby Emma was expecting, his fear. Emma's sense that she barely knew her husband.

'She doesn't know,' she'd said to Dan. 'I'm sure of it. His wife – his new wife. Emma has no idea.'

As she repeated it all to Kate, with sudden clarity Celia understood why Lucas Marsh had employed her, to keep Emma busy; she saw the darkness and violence that he was trying to hold at bay and she stopped. There was a stunned silence.

'My God,' said Kate, and Celia heard fear in her voice. 'My God.' She fell silent again and Celia could almost hear her thinking, putting two and two together.

'It's been in all the papers here, too,' she said, and in that moment Celia remembered the newspaper Emma Marsh had bought in the market and the small, indistinct photograph of Lucas Marsh's dead daughter she'd glimpsed on the front page. How long could she keep it from Emma? Kate's voice broke in on her thoughts.

'He wasn't called Marsh, though,' she said, calculating.

'Dan said he changed his name.'

'How does Dan know all this?' Kate's voice was sharp again, probing, and Celia found herself grateful for the brisk pragmatism that had throughout her life alternately infuriated and comforted her.

'Well,' she said slowly, 'I didn't know him then. But he told me he followed the investigation, or at least the public reaction to it, for – well, it's hard to explain – sort of poetic reasons. He thought it was a kind of crisis point for the national psyche.'

She put the words in ironic inverted commas, but actually, they had rung true. She paused, remembering her arrival in Italy all those years ago, the city a ghost town in the August heat whose dwindled population crept out of their shuttered houses to learn the awful news, their faces pale and crumpled with shock as they read the newspapers. 'And it was terrible.' Galluzzo had been shunned in the immediate aftermath; the swimming pool still was. She passed it often on the bus to Siena, its crumbling façade derelict, weeds sprouting through the tiles of the pool, and wondered why it was still there.

What Celia couldn't articulate to Kate was what the conversation had revealed to her about Dan. Could she even understand it fully herself? She had known none of this before, he had never mentioned it in their three years together and nor had anyone else. He had hidden it away, and when he had begun, haltingly, to explain to Celia how he had come to know Lucas Marsh so well that he could recognize him in the street fifteen years later his face had been white, his voice low as though he was making a confession.

'I thought – I had some idea of turning myself into a jour-nalist,' he'd said, and he shook his head. 'Not an ordinary journalist. I thought I could bring poetry into it, get to the heart of things, crack things open. Reveal truths, about grief, or violence, or something.' His voice was rich with self-disgust. 'God knows what I thought.' He paused, and in a moment of revelation Celia had understood that this was where the chip of ice in Dan's heart had come from, somehow.

'I – there's not necessarily anything wrong with that. Not with the impulse, anyway. Is there?' she asked. He'd stared at her then, looking for redemption for a split second and then turning away, refusing it.

'Maybe not,' he said, but there was no sense that he drew comfort from her words. 'But there was certainly something wrong with the execution.' He looked at her directly. 'I hung around the police station. I went to the swimming pool and tracked down the people who'd been lying on the next sun-loungers, I spoke to the man who worked the bar, the skinny girl who handed out the keys to the lockers, I even remember her name. Giulietta Sarto. I knew they were after Bartolo, so I sucked up to his mother and even got her to give me a cup of coffee in her kitchen while I listened to her going on about what a good son he was.' He stopped then, as though something was in his way, something he couldn't get around. When he spoke again his voice was so low she had hardly been able to hear.

'I found out where they were staying, the bereaved parents.' He shook his head. 'His wife was very ill with it, you could see. Even I could see, and I should have stopped then, but I was so full of myself for having found them. I was twenty-five.' Dan looked as though he wanted to cry, but he couldn't.

'He wasn't much older than me, thirty perhaps, but he looked like an old man when he came to the door of this place, some kind of police house. And I said, *How are you feeling?*' He put his face in his hands for a moment, then went on. 'I door-stepped him. And then he looked at me, and he said, *How am I feeling? How am I feeling?* And he took a step towards me, just one step, and he had a look of such complete desperation, as though he didn't know if he wanted to kill me or kill himself.' He laid his hands down on the table between them, then, and looked up at her. 'I left. I never saw him again, until today. But he's just the same.'

Celia had wanted to cover Dan's hands with hers but she

couldn't; she'd thought of Lucas Marsh's white face and she felt sick. She just looked at his hands on the table, then up at Dan, and she saw that he was getting old – there was a web of lines under his eyes that hadn't been there before, when she'd left him, or he'd left her. It didn't seem to matter much any more.

She realized she'd been gripping the telephone so tight her hand was half-numb; she couldn't remember what she'd been saying to Kate, only the meaningless phrase, *It was terrible*, rang in her ears. Then Kate spoke.

'Well,' she said, 'I suppose I can see that. A child dying . . .' She fell silent again and Celia knew what she was thinking. 'We're all afraid of it, you know,' Kate said abruptly. 'We all lie awake thinking about losing a child. That's why—' She broke off.

'That's why what?' There was something in Kate's voice, a wobbliness that Celia didn't recognize.

'I'm having another baby,' said Kate then, quickly. 'I know what you'll think, hasn't she got enough? What an idiot giving herself more work, what'll happen about the job . . . ?' She started out defiant, but then her voice caught and broke.

'Hey, wait a minute,' said Celia, astounded. 'What are you talking about?' She'd never heard Kate like this. On the other end of the line Kate burst into tears. 'But you – you do want the baby?' said Celia.

'Yes!' Kate sounded furious and hopeless at the same time. 'Yes, at least I think – yes.' She took a breath, then spoke hurriedly, as though confiding something she didn't want overheard. 'You don't know what it's like. At the back of your mind there's always the thought, what if I lose one? Slip one more in and I'll be safe.' There was a pause and then she laughed raggedly.

242

'Oh,' said Celia, and she didn't know what to say. A Kate she had never known materialized in front of her, anxious, insecure, appealing to her for help. It was an entirely unfamiliar sensation. 'Oh.' She thought a moment, dwelt for longer than she had ever dared on the thought of having a child of her own and what its loss might mean. 'I think I'd be just the same,' she ventured truthfully. 'I mean, how could I know, but it doesn't even sound that irrational to me. And – well. A baby!' She remembered her excitement when Imogen had been born. She even remembered regaling Dan (had she really? she couldn't help grimacing at the memory) with details from the delivery, nine and a half pounds, blue eyes.

Down the line Kate cleared her throat and sighed, and in the background Celia could hear Imogen's insistent, high-pitched voice, close to the receiver. 'Mummy, what's for pudding?' There was a muffled, weary exchange, and Celia imagined the two of them at the kitchen table in the yellow light shed by Kate's carefully chosen and saved-for French porcelain shades. When Kate spoke she sounded like herself again, perhaps even a little sharper.

'So, this Lucas Marsh flew in the day after the man they think killed his daughter is murdered? Sounds like a bit of a coincidence to me,' Kate mused.

'He called me a bit more than three weeks ago,' said Celia slowly, trying to make sense of it. 'His trip had been planned for longer, but he called me when he knew he was bringing his wife.' Lucas was coming to get him, to see the man who'd killed his daughter.

'It says something about a DNA test in the piece I read,' said Kate, pondering. 'Maybe—'

'I don't know,' said Celia quickly, and together they fell

silent, imagining Lucas Marsh meticulously making arrangements to return to the city where his daughter had been murdered. Like some kind of terrible ceremonial of remembrance, awaiting confirmation of his child's killer. Would he have come to look into the man's face, to ask him what he had done, why he had done it? So why was Bartolo dead before he arrived? Celia speculated wildly that he might have come earlier, in secret, to kill Bartolo with his own hands, but she knew that was impossible. He'd flown in with Emma. And then she remembered the drawing Beate had made of Lucas; she remembered the man he'd stood there talking to at the river's edge with his raw, big-knuckled hands, and her stomach contracted, wondering.

'Well, he's dead, anyway,' said Kate, deliberately brutal. 'I'd have killed him.'

'What if it wasn't him, though?' said Celia, still trying to make sense of what she'd seen.

'Well,' said Kate, 'no smoke without fire, if you ask me. It sounds like he was a creep. They use words like loner and misfit in the newspapers, but we all know what they mean.'

Kate's voice was bitter and Celia thought, this is the kind of thing you can't get out of your mind, once you have children. She thought of Kate doggedly going through the article, avid for information, and Celia had hardly been able to finish it, it had sickened her. There was a silence.

'Well,' said Kate after a bit, conciliatory. 'He's dead, so maybe it's all over.'

'Maybe,' said Celia, wondering what on earth this evening's dinner would be like. She didn't think it was all over, not at all.

'So,' said Kate. 'You're seeing Dan again.' And despite herself, Celia laughed.

Chapter Twenty-One

Luisa heard the phone ringing as she was unlocking the door and she fumbled with the key, groped her way down the dark corridor towards the sound. It rang loud and unfamiliar in the empty flat, a shrill, antiquated ring; Sandro had his mobile, she had one too somewhere although she couldn't get on with it, but since her mother died, no one really used the land line much. In Luisa's present state, at once tense and exhausted, her stomach sour with apprehension after leaving Lucas and Emma Marsh with their secret to unravel in the stifling luxury of a hotel room, the sound was ominous. She dropped the bag containing the dress Emma Marsh had bought for Celia Donnelly at her feet and picked up the receiver, standing stiffly as she spoke into it.

'Yes?'

'Can you put Sandro on?' It was Pietro, and his voice was terse.

'What?' In the dark Luisa swayed, feeling giddy, and she

reached out a hand to steady herself. She groped for the switch on the lamp by the phone. 'He's not here, Pietro.' She made a conscious effort not to betray the panic she felt like a rising tide in her throat, forced unconcern into her trembling voice. Pietro grunted, and she had the impression he was deciding whether to believe her or not. She looked around the little sitting room quickly for any sign that Sandro had been back, and saw none. The round mahogany table gleamed quietly, the sofa cushions were neat and plump, all undisturbed.

'I spoke to him a couple of hours ago,' she said calmly. 'He was with you, he said, out near the airport?'

'Yes,' said Pietro. 'We were there.' He spoke cautiously. 'Then we'd just got back to the station and before we even got inside Sandro suddenly said he was due a break, and he was off before I could ask him what the hell he was up to. I let him go because – well . . .' He sounded almost embarrassed, hesitating. 'If you want the truth I thought you and him – well, I thought you were going through a bad patch, thought you needed to talk.' He paused. 'I mean, he's been on the phone to you every five minutes, you've got to admit it looks funny.'

The flat suddenly felt suffocating, the ancient iron radiators silently, steadily blasting out heat. Sweat sticky on her back, Luisa thought about the irony of what Pietro had said. The bad patch had lasted fifteen years, and Pietro, a detective for most of that, had only just noticed. Never mind the irony that this was the closest they'd come in all that time, that those phone calls that had looked so suspicious to Pietro felt like a lifeline to Luisa.

'Well, I haven't seen him,' she said, passing no comment on the state of her marriage to Pietro. 'But I've been at work, haven't I?'

246

'Yes, well,' said Pietro, and she could hear just a hint of panic in his voice, 'it's more serious than that. Than whatever's happening between you and him.'

'Nothing's happening between me and him,' said Luisa distractedly, trying to get at what Pietro was saying. 'What are you talking about, Pietro?'

'I don't know if I can—' Pietro broke off, and then when he spoke again she could hear his breath as though he had his mouth up against the receiver. 'It's confidential. It's police business.'

Luisa waited, said nothing of what she knew. She didn't want to get Sandro into more trouble. She held on, waiting, then heard Pietro exhale. 'Look,' he said, 'you didn't get this from me, all right? But I've known Sandro twenty years, it's madness.' He hesitated only briefly. 'The thing is, after he walked off like that, I went into the station and all hell broke loose. Everyone wanted Sandro, they all started shouting at me at once. He'd been called into a meeting with the chief; that conniving little bastard Gemelli on paperwork found something in the photocopier and kept it. A letter to the father of the dead girl, signed by Sandro. There's a box at the post office, too. I suppose Gemelli thought he was showing he had the makings of a detective, tracking that down.' Pietro snorted. 'A detective!' There was a silence, then a heavy sigh.

'They'd been trying to get hold of him all afternoon; he'd turned off the police radio, and his mobile, and I never noticed.' His voice was leaden. 'There's going to be an official inquiry, anyway,' he said, then stopped. 'A bloody lynch mob – maybe I'd be running too if I had that lot after me.'

Luisa quailed. 'Do you think he's running?' She felt dizzy at the thought; where would he go? His parents were long dead. She and Pietro were all he had. She thought of all the shadowy characters he had had dealings with over twenty years as a policeman: informants, conmen, pickpockets, drug dealers. For a moment, thinking of how alone he must be, a worse thought occurred to Luisa than that Sandro might have left her, worse than the thought that he might have vanished for some foreign border. 'You don't think – he wouldn't—'

'No,' said Pietro quickly, a warning note in his voice, but then he stopped. 'Jesus, who knows? I don't think so, but I'm beginning to wonder. Did you know about any of this, Luisa? Because I didn't. Twenty years together, and I had no idea.'

The thought that she shared her ignorance with Pietro gave Luisa an odd kind of comfort, but – poor Sandro. The day he must have had. She tried to forget the horrible possibility that had been raised between them, that Sandro might feel he was at the end of the line. *He'd never leave me.* It came to her that if she didn't believe that, it was all over anyway. With a great effort she spoke calmly again. 'Not before yesterday, Pietro. He told me nothing before then, honestly. And he really isn't here, no sign of him at all. What are we going to do?'

The moment she put the phone down, of course, she dialled Sandro's number, but there was no reply; she heard the answering service and automatically hung up; she couldn't talk to those things. But what else could she do? She thought for a moment, called the number again, and blurted out the first thing that came into her head.

'Sandro,' she said urgently, hopelessly. 'Sandro, it's me.' How much time did she have, to say all that she needed to say? 'Call me. Call home.'

It was only after she'd put the phone down for the third time that she found it, a folded scrap of paper, sodden and dirty, left carelessly on the kitchen table for anyone to see. As she unfolded it she had the strangest feeling of having seen it before, dates, times, places, neatly word-processed by a diligent Florence City Guide whose blurred photograph was reproduced in the corner of the page. Wordlessly, she reached into her handbag and pulled out the page Lucas Marsh had given her with Celia Donnelly's address on it; they were the same.

Luisa sat at the kitchen table and stared at the page, tried to make sense of the illusion it offered. A romantic weekend to be spent wandering through chapels and gardens, idling hand in hand in the sunlit corridors of the Uffizi, no expense spared. She looked down to the last line on the page, circled in red. Dinner at the Palazzo Ferrigno, drinks at seven-thirty. She stood and paced the room, from the sink to the stove to the window, gazing at the props of her married life, the pots and pans and cupboards she had kept clean for twenty years, as though they might tell her something. *Where has he gone?* She dialled Pietro, but when he answered his voice sounded odd, wooden.

'I can't talk right now,' he said, and when he didn't say her name she understood he must be with someone, someone he was protecting Sandro from. In frustration she hung up.

Walking from the kitchen into the dark corridor, she stared down it, willing the front door to open and let Sandro in. She went into the bedroom and opened the wardrobe; there hung her husband's ironed trousers, his sports jackets, his sweaters. Something was missing though; she looked, waiting for it to reveal itself. His warm coat, black padded nylon, that should have hung in the corner. It was gone. She looked down: his snowboots were gone too. In a panic she checked the suitcase, the holdalls, the drawers, but everything else was there. He'd

been here, but he hadn't packed to leave. If he was going to —
if — surely he wouldn't need to keep warm if he was going
to . . . ?

No, no, no. She willed herself not to think about that; she
made herself think of Sandro dressing warmly for the weather,
prepared, not panicking. Had he taken the car? They had a
small Fiat they kept on the street, hardly ever used because
the days were long gone when they might have gone out on
a drive into the country on a summer evening, a Sunday. She
couldn't remember seeing it on her way home, but then she
wouldn't have looked; would they have the licence plate on
record at the station? Of course they would, they'd find him.
She went back into the sitting room.

The first thing Luisa saw was the bag. There it sat, incon-
gruously jaunty and hopeful, with Celia Donnelly's dress in
it. As she stood there and stared at it with not the faintest idea
of what to do, another wave of heat rolled over from the great
radiators; on the polished table the telephone sat silent. She
stared from the bag to the crumpled piece of paper and to the
bag again, and suddenly Luisa knew that if she stayed here and
waited in passive ignorance, helpless, she would go mad. She
took a small backpack and put the mobile she'd never used into
it, a torch, a packet of biscuits, a thin blanket she used in the
shop when it grew cold. She changed into trousers and put on
thermal socks and snow boots, then, padded and stifled in the
heat, awkwardly fitted her arms through the backpack's straps
and picked up the Frollini carrier bag.

As Luisa stood, padded like a polar explorer, and con-
templated her front door, she remembered something; she
went back into the sitting room and slowly picked up the
handbag she'd brought home from work. She reached into

250

it and brought them out, three little sacks like sandbags: the day's takings she'd never managed to bank. One of them was heavy with coins and she set it aside; from the other two she withdrew three, four, five fat rolls of notes and stowed them in the small backpack. What had she thought as she came out through the bank's security doors, *I could run away?* The time for running away was past.

In the city traffic was slowing almost to a standstill as the snow continued to fall, thick and soft and silent in the dark. Down to the south of the city the snowploughs had been through already and things were beginning to move. Great mounds of dirty snow lined the road that wound below the hilltop villas and ancient estates on the edge of the city, the Poggio Imperiale and the Certosa, Bottai and Impruneta and Galluzzo, and on the spattered, slushy tarmac cars made their way home. Where the roads to Rome and Siena met the ring road around Florence, miraculously the traffic was moving: slowly, but it was moving all the same, around the roundabouts and link roads.

Between the ring road and a nice, clean housing development, neat balconies and pale stucco and fresh paint, sat the crumbling concrete of the Olympia Club, an eyesore and an embarrassment. It had always been a squat, ugly building, built of reinforced concrete with a grandiose circular bar set on top of the gym complex and changing rooms, pretentious and ill-proportioned. The curved windows of the bar were all smashed now, inside the dark interior the concrete floor was littered with broken glass and the rusted steel of the building's reinforcements showed through the grey like dirty bones. Snow drifted against the wire link fence of the tennis courts;

the weeds that had long since forced their way up through the tarmac were blanketed with it.

The pools were still there, even after all this time, a long oblong and a small, shallow, round pool for babies and children, in summer a dismal sight, overgrown with weeds and rye grass and filled with pine needles and litter. Inside the building the indoor pool yawned horribly, falling away like a landslip, like some cavernous burial chamber waiting to be filled. For fifteen years no one had been able to decide what to do with them, but this evening outside at least the shabby disgrace of their cracked and mildewed tiles was softened and obscured, like everything else, by the snow.

Behind the Olympia Club the decaying farmhouse where Cesare Bartolo had lived sat squat and dark and empty, its grounds overgrown and neglected. The perimeter wall seemed the only part of the property to which attention had been paid. Close on two metres high, originally of brick, it ran along the side of the quadrilateral that touched the outside world and had been patched and extended with concrete and misshapen stone and breeze blocks to seal every gap. It was surmounted with some rusty link fence and irregularly stuck with broken glass that could be seen protruding lethally even through the six inches of snow that had fallen since dusk. Beyond the wall was a strip of narrow pavement, a dead-end of a road, two sulphur-yellow streetlamps and across the way the Bartolos' nearest neighbour, a villa with striped awnings, trimmed hedge and shuttered windows.

Outside the neighbours' house a car was parked. Even from what was visible under the snow – a rear-end sagging so low it scraped the road, one headlight smashed and a deep, rusted dent in the offside wing – it seemed unlikely that this car belonged to the neat little house, which anyway had its own garage. It might have belonged to Cesare Bartolo, except that he had never learned to drive; his mother hadn't thought it a good idea.

The car was an Opel, perhaps fifteen years old and without the ghost of a chance of an MOT, the kind of car driven by those to whom the need for tax and insurance was theoretical only: a car for the lawless. It was an uncertain brown or bronze in the yellow light, and it had Modena plates.

This backwater of Galluzzo was very empty, and aside from the perpetual, unvarying roar of the motorway on its elevated section beyond the river, on this snowy night it possessed a kind of unnatural quiet. The neat rows of housing blocks beyond the Olympia Club turned away from the Bartolo house, and the families who lived there told their children not to go near it. They didn't all obey, of course; the girls tended to give it a wide berth, but boys on the verge of adolescence would loiter below the wall to throw stones, and they got on one another's backs and ripped the wire link fencing to peer inside. They scrawled graffiti on the crumbling render along the wall. *Pedofilo.* At the end of the wall where the word tailed away a man was leaning.

An overgrown lad in an expensive-looking waxed motor-bike jacket, his short hair spiked and gleaming with gel, he had the appearance of a petty criminal or market trader; there was something cocky about his stance, something too new about his jeans. He was eyeing up the car. Slowly he pushed himself off the wall, thrust his hands deep in his pockets and walked up to it, knelt down quickly and flicked the dusting of snow from the licence plate. He rocked back on his heels for a minute and nodded, then he took out a mobile phone and punched in the number. 'Dottore?' he said. 'Sandro? It's Fausto. I've found it.'

253

Looking up and down the street, the boy spoke into the phone for a few moments in a quick, businesslike way, describing the street, the dent in the car's wing, the missing fender, the numberplate. When he'd finished he paused, then said curiously, 'So I got there before the police's fancy computer, did I? What's it all about, Dottore? Not like you to call in favours.' There was no audible response and after a moment the overgrown boy shrugged. 'You're the boss,' he said. 'You coming over to check it out, then? But you watch yourself. They're not polite like us homegrown lads, Russians aren't.' He clicked the phone shut, walked to the end of the wall into the shadows, and vanished into the night. Job done.

The shops were still open but on the slushy pavements people were walking home, cheerful in the snow; it hardly ever snowed in Florence and although it had taken most of them by surprise and their feet were wet, the weather seemed to have lifted everyone's spirits. They walked arm in arm, making impromptu arrangements for a Saturday night meal, talking about what they'd do at Christmas. Up the warm, carpeted stairs in the honeymoon suite of the Regale, Emma Marsh still sat at the great square table in the centre of the ballroom-sized drawing room that surely must have been daunting for the most deliriously happy of honeymoon couples. Only two of them in all this space, their voices echoing hollow under the high ceilings. There was something about the room that said two was not enough, and the claustrophobia of romance hung like pollution in the air.

Emma must have left the table since Luisa closed the door behind her, because she was undressed, but it was as though she had started to perform some ritual of bathing and preparation but had not been able to continue. The dresses she had showed Luisa still hung, untouched, from the bedroom door; the red shoes sat bright and expectant on the rug where she had left them. Her heavy black hair fell to her pale, bare shoulders, and with one hand she held a towel tight across her breast; the other hand was pressed across her mouth. She was staring down at the newspaper, where the photograph of a small girl with a chipped front tooth smiled back at her against a backdrop of impossible, perpetual blue. Outside on the balcony Lucas stood in the snow and stared into the dark, no more than an outline against the lit red roofs of the city that rose and fell beyond him.

Outside the Palazzo Ferrigno, where light blazed from the huge, unshuttered windows into the street below, there was a ceaseless passage now of shoppers on their way home. But the brazier where they might have warmed their hands, which might have been expected to be enjoying brisk trade, had been shoved half into an alley, its coals grey and dead. A handful of chestnuts still sat on the perforated tray but they were dusty with ash and there was no one there to offer them to passers-by. Jonas had gone.

Celia had showered at least when the buzzer sounded; she glanced at the clock as she headed for the door, dripping and impatient at the interruption, and saw that it was six o'clock. With a sigh she picked up the entryphone. It struck her as ironic that she had spent months in lonely isolation here, seeing only clients, glimpsing Beate or Gabriele in the street without the time even to wave, and now that there were any number of people turning up on her doorstep she just wanted to be left alone. She didn't want to see Gabriele, or Dan, or Jo Starling, she just wanted to get through tonight. She wanted her part in Lucas and Emma Marsh's exotic, dangerous lives to be over. Just a few more hours, and she would be back here, Celia told herself, but she wondered. She understood that she had been drawn into something she didn't understand, a dark and tangled story, and she didn't know yet how it was going to end.

'Hello?' She spoke warily, uncharacteristically apprehensive. This was the effect, she realized, of coming up close to violent death; you realized that the well-lit comfort of your home was no more than an illusion of security. A child had been killed, a hole punched in a happy family. Someone might come to your door one night, and it would all be over.

The voice on the street below crackled, obscured by the wasp-whine of a passing *motorino*.

'Hello?' At first Celia recognized neither the voice nor the name and struggled with an impulse to hang up, to slide the bolts shut and refuse to answer. She repeated the name to herself in bemusement and then she understood: Luisa, from the shop. She could not imagine what the woman was doing here, she didn't have time for this, she wasn't even dressed; she felt her nerves jangle, impatience and panic combining. But out of an ineradicable reluctance to be rude, Celia wearily buzzed Luisa inside. She reached into the hall to turn on the stair light, and left the door ajar while she ran for a dressing gown.

Out of breath on her return, Celia pulled the door open and came face to face with Luisa at the top of the stairs, holding out a white paper carrier bag with the shop's name looped across it in silver. Dumbly she took it: *This is some kind of a delivery, then, or did I leave something in the shop?* Celia stepped back instinctively.

'Please,' she said, standing aside and gesturing to Luisa to enter. With the automatic '*Permesso?*' no Italian can cross a threshold without uttering, Luisa tentatively came inside. In the hall she pulled off a mitten, took Celia's hand and gave it a quick, half-embarrassed little shake; it was not an Italian gesture, and it took Celia by surprise. They went into the small sitting room and sat, the bag between them, on the neat, comfortable little sofa.

'So,' said Celia with an awkward little laugh. 'What's this?' She pulled the bag towards her, curious. Luisa watched her, slowly pulling a small backpack from her shoulders which she set beside her on the sofa.

'Mrs Marsh – she asked me to bring it to you.' She paused as if to reconsider, frowned a little as if an effort at scrupulous accuracy. 'In fact, she didn't say I had to bring it, I could have sent it over in a taxi, but I wanted – well. I needed some fresh air. Please.'

She gave the bag a little push and Celia set it upright, unpeeled the silver sticker that held it together, pulled out something folded in white paper. 'Oh,' she said, as the emerald-green tulle and silk unfurled in her hands, ribbons slithered cool across her knees and hung to the floor. She held it up. 'Oh! This.' She didn't know what to say; she felt ridiculously overwhelmed, brought to the point of tears by Emma Marsh's gesture. 'Oh.' Spontaneously she held it against her chest and a faint waft of the shop's smell rose from it. Luisa smiled, but the smile didn't reach as far as her eyes; her thoughts were elsewhere.

'I think she wanted you to wear it for this evening,' she said, shaking her head a little as though in wonder, or despair. 'Signora Marsh. She is – she's very young.' Celia looked up at the sadness in Luisa's voice, at the oddness of the words.

'Yes?' she said.

Luisa shrugged. 'You know, when you're young you think it can be that easy. Dress up, go out, forget all your troubles.' The thought seemed to make her sad.

Celia put down the dress; in some sense, they were in this together, she and Luisa, trying to understand clients. 'You've just come from the hotel,' she said. She hesitated. 'Can I ask you – what – how did they seem to you?' Luisa looked at her for a long moment without saying anything, then she spoke.

'Look,' she said. 'That man—' She broke off.

'Mr Marsh?' said Celia softly.

'He wasn't called that then,' said Luisa slowly. 'You're too young to remember. It was a long time ago.'

'I'd just arrived here,' said Celia, and she held Luisa's gaze. 'It's a bit more than fifteen years. His daughter had disappeared. Then they found her.'

'I think Mr Marsh is in a lot of trouble,' said Luisa. 'He might even be in danger, that's what my husband thinks.' And Celia thought of the day they'd had; she saw Lucas's face again as he fought for breath in the windowless space between the Medici library and its snowy cloister, and she nodded.

Luisa put a hand into the pocket of her padded coat and pulled out two sheets of paper, one stained with the marks of having been folded many times, one clean and smooth. Carefully she unfolded them and set them side by side in front of Celia.

'This is you?' she said. 'These are their plans?' Celia frowned down at the page and nodded. *Someone knows where we are*, she thought. *Knows where we're going.*

'Where did you get these?' she asked slowly, and she knew that the answer would not be simple.

'Let me tell you from the beginning,' said Luisa. 'Let me tell you about my husband.' She saw Celia glance anxiously at the clock. 'You have time, before you go.'

Luisa hadn't meant to say anything, she had intended to hand over the pretty green dress and leave. But when she held it out to Celia Donnelly on the threshold of her warm little flat, she realized there was nowhere to go except back outside into the cold. Nothing to do but walk and walk until she was exhausted, with all of this going round and round in her head. Then the girl had invited her inside, and the flat seemed so clean and bright and empty compared with her own great dark, suffocating mausoleum of a place that she'd sat down. And when Celia had looked at Luisa and asked, straight out, about Lucas and Emma Marsh, she understood that the poor child was involved with this too, she had to go back in there and get through an evening with them. She needed to know. And Luisa had laid it all out, everything Sandro had told her, everything that had happened all those years ago, everything that had happened since. The relief was so great she found herself speaking faster and faster, words tumbling over themselves in their eagerness to be spoken.

'It seems a mess,' Celia had said slowly, speaking carefully and precisely and, to Luisa's great relief, not hysterical, not doubting. 'It's not just your husband who's in trouble, though, is it? Lucas Marsh is, too. Do the police know he's here?'

Luisa had shaken her head. 'I don't think so. Only Sandro.'

'And the men he came to see, to pay off for . . . ' Celia had hesitated. 'For whatever – whatever they've done for him.'

Luisa had nodded, looking at the girl intently, watching her calculate, saw her conquer the incredulity she felt, as Luisa did, at the thought of being immersed in this alien world of hitmen and torturers. 'Except he didn't pay them. It's not the police he's running away from, hiding from.'

'No,' said Celia, and she put a hand to her mouth. 'They're going to want the money, aren't they? Your husband – Sandro – he knows that.' She was pale, her blue-green eyes dark against her English skin. 'And Lucas Marsh goes home tomorrow.' She looked down then at the tattered piece of paper in her lap that spelled it out; where to find him and when. Her photograph on it, too.

'Where did he get this?' She stared at the image of herself. 'Your husband?'

'I don't know,' said Luisa simply. The grimy paper looked sinister suddenly; Luisa wondered how many hands it might have passed through, and she was fearful.

They both fell silent then, and suddenly Luisa felt sure of something at last: it became clear to her what Sandro would be thinking.

'I think Sandro will be there,' she said simply. 'I think he'll be wherever Lucas Marsh is. Because he got him into this – this mess, and he has to get him out of it.'

'You've got to tell the police,' said Celia suddenly. 'Give them this.' She thrust the piece of paper back at Luisa as though it was dangerous, an unexploded bomb.

'Yes,' Luisa said slowly, taking the page. 'I know. I – I will tell them.' *But not yet.* She'd stood up then, to go, and Celia had got to her feet too, the dress in her hands. 'Thank you for coming,' she'd said distantly, and Luisa had wondered if she was in shock. 'I hope you find your husband.'

'Here's my number,' said Luisa, uneasy at leaving her like this, and she scribbled it on an old receipt from her pocket.

'And here's Sandro's. You know, in case.' Celia had just nodded absently, as though her thoughts were already somewhere else.

At the foot of Celia Donnelly's building Luisa stood on the snowy pavement and breathed in the crystalline air. Around her the city sounded different, muffled, slow, and briefly the fresh, cold smell of the snow took her back to her childhood, to a cleaner world. Across the street a solid, handsome man was standing beside a big, shiny dark car and smoking a cigarette in a meditative sort of way; he watched as she pulled the door shut behind her. Luisa recognized him, one of the city's drivers, chauffeur to the wealthy; he gave her a brief nod and she returned it.

Walking away, thinking hard, Luisa took out the mobile but it told her there was no signal; here in the tight warren of streets at the foot of the hill that led up to San Miniato there was too much stone, ancient and impenetrable, walling her in. She needed height, and not just for the mobile signal; she needed to be able to look around herself, to get a clear view. Luisa made for the great stone gate that stood in the city wall just across from Celia Donnelly's flat, its crenellations iced with snow against the inky night sky, and headed up the hill.

Doggedly Luisa climbed the Costa dei Magnoli, the Via Monte alle Croci, crossed the Viale Michelangelo where the cars hissed past in the slush; she didn't pause for breath until she had reached the church itself and then, with its cool pale green and white façade at her back she turned and looked. Below her the great city was spread out, glittering in the darkness; a full moon shone from a clear black sky, and the lovely floating dome of the cathedral gleamed with an unearthly luminosity under its dusting of snow. The sight lifted Luisa for a moment and she even found herself thinking, *I must do this more often*. And then she heard the distant sound of a siren wailing in the tangle of dark streets below her, and she felt a tightness in her chest like a stone. She took out the mobile and dialled Sandro's number again. *Answer*, she pleaded silently into the cold night air as she listened to the ring: mindless, mechanical, it sounded in virtual space, nowhere. Sandro was nowhere. But then she heard his voice.

'Where are you?' he said quickly.

'No,' said Luisa, catching her breath. 'Where are you?'

He wouldn't tell her. 'It's better if you don't know.' He paused, then started again. He sounded contrite, but determined. 'I tried the flat, when I heard your message, but you weren't there.' His voice was strained; *he's worn out*, thought Luisa. She imagined her husband's body, so strong once, running for fifteen years on anger and adrenaline; she realized she couldn't remember the last time he'd laughed, or even eaten properly.

'You've got to come back,' she said. 'We'll get through this.' She told him she'd talked to Pietro, what he'd said about the things they were saying at the station.

'I've got the car,' said Sandro, and his voice was flat; the sound of it chilled her. 'Look, I've screwed it up. Bartolo's dead, the father, Marsh, he's in a bigger mess than I am, getting himself involved with these bastards, that's all down to me, my responsibility.'

'No,' said Luisa with urgency. 'You did what you thought was right, they'll understand that. Pietro understands.' It was a lie; she made herself believe, though, that eventually he *would* understand. Sandro had to believe he could get back from this. '*I* understand. Even if there's a trial, even if,' she swallowed,

262

'even if you have to go to prison for it. It can be done. We can do it. You've got nothing to be ashamed of.'

There was a long silence and Luisa made herself focus on the background sounds she could hear down the line, trying to get a picture of where he was. She felt as though she was betraying him as she listened, but she forced the qualm aside. She could hear a lot of traffic noise, a steady stream of cars, one after the other, slush, the regular rumble of heavy-goods vehicles, too. Not in the city, then. Somewhere above the traffic noise behind Sandro a church bell began a monotone clang summoning the faithful to Saturday evening Mass, a light, tinny bell, perhaps even recorded as they sometimes were in new, suburban churches. It was nothing like the deep sonorous sound of the old bells that would ring below her any moment, in the ancient bell-tower of San Niccolò. Did she know that bell? Some modern church. But even as she listened they began, the two sounds merging, one here in the real world, one in whatever bleak place Sandro was inhabiting, and she gave up.

He paused. 'I've got to protect Marsh,' he said. 'That's all I can do now.'

'He's going home tomorrow,' said Luisa, pleading. 'Is he really in danger?'

There was a long silence, and when Sandro spoke his voice was deliberately brutal. 'In Livorno, just last week,' he said, 'they found a torso in a barrel, washed up on the beach. A rich Milanese who didn't pay his Russian dealer for his drugs on time, he thought they'd indulge him, he was busy at work. Two thousand euros, that's all, the price of a secondhand car, and they killed him. They left one of his hands – the one with the wedding ring – in a padded envelope on the doorstep for his wife to find.' Sandro never spoke like this to her, never told these stories. Luisa understood that the time to spare her such details was past.

He went on, softer now. 'I – I've had a call. I think I can get to him – to the man who was working for Marsh, the man who abducted Bartolo. His car's been found. Of all the places—' He broke off as though something had occurred to him, then started again. 'I don't know if it's the right thing to do any more. I could stake out the Regale, or wherever they're having dinner, but – but I'm going to go for the car. Maybe I can stop him before he can get to Marsh. Maybe I can stop all this.'

Luisa's first thought was, *At least he's not planning to kill himself.* Her second was, *He could get killed anyway*, and she couldn't stop herself interrupting him. 'Not on your own,' she blurted, begging without shame. 'Get – what d'you call it, get backup, just Pietro even, get them to help you, please. Just tell me where you are.' She'd lost her grip; she knew it was hopeless. 'They'll find you,' she whispered. 'They'll trace the mobile, the car, they'll be looking for it.'

'I've got to go now,' said Sandro softly, and he hung up. Alone in the dark, high above the city, Luisa pressed the dead phone to her lips and began to cry.

Chapter Twenty-Two

In the bathroom Celia held up the green dress against her and tried to remember who it was who had worn red petticoats to the scaffold. Charlotte Corday? Mary, Queen of Scots? She could remember the picture in some ancient children's encyclopedia, an engraving of a woman on the wooden platform with her chin in the air, head held high; no doubt the reality had been somewhat different. Could she do this?

Celia had been too long out of the shower before dressing, sitting there on the sofa in a dressing gown listening to Luisa, and she felt cold. In the bathroom mirror she saw her own pale outline, her arms thin, her eyes wide and shocked. She was frightened. She wondered if she could go through with it; for the first time in her professional life she desperately wanted to run away, to give up. It was Emma who made that impossible, of course; her bright impulsiveness, her faith in a pair of new shoes, a party, to make everything better. Wearily Celia knew she couldn't let her down. *She's so young*, Luisa had said.

Not much younger than me, actually, Celia realized with surprise; perhaps she should remember her age more often. What Luisa had said went around in her head, the message that Lucas was in danger, but the danger stubbornly refused to become real. She thought of the thick walls of the Palazzo Ferrigno, built to keep out assassins. She had to get going.

Turning her back on the mirror, Celia stepped into the dress and pulled it up around her, drew up the tiny concealed zip and tied the ribbons loose in the small of her back. She felt the perfect cut of it comfort and enclose her; the lovely sea-green of the skirt floated, luminous and demure, around her hips. She began, frowning, to search for her turquoise earrings, a dab of lipstick; she brushed her hair and tied it back. Her arms felt very bare, and she dug in her wardrobe, grateful for the impulse that had at last led her to unpack – it seemed like a lifetime ago but must only be three days, Thursday, her day off. She found a little black satin jacket of her mother's from some long-forgotten era, still sweet with ancient perfume, and slipped her arms into it. It was unreal, dressing up like this for a life that didn't belong to her; for a moment, as she realized the jacket fitted exactly, she had an image from childhood of her mother leaning down to kiss her before leaving for a party.

Suppressing her reluctance, Celia decided she was ready; she found the right shoes, pulled on her good coat and reached for the phone to dial a cab, only it rang before she could pick it up. Even before he spoke she knew it would be Gabriele. 'I'm outside,' he said. 'You need a lift.'

'Hey,' he said, staring at her as she tucked her dress inside the car. 'You look—' He seemed lost for words, self-conscious;

she could smell the tobacco on his breath but she surprised herself by liking it.

'What?' she said, pulling her coat around herself. 'You're making me nervous now.'

Gabriele smiled then, his easy smile. 'You look gorgeous, that's all,' he said mildly.

Celia felt her cheeks burn, remembering the kiss, and looked out of the window into the dark. They drove in silence for a while, the traffic moving more freely now that the snow had stopped and the snowploughs had been round. But as they glided over the river abruptly Gabriele said, 'I saw your ex this evening.'

Celia stared at him. 'Who – you mean Dan?' Gabriele nodded.

'Do you know him?'

'Of course,' said Gabriele coolly. 'I told you, I know everyone.' Celia felt uneasy, wondering when he'd seen Dan, if he'd seen them together, and she felt, really, that this was ridiculous. Were they spying on her, the two of them? Was this what another relationship had to involve, all this hiding in corners, misunderstandings and jealous insinuations?

Gabriele went on, apparently oblivious to her body language, her knuckles white as she held the coat together across her exposed neckline and her white shoulders. 'I was just having a drink, not far from here actually, little place down there.' He nodded towards the bridge. She knew the bar he meant, a smoky little subterranean place that was always crowded with drivers and shopgirls and local tradesmen, where they turned to look at foreigners if they came in. Gabriele talked on as he drove, looking ahead, indicating, monitoring the street as he spoke. 'Anyway, I came out and I saw him under the streetlight, that's how I recognized him, the light was shining right down on him. Anyway, he was talking to this old girl on the corner, I thought she was – you know—' He darted a glance at Celia, then went on, 'On the game.' He paused, musing, 'But when I got up close she looked terrible, half her hair looked like it had been pulled out and a cheek-bone all caved in. Maybe he was, what d'you call it, doing research. Likes a walk on the wild side, does he?'

'Look, Gabriele,' said Celia suddenly, 'I don't know what you're getting at, and I don't want to know. Dan's nothing to do with you, is he? Or me, come to that, who he talks to, who he meets, it's none of your business.' Her voice sounded tougher than she had intended.

'I didn't—' Gabriele's eyes darted away and she knew she'd nailed him: this was about Dan, this was some roundabout way of doing him down. 'Look,' he said, sounding cornered, 'I know that girl. Anorexic prostitute works out in Galluzzo, not far from where I live. Giusi, Giuli, something like that. Do you really want anything to do with a man who sees whores?' He pulled up at the Palazzo Ferrigno. 'It's all right,' he said, turning towards her earnestly. 'Don't you see? I want to make sure you're all right.'

'I don't need it,' she said angrily. 'I can look after myself. Just – just – don't. Just don't.' Exasperated, she jerked the door open and climbed out on to the slushy pavement, in too much of a hurry to think about doing it elegantly. A paving stone tipped under her foot, soaking her leg with icy water. 'Thanks for the lift,' she said irritably, but Gabriele said nothing. She tried again. 'I'm sorry,' she said, but she knew she didn't sound it, didn't feel it, her voice still uneven with frustration. Slowly Gabriele leaned across and pulled the door shut. At her back Celia felt a figure standing in the arched gateway of the Ferrigno take a step towards her but she didn't turn to go in. She just stood there and watched with a feeling of helpless regret as the car pulled away and her own words rang ridiculously in her ears. *I can look after myself.* Her heart dipping, she supposed that now she was going to have to find out if that was true.

When they'd built the housing project down by the river in Galluzzo they'd made sure, it being a key problem in the city centre, that there was plenty of space for cars, and a neat, marked-up parking lot ran the whole length of the place. Sandro pulled in between a Mercedes and a van, both taller vehicles than his, and he was careful so as not to dislodge the burden of snow on his little car's roof that so neatly disguised it. He turned to look back at it; the little Fiat had settled in so well it might have been there all week. Sandro knew it would all end soon, they'd trace the car or the phone, but it mustn't happen yet.

Turning away from the car, Sandro walked across the snow with his hood pulled up; he paused outside the Olympia Club's gates, gauging the place with a policeman's eye. He could see where some of the corrugated iron sealing the lower windows had been prised up; it might have been done by kids, or vagrants, or travellers. There weren't many of those around here, though. He walked on, to his real destination; he could have taken a short cut by vaulting the fence around the Olympia Club, crossing the tennis courts and finding that gap in the link fence on the other side, but he didn't.

He had to go back to the main road; there was no pavement for the hundred metres back towards the city that he had to cover and the trucks roared past him, soaking his legs to the thigh with salted slush. Then there was a sharp, narrow turn down the dead-end that led to Bartolo's place and Sandro turned down it without hesitation; if he felt any quickening of the heart rate as he approached the farmhouse there was little external evidence of it. He did put one hand deep into a pocket as though he was checking something, and the hand stayed there, but otherwise he trudged steadily onwards until he rounded the crumbling, defaced wall and then he stopped. The dead-end ahead of him was empty and silent and the snow covering it glittered yellow in the streetlight, virgin except for a line of footprints that ran ahead of Sandro's own. Footprints he found himself following until he reached the railings that fronted a neat villa opposite Bartolo's place, where a dark, wet rectangle of tarmac marked where a car had stood. The car itself had gone.

From her window as she waited for the evening's guests to arrive Paola Caprese saw the dark Mercedes draw up below and the girl step out; she leaned forward to watch – something about the scene drew her attention. She caught the driver's profile as he moved off and she recognized him – she knew quite a number of the drivers, and he was handsome. The girl stood there in the snow, watching him go, and Paola felt sorry for her.

Around her the palace ticked into silence, the wood settling; the place was almost empty. It was a fine balancing act, staffing this place, you couldn't carry dead wood, and the guests wouldn't know, would they, that they were drinking champagne in a ghost ship, a *Marie Celeste* of a place.

Celia stood in the foyer and waited; she looked at her watch and saw that it was two minutes past seven. The concierge had come out from behind his glass screen – where he had, she saw, been watching the football on a tiny portable television – to inspect her as she stood in the great arched gateway. *So much for security*, was the thought that pricked her as she watched the concierge approach; he looked dozy, indifferent. He had not said, when she told him why she was here, whether the Marshes had arrived yet, and she assumed that they had not; the atmosphere of the place seemed too still and calm, as yet unruffled by the drama they seemed to carry with them. The concierge had ushered her in here and she was glad at least to be out of the icy, wet air; he returned to his post where she saw him dialling a number on an elderly Bakelite telephone.

Celia felt cold suddenly in the great empty room, although it was warm, and she walked to the wide glass doors. Looking into the arched gateway, she saw the concierge in his gate-house on her left, intent now on the tiny, coloured figures of the football players against their electric green background, moving ceaselessly to and fro. Then, as she watched, a shaven-headed man walked in from the street, rounding the corner easily, with confidence; he wore a long brown workman's overall, buttoned like a coat, with his hands deep in the pockets. As he passed the concierge he nodded through the little glass window, but the concierge wasn't looking and the workman didn't break step, just walked on past.

He made straight for a small wooden door in the wall beside the gatehouse that Celia hadn't noticed before; it looked to her now like a service entrance of some kind. He reached for the handle, but it didn't open; apparently it had been locked. The man turned away immediately, didn't pause to rattle the handle or knock, and in retrospect that was the first false note his presence there struck. He headed straight for Celia; startled, she took a step back and he pushed through the glass door and past her. She only had time to record a vivid impression of bloodshot, pale blue eyes, a roughened complexion, but he came so close she could smell the cheap tobacco on his breath. She saw the glitter of an earring, a sharp quarter-profile, and for a fraction of a second she wondered, *Have I seen him before?* A gust of cold air came in with him from the snowy street; as the glass door swung shut behind him one of the wood-panelled doors inside the room creaked ajar, but by the time Celia turned for another look he was through it and gone.

There was something about the little scene – not even a scene, it had lasted half a minute and what had happened? A workman had entered the building – that seemed wrong to Celia. What was it? Perhaps the silence; an Italian would certainly have made some kind of greeting, the language was loaded with such tokens of courtesy, *pregho, permesso, salve*. But she had an idea from his complexion, his light eyes, that the man hadn't been Italian. Perhaps it was the fact that he disappeared so fast that left her feeling she could have imagined the whole thing, even down to the cigarettes on his breath. But then the door through which he had disappeared swung open and the administrator Paola Caprese came in.

She inclined her head a little stiffly and held out her hand; Celia felt the woman's gaze take in everything from the bare hand she offered in return – she'd forgotten her gloves in the rush – to the quality of her coat's lining as it fell open, and she felt a weariness in this perpetual need to be presentable in Italy. But as she took the woman's limp hand she saw that there was something a little distracted about her; she wondered if she had bumped into the brown-coated workman and had had to reprimand him for an unauthorized cigarette break.

'There was a man,' she said suddenly, 'a workman, he just came in—' She broke off, not sure what to say.

'Yes?' Paola Caprese frowned at her.

'He – well. There was something not quite right about him. He was rather – he was rude.' It sounded lame, but for a fraction of a second Paola Caprese looked uncertain. Then she bristled, taking offence. 'Well, really,' she said. 'We do have workmen, yes, we don't send them to finishing school. Is that what they do in England?' And she laughed stiffly. Celia flushed, reprimanded.

Caprese looked down at her watch, changing the subject. 'Are you early?' she asked. 'No. You are not. But where are your – your clients? Our clients?'

'It's only five past,' said Celia quickly, on the defensive. Why hadn't she insisted she should arrange transport? They might be anywhere; for a brief, mad moment she succumbed to the ridiculous fears that had been pressing in on her since she found out who Lucas Marsh really was and pictured them lost, hijacked, dead. She forced the picture out of her mind: *They're just five minutes late.* She smiled as brightly as she could manage at Paola Caprese. 'I'm sorry. Is there some leeway, with the timing of the dinner? Ten minutes here or there?'

'Of course,' said Paola Caprese, but she sounded faintly disgusted, and Celia was surprised. In her experience of the very wealthy, and she imagined Paola Caprese's wasn't very different, they weren't unduly disturbed by punctuality. Part of the job was standing around waiting for the client, wasn't it? Suppressing any feelings of irritation at time wasted, rising above the small humiliation of it. *That's all it is,* she told herself again, *they've no conception of the time, it's our job to wait for them.* 'I'm sorry,' she said, and turned away from

273

Paola Caprese to look out through the glass, willing them to arrive.

In the concierge's booth the television screen still flickered; she could see a row of smaller, CCTV screens ranged on the wall above the portable, but even if the man's attention hadn't been elsewhere only one of them seemed to be functioning. The grainy black and white image of a broad, galleried landing showed no movement. Celia turned to Paola Caprese on impulse, remembering that Marsh had asked not once but twice about the security of the Palazzo Ferrigno. *Of course it's safe here*, she told herself robustly, *with a vanload of carabinieri just two minutes' walk away outside the British Consulate, police cars wailing past every five minutes, a thousand witnesses in the streets.* But all the same, what might Lucas Marsh say when he saw the concierge with his feet up on his desk? She had done no more than make eye contact with the administrator, though, she hadn't even opened her mouth to articulate her misgiving and it was already too late. They were here.

Jonas didn't even think, *That was close*, as he pushed open the door of the small cupboard at the foot of the service staircase and closed it behind him on the industrial vacuum cleaner, the brooms and mop bucket and ten different kinds of feather duster among which he had stood, as effortlessly still as marble, and waited for the steps to fade away. He had the perfect poise and certainty of a genius, a brain surgeon, a master criminal. The confidence of a fixed-up heroin addict. He listened on the stairs and it seemed to him he could hear everything, every creak and whisper in the building, and he thought, four, maybe five people, in a thousand square metres of corridors and salons and ballrooms. And, of course, he'd counted them

274

in and counted them out, he'd watched them trudge home out of the gatehouse in the snow, there was no substitute for thorough preparation.

In Jonas's pocket was the stubby knife he'd pressed against Giulietta's throat, a throat as stringy as a plucked chicken's. *Leave me alone.* She'd leave him alone now, that was for sure. He wasn't her knight in shining armour any more. Jonas moved his head slowly from side to side, trying to get her face out of his mind because it was spoiling things. The sharp bones of her jaw, deep, bruised eye sockets, her skin grey as a starved child's. Her forearms furred with fine hair, like an animal, like something feral; it gave him the creeps. She'd been useful to them at first, sitting there in a booth in the bar while he bought her sweet drinks, apricot nectar, amaretto, she'd told Jonas all her secrets once he'd put an arm around her waist and whispered promises in her ear. *Yes, he did this, he did that, I saw him. He called to the little girl, and she went to him. He saw me watching.* Shame the police didn't try that fifteen years ago when they were interviewing her, although you never knew, she might have turned on them. She might have bitten.

But she'd got Bartolo out of the house where she told them he kept the doors triple-locked, with homemade booby traps at the doors, sticks whittled to a point, buckets of slurry to trip intruders. She lured him out to Le Cascine for them, which had been very useful; Jonas didn't know what she'd said to get him there. Blackmail? She wasn't Bartolo's type any more, after all, although she could hardly be called a grown woman either, more an assembly of bones and string, titless, an ugly doll. She'd spoken to Bartolo in a little girl's voice that had made Jonas sick. How was he to know they'd never be able to get rid of her, afterwards?

On the stairs Jonas paused for a moment and breathed deeply, in and out, imagining all the stone and wood around him, a maze, or a tomb. *She's gone now, isn't she? I taught her a lesson.* A rich smell of cooking food came up from somewhere down below him. Venison, wild boar, pasta; with vague disgust he imagined an oily stew of vegetables and herbs. It slowed you down, all that food; Jonas didn't have time for food, but let them stupefy themselves with it, all the better. He moved on up the cramped stairwell; *You're mine, now*, he thought, addressing the great house. He felt like a king.

Chapter Twenty-Three

She sat there for a long time in the dark. There was a long stone bench under the trees along the busy ring road and she sat down and gazed out over the cold, glittering city. Lights were strung across its breadth like diamonds, except out to the east, where Le Cascine lay in darkness, absorbing light, giving out none. At first her thoughts were dull and aimless: only misery and a sense that her life was over.

Gradually it dawned on Luisa that the last time she had felt like this was when she'd been twenty, and Sandro hadn't called her after their first date; sitting there, Luisa made a little derisive sound when she realized. *He hung up on you. Poor little thing.* And although all she wanted was simply to fall asleep in the cold and not wake up, suddenly she couldn't. It niggled at her like a stone in her shoe. It scolded her like a mother for never having grown up. As though she was in her own bed at home and trying to sleep, those odd, tangential, obscure thoughts found their way into the counting of sheep and roused her. The insistent sound of recorded church bells, trucks thundering through slush. Luisa sat up. She knew that tinny peal of bells, the ugly spire of a modern church just off the Via Senese. Galluzzo. What had Sandro said, before he interrupted himself? *Of all the places.* He was out in Galluzzo, where the swimming pool had been, what was it called? The Olympia Club. Where the child had disappeared; where Bartolo lived. *Of all the places.*

The bus lurched and swung, agonizingly slow; a man's heavy body pressed against her shoulder and at every stop Luisa fought the desire to jump up and push through the crowded gangway until she found herself out in the cold air. She gripped the pole more tightly and with her spare hand groped for the rucksack on her back. Through the nylon she felt the compact wad of banknotes rolled tight in their thick elastic bands and felt oddly unmoved by the thought that she was a thief, after a lifetime's honest loyalty to her employer. If Sandro needed the money, if he needed to get away. They could go together. Luisa almost smiled. *Start a new life on one day's takings? Hardly.* She realized she didn't care about the money, it was just money; it was a sign. A sign that Sandro was more important.

Outside the windows the houses thinned as they reached the edge of the city. They passed the orchards of Impruneta, a row of gas stations planted along the main road, a yard full of terracotta pots under the snow. The bus swayed along in the dark, all lit up inside, its cargo of passengers blank-faced in expectation of their arrival home. Luisa looked out of the window and saw that they were nearly there. The river appeared on the right, winding up to the road and then veering away to where it passed behind Bartolo's farmhouse and the Olympia Club. She stood up.

As she watched the lit bus move away from her in the darkness Luisa felt a moment of panic. She was standing on a verge covered in dirty slush under a row of tall, leafless trees, their load of snow dripping silently in the dark. The nearest streetlight was a couple of hundred metres away, there was no pavement, and as she stood and wondered what to do next a truck came past so close she could have touched it, then another. She turned and listened to the rhythmic blare as each one passed and receded, the hiss of tyres.

Had he been here? Had Sandro been standing here? Luisa circled to get her bearings, waiting for her eyes to adjust to the dark. Opposite her there was a bar, closed up for the season, and behind it a straggle of houses up the slope; as she got used to the dark she saw the uplit outline of the modern church spire beyond them. It was ugly, too narrow, too pointed. To her right the road led back to a snarl of motorway junctions she knew well, the roads to Siena and Rome, and to her right, where the street-lamp shed its yellow light, stood an arrangement of apartment blocks, on the edge of the darkness. She stopped and looked. *There*, she thought.

It was better once she was moving; as she trudged along the verge Luisa was able to subdue the dread that lay like a stone in her stomach. She turned down the well-lit access road and looked up briefly at the apartment blocks; she saw the silhouette of a woman at a sink, or a stove. She supposed it was suppertime and felt a moment's longing to be in a warm kitchen herself, laying a table. Sandro reading the evening paper. What had once seemed like dull reality seemed an impossible fantasy now, that scene she had taken for granted all her married life.

Along the foot of the nearest apartment block cars were

parked neatly; on her right, in the dark, was a new car park for the overspill, and beyond it the dark. That was where he was, somewhere in there. She turned across the car lot; *I can't do it*, she thought, as the shape of the Olympia Club's high circular bar took shape in the shadows, its smashed windows blank and sinister. She faltered in the yellow half-light and leaned for support on the nearest car, a little Fiat wedged between two taller vehicles; her face felt clammy and she pulled off a glove and put her palm to her cheek.

What if he's not here? What if he was here, but he's gone back to wherever Lucas Marsh is, and I'm out here in the dark, on my own? The glove slipped from her hand and she bent to retrieve it; straightening, she registered the car's dented front bumper with the chrome pitted and flaking, the colour, battleship grey, which was once the colour of almost all these little cars. The colour of their car, Sandro's and hers. She squinted at the licence plate of the car and there it was, confirmation that she had been right after all. He was here.

Beyond the cars where the narrow access road led to the old pool complex it was dark, a dense blackness full of half-decipherable shapes; the snow-covered ground gave off an unearthly, low-level gleam of white. Where was the moon? Luisa stumbled on through the snow towards the sullen, looming shape of the Olympia; beyond it she heard the constant hum of traffic on the motorway behind its screen of trees. The road surface had been poorly maintained and the soft blanket of snow concealed potholes and stones; at the edge of the complex Luisa turned her ankle on one and let out an exclamation. Her voice was loud in the darkness and she stopped, her hand on the fence around the Olympia. It occurred to her that if Sandro was here, then whoever it was he was looking

280

for might be here too. Could they hear her? Beyond the fence there was no sound.

Luisa felt in her pocket; she wanted to take out the little mobile and call Sandro, she needed to hear his voice. She took out the phone. But what if he was watching someone, and the phone rang in his pocket? She'd be responsible. Luisa put the phone away and took hold of the cold iron of the railings, scanning the dark on the other side. The house must be there, somewhere. Luisa closed her eyes and told herself, in the daylight this is just a patch of abandoned ground; she peopled it, imagined buildings, trees, the Olympia's tennis courts. But when she opened her eyes the dark was still there, dense and alive, and what it contained was still hidden from her. Somewhere in there, whatever had happened here one scalding long-ago August was still hanging in the air. Between here and Bartolo's house and the river where her body was found, somewhere in this triangle a child's life was ended, seven years old. And suddenly it seemed to Luisa that there was nothing for her to be afraid of, by comparison.

Behind a door in the dark Jonas listened to doors closing and opening as they moved through the building. He'd heard them pass him on the landing, and even felt the displacement of air, but he heard no laughter, nor even what you'd call conversation. *Not much of a party, this*, he thought with grim satisfaction. Jonas didn't care about grief, or loss; these things happened routinely where he came from. Here they lived under the dangerous illusion their money and their police and their hospitals bought, that the world was a safe place and that their children could be protected, and so when it happens they're not ready. When what they call evil sees its chance and jumps out from the dark to take away the thing they love they're not prepared. But in the end it's so easy to kill. It only takes a moment, a gunshot, a well-placed punch, cancer, and it's all over. *They'd do well to understand that.* In his pocket he turned the knife over, and the feel of the knotted surface of its handle in his palm comforted him.

For a split second as Celia had stared out through the glass into the gateway she thought that Emma hadn't come. There stood Lucas Marsh, pale and impeccable in a dinner suit as far removed from a cheap hire outfit as a Titian was from a greetings card. He stood very erect, as though he was bracing himself against something, and to Celia as she pushed her way through the glass door to greet them, he seemed dazed. Then Lucas looked over his shoulder and she appeared beside him, and for a ridiculous moment Celia stopped short, imagining that he had had to find a substitute, this wasn't Emma. But of course it was.

Dressed in a close-fitting black dress with long sleeves, her gleaming hair coiled tight at the nape of her neck, Emma looked older but if anything more beautiful for it, the bones of her face more refined. She wasn't smiling: *Is that it?* thought Celia, realizing that since their first meeting, even when things had gone wrong and her expression had clouded, the smile would return, sooner or later, her fallback position. That ability seemed to have deserted her now, and with it some kind of innocence, and Celia knew that Lucas must have told her.

'I'm sorry,' Emma had said, holding out a hand to Paola Caprese. 'We're a bit late.' She smiled now, but it was nothing more than a reflex, and her eyes were somewhere else. A girl in a white lace apron materialized at the foot of the great staircase and took their coats off somewhere behind it. As Emma removed hers Celia saw that her pregnancy was clearly outlined by the smooth line of the long black dress, and to Celia it appeared vulnerable and exposed. As she took off her own coat she remembered what she was wearing with a flush of self-consciousness, and who had given it to her. Emma was looking at her with a frown as though she was trying to remember something herself.

'Oh – you, I'm sorry, I should have said before – thank you,' Celia said, faltering. She started again, looking down at the green tulle, and pulling the thin satin of her mother's jacket around her. 'You really shouldn't have.' It sounded formal and ungracious, and impulsively she put her arms around Emma. 'It's lovely. It's a dream.'

'Oh, the dress,' said Emma, and she sounded forlorn suddenly. 'You looked so pretty in it, didn't you? I just thought – it was going to be such a party. Anyway.' She turned away. 'Let's get on with it, shall we?' She spoke brightly to Lucas but to Celia she still sounded lost. And briskly Paola Caprese had led them across the baronial hall to the great staircase, and their last evening together, it seemed, had begun.

They paused on the magnificent landing, under a cupola that gave on to the black night sky. It was warm inside, a luxurious tide of heat rolling out from great iron radiators, but the palace seemed very quiet and they saw no one as they walked on past doors open on to dark and empty staterooms. They turned into the ante-room Celia remembered, between the dining room and the terrace; she looked through the long windows and saw that outside drifts of snow had been cleared away and the braziers lit. There was a tray of something on a table, glasses and a wine bucket; beside it long wax tapers were guttering in an evening gust and beyond them, across the river, rose the dark silhouette of the Strozzi Gardens. For a moment, looking at the flickering light on the stuccoed walls and considering the silent, secret agency of servants that populated the building, Celia felt as though she had walked into a gothic fairytale, something lovely and full of menace. But there'd been nothing beautiful about stories Luisa and Dan had told her, they'd been about a real child with a name and a mother and father, a little girl they'd let out of their sight for a moment and had only been returned to them broken and dead. This was real, and it wasn't over yet; somehow Lucas and Emma had to get through it.

Beside her Emma stopped at the window and looked, too, her hand up at the glass.

'How pretty,' she said, her voice light and unsteady.

Paola Caprese turned to consider Emma, and it was as though she was seeing her for the first time. Emma looked right here in this mysterious palace, thought Celia, she was the virgin bride, the beautiful serving girl turned princess. It was Lucas who looked out of place in this story as he stood stiffly beside his wife but, it seemed, didn't dare to touch her. He appeared exhausted; his face was very white and even his lips seemed bloodless, almost bluish.

Paola Caprese's gaze settled on Emma's belly but her face remained impassive. *Does she have children?* Celia thought that perhaps pregnancy became less extraordinary once you'd been through it; for herself, she could not help a stir of envy at the thought of the cells multiplying like magic, behind that firm curve of flesh. Whatever it was the administrator was wondering, she suppressed it, because all she said was, 'Perhaps a drink first? Really it is too cold, but you are English ...' When this

284

heavy attempt at familiarity drew no response, she changed course swiftly and began to talk to Lucas about the statuary outside as she pushed open the long doors.

The cold braced them as the door opened, fresh and sharp and clean. Celia turned to Emma, almost laughing with the shock of it in her thin satin jacket, the ridiculous flounce of the tulle hardly warmer than a slip, but when she saw Emma's face the laughter evaporated.

'In the nineteenth century, this wing was added,' Paola Caprese was saying as she turned to indicate the façade of huge arched windows opposite the dining suite, and Celia knew she should be joining in. But Emma took hold of her elbow and steered her away towards the table where the wine had been poured; the administrator's head turned slightly to follow them, and Celia could sense the curiosity in the woman's gaze, but she kept up her commentary to Lucas. He just stood there, passive and silent, as though paralysed in the face of some terrible catastrophe, but the administrator seemed not to notice.

Emma picked up two glasses of champagne, handed one to Celia and took a reckless gulp from hers. A strand of her hair had come loose from the tight black knot and it blew across her white face; she looked beautiful and wild, like a Fury, out for revenge. She drained the glass.

'What am I doing here?' she said suddenly. She swept a hand around the balustrade, the lovely, crumbling statues along the edge of the terrace, the glowing interior of the building behind the tall windows. 'I don't belong here.'

'Come on,' said Celia, as robustly as she could. 'You appreciate beauty. It's the first thing you said to me, that you liked beautiful things. That's all you need to belong here.' But she knew that wasn't exactly what Emma meant; she didn't even know any more if it was true, either. You had to take the whole package, not just the pretty hills and the paintings; you had to take the bad drains, and the larceny, and the fast-food cartons in the gutter, a city despoiled by tourism, overrun by strangers, angry.

Celia turned away a little and gazed out at the dark hills across the river with the empty glass to her lips. They stood there side by side in silence for a long moment, the sound of Paola Caprese's voice indistinct but persistent in the background as she went on talking to Lucas. Then Emma spoke again.

'He's been lying to me,' she said, unflinching. Celia looked down, ashamed; she couldn't pretend she didn't know. 'I see,' said Emma. 'Does everyone in this city know, but me? Does she?' She nodded towards Paola, whose back was turned to them.

'No,' said Celia, desperate. 'Of course not. I didn't know, either, not until this evening. I – yes, there are people here who remember, him. People who were involved. I don't think ... the only person who has kept it from you deliberately is Lucas. He – he must have his reasons.'

Without a word Emma turned away and Celia could only see her profile, head held high on her long, white neck as she stared out into the darkness. 'My father had another family,' she said suddenly, her voice sharp and clear and angry. 'He was a bigamist. He kept them secret, the others. Three children.' She turned to face Celia. 'My mother stayed in bed for two years after she found out, and he left. Before, she was the most beautiful woman you ever saw, clever and funny, she could paint—' Then she stopped. Started again. 'I chose Lucas because he was the opposite of my father. Completely straight,

286

not a conman like my father, not someone who'd tell the lie he thought you wanted to hear. That was what I thought.'

'And now?' Celia didn't dare say any more.

Emma's eyes glittered in the light of the flare. 'I won't put up with it,' she said. 'I won't be lied to.' Her voice rose, and now both Paola Caprese and Lucas had turned towards them. 'Why did he bring me here? I was just in the way. An inconvenience.'

It was unbearable, inexcusable; Emma was right. But at the same time Celia could see what Emma was too angry to see, that Lucas Marsh had had no time to spare, no emotion, for anything except finding the truth; he'd started on a path he couldn't change, not even for Emma. She'd opened the envelope she shouldn't have seen, taken out a ticket to Florence, and he hadn't paused, he'd swept her up with him and carried her along.

Paola Caprese bustled over then, getting between them. 'It's too cold,' she said, looking narrowly at them, sensing trouble. 'Let's go inside.'

The table was laid with candles and silver and some fine old porcelain with hints here and there of faded gold and painted flowers. As they shuffled into the room Celia felt a tiny lift at the thought of seeing the painting again; this, at least, couldn't go wrong, this could only seduce the Marshes, might even bring them round, she told herself. It was only as they approached it – it was much smaller than she remembered, and Paola Caprese brought them up close – that she remembered the story behind the picture and felt a misgiving that stirred and grew.

As Celia took another step forward and the picture came into view, the feeling that this could only go badly could no longer be ignored. This was what had been nagging at her, wasn't it, since she first saw Emma Marsh. The *Madonna of the Lilies*. This, too, was what Paola Caprese saw when a moment ago she had studied Emma with that look of bemused recognition. The perfect white oval of the Madonna's face, the red lips, the black hair shiny as liquorice and even bound at the nape. The Titian in the Uffizi had had similarities but this was striking; the *Madonna of the Lilies* was just like Emma, she had the tenderness, the vulnerability, the longing as well as the voluptuous beauty. It seemed to stir something up in Emma and a flush appeared in her cheeks. She said nothing.

Paola Caprese began to speak and what she said was innocuous at first, pointing out the symbolism of the myrtle and the lilies, and Celia thought for a moment of false hope that she would leave the story of the real-life model out. She must have noticed Emma's pregnancy and out of consideration would at least not mention the death of the child the Madonna was holding so tenderly on her lap. But diligently, inexorably Paola Caprese fulfilled her duty, and with increasing desperation Celia tried to think of a way of deflecting her; for a mad moment she thought Caprese must be doing this on purpose, out of some long-nurtured grudge against foreigners.

It was as she drew to a conclusion, though, that Celia understood that it was all just some awful coincidence. In latter years, said Paola Caprese, pleased with having marshalled all the facts and even some interesting anecdotes into the bargain, the *Madonna of the Lilies* had become the patroness of lost children. Prayers were said to her postcard image when children went missing; flowers were even occasionally laid at the palace's door. With satisfaction she turned to her small audience, expecting acknowledgement, but for a moment no one said anything.

Paola Caprese couldn't have known who she was talking to, couldn't have known Lucas Marsh had lost a child. But as Celia looked at his white face she couldn't help but be aware that she, Celia, *did* know, though, she knew what Lucas had gone through, and had no right to. One look at her face and Lucas, like Emma, would see through her. She felt hot shame at being an unwilling voyeur of their grief; she wanted to run away but some awful sense of duty restrained her. And then she looked at Emma. She was gazing at the picture, her blue eyes curious.

'She looks like me,' she said quietly. 'Isn't that funny?' She turned to Lucas. 'Did you know?'

'I didn't know,' said Lucas, and he sounded broken. 'I've never seen her before. I knew she'd be beautiful.'

And they stood there, Paola Caprese with her back to the Titian as though to shield it, while Emma stared at her husband. Celia saw everything in the look she gave him: saw her anger at being lied to, her unhappiness at not being trusted, her disillusionment as her marriage, all those intimate things that she thought tied her to Lucas, began to dissolve. It wasn't, after all, simply a sin of omission born out of a desire to protect Emma, like a child, from something unpleasant: this awful thing had eaten away at him for fifteen years. He had had a daughter, and he had hidden her away.

For a moment too Celia saw Emma panic, a girl who had fought and worked for what she had and realized the dream was ended; she wondered for a second if Emma was going to turn and run. But she stood her ground.

'Could I have a moment?' Emma spoke quietly, staring at Lucas. He stood there, mute and blank, he didn't protest, but he didn't move, either. Celia thought he might be suffering

289

some kind of shock reaction, and she felt a shadow of anxiety. 'Please. I'll see you in a minute, Lucas.' Emma was polite, but there was no room for argument.

'Come on,' said Celia, and gently she took Lucas by the elbow. 'A breath of fresh air.' At the door she looked back and saw that neither Emma nor Paola Caprese had moved. They stood beside the painting as though it held them there, a life-line, or a millstone, or the answer to something.

Chapter Twenty-Four

The emergency room of Florence's dilapidated central hospital, Santa Maria Nuova, was in chaos. There had already been twelve road traffic accidents since the snow began to fall – most of them minor, two involving fatalities – and although the critical cases had been sent over to the big modern trauma centre on the northern edge of the city the waiting room was full of the non-urgent. The plastic chairs were all occupied by the walking wounded awaiting treatment for mild concussion and lacerations from coming off *motorini*; half a dozen befuddled elderly folk had cracked ribs and broken wrists after going over on the ice. If only they knew, thought the staff nurse, that at their age a broken wrist or a dislocated hip could be the end of them, what with the bed sores, the dehydration and the depression. It's not what you imagine, when you're young, she often thought, that you could be so easily finished off.

There was one, though, sitting behind the curtain at the end of the observation ward and awaiting specialist assessment, whose injuries could not, in the opinion of the staff nurse, be put down to a slip on an icy pavement. The smashed cheekbone, the broken nose and the two ripening black eyes might, at a pinch, have been sustained coming off a *motorino*, but not the rest. The deep lacerations on each cheek, ragged but symmetrical, had been put there by a human hand, they were signs, they were a punishment. There was worse, too; this woman hadn't been right for years. As she passed back down the ward towards the drawn curtain a weak, quavering voice called her: 'Nurse, nurse.' An old man's thin white arm held up a bottle to be emptied: *Not my job*, she thought, but she took pity and turned back.

She emptied the bottle, put it in for sterilizing, scrubbed her wrists and forearms. She was surprised, even with her experience, how much punishment the human body – some human bodies – could take before they gave up. They'd undressed the woman, a body yellow and sunken with hepatitis and malnutrition; you couldn't help wondering what she was holding on for. You didn't put your body through all that if you loved life. It was hard to tell how old she was, somewhere between forty and seventy, but certainly younger than she looked. An anorexic since puberty, perhaps even earlier, would have been the nurse's assessment; these days you saw enough of them to be able to make a judgement. A modern plague, half the population obese, and others, it used to be just girls but now you saw grown women too, terrified of food. A drugtaker into the bargain, probably; her arms, no more than bones strung with veins, were bruised and scarred, but that might be self-harm. Who knew where these things began? A word, a touch. Abuse. The psychological evaluation she was waiting for certainly wouldn't get to the bottom of it, not after all this time, although the police might.

A foreigner had brought her in, though one of those who'd made Florence his home as his Italian had been near-perfect. The nurse prided herself on judgement, you had to be able to tell at a glance after thirty-five years on the front line, and she'd thought him a decent person. He found her collapsed in the street, he said, he'd been waiting for someone outside the Palazzo Ferrigno and she asked him for help.

He'd frowned then, deciding that he should tell her the full story. 'I thought she was an addict,' he said. 'But when she stood up I saw she could hardly walk. And . . .' He'd looked away then. 'When I had a good look at her, I realized I'd met her before. A long time ago. She's called Sarto, Giulietta Sarto.' The nurse had nodded then, sympathizing; it must have been a shock, seeing anyone in that state after you'd lost touch would be a shock. She decided it wasn't her job to pass judgement, to wonder if they'd been lovers, nothing like that. Not many people would have bothered to give the girl a second look, and he was a Good Samaritan in her book. *Have you got somewhere to stay?* he'd asked, his voice gentle. *Somewhere to go back to?*

She'd left them alone for a bit, and heard the woman whispering to him through her broken teeth, on and on, urgent, insistent. She'd heard it all in here, when the overdosers came in and they woke up, the stories they came out with: the husband attacked her with a carving knife while she was asleep, forced her to have an abortion, raped her thirteen-year-old daughter. She'd had people sectioned before now. So when she heard Sarto say, 'He's been inside the building, he's got it all planned. He's going to kill someone,' she didn't break step. Let the police deal with it.

He'd been meticulous, left his name, address, two numbers he could be reached on; he'd had to leave, though. To begin with he'd kept coming and going to call someone on his *tele-fonino*, the only person in the hospital to obey the injunction against use of mobiles in the building, becoming more and more impatient and anxious, and then, *Sorry*, he'd said. *Please excuse me, I must – there's something I have to do, give my name to the police.* Laboriously he had written his name down to save her spelling out the foreign syllables. Daniel Strickland, with an address in San Frediano.

She walked on with a slow, heavy tread, reached for the curtain and pulled it back, but even before the bed was revealed she had a premonition. *She's gone*, she thought, and the curtain rattled back, steel rings along an aluminium pole. The bed was empty.

The match was over but the Palazzo Ferrigno's concierge, yawning to his feet, had his back to the monitor and didn't see the figure, grey and insubstantial as a shadow, that it showed slipping out from a darkened stateroom and along the great landing towards the private dining suite. Pressed close to the wall, the figure's silhouette was indistinct, but certainly male; he was tall, and he moved quickly. The concierge had been summoned to his window by some late-night visitor, and he was taking his time answering such a rude summons. The man was no doubt a tourist under the misapprehension that his needs should be answered even though it was close to eight o'clock and the palace was not a public museum but a private asset. The man rapped on the glass for the second time.

English, thought the concierge, eyeing him judiciously. The man's heavy jacket was shapeless and might have been thirty years old, and he wasn't very careful with his razor. About forty, maybe forty-five. Didn't look like a tourist though.

'I need to speak with one of your guests,' said the man.

'Urgently.' He paused. 'Celia Donnelly. Or – or Mr Lucas Marsh. My name,' and at this he produced a dog-eared card, 'is Daniel Strickland.'

The concierge frowned down at the card. Mr Strickland, it seemed, had an official connection with the British Council, but there was something about the man, some air of barely concealed desperation, that combined with the shabby coat and stubble to give the impression of instability. He might be a vagrant, even, a schizo, a psychopathic street person. The concierge drew himself up; he had to consider his responsibilities, he couldn't be too careful. The man certainly wasn't dressed for a social occasion, or even a casual visit, in a house like this.

'I don't think so,' he said, handing the card back. 'This is a private function. Very private. A dinner.' He glanced sideways at the appointments book; the guests *had* been booked under the name of Marsh. Behind him the single functioning CCTV screen flickered, but the concierge didn't look around.

Strickland took a step away from the window in apparent frustration, then stepped back. 'Perhaps you could check,' he said with exaggerated politeness, his face up against the glass. 'I'll wait.'

The concierge looked at him, expressionless, but the man held his gaze and it became uncomfortable. He leaned back and made a play of pulling out drawers, riffling through the visitors' book, and eventually he picked up the intercom that was connected to the landing. Ponderously he dialled, keeping his eye on Daniel Strickland.

As he watched, Strickland took out a *telefonino* and frowned down at it, half-turning away and jabbing angrily at the keypad. The concierge put a hand over the intercom receiver; no one was answering, but he hung on.

'Mobiles don't work down here,' he mouthed at Strickland through the glass, with some satisfaction. He gestured around at the massive stone arch of the gateway. He shook his head, wagging a finger in a pantomime gesture. He was taken aback by the furious glare he received in return. *Right*, he thought with indignation. *No way are you coming past me.* He replaced the phone. They must be busy up there, he thought. Or out on the terrace.

'If you insist,' he said, enunciating clearly as if addressing an idiot, 'I will have to ask someone to go up there and find Signorina Donnelly. But we are very busy. It may take some time.'

Daniel Strickland said nothing; he inclined his head and then stood, immovable and with his arms folded across his chest, in front of the glass. The concierge picked up the intercom again and dialled down to the kitchen. He wasn't going to let on to this thug that there were no more than a handful of staff, three if truth be told, and both the waitresses would be out at the tradesmen's entrance enjoying a pre-work cigarette until the very last moment. He fixed a fake, servile smile on his face as he held Strickland in his sights.

'Ah, Signorina Chiara,' he said when eventually he heard the waitress's voice, petulant at the interruption. 'There is something I need you to do.'

Luisa stood at the entrance to the Olympia Club in the dank, freezing dark beneath a slab of concrete awning, pillars to either side of her. Mindlessly she rehearsed what she could see of the detail of her surroundings, as though to persuade herself that she wasn't standing here in the dark alone, pretending she knew what was out there. But the truth was she could hardly see a thing. She stood and waited for her eyes to adjust; to her left was a decaying piece of plywood half concealing the smashed glass of a lobby door. As she moved, yellow light gleamed off it, the same sliver of light repeated in a fan of shards, but she couldn't see what was behind it. Involuntarily she stepped back. She didn't want to go inside.

There was a wall. Groping her way, Luisa followed it around the side of the building. A kind of tunnel yawned in front of her, empty doorways on either side of it, and set in the wall to the left of the tunnel's entrance was a rectangular hole. Luisa stopped and tried to make sense of it. It was like archaeology, like entering a place walled up for centuries. With a surge of relief she remembered the torch and pulled the rucksack off her back; as she did so she thought she heard a scuffle some-where off to her right, in the dark. Luisa stopped moving and listened, hardly daring to breathe, but she heard nothing more. All the same, she didn't want to draw attention to herself by flashing a light around right now; she removed the small but reassuringly heavy torch from the bag, slipped it into her pocket and carefully slid her arms back into the rucksack's straps. Cautiously, reluctantly, she took a step, then another, towards the rectangular window-space, set her hands on the low sill and leaned inside.

This was as far as she was going to go, Luisa told herself, and this was already too far. She could see nothing, but she could smell it: chlorine and stale, damp clothes, old socks and urine. And behind it all the river, she could smell the river even in here, cold and sluggish, where a child's body had drifted and circled, sank and rose, for almost a week, and suddenly it wasn't just the smell of an old pool. She felt it choke her, this fog of something old and stinking and horrible, and fumbling, she reached for the torch. She shone it into the corners of the cramped space behind the low window. *This is where you hand in your ticket, they give you a wire basket for your clothes.* A rail to hang the baskets from, a dirt-crusted floor of dimpled tiles with a couple of baskets still lying there, discarded. Below the sill a stool for the girl to sit on. The girl who takes your ticket. That girl.

The torch flickered and went out, and as though something had reached for her out of the darkness to take her by the throat, Luisa pulled back hastily out of the window space and pressed her back into the wall. Her heart bumped so hard and loud she could feel it at the base of her throat. And then she heard the sound again, over the thudding in her chest, over her ragged breath, a careful footstep crunching in the snow, and then another.

Paola knew instantly what was coming when she saw him step through the door, and somehow it all came together; perhaps this is always how it ends. Her nemesis, like a sixteenth-century assassin, seemed to fit in better than any of them here, making his stealthy way between the enfilade of staterooms with a knife. *We're no more than squatters*, she thought, *play-acting, but he's for real.* Deliberately Paola stepped to place her back to the *Madonna of the Lilies*, protecting her. At her side the black-haired wife of the English millionaire had gone very pale and Paola put out a hand to calm her, a gesture that would not under normal circumstances have come naturally to her. She thought of her children, and lifted her chin. *They're grown now, they'll live.* She faced him. 'What do you think you're doing here?' she said bravely. He laughed.

*

298

They stood in the cold beside the brazier. Lucas still hadn't said anything, and Celia hadn't known where else to take him. Was this it, she wondered, was this what she had feared would happen? Or was there worse to come? She held on to Lucas's arm; he seemed unsteady. She looked around for a chair: beyond the brazier there were some padded wooden seats around a table under white damask and she led him to them. He sat down heavily. On the table was a tray with glasses and a champagne bucket; brandy would have been better, she supposed, as she poured a glass; she saw that her hand trembled as she held it out to him. But this was supposed to have been a celebratory drink; it seemed so long ago that she'd arranged it all, the champagne, the dinner menu. Lucas looked at the glass as though he didn't know what it was. 'Go on,' she said gently. 'Have a sip, at least.' Lucas took the glass from her hand, looked at it for a moment, then knocked it back with a kind of recklessness. He set the glass on the table and sat back heavily in his chair, staring at Celia; he didn't look any better but his eyes seemed to have gained focus. *Where is everybody?* Celia thought with indignation, and for a second the professional in her decided she'd never book the Ferrigno again, it was obviously a shoestring operation, they weren't supposed to be out here yet. But just then the girl who'd taken their coats appeared in her apron at the long French doors, seeming agitated. Lucas didn't seem to register her arrival; he was still looking at Celia, and it made her nervous.

'You know, don't you?' he said suddenly. 'How do you know?'

'I – I—' Celia was flustered. There was no point in denying it, but she was afraid of the emotion she heard in his voice. *If it was me*, she thought, *I'd hate that, being other people's property, the subject of other people's whispered conversations. Poor thing. How must she be feeling?* 'I'm sorry,' she said. 'I heard. You were recognized.' Almost involuntarily she looked away, and saw the waitress a couple of yards away hanging back. Celia turned back to Lucas; he was looking at her hungrily, as though she had something he wanted. It occurred to her that he had not had anyone to talk about this to in fifteen years since his wife died, or perhaps even before. She took a deep breath.

'It was – a terrible thing,' she said. Cowardly, she didn't want to name it more precisely. 'A lot of people here were affected by it. They still remember it, I suppose they remember you.' Lucas just nodded grimly. *Where is Emma?* Celia thought desperately, with an awful stirring of dread, *she should be here.* Out of the corner of her eye Celia saw a waitress take a step towards them. *Damn them*, thought Celia, and she no longer cared about holding anyone up, no longer cared what any of them thought about this catastrophic mess of an evening. Lucas Marsh had paid, after all. She held up a hand to stop the girl coming any closer.

Perhaps it was the girl's presence, or Celia's gesture, but Lucas's look had changed by the time she turned back to him, as though a shutter had come down. 'It's none of your business,' he said bitterly. 'It's nothing to do with – with anyone but me, now. My wife died, I suppose you knew that? My first wife. Everyone wanted to know how we felt. Not that they really want to know, do they? They're just glad it's not them. Let it happen to him.' His anger seemed to be exhausting him; his handsome face looked grey and ill. Celia just gazed at him, frozen with shame. He was right, of course. Not her business. But she couldn't keep silent.

'But what about Emma?' she said. 'You should have told her.'

He looked away then. 'Emma,' he said, repeating her name to himself. 'Oh. Emma. Yes. I couldn't.' His voice was flat and cold. 'Don't be ridiculous. How could I tell her? You have no idea.' He looked away. 'It's like a black hole. It drags everything down with it, swallows it up.'

'She knows now, though,' said Celia. He said nothing, just gazed away from her into the darkness across the river, the reflection of the lights along the embankment glittering in his eyes. On impulse she tightened her grip on his icy hand, in defiance of his hostility. 'But that doesn't mean it's too late,' she insisted. She leaned forward, wanting him to believe her, even though she didn't believe it herself.

'No,' said Lucas. His voice was a dry whisper. 'You don't know what I've done.' The waitress darted forward, seeing her chance.

'Excuse me,' she said to Celia. 'Please. There is someone who needs to speak with you downstairs. His name is Strickland? He is waiting at the gate.' She stared curiously at Lucas. 'Is all right? Signore?'

'Yes,' said Celia, 'we just need a moment, please.' She felt for her mobile and realized she'd left it in her coat. Had Dan been trying to get hold of her?

At the edge of her vision she caught a movement; one of the French doors swung open as though another door had been opened somewhere else in the building and it banged, shockingly loud, back against the wall. The waitress exclaimed something under her breath and hurried away from them, towards the sound. She disappeared inside and they watched her go.

'I'm getting cold,' said Celia after a moment, wondering

301

again, *What does Dan want?* He'd been following her all day, stalking her, and this evening Gabriele had seen him talking to a woman who'd been beaten up. Or said he had. Celia wasn't sure she wanted to see him, to see either of them for that matter. Dan would have to wait.

'Shall we go back in now? Let's go back,' she said. They had to put this all back together, somehow. Start again. It seemed a remote possibility, for all of them; out here in the raw night, as a wind got up off the river, the terrace seemed a bleak and inhospitable place. The damask tablecloth fluttered in the wind; hunched in his chair, Lucas looked half-frozen.

Slowly, stiffly, he got to his feet, but before they could take a step after the waitress they heard a phenomenal crash, as though not just a trayful but a whole cupboard of glass and china had toppled to the floor. And then came a high-pitched sound, a long, wailing scream that hung in the icy air. Lucas took a step towards the door; blindly he groped with a hand and Celia seized it. 'It's Emma,' he said. Isn't it? It's Emma.'

Down at the gatehouse Dan Strickland, who was still standing in front of the concierge's window with his arms folded, saw something on the monitor behind the man's head. He took a step closer, peered up at it, and reflexively the concierge stood up to block his view. He wagged a finger. 'Oh no you don't,' he said. 'You just keep your distance.'

'What the hell's going on here?' said Strickland. 'Look, *sciemo*. You idiot. Look up there.' And in spite of the man's failure of respect there was something in his voice that made the concierge turn his head. '*Porca miseria*,' he whispered with dawning horror, and now all his authority was gone. 'Shit. Oh, shit.'

*

302

He came out of the darkness from where Luisa had imagined Bartolo's farmhouse must lie and for a moment she thought it was him, thought that she would see the filthy old man coming out of the dark towards her with his throat cut. And then he whispered her name, hoarse and disbelieving. 'Luisa?'

Blindly she stumbled across the snow towards the sound of his voice and threw herself at him, sobbing. She could hear the noise she was making but she couldn't help herself. It was Sandro.

'Darling, darling,' she said over and over again, and she held on for dear life while he stood there, solid and immovable and warm. The endearment was unfamiliar on her lips but it was the only word she could find and it seemed to be the right one. She patted his arms, his shoulders, put her mittened hands on his cheeks, needing to reassure herself of his reality, and then she looked into his face, half-laughing, half-crying. 'It's you,' she said; she should have been scolding him for frightening her and deceiving her, but she couldn't find it in herself.

Gently Sandro propelled her in front of him to the shelter of the wall. She moved away instinctively from the empty window where the girl who took the tickets had sat; it yawned beside them, dank and empty.

'What are you doing here?' he said roughly, but she could tell he wasn't angry. 'How on earth did you think to come out here? You shouldn't be here.'

'It was something you said,' said Luisa, distracted by her relief and by the warm pressure of his hands on her shoulders, 'and I heard the bells in the background. I had to find you, didn't I, before, before—' She stopped, not wanting to think about what might be going to happen to Sandro next. Would

303

they arrest him? 'You should have told me,' she said. 'All the trouble you were in. I had to find out from Pietro.'

'Yes, yes, I should,' said Sandro. 'You're right, but I haven't got time for all that now, don't you see?' He kept both his hands on her shoulders as though she might make a break for it, looking into her face. 'I haven't got time now. The car was here, I had this idea he was hiding out in Bartolo's place, but there's no sign of him, and the damned car's gone. At first I thought I'd got the wrong street, but it's gone and I've wasted too much time already. We've got to go back, don't you see? To wherever Lucas Marsh is, damn it, I had the blasted itinerary—' He broke off, his face in his hands. 'It's all falling apart. I've got to get him before he—' Then he broke off again in frustration at the effort of explaining.

'It's all right, I know,' said Luisa. 'I've got the piece of paper, the what's-it-called, itinerary. It was at home, you must have dropped it.'

'You – oh damn,' he said, passing a hand over his face, desperately calculating. 'But – all right, all right, let's think. And that's where she is now, at that whatever it is, dinner at the Ferrigno? They're there?' Luisa nodded.

He looked at his watch. 'Eight,' he said. 'We've got time, they'll be inside, eating, he'll wait until they leave. We've got to go back.'

'Yes,' said Luisa slowly; she knew she was stalling and could feel his impatience. But this had been the right place to come, she knew it instinctively, the answer was here. With reluctance she thought again of that foul-smelling, dismal hole she'd looked into and had seen something, smelled something. If they went back into the city, to home ground, she'd lose track of it. She remembered how Sandro had described the interior

304

of Bartolo's house: clean as a whistle. But next door, in the Olympia, what was there, among all the putrid rubbish?

But Sandro was already two, three metres away from her, heading for the light and the car. 'Wait,' said Luisa, stumbling after him in the dark, losing faith even as she spoke. She could see him slipping out of her grasp; was that why she wanted him to stay?

Breathless, she caught up with him at the car. 'Get in, I'll drop you at a bus stop,' he said distractedly, fumbling with the ignition. 'It's too dangerous for you to come with me.' Luisa climbed in, her face wooden with disappointment, apprehension at what Sandro might be planning to do without her beginning to coil in her stomach. Sandro turned the key, and the car coughed and fell silent. He tried again, but this time there was no sound at all. The car was dead.

Service staircase, thought Jonas, the escape route he'd planned illuminated inside his head like an underground map. He had a photographic memory, always had had, in school he could have read a page of telephone numbers back to you, just like that, not that it had got him anywhere. *Out on the landing and along the gallery, quick down the back staircase, double back at the bottom and the door straight ahead opens on the little stinking courtyard where they keep the bins. Double wooden doors with a padlock but eaten away from the ground up with worm and rain, just kick them down.* The wood splintered with a soft, rotten sound and he was out in the alley between the Ferrigno and a market trader's lock-up, an alley no more than one man wide and hardly visible from the Lungarno, where the traffic hummed and twinkled in the streetlights. Somewhere down there a siren wailed and he cocked an ear. *Ambulance, not police. Is that for her?* Jonas hefted his unresisting burden in front of him and headed away from the river. *You're too late.*

Celia went first, out of some instinct to protect Lucas, but to begin with as she pulled the tall French door back she couldn't make sense of what she saw; she rubbed eyes made bleary by the icy wind. Beside the door that led into the dining room the waitress was pressed against the wall as if some invisible force held her there. She stared at them with glazed, wide eyes as they came in and tried to speak but she made no sense, the words seeming to choke one another in her throat. Her face was red, like that of a child who'd screamed herself into hysterics. Beside her the door was ajar.

Celia stopped; she knew she had to walk on, push open the door into the dining room and find out what had happened but her legs resisted, leaden with fear. The door moved a little, as though in a draught, and then suddenly she was terrified, inside her head she screamed, *There's someone else here.* From behind her she heard Lucas say, 'Emma,' and in his voice she heard an awful, dull certainty Was this something he had expected? Did he think he deserved this?

'No,' she whispered, 'You don't know.' *Move,* she thought, and with stupid slowness she took a step then, but Lucas shoved past her and half-falling, half-stumbling, he hurled himself towards the door. Beside it the waitress shook her head, *No, no, no.*

The table was on its side in its own debris, cloth, overturned chairs, smashed glass and shards of crockery, cutlery scattered across the stone floor. Lucas had stopped in the doorway, apparently unable to go on, and Celia couldn't get a clear view. *Where were they?* Then she saw Paola Caprese, pressed small

306

against the wall next to the painting, her shoulders hunched and her hands pressed into her stomach. There was a lot of blood; her shirt was bright with it.

'What on earth . . . ?' said Celia, astonished. 'Call an ambulance,' she said urgently over her shoulder to Lucas, but he didn't move. She shouted in Italian and then crossed the room at a run; Paola Caprese just stared at her, then down at the blood dripping between her fingers. The girl appeared in the doorway. 'Go and call an ambulance, now, please,' Celia said, forcing herself to speak slowly and loudly, and the waitress ran from the room like a terrified rabbit.

'Where's Emma?' said Celia. 'For God's sake. Where's Emma?' Nobody answered; only Paola Caprese made a small, startled sound, her lips moving but unable, somehow, to form words.

Gently Celia lifted Paola's hands from her stomach; they were limp and white. She couldn't see where it was coming from, all this blood. She groped for a napkin, a cushion, from the debris on the floor and came up with a hank of tablecloth, and she held it across the woman's stomach, heard a dry sob and felt Paola lean heavily on her. From somewhere in the building came the sound of hoarse shouting and footsteps that came and went in the labyrinthine corridors.

'Where's my wife?' Lucas was beside her now, and he wasn't talking to her but to Paola, his voice savage and urgent. 'Where's Emma?'

'She's gone,' said Paola through dry lips, her voice barely audible. 'He took her.' And her head swayed and her eyes grew strange and distant. Celia tightened her grip on the cloth between her hands and looked away in desperation. She stared at the walls, the windows, the painted ceiling; she looked up

307

at the *Madonna of the Lilies* hanging above her and before she could stop herself she begged for Paola Caprese not to die. She thought of Emma Marsh, and her unborn child, and blindly she asked this inanimate confection of oil and wood and canvas for mercy. The painting had not even been disturbed from its position on the wall, and as she held Paola up as though her own life depended on it Celia saw that whoever had come here had not come for the Madonna. There she still sat among the lilies and the myrtle with her lips against her doomed child's hair, and she gazed over the bloody, ruined room with knowing eyes.

Sandro turned the key again, and again; the car whined once, coughed, and died again. He hit the steering wheel and swore, and Luisa could see that he was almost crying. He wrenched the door of the car open and got out; Luisa followed him. He kicked the wheel. The moon came out from behind a cloud and gleamed off the smashed windows of the Olympia, and as she remembered looking in through that window something fell into place in Luisa's mind, a connection sparked.

'Wait a minute,' she said. 'Just a minute. The girl. The anorexic girl who took the tickets and gave out the baskets, the one who thought she'd seen Bartolo then changed her mind? Where is she now?'

'Her?' said Sandro, brought up short, still raging with frustration. 'God, I don't know. I can't even remember her name, Sardo, Sarto, something like that. She'll be dead; she looked close to it even then. Starved herself to death, or overdosed, that's what happens.'

But Luisa was shaking her head. 'No,' she said. 'I don't think she's dead. I think I saw her this afternoon, outside the Regale.'

Sandro stared at her, disbelieving, shaking his head. 'No,' he said. 'How could you possibly have recognized her? She'd have been dead within a year, that girl. Half dead then.'

'I might not have recognized her,' said Luisa slowly, 'a year ago. But when all this got stirred up, seeing him, Marsh, in the shop – I'd been going over it, these past two days, over and over. She was on the news, wasn't she, all that time ago? I remember her all right. Some faces don't go away.'

Sandro was shaking his head, staring at her.

'And you don't know she's dead, do you?' said Luisa. She trod carefully, trying not to sound accusatory. 'Did you have to follow her up? She was a witness, wasn't she?'

'Yes,' said Sandro uneasily. 'But – there were twenty, twenty-five witnesses, people who saw the little girl leave her parents, saw her earlier getting an ice-cream, saw her going inside the building. And she – Sarto – even if she hadn't changed her story a couple of times she was out of it, she would have been rubbish in the witness box. Sometimes she was out of it completely, vacant. And then she'd turn into a stubborn child. *No, I don't remember, no, you can't make me!*'

He looked away and Luisa saw a streetlight reflected in his eyes. She thought he was searching his memory for something, trying to be a good policeman, searching for accuracy. He spoke slowly. 'I thought – it was some kind of sick way of getting attention. She said she'd seen him inside the fence, inside the swimming-pool compound.' He nodded into the darkness, and Luisa wondered if he knew the place by heart. 'Over there, leaning against the fence by the changing rooms. I said to her, you know how important this is, don't you, think of her parents, they're out of their minds. And she just stared back at me and clammed up. She was like a little kid, sticking her lip out, you know, shifting from one foot to another like a kid does when you pin them down with a story. Then she said, no. I was wrong. That was yesterday, I saw him. It was useless.'

He stopped then, his voice full of fifteen-year-old anger. 'She made my flesh creep, she was all bones, great big eyes, she'd stare at you but there was no one home, if you see what I mean. Useless.' He looked down at his hands, and Luisa saw him chew his lip. 'And then, when we were doing some routine follow-up a year later, we found out she'd gone. Her mother – she was a prostitute who worked the Via Senese – said she thought she might have gone off with some travellers headed up north, in one of those camper vans painted up, dreadlocks with a dog and an accordion and a couple of gallons of cheap wine.'

'Didn't she care? Where her daughter had gone?' Luisa couldn't subdue her indignation, and behind it was the guilty memory of that look the starved woman had given her at the door of the Regale. *Do I know her?* And she'd just walked past.

Luisa could feel Sandro's eyes on her in the dark, then he reached up a hand and touched her on the cheek. 'They're everywhere,' he said. 'The ones no one cares about. They just keep moving, they sit outside the *misericordia*, they take drugs, they sleep on benches or in hospital emergency rooms or in the gutter, they shit in the street. And pretty soon they die and there's nothing you or I can do about it.'

There was a long moment of silence and they stood there in the strange half-light, a luminescence that rose off the snow, with at Sandro's back the great dark shape of the ruined Olympia. It seemed to harbour a deeper cold even than the snow-covered wasteland around it. The traffic sounds had been reduced to no more than a low rumble by the snow, the impatient hiss of air brakes as the trucks inched forward on the ring road. Behind it all Luisa could hear the wind rustling in the dark beds of rushes and bamboo down where the silent river ran, and she shivered.

'That little girl,' said Sandro to her out of the darkness as though he knew what she was thinking, 'the one Bartolo took, and killed. At least someone cared about her, someone saw she was gone. She was loved.'

'She was loved,' repeated Luisa, and the bitter irony of it was like a pain; the terrible, immovable fact of the beloved child's death gripped her. She thought of the price of love, the mother who would not survive the loss, the father wandering among the sunbathers where now the snow lay, softening the outlines, concealing the past, calling his daughter's name in the scalding August heat. She felt the scene take hold of her, paralysing, immobilizing: *I'm too old, it's too long ago, too sad, too hopeless. Let's go home.* But something tugged at her, refusing to let go: Sarto might not have been loved but she wasn't dead; by some miracle she was still alive.

'All the same,' she said stubbornly, 'it could have been her outside the Regale, why not? Sarto. She was arguing with the doorman because ...' Luisa frowned, trying to remember. 'There was someone inside she had to talk to. She said it was urgent.'

Sandro took hold of her shoulders and turned her so that what there was of the light fell on her face; his was in darkness. 'The Regale? Where Marsh is staying?'

Slowly Luisa nodded, waiting. Sandro stood very still, his hands warm and heavy on her shoulders, thinking. Beyond the silent car park she could see the lit-up windows of the neat new housing project, tiny figures moving across them to pull shutters closed, some of the windows bright with Christmas lights. Despite the snow, Christmas, like the vision of home comfort the apartment block offered, seemed a long way off. At street level a big dark car cruised into its allotted space and a man climbed out and entered the bright foyer, a dark silhouette, going home.

'Out by the airport where they were sleeping,' Sandro said, thinking hard. 'There was a thin woman, the Romanian said, hanging around with the Russians like a starving dog. They couldn't shake her off.' He paused.

Luisa said nothing, but she thought of the emaciated figure she'd seen. She couldn't be more than forty; she should have been a woman in her prime, not a starving stray ready to lick the first hand that throws it a bone.

Sandro went on. 'They could have used her to find out about Bartolo,' he said slowly. 'God knows where they found her.' He sounded uncomfortable; after all, he hadn't been able to find her. He went on angrily, 'And when they finally managed to dump her – she went to find Lucas Marsh.' He was talking to himself now, thought Luisa; she might as well not be there any more. 'What was she going to tell him? How much did she know?' He dropped her shoulders abruptly and spun away from her in the dark.

'It's time to call Pietro,' he said, and Luisa thought, *at last*. But when Pietro answered, it seemed that they were too late.

Chapter Twenty-Five

They all seemed to arrive in the room at once. Two paramedics in fluorescent tabards, unshaven and red-eyed after a long shift, perhaps, but they moved fast across the room and took Paola gently and lowered her into a chair. Celia stayed there with her hands on the hank of tablecloth, doggedly unwilling to let go. The administrator was still conscious, at least, and with the paramedics' arrival her eyes had come back into focus but she wasn't talking. Three policemen in their blue-grey uniform were halfway through the doorway, one of them talking in fast and animated Italian she couldn't follow to the concierge who had accompanied them upstairs. The man's eyes were flicking nervously around the room as he answered their questions; he seemed submissive, and beneath his five o'clock shadow he looked pale and uneasy. *And so he should*, thought Celia, anger rising at the memory of him sitting there with his feet up. She could hear someone shouting far off in the building, a door slamming, and outside more sirens, one after another.

The building vibrated with heavy footsteps, but no one came to tell them Emma was safe.

The policeman's mobile went off and she thought, *For Christ's sake. Don't answer your phone, find her.* 'What?' the policeman shouted into it. He said a name, *Sandro.* Luisa's Sandro? 'Where are you?' He saw her looking at him, and he left the room.

'Here, Signora,' said one of the paramedics, reaching across her; for a moment as she stared at him Celia thought he could hear the pounding in her chest. 'Let me,' said the man, and deftly he took over. The floor was tacky with blood and she recoiled from it, stepping back with awkward haste. Stumbling, she reached behind her for support, a chair, a wall, anything, and then she found herself held up by a warm, steady hand under her elbow and turned to face her rescuer. It was Dan, and at the sight of his familiar face, pale with concern, she felt her knees buckle. She held on tight to his arm with both her hands.

'I thought it was you,' he said, staring. 'I saw – I thought . . .' And he faltered.

'Where is she?' she said. 'Where's Emma? Have you found her? Where is she?' In the doorway she saw the policeman's head turn at the insistent note of panic in her voice, and in the abrupt silence that followed they all heard a soft exhalation, almost like a sigh. All of them, Celia, Dan, the policemen, even the paramedics on the floor, turned towards the sound and saw that it had been made by Lucas Marsh, standing against the back wall of the dining room and facing the little Madonna.

'He's taken her,' said Lucas. He seemed to be having difficulty speaking, and Celia took a step towards him. 'He's taken my wife.' His face sagged with disbelief. 'His name is Jonas.'

314

'Who's taken her?' said Celia, and then Dan spoke.

'I saw him,' he said. 'On the CCTV in the gatehouse, a man carrying something along the landing. Carrying someone. He had a shaven head, I didn't see much. Big hands on her back. I thought it was you – I thought he had you.'

Celia remembered the big shaven-headed workman in his brown coat, smelling of cigarettes, and felt sick; she should have insisted, she should have sounded the alarm. She put her hands to her head. 'How long ago?' she said. 'He can't have got far, he must be still here, still inside.'

Dan shook his head, distracted. 'They've sealed the place off,' he said. The road, too, and the Lungarno. There's twenty, twenty-five of them in the building carrying out a search, they're looking right now. They'll find her.'

'I'm going to look, too,' said Celia, 'I can't stay here. She's pregnant, for God's sake, do they know that? Come on.' She looked from Lucas to Dan, and back again, listening for the sound of Emma's voice somewhere in the great echoing building, praying for it.

'I should have paid,' said Lucas. 'It's my fault. My Emma. I should have paid.' And as they turned to see him standing in the corner of the room they saw his shoulders contract in some awful spasm and he canted to one side and slid, a sickening deadweight, to the floor. All Celia saw were lips turned grey-blue in a face blank and upturned as he went down without even putting out a hand to save himself, and then he was on the ground, and he wasn't moving.

In his car Jonas was king. He felt as though he was gliding, weightless, through the dark streets in his chariot, and outside the faces seemed to turn towards him in slow motion, nodding

315

approval. He breathed in the familiar smell of old cigarette smoke and plastic upholstery, the faint burning odour of the defective heating. Air-freshener from the cardboard pine tree that dangled from the rear-view mirror. He kept it clean, this car; paid a scrap dealer up on the Brenner Pass near the Austrian border twenty-five euros for it because he liked the colour, but he wouldn't let the others even use the ashtrays. One of them – Piotr? – had spilled coke on the carpet and Jonas had had to show him it wasn't acceptable. He had his standards. He'd cracked Piotr's cheekbone without even turning around. He did like the colour. Bronze. A warrior's chariot.

Only now of course there was a woman in it, that did spoil it. Jonas shifted in his seat; the funny thing was, he'd been so high, not just the drugs but the thrill of it, walking straight into a fortress like that to claim his prize, that he'd almost forgotten he still had her. Had to do something with her. At the lights he drew carefully to a stop – it wouldn't do to attract attention – and lightly tapped his fingernails on the worn rubber of the steering wheel, listening to the imaginary music. The boot had stuck, of course, when he tried to open it one-handed with her body slung over his shoulder, but he hadn't freaked. Patiently, *easy does it*, he'd tried again and it had sprung open and he'd just dropped her in. Of course, she could be dead already. He thought the shock of seeing the knife might have done the job for him, she'd gone so pale when he brought it out, let alone seen what he could do with it. He hadn't hit her too hard, a little rabbit punch to the back of the head when she opened her mouth to scream, but she'd gone down like a sack of potatoes and pulled the table over after her. He'd had to be quick then, with the noise.

Had he meant to kill her, the other one? Jonas couldn't

remember now. It didn't matter, anyway, he could see now that he didn't need a plan, he could play it by ear, light as a dancer on his feet and as quick. It had been the look on her face when he walked through the door as though he owned it, she'd raised herself off the floor, fat little feet in high heels, and opened her mouth to order him out, *What do you think you're doing here?* and he'd just thought, *I don't need this*. Slash, slash, across one way and back, hoped he'd got that big artery in the pelvis.

There was no sound from the boot. *Even if she is dead*, thought Jonas, *I've taught him a lesson, haven't I? Dispose of the body somewhere and off out*. But the thought of meeting the others up on the Brenner without the money nagged at him, infuriated him. A bloody liberty, not paying up. They'd think he was losing his touch. But then, that power, life and death, that's not nothing, is it? That's not losing your touch. He weighed it up: dead, alive, what's the difference? Keep her alive, negotiate for the money, you have to organize a dropoff, it's a hassle, but you've got the cash to hand out, a wad of warm, dirty banknotes. Kill her, dump her, on the other hand, no hassle at all, home free. It's a win-win situation.

There was a police car behind them, edging forward in the gridlock with its lights flashing. The siren began to whoop and reluctantly the cars behind Jonas turned into the kerb to open up a space. The police car was right on his tail now, and Jonas turned the wheel, felt the resistance of the kerbstone under his front wheels. He gazed incuriously ahead as the light blue saloon drew alongside; on his side a slab-faced man, heavy moustache, peaked cap, turned towards him, talking into a radio. Jonas made another inch or two up on to the kerb and they were past. *I walk on water*, thought Jonas, triumph bubbling up in his chest, but he kept his face straight. *Need to get off the road, though*, and he nodded to himself, thinking. *I know where.*

'He's taken Marsh's wife,' said Sandro, and Luisa saw that his hand was trembling as he tried to put the phone away, his face wiped clean of anger and now blank with shock. 'The Russian. Pietro wouldn't tell me any more, said leave it to them. Said, hadn't I done enough harm?' He turned to her.

'It's all right,' said Luisa, clinging to the only shred of guilty comfort, that it wasn't Sandro's responsibility any more. But what about the girl? She closed her eyes to blot out the image she had of that pale, determined, heart-shaped face, the little foot in a red shoe, and felt the world spin around her.

They got back into the car and sat there in the dark, Sandro with his head in his hands, and ridiculously, Luisa found herself wondering how long it was since they'd been in here together. She remembered, distantly, a visit out to Vinci, a walk through the olive terraces to the house of Leonardo. Had they been happy then? How long ago had they last been happy? Beside her Sandro let his hands fall, and turned towards her.

I'm sorry,' he said. 'I screwed it up, didn't I? What did I think I was doing, coming out here like the bloody Lone Ranger?' He passed a hand over his face. 'I'll call Pietro again, tell them where we are. They'll come out and get me, and finish the job.' He took the mobile phone from his pocket and looked at it, but he didn't dial.

Luisa looked at him. 'It sounds as though they've got enough to do at the moment,' she said, and frowned, thinking hard. 'Will they find her?' Sandro looked at her, and she saw no hope in his eyes. 'I don't think you were wrong, coming here,' she said finally, feeling it was urgent, there was something they could still do, something to be found here. 'The car was here. Did you tell them that? Did you tell Pietro that? And Sarto's from Galluzzo, isn't she?' Sandro looked at Luisa, frowning, but he said nothing and suddenly the dark outside the little car seemed palpable, full of ghosts.

'I've spent fifteen years,' said Sandro suddenly, out of the blue, 'going over and over the detail, a scratch, a bruise, time of death; we couldn't let it go, together we kept this going, me and Marsh, and this is where it's ended up. Was it the right thing to do?' He shook his head. 'Because the facts aren't everything, sometimes they get in the way. The post-mortem – you see, it doesn't tell the truth, not the whole truth. It doesn't say, this girl woke at six-thirty every morning and climbed into bed with her parents, she liked dogs, or cats, or chocolate ice-cream. I should have been helping him put it behind him, how she died, not sending him post-mortem pictures.' Sandro passed a big hand over his eyes.

Luisa stared ahead, out through the windscreen, and thought of her own baby. She imagined something drifting away from her like one of those balloons blown loose from a fairground. Beside her Sandro had pulled something out of his pocket; she turned to him and he held it out to her. It was something cut from a postcard, dogeared; Luisa held it up to the window and found herself looking into her own face, or what she had been once, nearly forty years earlier, standing outside a jeweller's window on the Ponte Vecchio.

'I'm sorry,' said Sandro. 'I'm sorry it hasn't – I haven't – been what you wanted.' Luisa shook her head, unable to speak; she took his hand and looked away, out of the window.

'It's all right, now,' she whispered at last. And it seemed to her that it was. She looked away, and gently Sandro took the picture from her and put it back in his wallet. She heard him clear his throat.

Dazed, Luisa looked out of the window, wondering what would happen now. She could see a line of cars moving slowly past them along the highway, and a long bus, all lit up, like the bus she'd ridden out here. She could see the outline of an old lady hunched against the window, a bunch of standing figures clustered at the folding doors, a long arm strap-hanging as the bus lurched and swayed to a stop under the snow-laden trees. Luisa stared but she wasn't really seeing anything; she only barely registered the spidery outline of a passenger detaching itself from the bus where she herself had got off. She heard the hiss of the pneumatic doors and then she picked up the figure and followed it as, with painful slowness, it moved down the access road towards them.

A drunk, thought Luisa, a Christmas drunk rolling home, as she saw how unsteadily the figure progressed. It staggered a little and came to a stop beneath a street-lamp, leaning against the concrete pillar for support. A face came into the light, and Luisa saw that this was a woman, just. The hair was long but as fine and wispy as candyfloss, the jaw was fleshless and prominent and the eye sockets were deep shadows in the yellow glare. Luisa sat up in the passenger seat and groped for Sandra's shoulder.

'Look,' she said. 'Look.'

Suddenly alert, Sandro followed her gaze; he held up a hand to keep Luisa still, a finger telling her to stay in the car. They watched as she pushed herself up again off the pillar and walked on, as fragile as a matchstick figure. A puppet, she seemed to Luisa; it seemed barely possible that body had enough reserves of energy to propel itself. *How do you get like that?* And she knew, deep down, something terrible had happened to that girl, something terrible enough to turn her into a walking skeleton. Something that had frightened her out of her wits.

'Had he done it before?' she whispered, and Sandro turned his head a fraction. 'Bartolo. Had he done it to her?' Sandro shook his head a little, his eyes on the woman outside, past the car park now and edging along the darkness. She got to the Olympia's front gate and leaned down behind it, reaching for something. 'I don't know,' he said. 'I don't know.' And she was inside.

It came back to Celia in a rush; she should have known the moment she saw his face in the Medici library, this wasn't a panic attack, a mild claustrophobic reaction, the story he'd given them. There was nothing mild about this; she shouldn't have swallowed his explanation, she was responsible. The way his left arm stiffened and his shoulders drew together; the awful blue lips. She thought of her father standing up at the breakfast table, his chair falling back and that precise look of astonishment on his face she'd seen pass over Lucas Marsh's, and then, like Lucas, he'd gone down.

But Lucas was still alive. The paramedics had been on him without a second's pause while the rest of them sat back, shocked into silence by the violence of it, Lucas's body manhandled, his clothing torn back and the ambulanceman's hands, one folded over the other and thumping *down* into his chest as he counted. *One,* two three.

'Who's coming with him?' the paramedic had called back over his shoulder as they stretchered him down the great staircase with a perspex mask obscuring his face. *'Lei é la moglie?'*

Celia shook her head, *No, I'm not the wife*, but looking around her she realized with desperation that there was no one else. 'Dan?' she said.

'I've got to talk to the police,' he said helplessly. 'I'll be there when I can.'

And after that everything seemed to happen at a run. Celia snatched her coat from the rail, more for the mobile in its pocket than for warmth, and then folded herself into a corner in the back of the ambulance, her thin shoes soaked, the gorgeous green dress streaked and crumpled as she tried to keep out of the way. It was a grim interior, plastic seating, dials and metal instruments and tubing that swayed as they set off, and the paramedics spoke brusquely to each other in a language she didn't understand, a vocabulary of pressure ratios and drug volumes and beats per minute. They asked her if he had a history of heart trouble, and all she could do was shrug helplessly, she thought perhaps he did. *And his wife's been snatched, she's pregnant and she's somewhere out there in the cold with a man with a shaven head, she could be dead*, she wanted to say, but what could they do?

Inside the hospital they were still running. Clutching her coat around her, Celia followed the gurney at an awkward jog; they went through a heavy plastic door into the *pronto soccorso*. She held on to the metal rail around the gurney, and stared at the clouded mask that covered Lucas's face as they ran through the grey corridors of the hospital. This is where people come when life has crashed in on them, when the worst happens, the car accident, the stroke, the heart attack. *Where's Emma?*

They were slowing now and Celia caught her breath; she

felt as though she'd been holding it since she climbed into the ambulance. The paramedics and a white-coated doctor who'd joined the procession steered the gurney around a corner and into a room with a door. The doctor exchanged a few words with the paramedics, quite calmly, as he fixed some kind of monitor to Lucas's chest; Celia saw Lucas's pale smooth skin, a dusting of chest hair, exposed and vulnerable. *You have no control in the end*, she thought. *You have to be ready for that. All the planning, all the looking forward, and suddenly it's in someone else's hands. In a foreign bed, strangers taking hold of you and speaking their language around you.*

A nurse came in and the paramedics left, nodding to Celia; they looked grim and exhausted, and she wondered where they would be going next, or if they could go home now. They'd just saved a life, temporarily at least. The doctor leaned up to switch on the screen on the wall; a green line appeared on it; it jumped and hiccuped across the screen, then seemed to settle. He turned to Celia then, and as he seemed to register her for the first time, he frowned. He was a handsome man in late middle age, spare, with silver hair that stood up from his forehead. Aware suddenly in the clean room of her party dress and bloodstained hands, she pulled her coat around herself defensively.

'Are you hurt?' he asked, distracted by the blood from whatever it was he had been about to say. She shook her head.

'No,' she said. 'It's not my blood.' She saw him glance towards Lucas. The nurse was deftly easing off a sleeve, the expensive dinner suit, the shirt ripped where the paramedic had torn it open to pound on his chest.

He began again, 'Your husband,' and she shook her head a little; the doctor shrugged and went on, marital circumstances being nothing to do with him either. 'Signore,' he began again, consulting the chart he held in his hand, 'Signore Marsh. Lucas. He has suffered a heart attack.' He spoke slowly, in Italian, and she nodded to show that she understood. 'He was very fortunate that the paramedics were exactly there; although this would not certainly have been fatal, it might have been. And with the heart, prompt action makes a very great difference, to survival but also to long-term effects. Brain damage, for example.' Again Celia nodded, the coat wrapped tightly around her.

'So – will he recover? Can he – can he talk?' What would she say to him, if he could answer? The doctor put his head on one side.

'We have given him a sedative,' he said, and Celia wondered which of the many needles she had seen filled had sedated him. As if he could see what she was thinking the doctor said, 'And some drugs to make it easier for his heart. Aspirin, to thin the blood, for example. And soon we will have to do some tests to assess the damage to the heart and the treatment. But when the sedative wears off he should be able to speak, yes.'

Celia felt the hairs rise on the back of her neck as the full horror of the situation rushed at her, like an express train. If they didn't find Emma soon, Lucas Marsh might as well have died on the floor of the Palazzo Ferrigno. If he lost her, and with her this new child, he would never recover.

'So,' said the doctor, looking at her curiously, 'you will stay?'

'Yes,' said Celia. 'I'll stay.'

The doctor said something to the nurse and she left the room, returning with a hard-backed chair, which she set down beside the bed. Then she retrieved something from the chipped bedside cabinet and held it out to Celia.

'From his pockets,' she said. 'His things. Personal effects. For safekeeping.' Her expression, proud and guarded, spoke of late-night conversations with relatives complaining of missing valuables, accusations fielded across the still bodies of the dead and dying. 'I – all right,' said Celia, and she took the bag, which was surprisingly heavy, with reluctance. The same accusations, after all, might be levelled at her: what right had she to Lucas Marsh's personal effects? It seemed an intrusion, presumptuous, she thought he would hate it. She thought of her father, stretchered away with a zip over his face after the doctor had come. Suddenly overcome by a sense of weakness, she sat down abruptly on the chair, the clear plastic bag on her lap.

'Thank you,' she said faintly, and the nurse turned away. After one last, curious look at Celia the doctor nodded brusquely and left. The nurse moved around the room, checked a gauge on the monitor, flicked a tube feeding something into Lucas's arm, and after a while she left too.

Celia sat there for a long time, watching Lucas's chest rise and fall; his hand lay, clean and pale, beside his body. After a while she put out her own hand and rested it on his.

'I'm sorry,' she said. 'I'm so sorry.'

Chapter Twenty-Six

'That was her,' Luisa said at last. 'That was Giulietta Sarto. She went in – she went—' She couldn't finish the sentence, trying to imagine what she could want in there, in the dark.

Sandro, who seemed to have been struck dumb, nodded. When eventually he spoke, his voice was flat with self-disgust. 'She's come back home,' he said. 'Was she here all the time? I thought she was dead, overdosed in some travellers' shitty cara-van years ago. Why? Because I didn't like her, maybe. Because I thought that was all she deserved. Because she made my skin crawl. But all the time she'd come back here.'

He fell silent then, and Luisa saw that he was thinking, trying not to be side-tracked by his own failure. When he spoke again his voice was dogged, the voice of a policeman with not much imagination but a great deal of persistence.

'This must have been where they came when they left the airport,' he said slowly, 'both of them. This was where the car was. Sarto came home to Galluzzo, and she brought Jonas back with her. He must have come here before anyway, looking for Bartolo; Galluzzo must have been where he picked Sarto up in the first place, trawling for information. Maybe he thought this was as good a place as any to hide.'

'What shall we do?' said Luisa. 'What if – what if Jonas comes back here?' But she knew what Sandro was going to do. 'Please, Sandro. Call the others. Call Pietro, you can't do this on your own.'

Bitterly he turned to her. 'I've got to,' he said. 'I've screwed this up all the way down the line, don't you see? Giulietta Sarto knew something, all along. Why didn't I nail her before she disappeared? Why couldn't I make her tell me what she really saw? I – I just couldn't.'

Luisa shook her head slowly. 'You don't know what happened to her,' she said. 'To make her like that. Think of how much willpower it takes not to eat, to starve yourself. Just not telling might be easy by comparison, if you were angry enough.'

'I could have stopped all this, fifteen years ago,' said Sandro.

'You don't know that,' said Luisa, but he was already out of the car.

'I'm going in there,' he said, 'and I'm going to make her talk this time. Wait here.' But she was after him before the door closed.

'Absolutely not,' she said. 'You're not leaving me here.'

'Luisa,' he said sadly. 'This isn't a game. It's not safe.'

'I know that,' said Luisa; she had no intention of telling him how afraid she was of going in there. 'Don't you think I know that? I'm not stupid, I won't go barging in shouting the odds. But – if you go – you're all I've got.' She shut up then; she didn't want him to think she was getting sentimental.

'Come on, then,' was all he said.

Inside the dark was absolute, the air soft and rotten like mould; the stale, putrid smell of chlorine and damp was almost palpable. Wet and suffocating, the walls seemed to close in on Luisa and she blundered into something. Blindly she put her hands out to keep the walls away, and encountered a wooden partition, slimy with mildew, and then it gave under her hand and swung away. Just as a whimper she couldn't suppress rose in her throat, groping in the dark she felt Sandro's hand; firmly he took hold of her and at last she felt as though she could breathe, felt something lifesaving, like oxygen, enter her system, and took a lungful. Sandro held her still for a moment, by the wrist; he was listening.

It was quiet but not silent; around them Luisa imagined chambers like in a heart, pulsing and echoing. Some way off something dripped, the sound magnified as though it was falling into a great space. Where they were standing the sound was different, though; their footsteps didn't echo, they were muffled by some interior structure. Luisa thought of the slimy board that had given way under her hand and realized they must be in the changing rooms, and what she had pushed was a swing door. She might have felt triumph at her deduction, but instead she felt her claustrophobia intensify at the thought of the cubicles around her like a labyrinth, behind every door a deadend, or something dead. She scrabbled in her backpack and got out the torch, pressing it into Sandro's hand.

'We can't do this in the dark,' she whispered, her mouth at his ear, and at the sound of her voice something scuttled in a corner. Luisa grabbed for the torch and turned it on.

She'd been right, they were standing at one end of a row of changing cubicles, their melamine doors spotted with mould and scrawled with obscenities and endearments, *I love, I want to, call me*, some hanging from their hinges, a couple missing altogether. The floor was thick with a kind of scabrous grime and the plaster on the walls was pitted and crumbling. Luisa shone the torch along the row of doors to see how to get through and tentatively Sandro followed the light; as the beam hit the corner of the room something low down on the ground moved, horribly fast. A pair of tiny eyes gleamed red in the torch's beam and it was gone, under a partition; Luisa clamped a hand to her mouth to stifle her own noise.

'Here,' said Sandro in a whisper, and pulled her after him, through a door. Luisa held her breath. Of course, Sandro must know this place like the back of his hand, she thought, remembering that first day when he came home after twelve hours here sealing off areas, interviewing, searching. And had gone back, and back, dozens of visits she knew about, and no doubt others she didn't. Luisa felt something soft and wet under her feet, dragging her, and with revulsion she swung the beam down to see she'd trodden in a discarded towel, wet and filthy. An old beach towel with the long eyelashes of a faded and coquettish Minnie Mouse blinking up at her out of its sodden folds; how long had that been here? Luisa felt a sudden rage overcome her, when were they going to bulldoze this place, grind all this into landfill, burn it clean? Sandro pulled her behind him through a shower stall and they were in the great hall that held the indoor pool.

It was not, after all, quite dark. The moon had come out beyond the high, mildewed skylights and a thin light filtered down into the drained pool. It seemed huge, a great, empty space as big as a football pitch and deep, and on its edge Luisa felt as though she was somewhere high up, and afraid of falling. In the sudden silence as they stopped she heard something. A distant, stifled sound, and human. Luisa listened, her head cocked. She took Sandro's arm and pointed, up, and he nodded.

They'd almost reached the top of the gangway, Sandro half-turning to help Luisa, when the handrail he was leaning on, its wood rotted beyond repair by the damp, gave way with an awful soft, splintering sound, and he swore. Luisa clutched at him, half to steady him, half to shut him up, but it was too late. The crying had stopped.

'Quick,' said Sandro, and they ran along right under the roof, heedless now of the noise they were making as it rang around the huge space below them, through a door at the end of the high walkway.

They were in the bar. The semi-circle of its fancy panoramic window curved away from them and through what was left of the glass the moonlight shone on a shambles of broken bottles and smashed-up furniture. The bar itself had been ripped apart and looted long ago; in the moonlight it all looked black and white like an old photograph, and there was no sound. But as Luisa looked, feeling strangely calm now, she saw something. Not a person but an impression, something about a collection of shapes in the corner furthest from where they were standing that stood out from the chaos. Without hesitation she crossed the room, Sandro now the one hurrying to keep up. She stopped.

Four sections of the bar's squat, wide leatherette seating had been pulled together here, a small table had been dragged across and set at one end, and a nylon sleeping bag had been unzipped and spread across the seats. Luisa saw what it was straight away, an attempt at constructing a bedroom, complete with bedcover and sidetable. A marital bed, room for two. Luisa turned to Sandro.

'She must be here somewhere,' she said. 'This is where she's been living. This is her home.' And as she said it, suddenly from somewhere far below them a door slammed, a sound heedlessly, shockingly violent, and a man began to shout.

Celia stared at her mobile phone, willing it to ring. 'We know where to find you,' the policeman had said kindly as she thrust the number at him. 'As soon as there's any news, of course we'll call, straight away. You stay with him. Keep him calm.' *Emma, Emma, don't be frightened*, she prayed silently. *They'll find you.* Celia's neck was rigid with tension, her jaw stiff; she felt like screaming but she didn't even dare make a call. There were signs everywhere telling her to turn the phone off but she couldn't do that, because what if they called?

A nurse told Celia she should go and get a coffee. Lucas was stable now, out of danger; he would be coming round before too long and Celia should take her chance now. She spoke kindly and Celia just looked at her blankly for a moment, barely able to understand. The silent room with its machines and its shiny grey walls was like a flotation tank, a place of sensory deprivation, and she felt disoriented, as though she'd been there for hours. Then she nodded, *yes, thank you, I will*, and the nurse went out again.

Celia stared at the screen beside Lucas's bed; the green line spiked and blipped across it, persistent and indefatigable and regular now, Lucas's body reasserting its right to survival even while he lay there motionless on the bed. Then under hers his cool hand fluttered, and Celia sat bolt upright, holding her breath. On the screen the hiccups quickened a fraction, and the numbers on a quartz display beside it ran on, changing incomprehensibly. But no alarms sounded, and no nurse ran in; Celia let out a cautious breath, watching him. His eyes opened, a hand lifted and fell back to his side, and he turned his head to look at her.

The nurse bustled in then, alerted perhaps by some external machine, and Celia moved back as she leaned over Lucas, murmuring a gentle question, soothing. She heard his voice, hoarse from underuse, but she couldn't make out what he was trying to say, nor even whether he was speaking in English or Italian. Nor, apparently, could the nurse, who turned to Celia with an expression of helpless impatience on her round, kind face.

'You talk to him,' she said sternly, seeing that Celia had not gone for her coffee, as instructed. 'Reassure him. Then let him rest.' She turned back to her patient and with infinite care she detached the oxygen mask from his face, giving him a little pat on the arm as she left.

Reassure him. Celia felt herself begin to panic, because what on earth could she say to reassure him? But she stopped herself, right there; you'll think of something. She took his hand and waited for him to speak again.

'Hello,' he said, and perhaps it was whatever drug they'd given him but to Celia his voice sounded extraordinarily changed. To begin with as he looked at her all that vigilance, that guardedness she'd seen in him before had disappeared and instead there seemed to be a kind of exhausted quiet; it was as though something inside him that had been wound tight had loosened.

'How are you feeling?' she said cautiously.

'Oh,' he said, 'like I've been kicked by a horse. Not bad.' He fell silent then but she could tell he was preparing himself to speak again. 'Where's Emma?' he said and he struggled to raise himself, but his eyes were clouded, confused and she could see he couldn't remember what had happened. 'We – we were – were we having dinner?'

'You hadn't got that far,' said Celia, gently lowering him back to the bed, and with a sureness that took her by surprise she told the lie. 'Emma's fine. They're looking after her, keeping an eye on blood pressure. You gave us all a shock, you know.'

'I know,' said Lucas vaguely, his eyes wandering as he thought back. He laid his head on the pillow. 'It's my fault,' he said. 'I didn't know what I was doing.'

'You mustn't worry about it,' said Celia, trying to lead him away from the moment when he'd said that before, in the wrecked dining room. 'Really. Emma's not upset, they're just checking on her. You'll be able to see her soon.' She felt her face stiffen with the lie, forced her mouth into a smile.

'No, you don't understand,' he said, frowning. 'I – did I tell you? You know, don't you, I remember, we went outside. It was very cold.'

'About your daughter,' said Celia. 'Yes. I know, and Emma knows. It's all all right.'

'Emily,' he said. 'She's called Emily.' He spoke the name so quietly it was barely audible. 'It seems a long time ago,' Lucas said after a while, and his voice was far away. 'I couldn't let myself picture her face, because I knew I wouldn't be able to go on if I did. My wife died, you know.'

She waited for him to go on, not wanting to interrupt; she barely dared take a breath.

'I badgered Sandro Cellini, the policeman, I made him send me everything, every last piece of paper. I had a filing cabinet. I suppose it kept me busy. And then one day I realized I couldn't remember. I couldn't remember her face any more, even if I wanted to.' His voice was hollow. Celia thought of the picture he kept in his desk drawer, the photograph of a girl he'd told Emma was his god-daughter.

'It's all right,' she said, wanting to cry, and she lifted his hand to her cheek. 'It'll be all right.'

He parked as far from the light as he could, round the side of Bartolo's place. The air was fresher, wetter when he climbed out and he could tell the snow would be gone by morning. Just as well, too. Snow might make everything look pretty but he didn't want anyone following his tracks. And it always turned to slush and scum, in the end, his feet were wet with it already. He opened the boot. Alive, then. She looked up at him with her bruised face from over the dirty rag he'd tied around her mouth and he felt anger stir in his belly. She was scared, that was for sure, but there was some fight left in her too. He wanted her more than scared, though, he wanted her terrified into total submission, he'd seen them like that, like she was under hypnosis, and he could see from her eyes that she hadn't got there yet. Bloody women, bloody women hanging on beyond all reason, clinging to life, clinging to him, don't they know when to give up? He shut the boot again and lit a cigarette, leaning against it. That'll teach her. Stay in there a bit longer. He felt in his pocket, mobile phone, knife. He took out the knife and fingered it, running a thumb down the short, lethal blade.

He'd have liked a gun. He'd had one once, at the beginning, bought it in Odessa for hard cash. Liked feeling the weight of it in his pocket, cool and solid, he would place it against his

334

cheek. He'd never used it, but he could have done. And that idiot Piotr had got drunk and started firing at cans out by the airport, drawing attention to them, so he'd had to ditch the gun. That was why it was better to be on his own. He didn't fuck up, Jonas never fucked up. He looked up and down the quiet cul-de-sac; no one. The villa opposite was empty, they'd gone away for the holidays, that was a piece of luck. He turned and looked at Bartolo's place. It occurred to him he could take her in there, it was that bit closer, after all, but then he saw a piece of striped police tape fluttering from the gate and thought, maybe not. It was one thing to park the car under their noses, a laugh, but he didn't fancy being holed up in that place, you'd be trapped for sure if they came back for another look. And it gave him the creeps, he couldn't help thinking of the old guy, mumbling to himself in the back of the car as they drove off to Le Cascine. The stink of him.

'Let's do it here,' he'd said to the girl. *Why drive him off there for Christ's sake, I'm in charge here? There's the place right next door, we can do it there. Do it in his own house.* But she'd shaken her head, *no.* 'I know him,' she'd said. 'He'll scream like a pig if you make him go into the Olympia, he's scared of the place, and you don't want to do it in his house, on home ground. He'll say nothing there.' It might have been that she hadn't wanted to go into his house herself, Jonas knew that from the way she squirmed and pulled away at the gate. He'd let her have it her way, though, she'd been right about everything else where Bartolo was concerned, after all. Had it been a piece of luck, meeting her in the bar? He wasn't sure. But you had to be bold, take the initiative. Take a risk.

He pushed himself off the car and flicked the cigarette into the snow, a dark fleck on the white. He stretched and flexed, preparing himself; he had to do this quickly, no hesitating. There was a thump from inside the boot, and his anger flared. Now.

Over his shoulder she bucked and twisted, but she had no chance, his arm was clamped across her thighs. Jonas worked out, a hundred press-ups night and morning, ran five miles a day, pull-ups when there was a bar, and his forearms were like steel cable. You had to stay in condition. She was heavier than he'd thought, though; she only looked small with that pointed chin, the little wrists and ankles as he'd bound them, but her stomach was firm and solid against his shoulder. He was over the fence, walking without hesitation in the dark up to the back of the Olympia, shoved the piece of hardboard across the back door aside and he was in.

She was making a racket now, spitting and screaming through the rag, and unceremoniously he let her slide to the floor and stood astride her.

'Shut up,' he said in a soft voice. He knew English, that much, at least. Man of many talents. Then he leaned down and put his face an inch from hers and shouted as loud as he could, 'Shut. Your. Mouth.'

Celia paced, found herself at the end of the blue corridor, lost. The nurse had scolded her to get a rest when she came in and saw her still there; what must she have looked like? She felt shaky and cold, even though she had put her coat back on and the hospital was warm around her. Perhaps it was the smell, of iodine and surgical soap – this was a place of extremity where there was no time to waste on fragrance. Her feet in the thin shoes slapped loud on the speckled marble of the floors.

'Something to eat, at least,' the nurse had said, eyeing her. 'The bar's down one floor. Surely there's someone else can sit with him for a bit?'

That was when Celia had begun to shake at the thought of what she had said, that it would be all right and soon he would see Emma again. The nurse had looked at her trembling hands and sent her out.

'He's being looked after,' she said. 'Take an hour or two off. Go on.'

Celia arrived at a set of double doors and, pushing them open, found herself on a cold concrete landing with two lift doors and a stairwell. She stood in a daze, staring at the light over the lift door and trying to understand what it meant, up or down. She put her hands to her face, leaning back against the wall in the stairwell. She *was* tired. But she couldn't go home, couldn't rest; Lucas was lying there, halfway between alive and dead, and Emma was gone. Opposite her the lift pinged again and the door opened; dazed, she registered faces, one of them moving towards her and – Dan was there. She swayed, wondering if he was real, and then his arms were around her and she could feel his breath in her hair.

'Have they found her?' she whispered; nothing else seemed to matter suddenly. 'Please let them have found her.' She extracted herself from his arms, his closeness oddly distracting suddenly, and stood back, searching his face.

He shook his head slowly. 'Not yet,' he said, and she put her hands to her face. 'Come on, come on,' Dan said, and Celia realized that the funny choked sound she could hear was coming from her own mouth. 'It's all right. It'll be all right'

He looked over her shoulder, through the swing doors

and down the corridor that led to Lucas's room. 'How is he?'
he asked.

'He's okay,' she whispered, feeling a tiny stirring, a step out
of despair; at least he was alive. One step at a time. 'He's going
to be all right,' she said, then stopped. 'At least, as long as—'
And she looked up at Dan, stricken. They were a long way
from it all being all right.

'Here,' said Dan, turning her towards the stairs. 'The bar's
one floor down, isn't it?'

The warm coffee smell enveloped her at the doorway,
erasing the institutional odours of disinfectant and sickness. A
long glass cabinet full of stuffed toys and boxes of chocolates
ran along one wall, and a gang of ambulancemen still in their
fluorescent jackets were leaning against it drinking grappa.
At the bar a young, unshaven doctor, his white coat hanging
open, was staring into the dregs of a coffee cup, his eyes glazed
with tiredness. Celia realized she had no idea what time it was
and looked around; a clock above the till said eleven-thirty.
Dan went to get a ticket and she leaned against one of the
small, high, round tables, barely able to stay upright herself.
There was something bulky stuffed into one of her pockets;
she felt it press into her thigh and, puzzled, she fished it out
and set it on the table with a clatter. Lucas's personal effects,
in their plastic bag.

Celia felt guilt creep up on her, as though she'd shoplifted
them. But what else could she have done? She tilted her head to
one side, studying the contents of the plastic bag. Keys. Wallet.
A mobile phone – no. Two mobile phones. Dan arrived at her
side and set down two cups and two tumblers of some viscous
white spirit, but she was still staring, puzzled, at the bag. Was
one of the phones Emma's?

'What's this?' said Dan cheerfully.

'Oh,' said Celia, hesitating. 'It's—' Could she trust Dan, with his journalist's instincts? Was he using her? She realized that she was going to risk it. She sighed. 'They're Lucas's things. They emptied his pockets, told me to look after the stuff.'

Dan's expression turned serious. 'Oh,' he said thoughtfully, eyeing the bag; with that look she knew he wanted to grab it and shake out the contents, but he didn't. He picked up his coffee and drained it, then the grappa. It occurred to Celia that she had no idea why Dan had turned up at the Palazzo Ferrigno in the middle of the Marshes' dinner.

'What were you doing there?' she said. 'Why did you come?'

Chapter Twenty-Seven

'Here,' hissed Sandro. 'Come *on*.' He half-dragged Luisa across the room, stumbling ahead of her across broken furniture, behind the bar and down on to the floor. It was tacky with ancient spillage, and there was a rancid smell of sour alcohol and something nastier, more like bile, stomach acids, some disgusting bodily fluid. Beside her Sandro crouched, waiting.

They could hear him moving through the building below them. 'Is he coming up here?' whispered Luisa with horror, and Sandro shushed her. 'Wait,' he said. 'Quiet.' She felt his hand squeeze hers, though, and she thought, *We're in this together*. She concentrated on keeping very still; absurdly she thought of childhood games. Murder in the dark. She heard the clang of the steel stairway beyond the door, echoing tinnily in the great space underneath them.

There'd been another voice, too, higher-pitched, frightened, after the shouting. Was it a woman? Was it Sarto? Beside her Sandro's head was down as he concentrated on something in his lap. Luisa blinked, trying to force her eyes to adjust to the deep shadow behind the bar so that she could see what he was looking at. She put out a hand in the dark and felt something cold and metallic, then his hand on hers to stay it, and she knew what it was, the memory of it in her palm, of ridges and furrows. A gun. His police issue gun, not to be fired, never to be fired, that was what he'd once said to her. *I'd never use it.* And now – he'd gone AWOL, and he'd hung on to the gun – what kind of trouble could that get him into? Did he even have bullets for it? Luisa felt sick.

She heard the footsteps closer then, and different, no longer on the ringing steel of the steps but a more muffled, solid sound. He was stamping along the walkway towards them, a scuffling behind as though someone was being dragged, and then the door banged open. *How are we going to get out?* The thought crashed around inside Luisa's head. On the other side of the bar where they crouched there was a moment's silence, then a thump as something fell heavily to the floor and some swearing. Whatever he was saying in his thick, guttural accent, he was repeating over and over obscenities from another world.

As she concentrated on staying absolutely quiet Luisa saw something on her pulled-up knees. It was a thin shaft of pale light and she turned to see how it was getting through. At her shoulder a crack split the cheap wood of the bar where it had been ransacked and turning slowly, cautiously, she leaned close, pressing her eye to the opening. She could hear her own breath in the enclosed space. At first she could see nothing, squinting from the dark into the silvered moonlight, but then there was the silhouette of a man against the window. He was stubble-headed and huge in the shoulders, like a minotaur, and he was looking down at something, or someone.

341

'Bitch,' he said in English, and at his feet she scrabbled upright, a pair of shoulders set small and square against the moonlight, a thick head of hair that shone blue-black. She turned her head to look around, the girl Luisa had last seen in the honeymoon suite of the Regale contemplating red and silver shoes; now she looked up at the man who'd dragged her here and her face was blank with fear. For a moment they stared at each other, the girl and the bull-necked man, and Luisa thought how bravely she held his gaze. *But don't make him angry*, she prayed silently; she knew the rich, knew how carelessly they could act because they were used to silent obedience, their arrogance never corrected. This one wouldn't say, *Yes ma'am*, would he, and smile to hide the fact that he'd been insulted, as Luisa had to do day in, day out. He'd cut her throat as easily as if she was an animal.

'Don't hurt me,' said Emma, her voice like a bell after his obscenities. 'Please.' Luisa could see that her arms were bound to her sides and there had been something covering her mouth that had slipped down around her neck. Trussed, she was tense with the effort of staying upright. 'I—' She hesitated, and Luisa knew she was struggling with whether or not she should tell him she was pregnant. *Don't*, she thought, closing her eyes as she imagined what the man might do with the information, and as though Emma had heard her, she stopped. Luisa felt a hand on her arm and stiffened; she turned her head and saw that it was Sandro, of course. She pointed to the crack and mouthed in his ear, hoping that he would hear. The wife,' she said. 'He's got Lucas Marsh's wife.'

Sandro looked down at the gun and Luisa seized him by the wrist, shaking her head violently in the dark. She held up

342

a hand to tell him, *At least wait.* He stared at her but he didn't move, the gun weighed in his hands.

'I'll hurt you if I want,' said the man, and he took something from his pocket and looked at it. 'He thinks he can treat me like this.'

'He – he lost his daughter,' said Emma, her voice trembling. 'He doesn't know what he's doing.'

'Fifteen years ago,' said the minotaur with deep scorn. 'That's weakness. He should have killed the man himself and then, forget it. Start again. That's how you do it.'

'He's not weak,' said Emma, and Luisa saw her chin rise, her voice choked. 'You don't know him.'

'Don't I?' said the man. 'We find out, eh?' And he took something from his pocket, jabbing at it, then raised it to his ear. 'We find out.'

'I saw someone,' said Dan. 'In the street. Someone I recognized from all that time ago, when I was hanging around the Olympia watching the police, seeing who they were talking to. They brought her in for questioning five or six times, so they must have thought she knew something.' He was frowning. 'I couldn't believe it when I saw her this afternoon, really, looking just the same; not that she looked young, more that she looked ancient when she was twenty-five. I suppose anorexia does that.'

Anorexia? Something chimed in Celia's head and she thought, *Where have I seen a girl like that?* Dan was still talking. 'She was in a bad way,' he said. 'She'd been beaten up.' And Celia remembered. Beate's sketchbook. And she saw the man Lucas had spoken to, with his earring and his big-knuckled hands; as she'd turned the page there he'd been again, towering over a girl so thin she might have been made out of paper herself.

343

'She didn't want to talk to me at first,' said Dan, staring into the distance. 'But when I mentioned the Olympia all the fight seemed to go out of her. She said she'd got involved with a Ukrainian called Jonas who turned up in Galluzzo one day, looking for Bartolo, and found her first.'

Celia nodded dumbly. 'Lucas sent him,' she whispered, and Dan turned to look at her.

'Yes,' he said. 'She said she'd help him get Bartolo, because he talked nicely to her. But something went wrong, she said, and Lucas wasn't paying up. *Stop him*, she said. Jonas. *He's down at the Palazzo Ferrigno, and he's going to kill someone.*'

'Luisa warned me,' said Celia, her voice shaking. 'She told me Lucas was in trouble. But I didn't really understand. I thought, all we've got to do is get through that dinner, I thought we'd be safe while we were inside, in the Ferrigno. Only one last evening, and they'd be going home. Just get through the evening.' She put her face in her hands. 'Is he going to kill Emma?' Then she stopped. 'Wait,' she said. 'Wait. Where is she now? The anorexic.'

'Giulietta Sarto,' said Dan quietly.

'You brought her here, didn't you?' Celia got to her feet, desperate to go. 'She's here. She can find them, she must know where they are. Have the police spoken to her?'

But Dan was staying where he was, and slowly he was shaking his head. 'No,' he said.

'What?' said Celia. 'Why not?'

'Because she's gone,' said Dan. 'I—' He looked shamefaced. 'I went to the ward where I left her, on my way up here, and they told me she'd done a runner just after I left.' He passed a hand over his head. 'I should have known she wouldn't wait around for the police, shouldn't I?'

344

Celia felt the hope ebb, and almost gave in, almost sat down and cried at the disappointment of it. But she stayed on her feet. *No*, she thought. *There must be something.* 'Think,' she said to Dan. 'What did she say to you? Did she tell you anything, I don't know, about where they'd been living? We can find Sarto. We've got to find her.'

Dan shook his head with maddening slowness, trying to remember, to shake things into order. 'I did ask her if she had somewhere to stay,' he said slowly. 'Somewhere to go back to. *I'm back in Galluzzo*, she said. She said something odd, what was it? I thought she was in shock, you know, not making sense. *It's cold there*, she said,' Dan repeated slowly as though trying to remember it verbatim. '*He doesn't like the damp but it's quite safe now. No one goes there any more.*'

Celia stared down at the bag on the table, but she wasn't seeing it because she was trying to think. Then suddenly she couldn't stand it any more, the waiting, the inaction. She grabbed the bag and scooped the contents out, spreading them across the table. For a moment they both looked in silence at the small, innocuous assortment, then Dan spoke, frowning.

'That's odd,' he said, and put out a hand. Two mobile phones, one sleek and tiny and silver, the other scratched and battered. Dan picked it up, the odd one out. 'This isn't his phone, is it?' he said, but it wasn't really a question.

Celia shook her head. Dan flipped it open and the tiny screen lit green. Celia picked up the wallet; it was very soft black leather, and felt light, not stuffed, as hers was, with receipts and crumpled notes. Perhaps if you were very rich you didn't need cash. She opened it. A credit card, black; she'd never seen one of those before. A five-hundred euro note; she hadn't seen one of those, either, and she couldn't imagine how much use it would be; you could hardly use it to buy a bus ticket. There was no picture of a small girl, smiling against a blue background, one front tooth chipped. But as Celia dug deeper she did find something printed on photographic paper, hardly bigger than a credit card. The image on it was blurred, and she turned it this way and that, and then she saw emerging from the black and white pixels the unmistakable, tiny jointed curve of a spine at their centre like a fossil, a curled ammonite in the desert. A scan picture, dated 1 December, a week ago. Emma must have given it to him.

Beside her Dan was very still, staring at the phone.

'Wait,' he said. 'Hold on.' He pressed a button, then another. Celia, barely used to the simplest functions of her phone, had no idea what he was doing; he scrolled down, *gallery, video clips*. A picture, fuzzier even than the scan photograph, appeared, and a huge hand almost filled the screen, then was withdrawn. Then there was just a face in the dark, unshaven, blunt features, small eyes, thin, wet hair plastered across a broad forehead. 'I am Cesare Bartolo,' it repeated clumsily, stupid with fear. 'I am the killer of the girl.'

They stared at the thick lips that moved for ten, perhaps fifteen seconds. *I touched her. She made a noise. I didn't mean to do it.* It was crude, a forced confession, but it sounded like the truth. And yet the words were so few, it was over so quickly, that Celia thought, *Is that it? Is that what all this was for?* She looked at Dan.

The phone rang.

The bull-necked Russian's face was turned to the light, the phone pressed to his ear as he waited for an answer, and Luisa could see the broad, flat planes of his cheekbones, the irregularities in his skull under the fuzz of stubble. He seemed to her more like an animal than a human being, savage and unpredictable. Her neck ached with the effort of pressing her face against the crack, and her legs were cramped underneath her, but she couldn't look away.

'Where is Lucas Marsh?' He spoke quickly, turning as he did so, and his face was in shadow again. 'No,' he said evenly. 'You're lying.' Even from where she was sitting Luisa could hear the urgent crackle of a woman's voice, pleading down the line. 'What a shame,' he said, and his voice grew dangerously quiet. 'That's too bad for his poor little wife, then. Perhaps he doesn't give a shit about her, though.' The voice on the other end was higher now, with a note of desperation. 'Ten minutes,' said the Russian, and hung up.

Shit, thought Jonas. And who was she, answering the phone? A policewoman, or a nurse? *He's in intensive care, he's unconscious.* Below him the woman stared up at him, trying to understand.

'What is it?' she said, and he could hear she was close to breaking now. 'What's happened?'

'Your big strong husband's in the hospital,' he said. 'Unconscious. So where am I going to get my fucking money now, eh? What am I going to do with you now?'

The woman's mouth trembled, open; a pretty mouth, he thought without warmth. She was crying quietly, and she turned her head a bit so that he wouldn't see. It didn't move him, maybe she could tell; some women might have worked it, begged and screamed; perhaps she wasn't like that. For all she looked dainty and delicate, there was something harder underneath; he thought of the solid weight of her over his shoulder, bucking and twisting. Or perhaps she was clever. She turned back to look at him and her eyes glittered.

'What did he ask you to do for him?' she said. He narrowed his eyes.

'Didn't he tell you?' he spat, surly; did she have the right to talk to him like that? 'He didn't tell you much, did he?'

'He was protecting me,' she said. She was defying him; Jonas felt anger stir in his gut, like a sickness. He'd had enough of her, answer for everything. She didn't see it, though, couldn't tell that it was coiling inside him, getting ready. He stared at her.

'Lucas isn't a murderer,' she said, and she struggled to get upright but her hands tied behind her kept tipping her over. Jonas looked at the gag that had fallen down to her collarbone. He'd just have to reach behind her and twist, two turns with his strong hands and it would be over. He'd quite likely killed one woman already, what was another one, after all? He thought of the trailer park out by the airport a week ago, those freezing nights when they'd lit a fire of old fence posts and watched it burn down, the cold, fresh air, the smell of gasoline, the men's faces around him. They'd never have believed it was his first time, sticking the knife into the little woman on her high heels; they thought he was a warrior, a fighter. He felt the sickness burn in his stomach; he was queasy at the thought of the painting on the wall, the woman's face looking down as he pulled the knife across. Jonas could feel the damp on his skin and it was like being buried alive in here. The money felt like an obstacle now, something in the way of freedom. *Just kill her, and run.*

She couldn't hear it though, that voice of warning; she kept on. 'He wouldn't pay to kill someone,' she said, her face white; she seemed to have run out of breath. 'He won't – he won't – you won't get any money. You'll never—' Jonas leaned down and thrust his face in hers, so close to losing it.

'I told him, your hus-band.' He spat the word, contemptuous. 'How many times?' he said. 'How many times? *I don't kill Bartolo. Did not kill him.*'

For a moment it was quiet, so quiet he could hear the building around him, almost as though it was breathing. Or was that him? He turned his head; was there someone else here? But then she spoke again. *Too far,* he thought, *you've pushed it too far,* and in a small voice Emma Marsh said, 'So who did? Who did kill him?'

He was ready then, his hands were on the gag and twisting, but then he saw something out of the corner of his eye. He turned and she came at him out of the dark, from where they'd slept the night before, a skeleton from the ghost train, and her bruised lips moved to answer the question but he didn't hear, because at that moment all hell broke loose.

'Ten minutes?' said Celia, numb with disbelief as she stared down at the phone. She turned to Dan. 'He's got Emma,' she said. 'What did he mean, ten minutes?' But she could see in Dan's eyes what he had meant. 'We call the police,' said Dan, getting to his feet. 'Now.'

Celia nodded, yes, of course, yes, and put her hands to her mouth as the panic rose; she could see Dan glance at her as he took out his own phone. She thought of the thick foreign accent, echoing in a deserted space, and the sound of water, dripping. She felt sick; it had sounded cold, somehow, poor Emma in the cold.

Where are they? Then something came back to her, something insisted she remember. What was it Sarto had said to

Dan? *Somewhere cold, and damp.* She repeated the words to herself in despair and Dan turned to hear what she was saying, paused even as he dialled.

'What?' he said, and they looked at each other. 'Sarto had gone back to Galluzzo with him,' she said. 'Galluzzo's where it all started,' and she hardly dared to trust herself. 'Isn't it? And somewhere cold and damp—'

'The Olympia,' said Dan, and in his face she could see aversion to the very name, but even as he shook his head she knew they'd got it. The Olympia. 'Now we call the police,' he said, and he handed her the phone.

They put her through to Pietro in the end. *That's all I need*, he thought as he climbed into the patrol car out on the wasteland beside the airport, but the Russian hadn't gone back there, he'd thought it was too good to be true. And now this, some crazy Englishwoman thinks she's Sherlock Holmes. But as the woman spoke, keeping calm, setting out the theory, an uneasy feeling persisted that she could be right there, she could have a point. And when she came to it, said, *Look, I know it sounds crazy but couldn't it be? The Olympia Club in Galluzzo, it's abandoned now, isn't it worth a look? Please, the man said ten minutes and it's been that already and more, please.* Pietro thought of the place, the dirty wasteland next to Bartolo's place where he'd been with Sandro only yesterday, the ugly, boarded-up buildings and he thought, *Maybe. Maybe. If there's even a chance we track Sarto down out there, that's something, and let's face it, it's all we've got and if the worst comes to the worst, we've wasted half an hour.* He tried not to think of what might happen in half an hour. 'Okay,' he said. 'I'm on my way.'

*

Luisa heard it; she wondered if she was the only one. She saw the big man with his hands around Emma's neck turn his head as Sarto came out of the dark and Luisa had thought for a second of the little mermaid walking on knives. She said those three words and Luisa heard, and then Sandro's radio went off beside them and everything happened at once.

After Sarto's whisper the harsh crackle of the radio sounded deafening, the sound of a voice distorted with static shouting down the line, *Location, give your location*. Jesus, thought Luisa, who never swore, and found herself bracing herself behind the bar, head in hands, as though for a plane crash. *We're dead*, she thought, *we're all dead*. But Sandro must have switched it on deliberately, it must have been thought out in advance because he was ready; she felt a movement from her side and looked up and he had gone. She came around from behind the bar on her knees on the sticky, filthy floor and there he stood, legs braced, shoulders square, his gun pointing at the big man.

'Let her go,' Sandro said, and the Russian, whose face was white and blank as a sheet, turned to look at him. Then he took his hands away from Emma's neck and held them out to Sandro as though they didn't belong to him. Luisa scrambled to her feet, made it to the plastic seating and pulled Emma against her, away from the big man, feeling her tremble. Then they were all looking at Giulietta Sarto.

What did you say?' said Sandro very quietly, and Luisa saw his hands tremble so you could barely see it.

'I said, I killed him,' she said, and her voice was light and cool as though it was trying to float free from her body, where the bones pressed painfully against her paper skin. Outside a siren screamed in close, and another, and the flashing blue of a light swept around the bar.

Chapter Twenty-Eight

By the time Celia and Dan got there they'd taken him away, that was what they gathered from the small crowd that had materialized in the car lot. A drooping strip of police tape stretched across the road. 'Big as a house,' an old woman had said, a crumpled handkerchief held to her mouth. 'A monster.' An ambulance stood with its rear doors open, empty inside, and three police cars, their blue lights still idly rotating, were parked on the kerb outside the Olympia. A burly police officer gave them a glance from where he stood leaning against one of them and talking into a radio at his shoulder. Dan nodded, and Celia recognized him then; he must have been one of the officers who'd turned up at the Ferrigno, what seemed like a lifetime ago. They pushed through to the tape, and the policeman jerked his head up, giving them grudging permission to approach.

'Have you got her?' said Celia. 'Is she all right?' She'd gone back to Lucas before they left the hospital. 'I won't go,' she'd said to Dan at the door to his room, thinking the worst once she'd hung up from talking to the police, thinking, *She'll be dead, someone will have to tell him, when he wakes up.* Dan had let her go in alone; he'd stood at the door as she went to the bed and took hold of Lucas's hand. The line on the screen held steady, and gazing at it she'd realized she had to know, now. 'Come on,' Dan had said gently from the doorway, as if he'd read her mind. 'We'll come straight back.'

Now the policeman looked at her consideringly. 'The Englishwoman?' he asked, and in an agony of impatience now Celia wondered, *Who else?* 'Yes, we've got her,' he said. 'She's all right. They're bringing her out.' And as he spoke from behind him Celia heard voices, saw movement through the overgrown laurels behind the fence, then Emma was there, wrapped in a dun-coloured blanket, pale and weary but upright.

'Emma,' said Celia tentatively, and perhaps at the sound of an English voice, because she hadn't spoken loudly, Emma looked across at her. 'He's okay,' said Celia. 'Lucas is okay. I told him he'd see you soon.' And seeing Emma sway, she broke away from Dan and crossed over to her at a run. 'Really,' she said, her face pressed against Emma's, 'he's going to be all right?' She held on tight and whispered, 'It's going to be all right.'

'They're going to take me there now,' said Emma. 'To make sure everything's – to make sure the baby—'

Celia thought of the tiny, fuzzy photograph in Lucas's wallet. 'It's not—' she said, feeling her throat closing, preventing her from finishing the sentence.

'No,' said Emma, and at last she smiled. 'No. We're fine. We're all fine.'

At her side the paramedic said, 'Signora. Please.'

As Celia watched the two yellow-coated ambulancemen help Emma gingerly into the back of their vehicle she suddenly felt very tired. 'I want to go home now,' she said to Dan. 'Is that all right?'

They retraced their steps to Dan's car, which they'd left in the shadow of the handsome new apartment block; as they crossed the crowded parking lot towards it Celia became aware of someone standing on the steps at the entrance of the building, watching them. He took a step forward into the light, and as she saw that it was Gabriele it came to Celia that this was where he lived. She stopped, and Dan stopped too; she half lifted a hand to wave. Gabriele stood there for a moment, looking from her to Dan, then abruptly he raised his own hand in an awkward response.

'Thanks, Gabriele,' Celia called.

'No problem,' he said, 'I'll see you.' And he turned and went inside.

As they passed through the great sombre gate of the Porta Romana and entered the narrow streets of the city that had grown quiet at last, suddenly Celia knew where she wanted to be, and who she wanted to be with.

'I'm going home for Christmas,' she said, looking straight ahead and feeling a great bubble of pride and certainty buoy her up. 'To see my sister. She's having a baby, you know.'

'Okay,' said Dan, equably, shooting her a sidelong glance. 'As long as you come back.'

Epilogue

Sandro took early retirement, it turned out to be as easy as that. And just as well, because Luisa needed him.

Giulietta Sarto spent eighteen months in a big new psychiatric unit outside Bologna, and Luisa visited her twice a week. It was nothing like the old lunatic asylums of Luisa's imagination; it was in a modern building of glass and *pietra serena*, grey and calm and very quiet. There was a vegetable plot, and a walled rose garden where Luisa was allowed to sit with Giulietta. Over the weeks she filled out, put on perhaps twenty kilos, and one day Luisa noticed that the dark fuzz of hair on her arms had gone. To begin with, Giulietta hadn't talked at all, only Luisa. She'd tell her what she was planning to cook for dinner, how the train had been up from Florence. Even when Giulietta began to answer, to tell her about the doctor who treated her and about the weather and the work she did in the vegetable garden, they didn't talk about what had happened. They didn't need to; Luisa knew already, from Sandro, who knew from Pietro. And Giulietta knew she knew.

Pietro had called Sandro up one hot June evening when the psychiatrist's report came in and said, come for a drink. They sat on a bench in the park outside Pietro's apartment block and Pietro told him everything, and when he got home Sandro told Luisa at the kitchen table, with the windows wide open and the scent of jasmine coming in from outside.

'From the age of seven to the age of thirteen, when she stopped eating,' Sandro had told her, 'Giulietta Sarto was abused by Bartolo. Her mother, who was an addict and a prostitute, took money from him.' He'd shaken his head slowly to and fro, and Luisa was glad he was out of it, glad he didn't have to hear such stories any more.

'Sarto remembers it all,' Sandro had said. 'Like she'd locked it away, every detail, in a little box until it was time to get it out again. The psychiatrist said it could happen that way, a result of trauma, or guilt, or both.' He'd sighed. 'That day, she was working in the changing rooms as usual; it was a summer job, the only one she could get, and it was better than doing what her mother did, even if she did have to sit five metres from Bartolo's house. It's a small place, Galluzzo; she couldn't avoid him.' Luisa tried to imagine how it would have felt. Had it felt like revenge, to sit there and show him what he'd turned her into? Deep down, was she still afraid of him as he went about his business behind the fence, as monstrous and brutal as he had been to her as a seven-year-old?

'That day she saw Bartolo leaning against the fence; she turned away, she said, she read her magazine to show him she didn't care. He hadn't touched her since she got thin, and she said she made herself sit there, pretending she wasn't still afraid of him. She heard him talking to someone at the side entrance to the changing rooms, the emergency exit they leave open when it's very hot, she said, but she didn't look up. She didn't want to look at him, she said.' Sandro had cleared his throat, a painful sound.

'About fifteen minutes later, maybe twenty, she heard the mother, in the changing rooms, come to look for her daughter, calling. She went on reading her magazine, she said it had made her angry, the sound of the woman calling, on and on. No one had ever come looking for her when she got lost, you see, no one had ever called her name like that. The manager came round, saying, have you seen a little girl come through here, and she said, no, which was true. She said she really didn't understand, then, what had happened, didn't connect it with Bartolo. It was forty-five minutes before they called the police.

'We interviewed about eighty people, but none of them had seen anything useful. It was very crowded, and very hot. There was a young officer talked to Sarto. By then we'd been round to Bartolo's house, but we didn't have a warrant, and his mother was there in the kitchen, shouting at us to leave her son alone, he'd been with her all afternoon. But we knew, even then, what kind of a man he was. So this young officer asked Giulietta Sarto if she knew who Bartolo was. She said yes. He asked if she'd seen him that day, and she said she wasn't sure, which he took to mean yes, and then we thought, nail her, pin her down. She told the psychiatrist she just felt scared then, in a panic, terrified of Bartolo, scared of the police in case they blamed her for letting him talk to the girl. Like it could be her fault.' He'd sighed then, a long, sad, weary sigh.

'So they asked me to talk to her, and in I went, saying, if you saw him you've got to tell us, think of that little girl's parents, think what they're going through. The psychiatrist says Sarto thought, when I said that . . . ' He paused, swallowed, and Luisa had been able to see that it was beyond him to understand. He started again. 'She thought, it's not fair. No one looked out for me, no one cared about me. And that's when she looked at me and said, *No, I didn't see him, I was confused. Not today, I didn't see him today.* And the more I went on about the parents, the more stubborn she got. *I said I didn't see him!* Luisa had nodded, cold with the horror of it. And then, it was too late.' He had to get it out of his system, she could see that. Doggedly he had gone on, looking Luisa in the eye.

'It would have been too late, anyway,' he said, picking at the timing of it. 'The girl was almost certainly dead before we'd even arrived at the Olympia Club. But after that Giulietta Sarto spent fifteen years trying her best to die, taking drugs, starving herself. But she didn't die, did she? And eventually . . . ' He paused. 'Eventually, when Jonas Godorov came along looking for Bartolo, it was as though someone had come along to rescue *her.* She got him out to Le Cascine for them, and they got him to confess, and then it came to her, what she had to do. They went off to find a beer to celebrate; they didn't notice she wasn't there any more, because they didn't give a damn about her, did they? She went back to where they'd left him, and she cut his throat.'

In the scented rose garden Luisa sat beside Giulietta and took her hand. The roses were out and the air was full of their scent; it was July, and she'd been here more than a year. The psychiatrists had delivered their report, and there would be no trial.

'I thought, when you come out,' said Luisa, 'you could come

358

home with us, for a bit.' Giulietta said nothing. 'It's all right with Sandro,' said Luisa. They looked at the flowers, the buds bursting with colour in the sunshine.

'Okay,' said Giulietta. 'If you like.'

Celia walked along the Arno in the spring sun, the Ponte Vecchio behind her, with its burden of tourists, moving to and fro as they did every day of the year, but for a while, she thought, they were no business of hers. Next year, maybe, she and Beate would go into partnership doing painting tours that would only take them, they'd agreed, to the secret corners of the city, cloisters and rose gardens. That was the plan. But for a while, Celia would have other things to occupy her.

She looked ahead, along the river at the blue Casentino hills, and the swallows soaring against a great smoky thunderhead of cloud. She thought of Emma Marsh, who that morning had emailed her a photograph of their son; he looked just like Lucas, on whose knee he had been sitting, although Lucas himself had been barely recognizable as the pale, stern figure she had last seen. His hair had grown down almost to his collar, and seemed somehow darker; his eyes were creased with happiness. 'He's stopped work,' Emma had written. 'We've moved to the country. I want another baby.'

And then Celia thought of her own news, the piece of paper she'd just collected from the laboratory up at Santa Croce, the crowded little clinic full of people anxiously awaiting blood-test results. And, although she already knew because she'd done her own test, the white plastic baton with its blue line, her doctor had insisted that this was how it was done here, you had to have the official test too. And hers was positive.

Beside her a swallow rose up above the parapet until it was

level with Celia's face, then it rose and her heart rose with it. She walked on, back to the flat that no longer belonged to the Venezuelan because her name was on the lease now, official; the flat where Dan was waiting for her, and her news.